Disney·Pixar

MONSTERS, INC.

Art by: Hiromi Yamafuji
Cover by: Phillydelphy

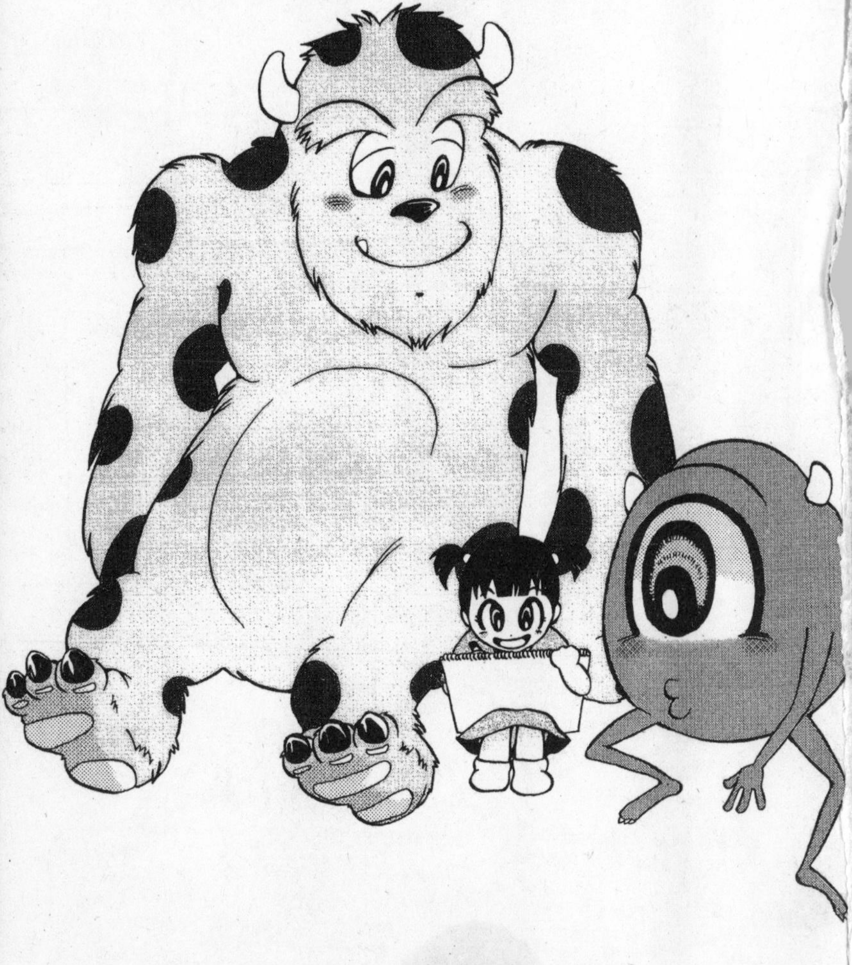

Disney·PIXAR

MONSTERS, INC. CHARACTERS

PART 1

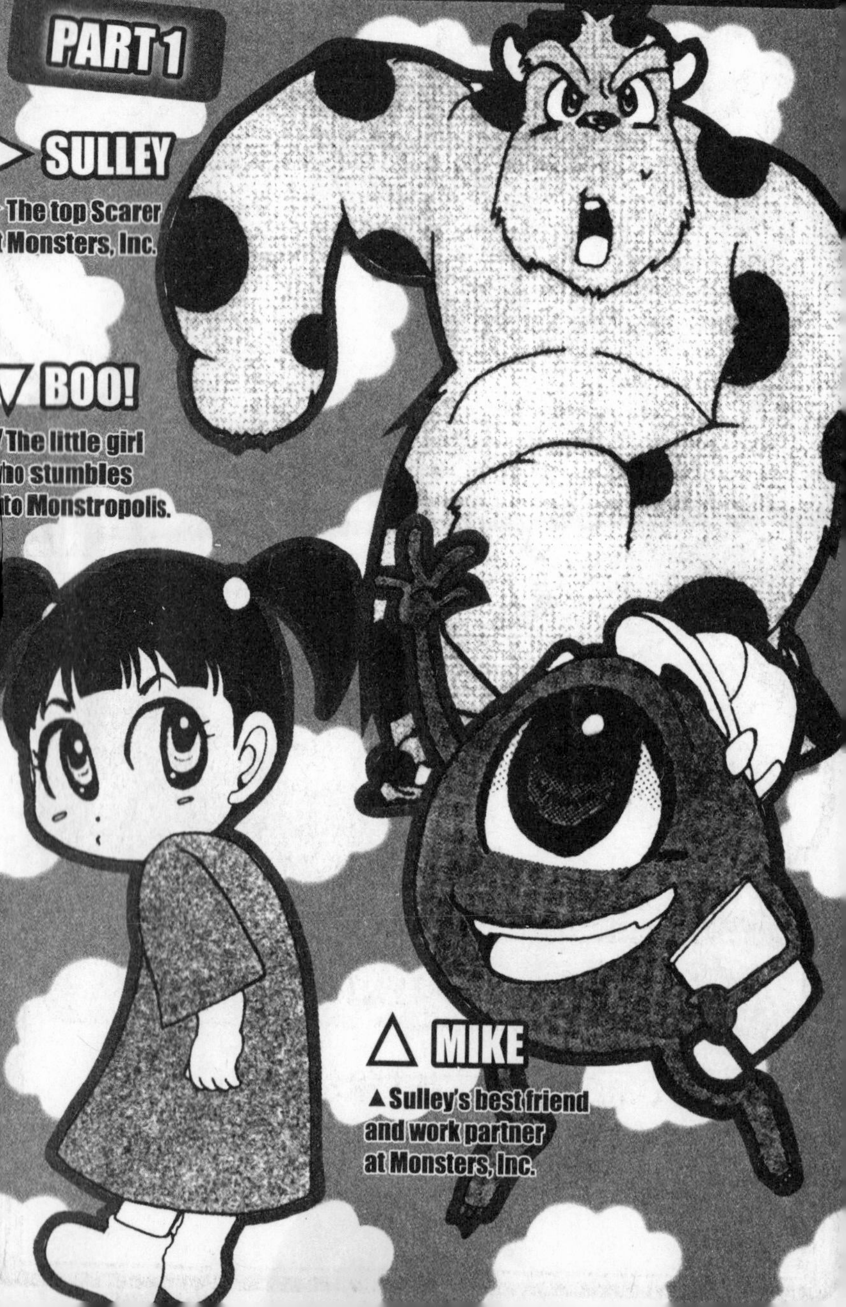

▶ SULLEY

▶ The top Scarer at Monsters, Inc.

▽ BOO!

▼ The little girl who stumbles into Monstropolis.

△ MIKE

▲ Sulley's best friend and work partner at Monsters, Inc.

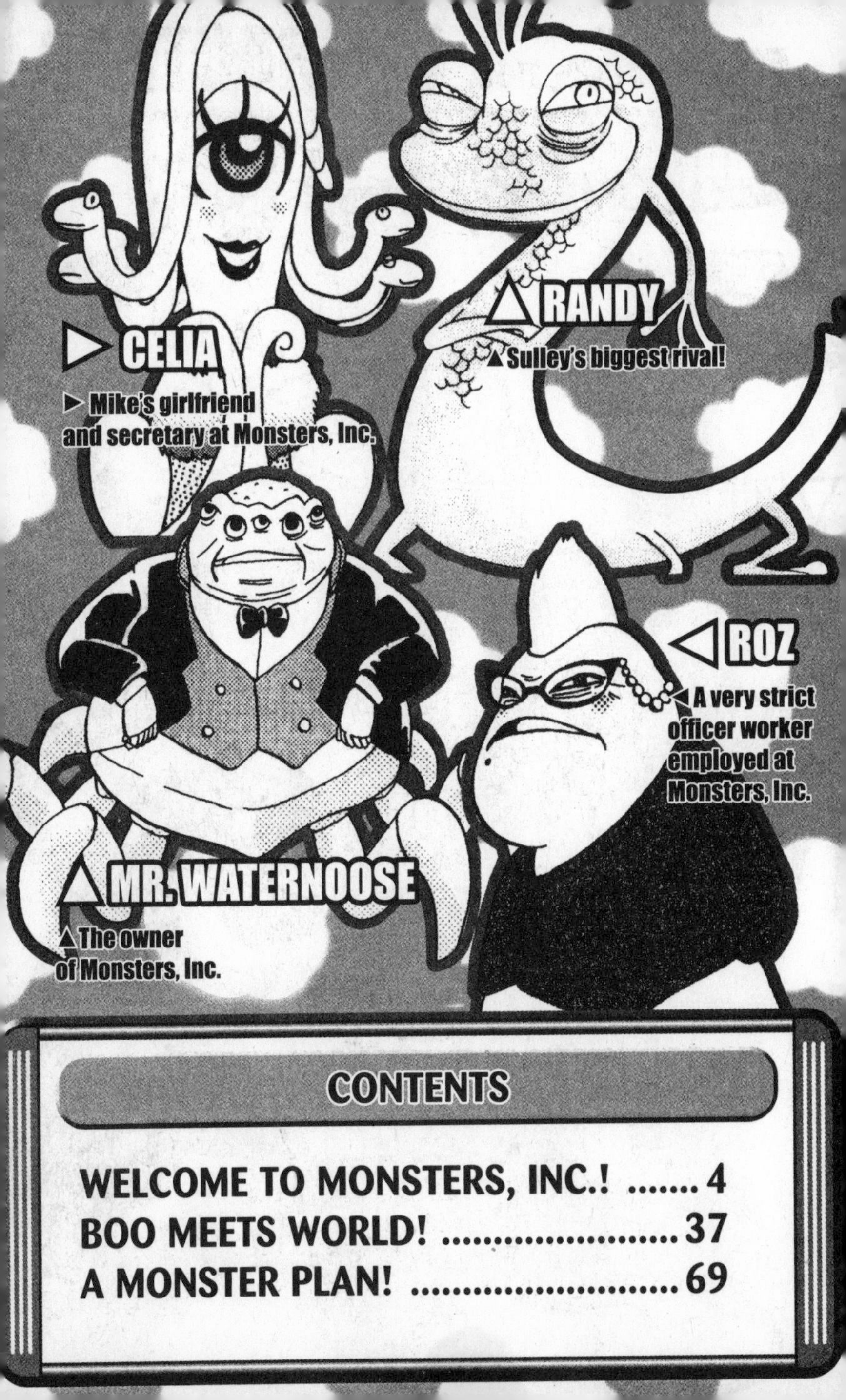
RANDY
Sulley's biggest rival!
CELIA
Mike's girlfriend and secretary at Monsters, Inc.
ROZ
A very strict officer worker employed at Monsters, Inc.
MR. WATERNOOSE
The owner of Monsters, Inc.

CONTENTS

Chapter 1

WELCOME TO MONSTERS, INC.!

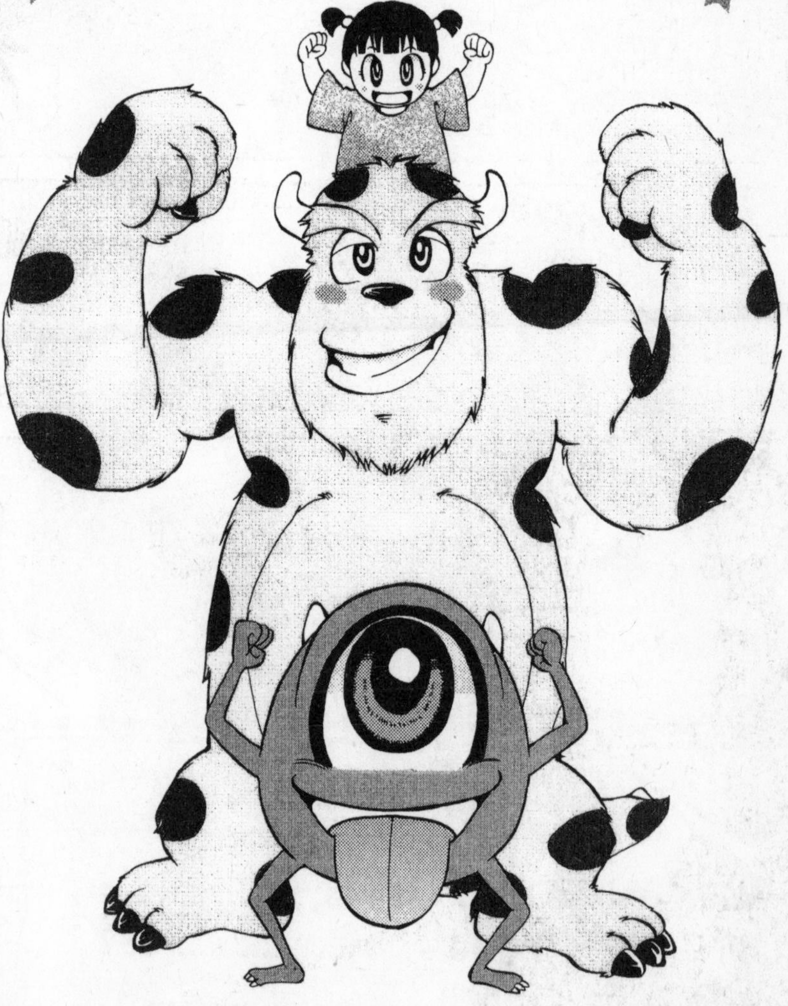

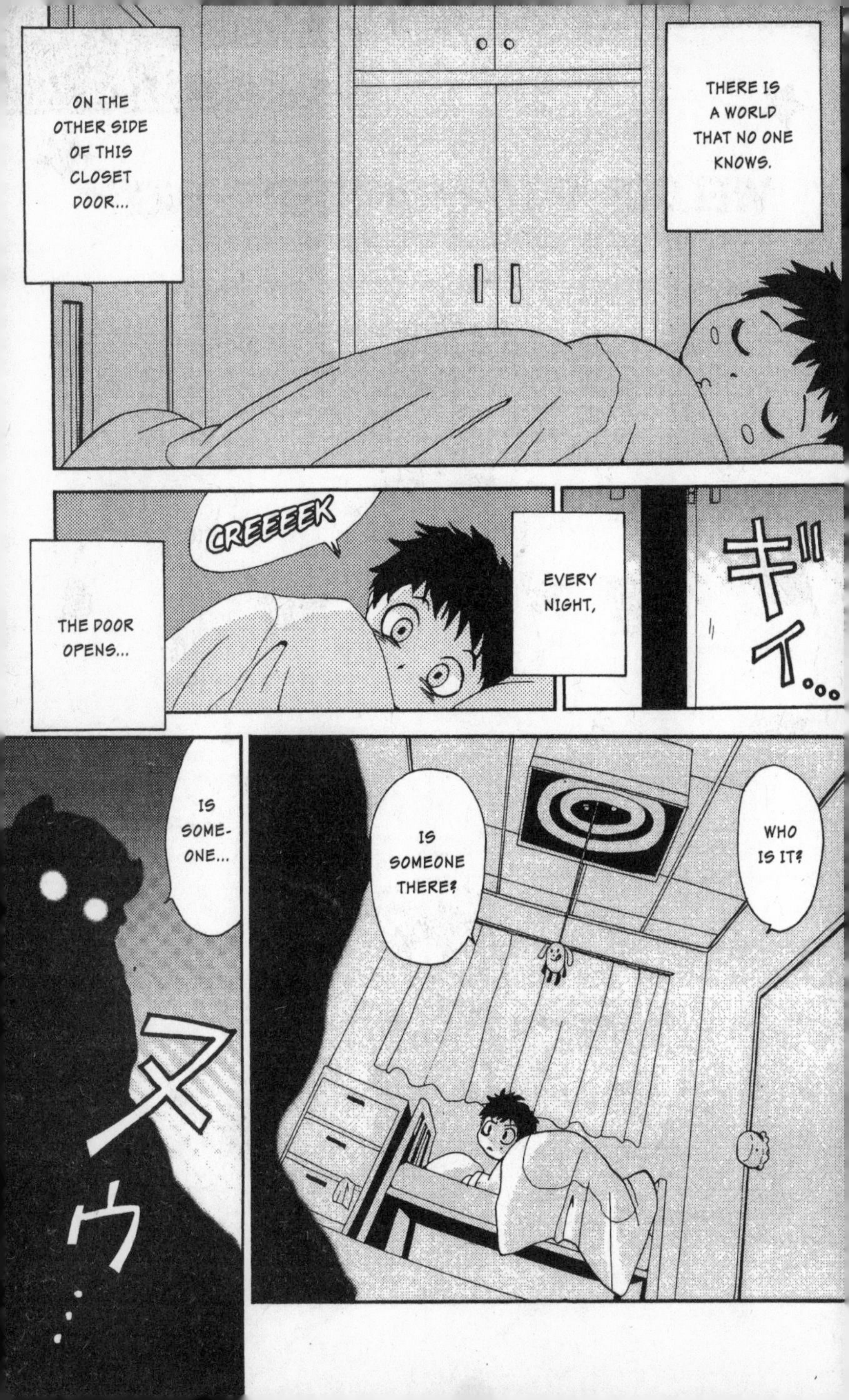
THERE IS A WORLD THAT NO ONE KNOWS.
ON THE OTHER SIDE OF THIS CLOSET DOOR...
ギィ…
EVERY NIGHT,
CREEEEK
THE DOOR OPENS...
WHO IS IT?
IS SOMEONE THERE?
IS SOME-ONE...
ヌウ…

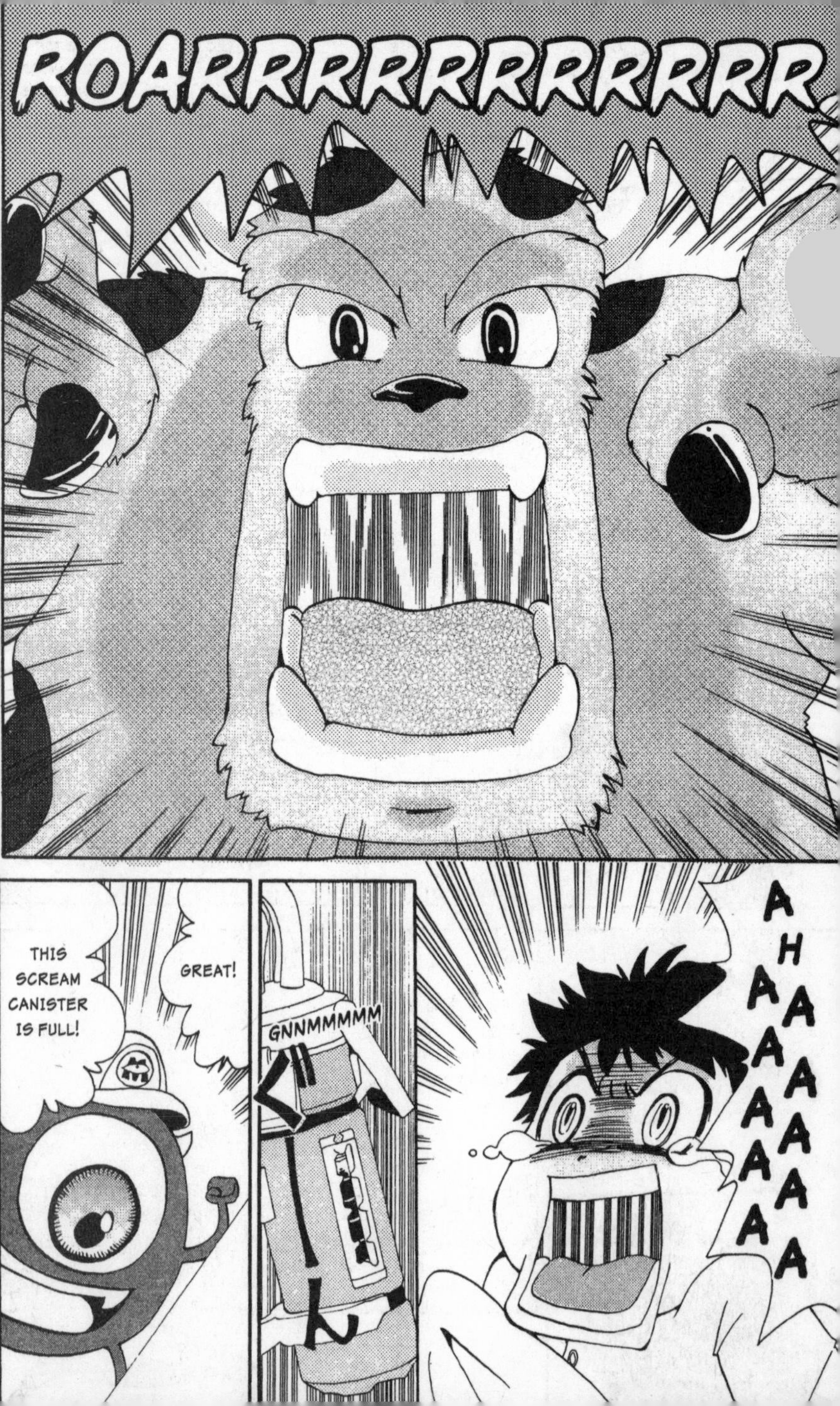
ROARRRRRRRRRRRR
AHAAAAAAAAAA
GNNMMMMM
GREAT!
THIS SCREAM CANISTER IS FULL!

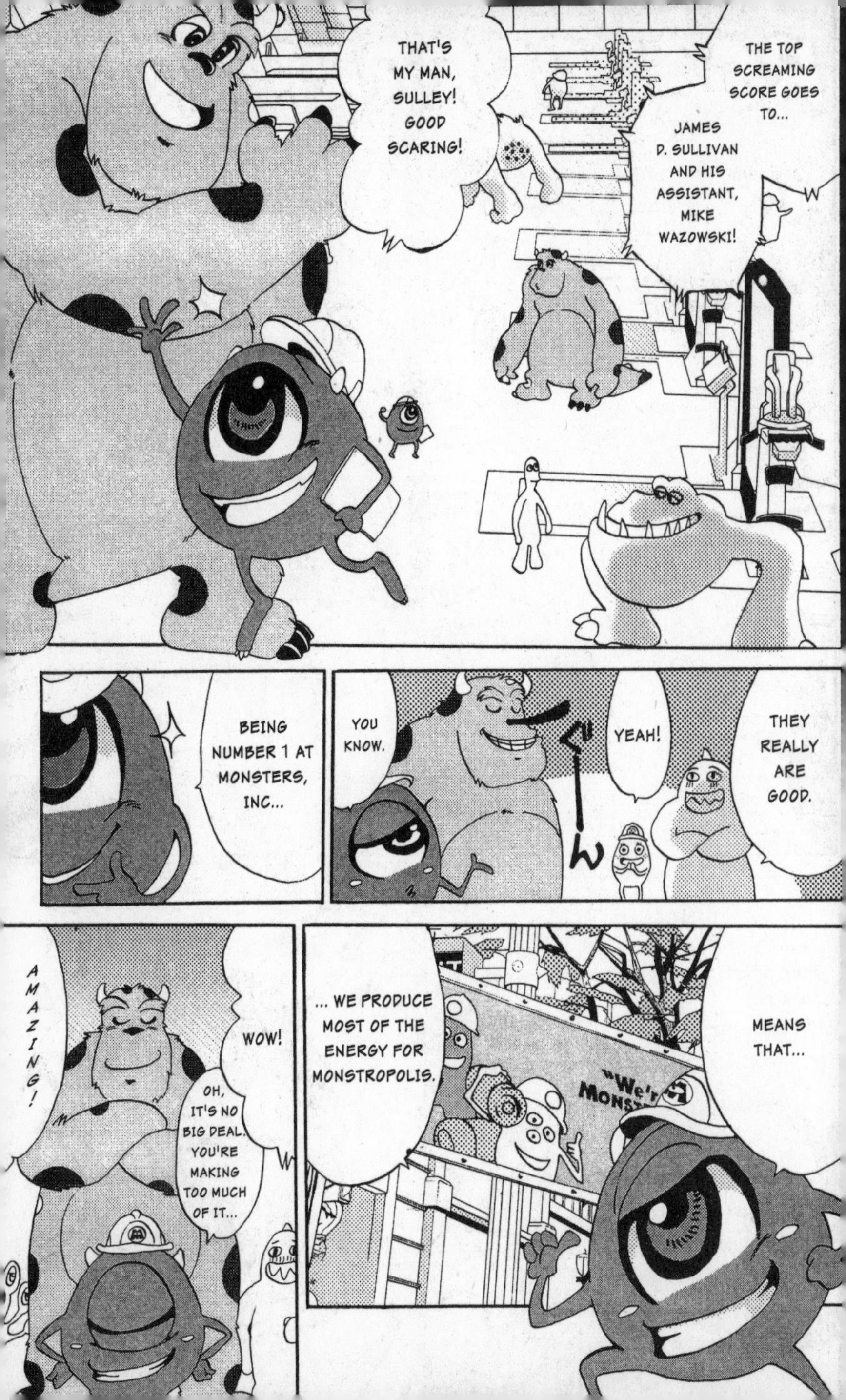
THE TOP SCREAMING SCORE GOES TO...
JAMES D. SULLIVAN AND HIS ASSISTANT, MIKE WAZOWSKI!
THAT'S MY MAN, SULLEY! GOOD SCARING!
THEY REALLY ARE GOOD.
YEAH!
YOU KNOW.
BEING NUMBER 1 AT MONSTERS, INC...
MEANS THAT...
... WE PRODUCE MOST OF THE ENERGY FOR MONSTROPOLIS.
WOW!
OH, IT'S NO BIG DEAL. YOU'RE MAKING TOO MUCH OF IT...
AMAZING!

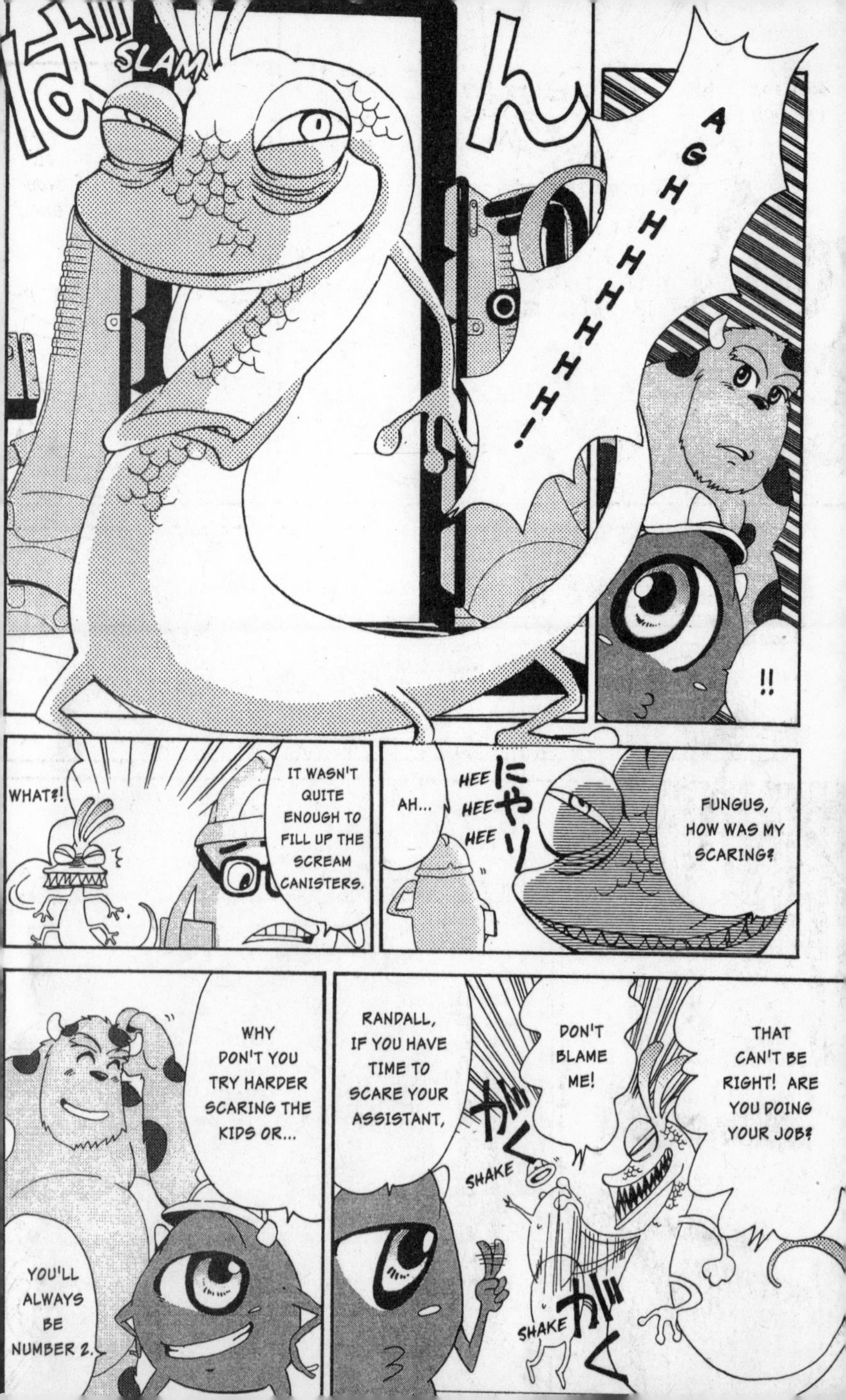
ばん
SLAM
AGHHHHHHH!
!!
FUNGUS, HOW WAS MY SCARING?
にやり
HEE HEE HEE
AH...
IT WASN'T QUITE ENOUGH TO FILL UP THE SCREAM CANISTERS.
WHAT?!
THAT CAN'T BE RIGHT! ARE YOU DOING YOUR JOB?
DON'T BLAME ME!
がくがく
SHAKE
がくがく
SHAKE
RANDALL, IF YOU HAVE TIME TO SCARE YOUR ASSISTANT,
WHY DON'T YOU TRY HARDER SCARING THE KIDS OR...
YOU'LL ALWAYS BE NUMBER 2.

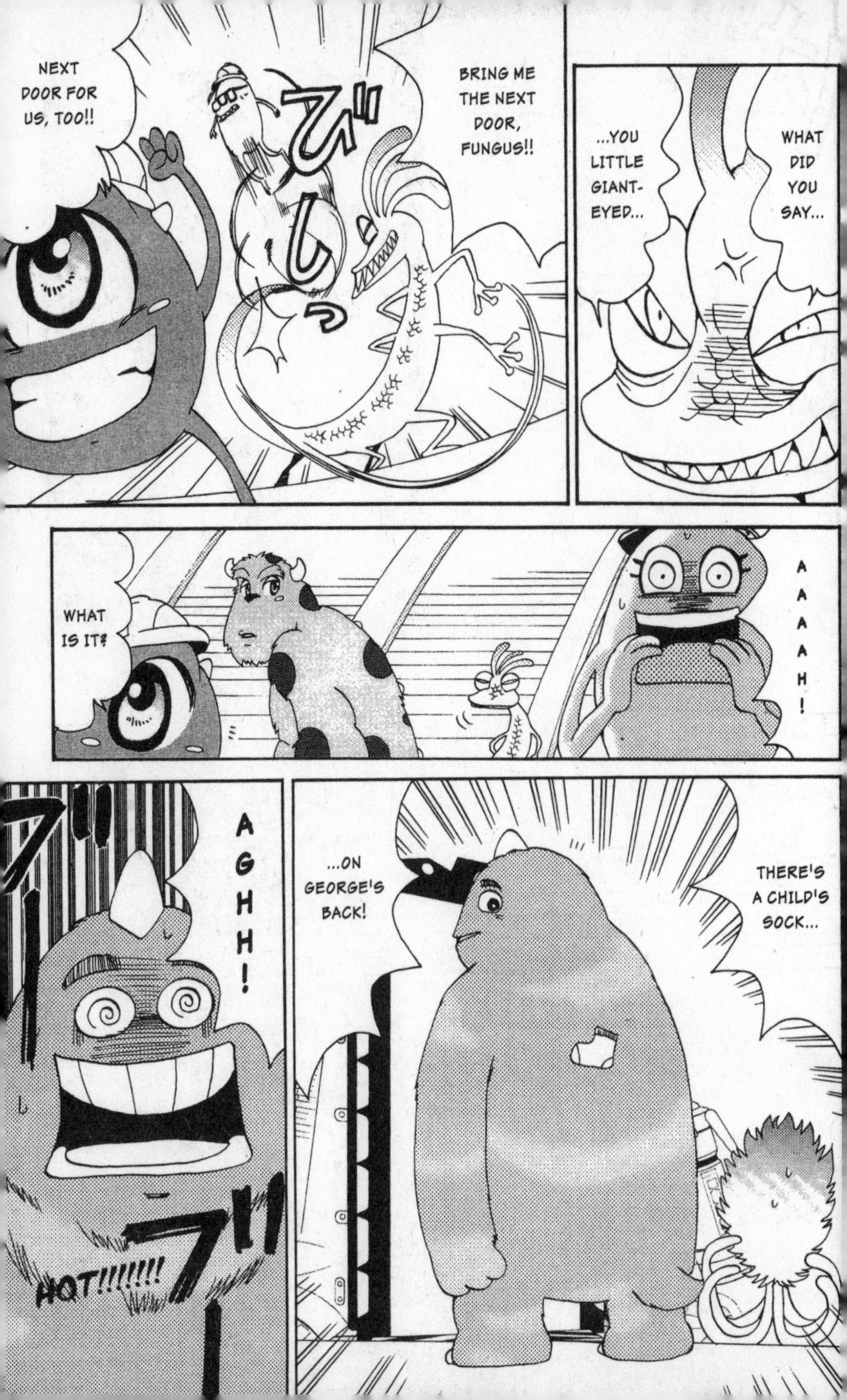
WHAT DID YOU SAY...
...YOU LITTLE GIANT-EYED...
BRING ME THE NEXT DOOR, FUNGUS!!
びしっ
NEXT DOOR FOR US, TOO!!
AAAAAH!
WHAT IS IT?
THERE'S A CHILD'S SOCK...
...ON GEORGE'S BACK!
AGHH!
HOT!!!!!!!

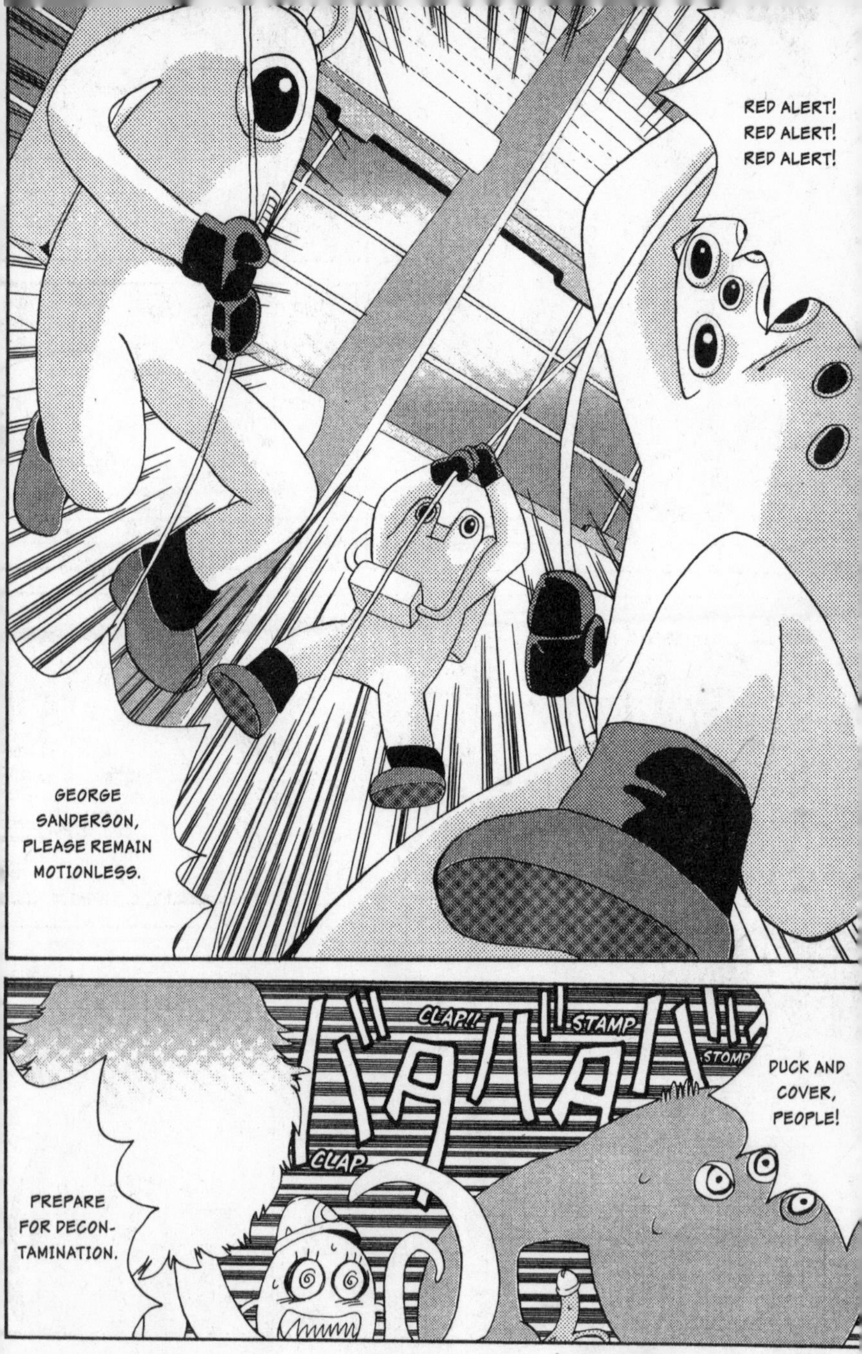
RED ALERT!
RED ALERT!
RED ALERT!
GEORGE SANDERSON, PLEASE REMAIN MOTIONLESS.
DUCK AND COVER, PEOPLE!
STOMP
STAMP
CLAP!!
CLAP
PREPARE FOR DECON-TAMINATION.

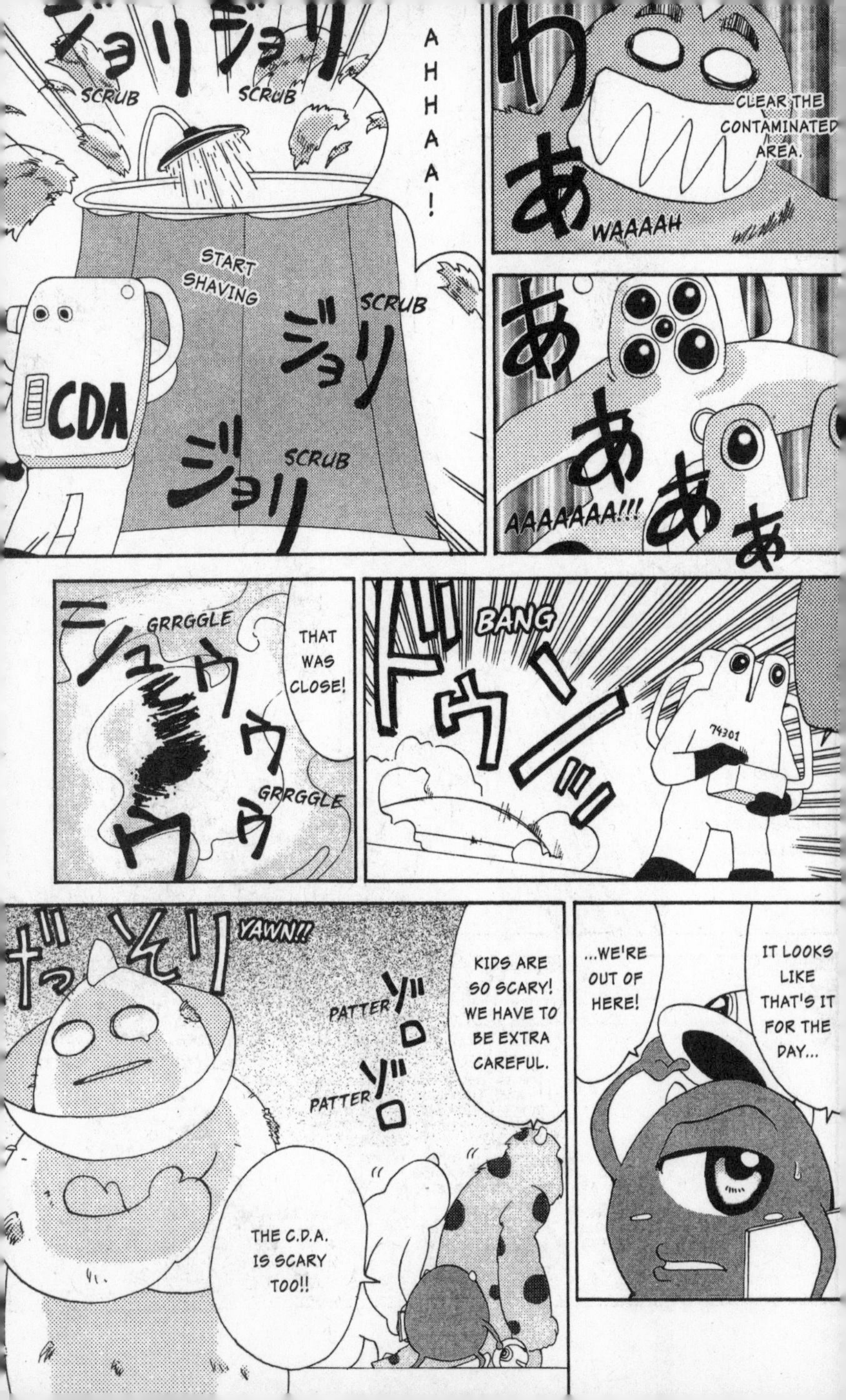

わあ
CLEAR THE CONTAMINATED AREA.
WAAAAH
あああぁ
AAAAAAA!!!
ジョリジョリ
SCRUB
SCRUB
AHHHAAA!
START SHAVING
CDA
ジョリ
SCRUB
ジョリ
SCRUB
ドウーン
BANG
74301
ニュウウウ
GRRGGLE
THAT WAS CLOSE!
GRRGGLE
IT LOOKS LIKE THAT'S IT FOR THE DAY...
...WE'RE OUT OF HERE!
げっそり
YAWN!!
KIDS ARE SO SCARY! WE HAVE TO BE EXTRA CAREFUL.
ゾロゾロ
PATTER
PATTER
THE C.D.A. IS SCARY TOO!!

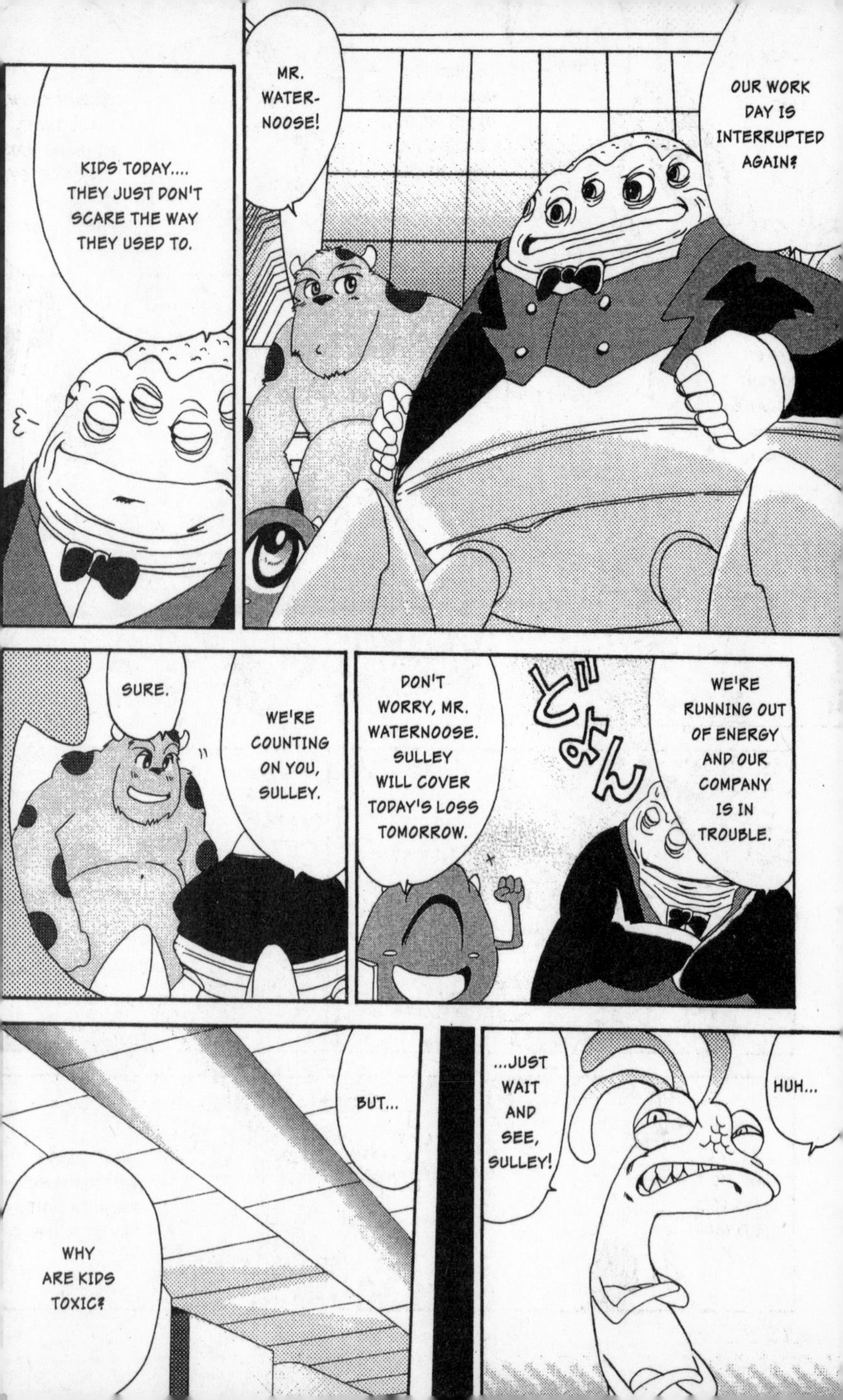
OUR WORK DAY IS INTERRUPTED AGAIN?
MR. WATER-NOOSE!
KIDS TODAY.... THEY JUST DON'T SCARE THE WAY THEY USED TO.
WE'RE RUNNING OUT OF ENERGY AND OUR COMPANY IS IN TROUBLE.
どよん
DON'T WORRY, MR. WATERNOOSE. SULLEY WILL COVER TODAY'S LOSS TOMORROW.
WE'RE COUNTING ON YOU, SULLEY.
SURE.
HUH...
...JUST WAIT AND SEE, SULLEY!
BUT...
WHY ARE KIDS TOXIC?

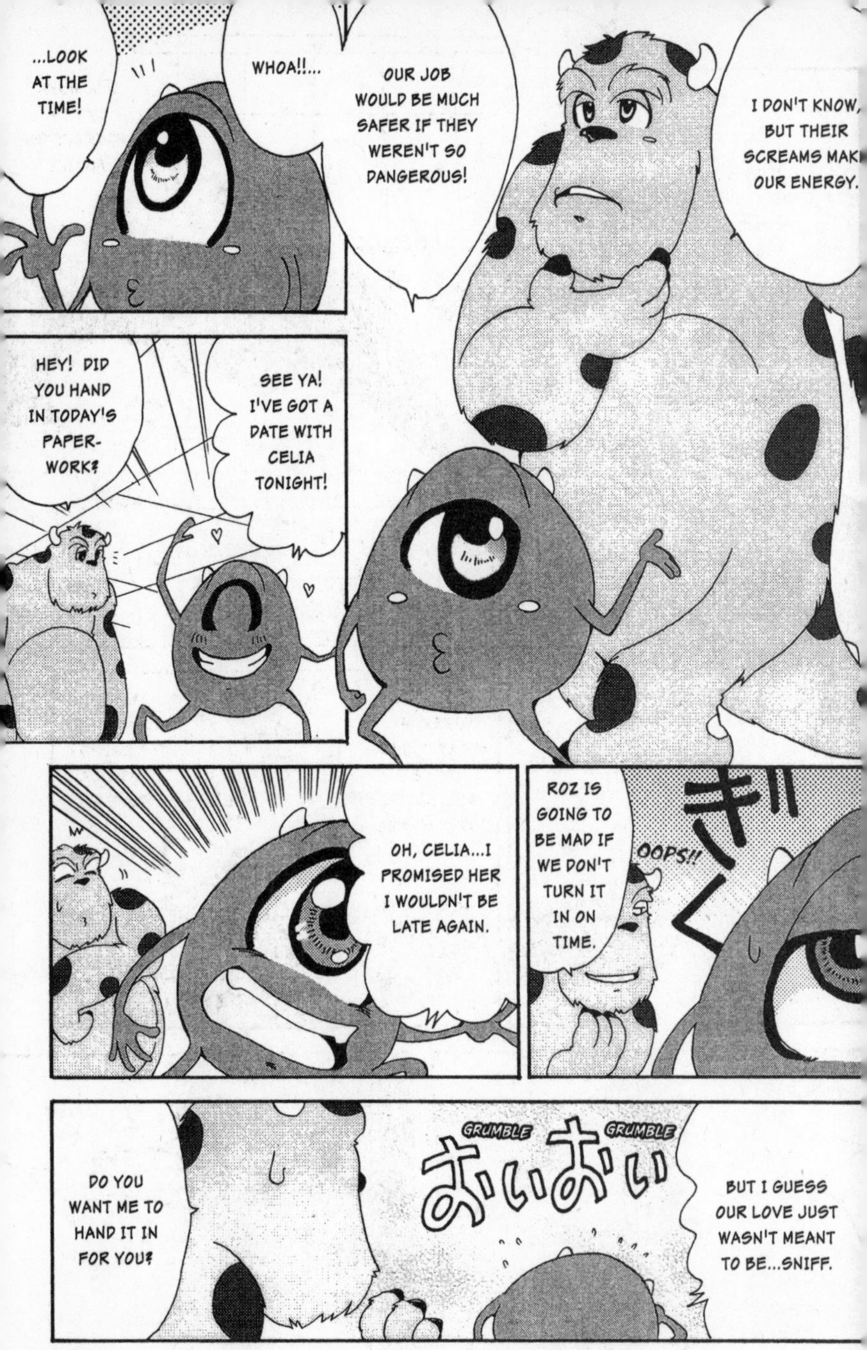

I DON'T KNOW, BUT THEIR SCREAMS MAK OUR ENERGY.
OUR JOB WOULD BE MUCH SAFER IF THEY WEREN'T SO DANGEROUS!
WHOA!!...
...LOOK AT THE TIME!
SEE YA! I'VE GOT A DATE WITH CELIA TONIGHT!
HEY! DID YOU HAND IN TODAY'S PAPER-WORK?
ぎく
OOPS!!
ROZ IS GOING TO BE MAD IF WE DON'T TURN IT IN ON TIME.
OH, CELIA...I PROMISED HER I WOULDN'T BE LATE AGAIN.
BUT I GUESS OUR LOVE JUST WASN'T MEANT TO BE...SNIFF.
GRUMBLE
GRUMBLE
おいおい
DO YOU WANT ME TO HAND IT IN FOR YOU?

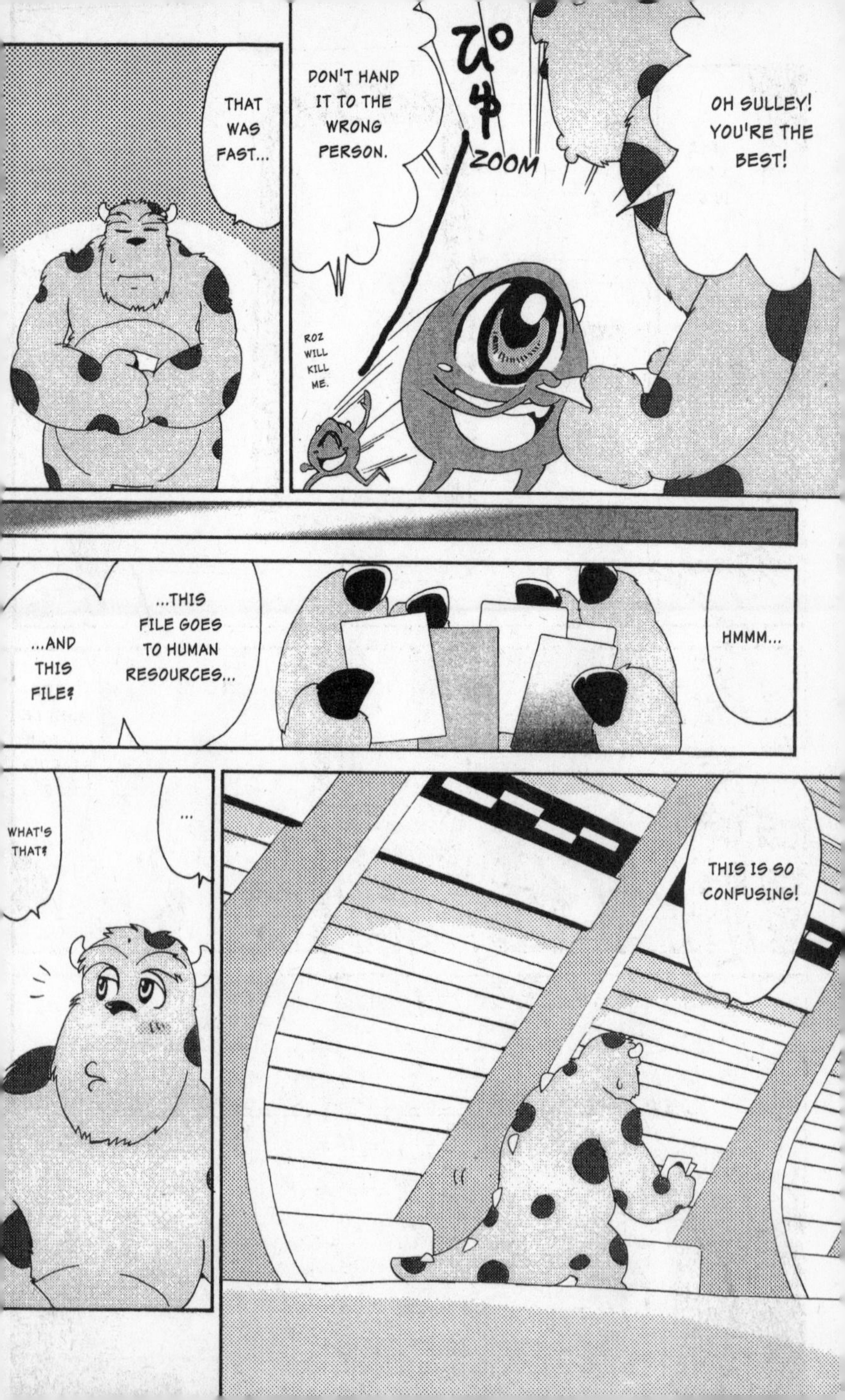
OH SULLEY! YOU'RE THE BEST!
DON'T HAND IT TO THE WRONG PERSON.
ZOOM
ROZ WILL KILL ME.
THAT WAS FAST...
HMMM...
...THIS FILE GOES TO HUMAN RESOURCES...
...AND THIS FILE?
THIS IS SO CONFUSING!
...
WHAT'S THAT?

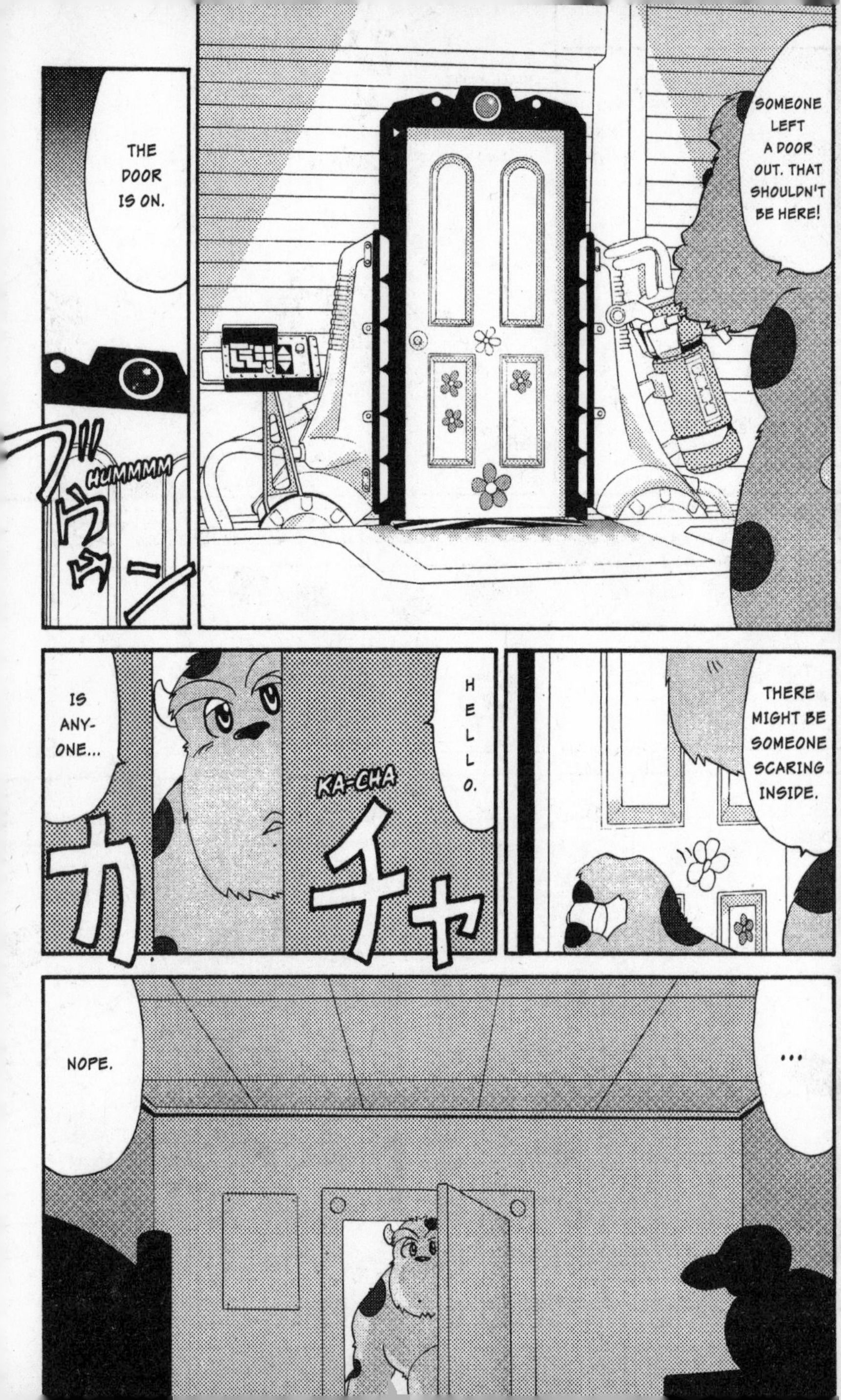
SOMEONE LEFT A DOOR OUT. THAT SHOULDN'T BE HERE!
THE DOOR IS ON.
HUMMMM
THERE MIGHT BE SOMEONE SCARING INSIDE.
HELLO.
IS ANY-ONE...
KA-CHA
カチャ
...
NOPE.

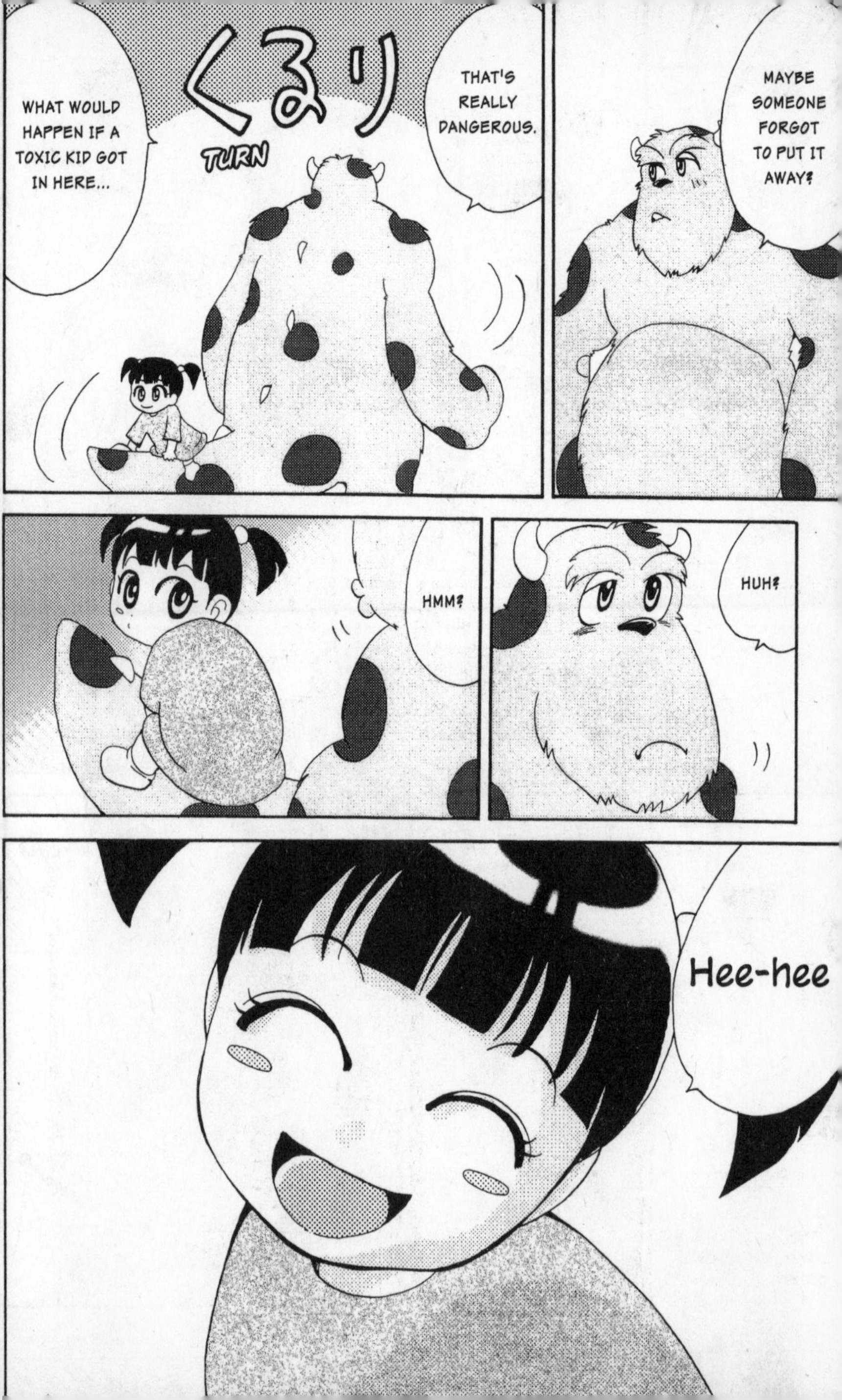
MAYBE SOMEONE FORGOT TO PUT IT AWAY?
THAT'S REALLY DANGEROUS.
くるり
TURN
WHAT WOULD HAPPEN IF A TOXIC KID GOT IN HERE...
HUH?
HMM?
Hee-hee

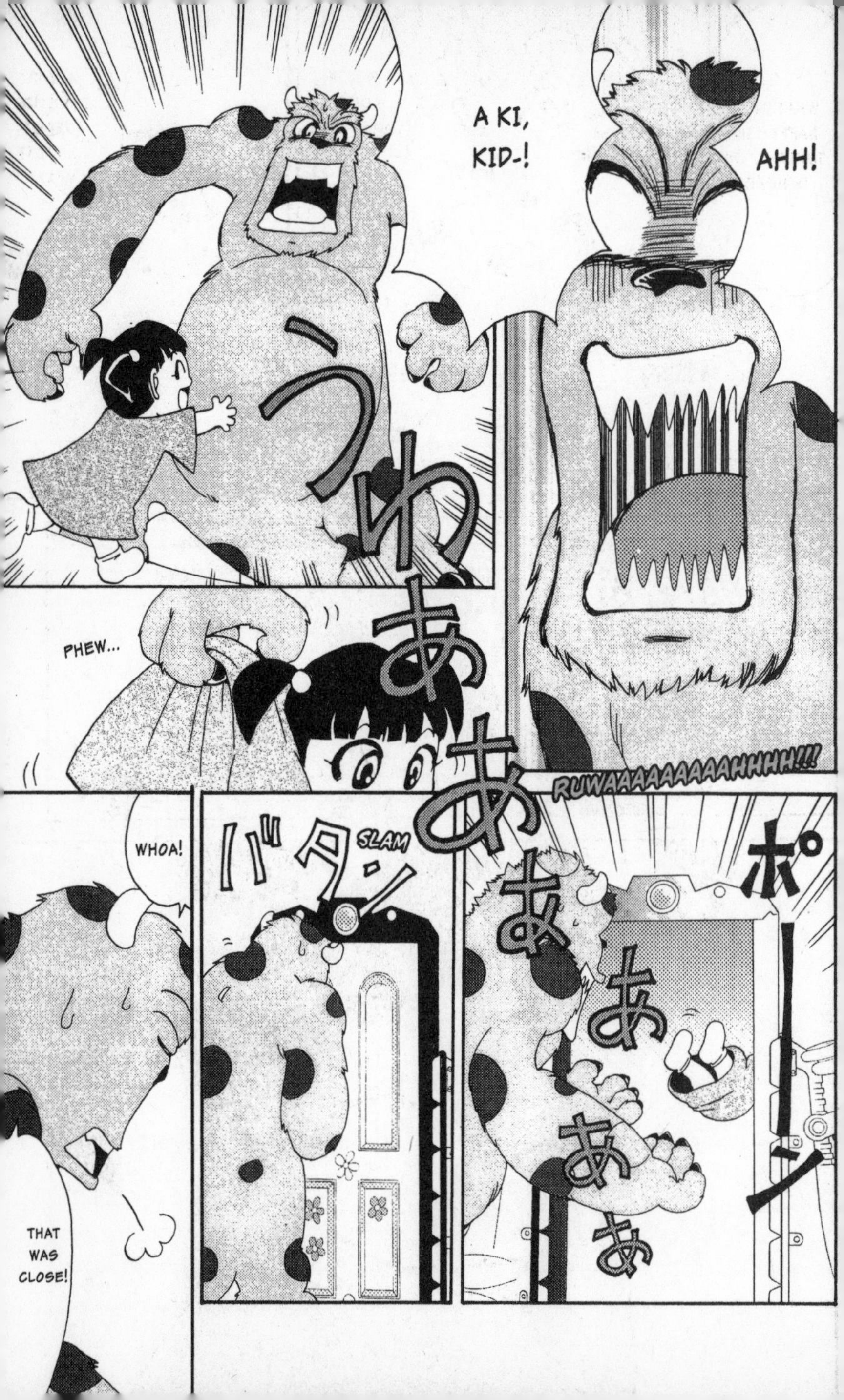
AHH!
つわああぁぁぁ
RUWAAAAAAAAAHHHH!!!
A KI,
KID-!
PHEW...
ポーン
バタン
SLAM
WHOA!
THAT WAS CLOSE!

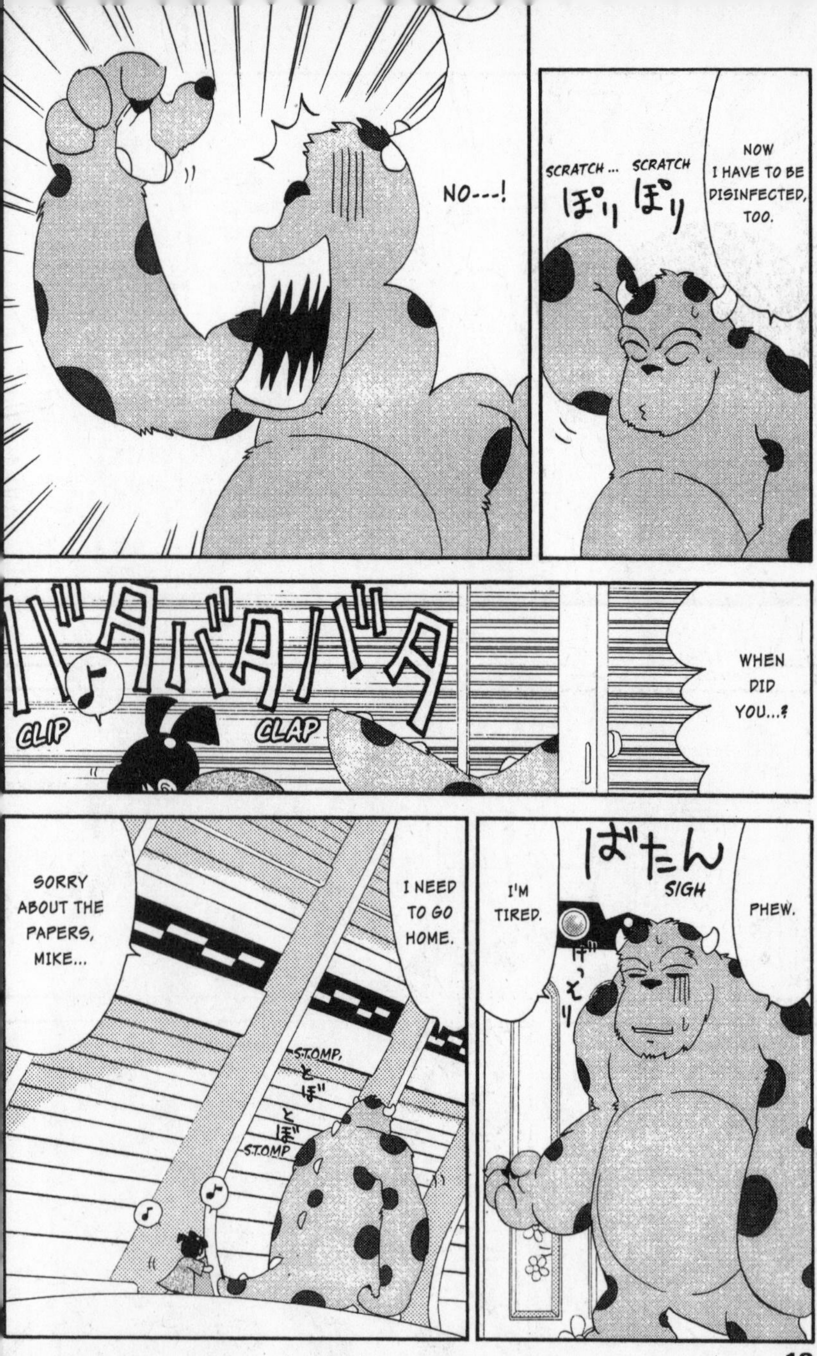
NOW I HAVE TO BE DISINFECTED, TOO.
SCRATCH ... SCRATCH
ぽり ぽり
NO---!
WHEN DID YOU...?
バタバタバタ
CLIP CLAP
PHEW.
ばたん
SIGH
I'M TIRED.
げっそり
I NEED TO GO HOME.
SORRY ABOUT THE PAPERS, MIKE...
STOMP, とぼ とぼ STOMP

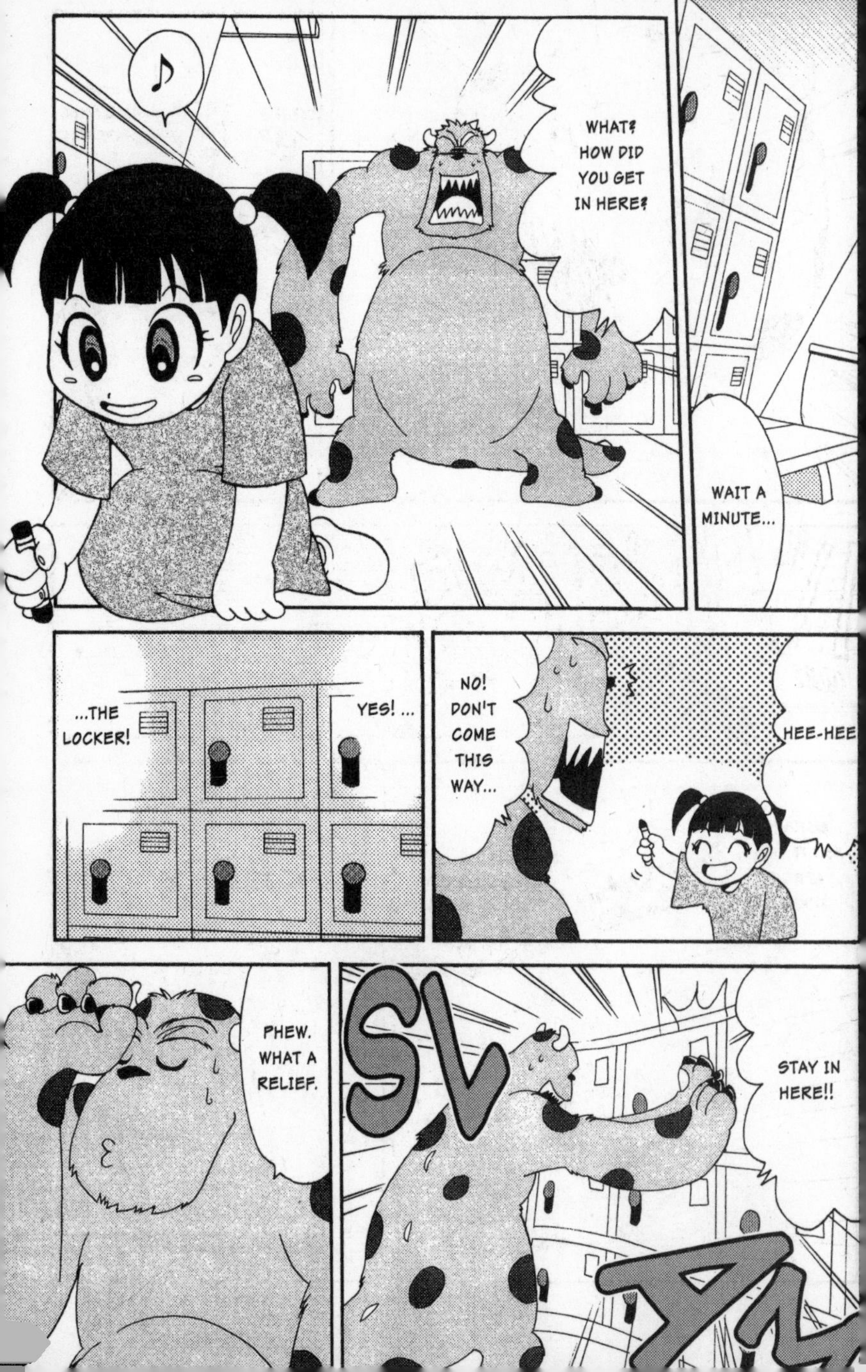
WAIT A MINUTE...
WHAT? HOW DID YOU GET IN HERE?
♪
HEE-HEE
NO! DON'T COME THIS WAY...
YES! ...
...THE LOCKER!
STAY IN HERE!!
SL
AM
PHEW. WHAT A RELIEF.

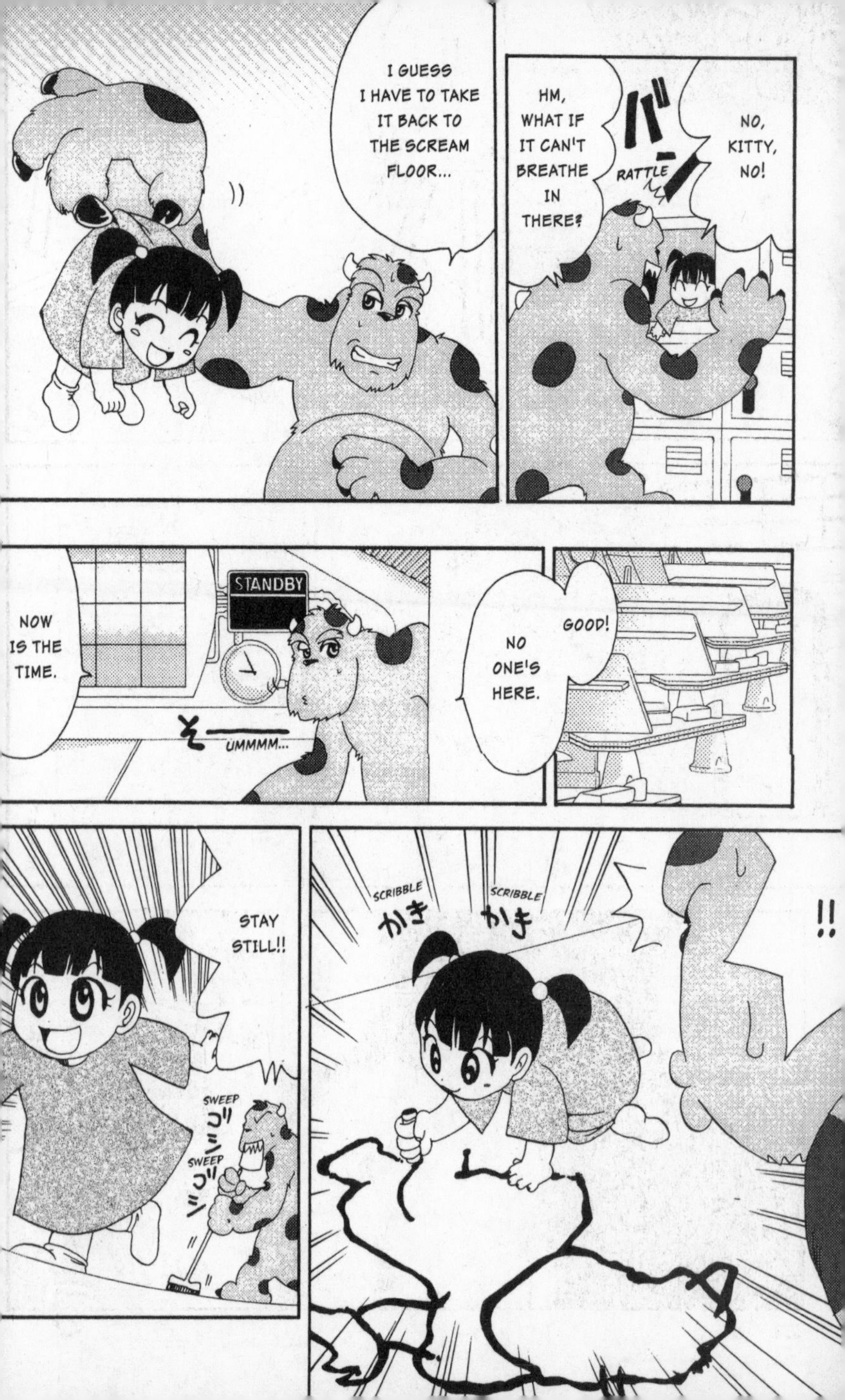
NO, KITTY, NO!
バ
RATTLE
HM, WHAT IF IT CAN'T BREATHE IN THERE?
I GUESS I HAVE TO TAKE IT BACK TO THE SCREAM FLOOR...
GOOD!
NO ONE'S HERE.
STANDBY
NOW IS THE TIME.
そ
UMMMM...
!!
SCRIBBLE
かき
SCRIBBLE
かき
STAY STILL!!
SWEEP
SWEEP

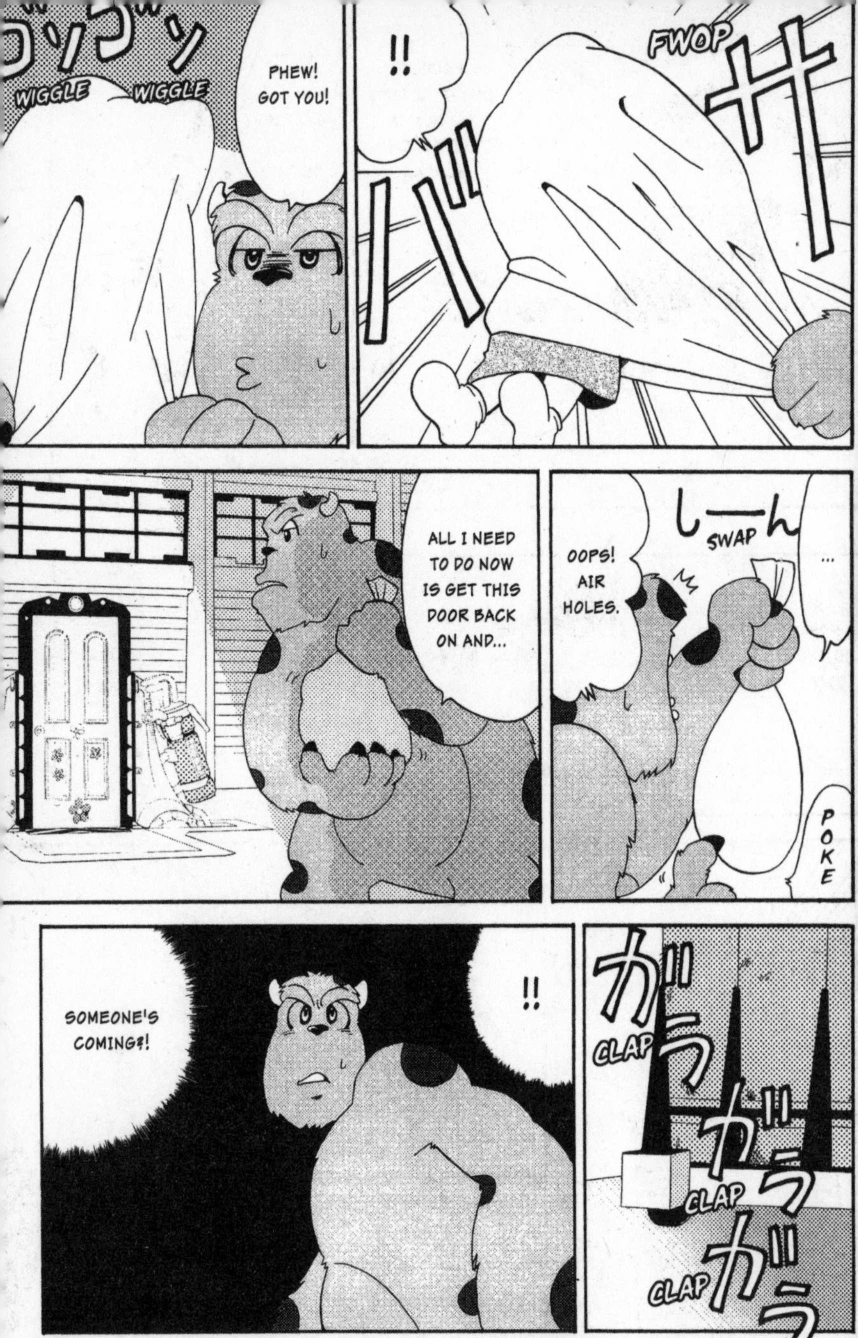
FWOP
!!
WIGGLE WIGGLE
PHEW! GOT YOU!
しーん
SWAP
...
OOPS! AIR HOLES.
POKE
ALL I NEED TO DO NOW IS GET THIS DOOR BACK ON AND...
がら
CLAP
がら
CLAP
がら
CLAP
!!
SOMEONE'S COMING?!

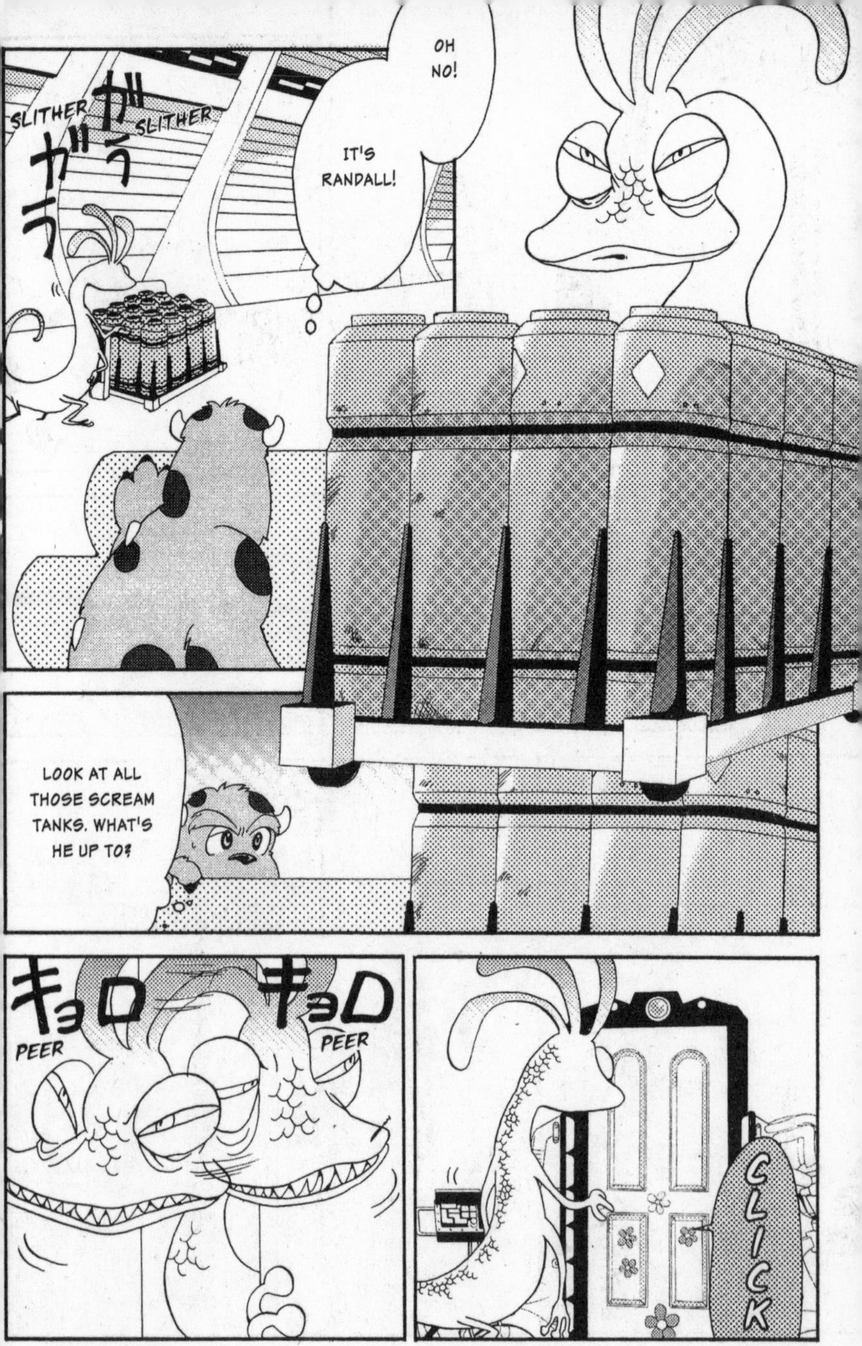
OH NO!
IT'S RANDALL!
SLITHER
ガラ
SLITHER
ガラ
LOOK AT ALL THOSE SCREAM TANKS. WHAT'S HE UP TO?
CLICK
キョロ
PEER
キョロ
PEER

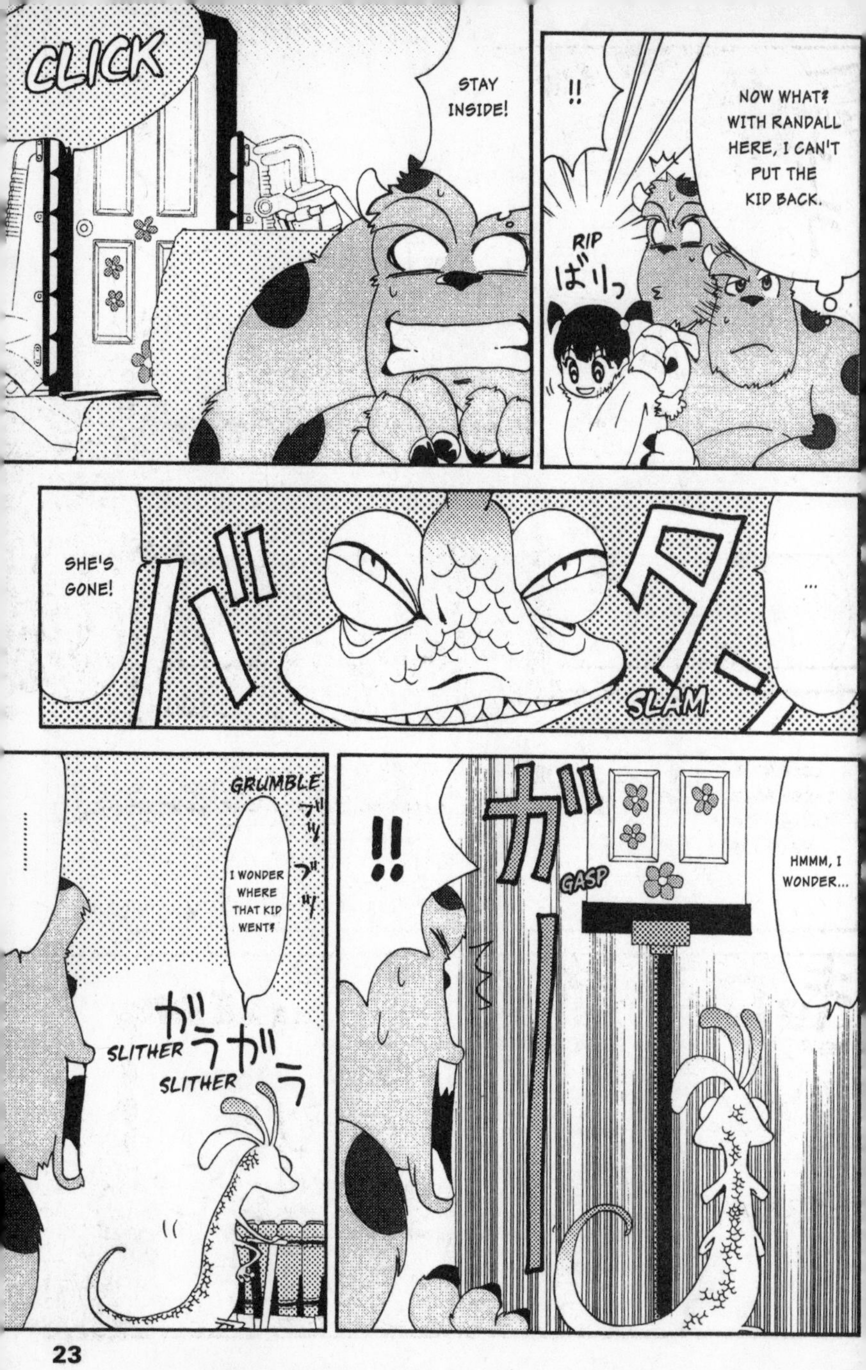
NOW WHAT? WITH RANDALL HERE, I CAN'T PUT THE KID BACK.
!!
RIP
ばりっ
STAY INSIDE!
CLICK
...
バター
SLAM
SHE'S GONE!
HMMM, I WONDER...
ガー
GASP
!!
GRUMBLE
ブツブツ
I WONDER WHERE THAT KID WENT?
....
SLITHER
SLITHER
ガラガラ

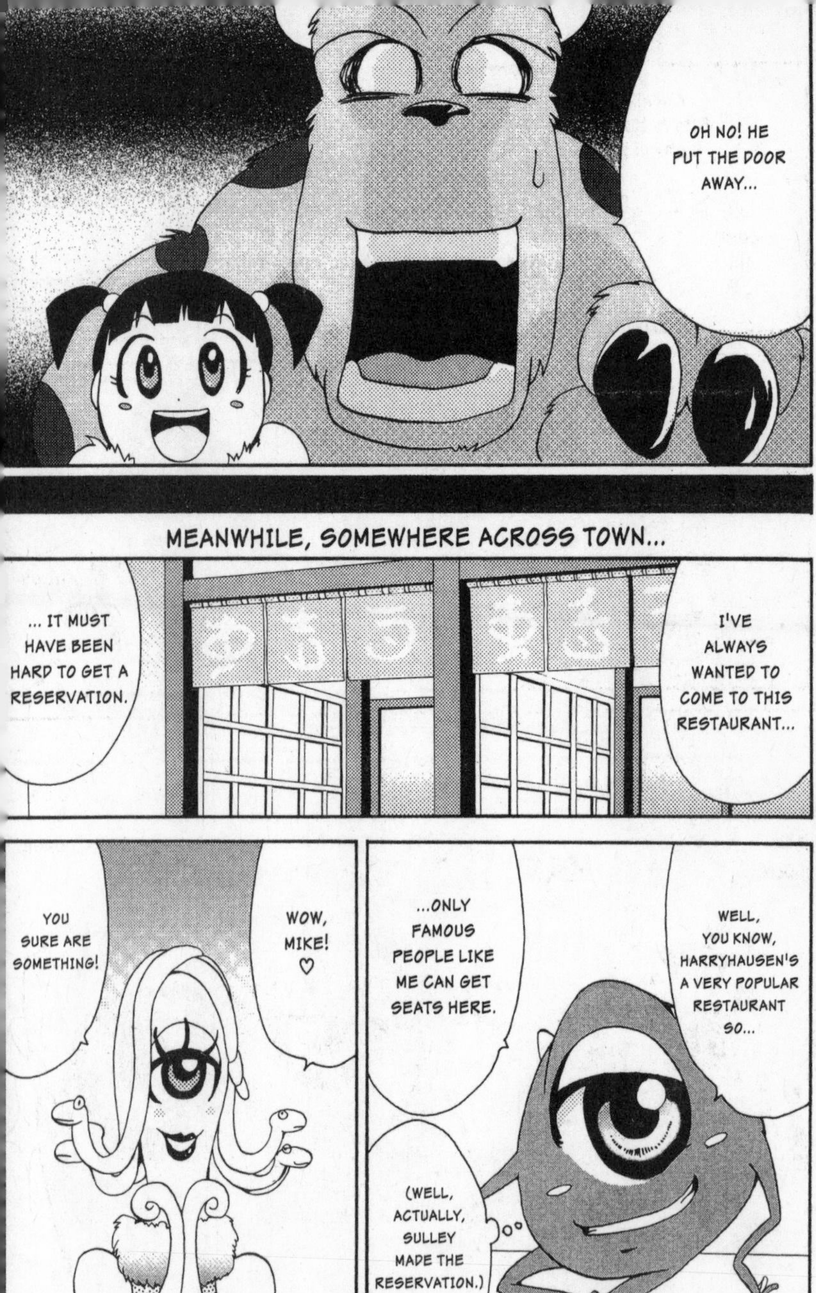
OH NO! HE PUT THE DOOR AWAY...
MEANWHILE, SOMEWHERE ACROSS TOWN...
I'VE ALWAYS WANTED TO COME TO THIS RESTAURANT...
... IT MUST HAVE BEEN HARD TO GET A RESERVATION.
WELL, YOU KNOW, HARRYHAUSEN'S A VERY POPULAR RESTAURANT SO...
...ONLY FAMOUS PEOPLE LIKE ME CAN GET SEATS HERE.
(WELL, ACTUALLY, SULLEY MADE THE RESERVATION.)
WOW, MIKE! ♡
YOU SURE ARE SOMETHING!

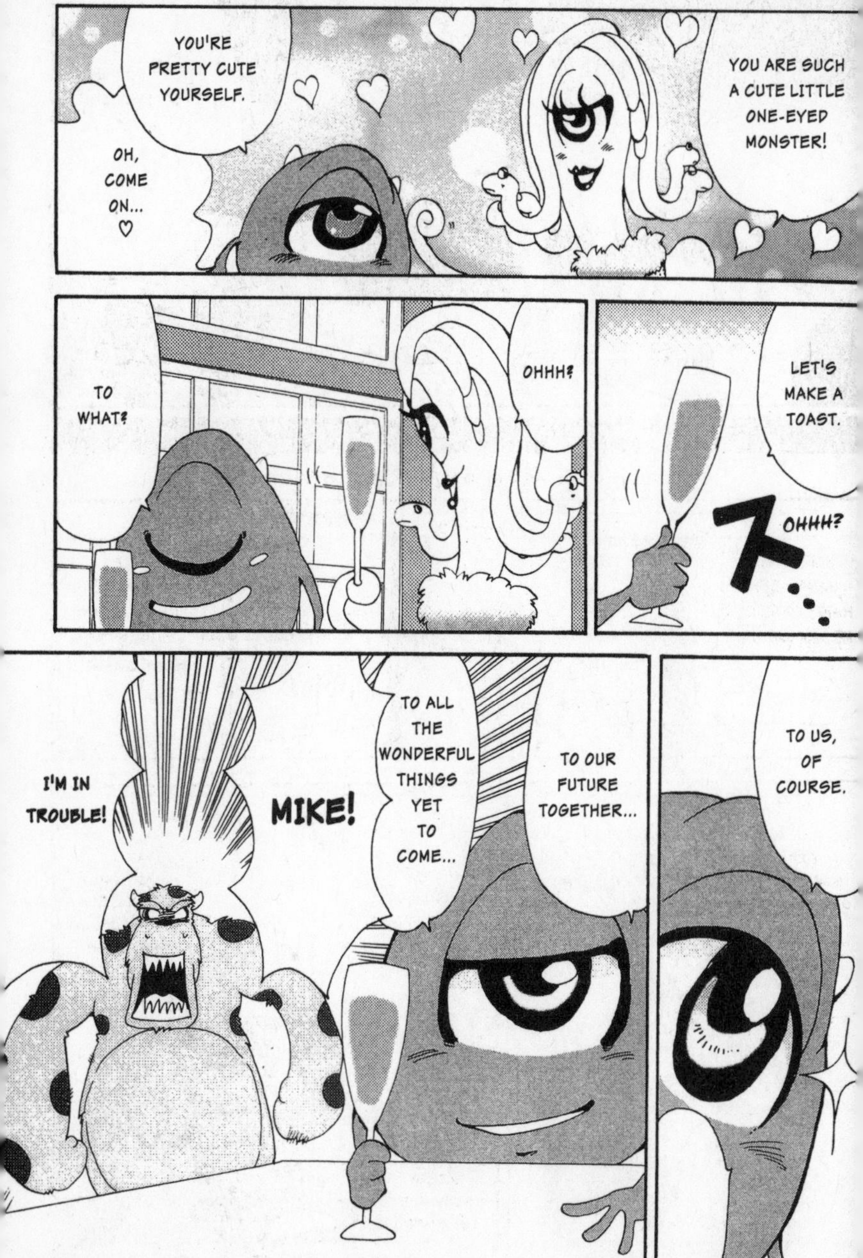
YOU ARE SUCH A CUTE LITTLE ONE-EYED MONSTER!
YOU'RE PRETTY CUTE YOURSELF.
OH, COME ON... ♡
LET'S MAKE A TOAST.
OHHH?
OHHH?
TO WHAT?
TO US, OF COURSE.
TO OUR FUTURE TOGETHER...
TO ALL THE WONDERFUL THINGS YET TO COME...
MIKE!
I'M IN TROUBLE!

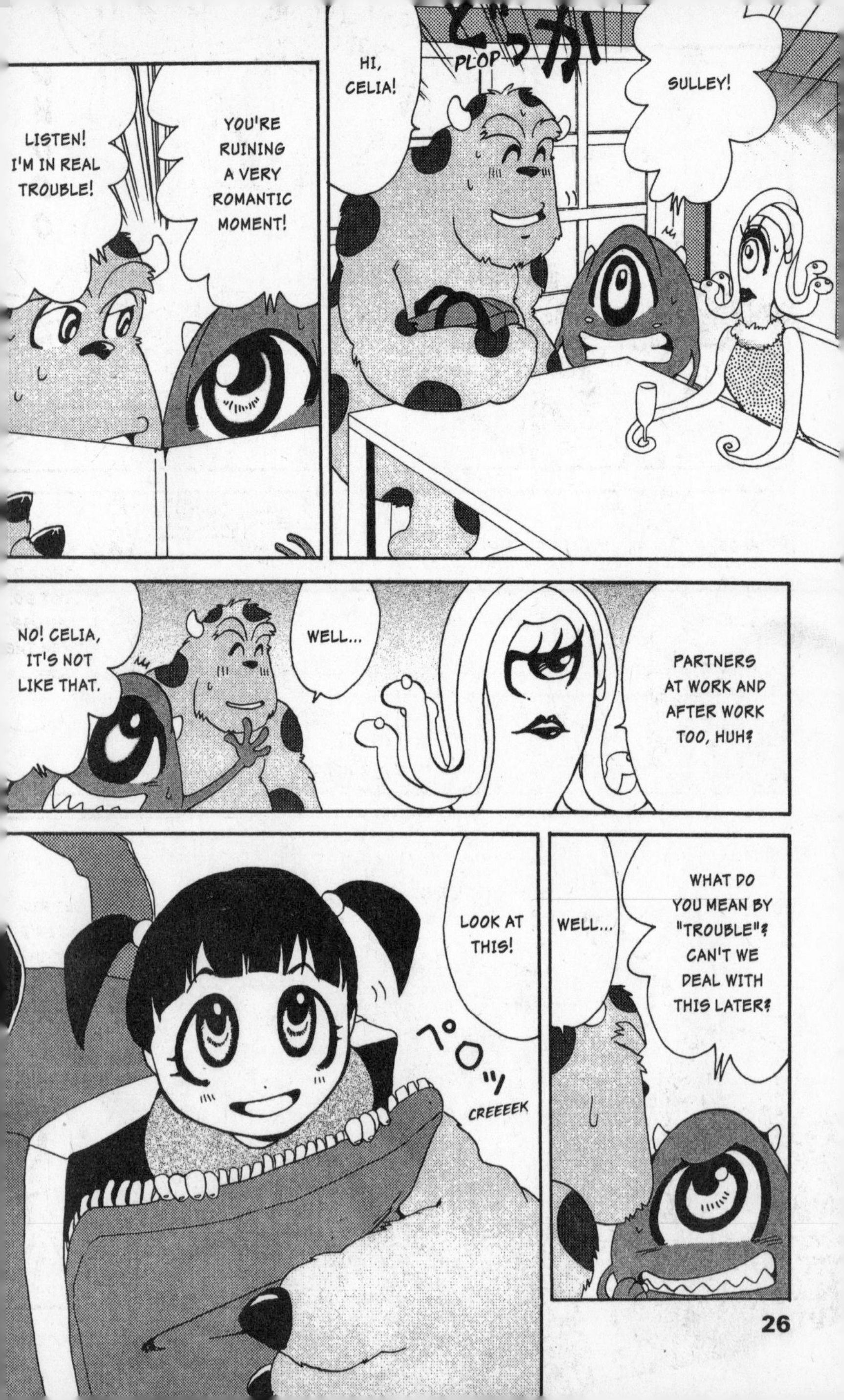

どっか
PLOP
SULLEY!
HI, CELIA!
YOU'RE RUINING A VERY ROMANTIC MOMENT!
LISTEN! I'M IN REAL TROUBLE!
PARTNERS AT WORK AND AFTER WORK TOO, HUH?
WELL...
NO! CELIA, IT'S NOT LIKE THAT.
WHAT DO YOU MEAN BY "TROUBLE"? CAN'T WE DEAL WITH THIS LATER?
WELL...
LOOK AT THIS!
パロッ
CREEEEK

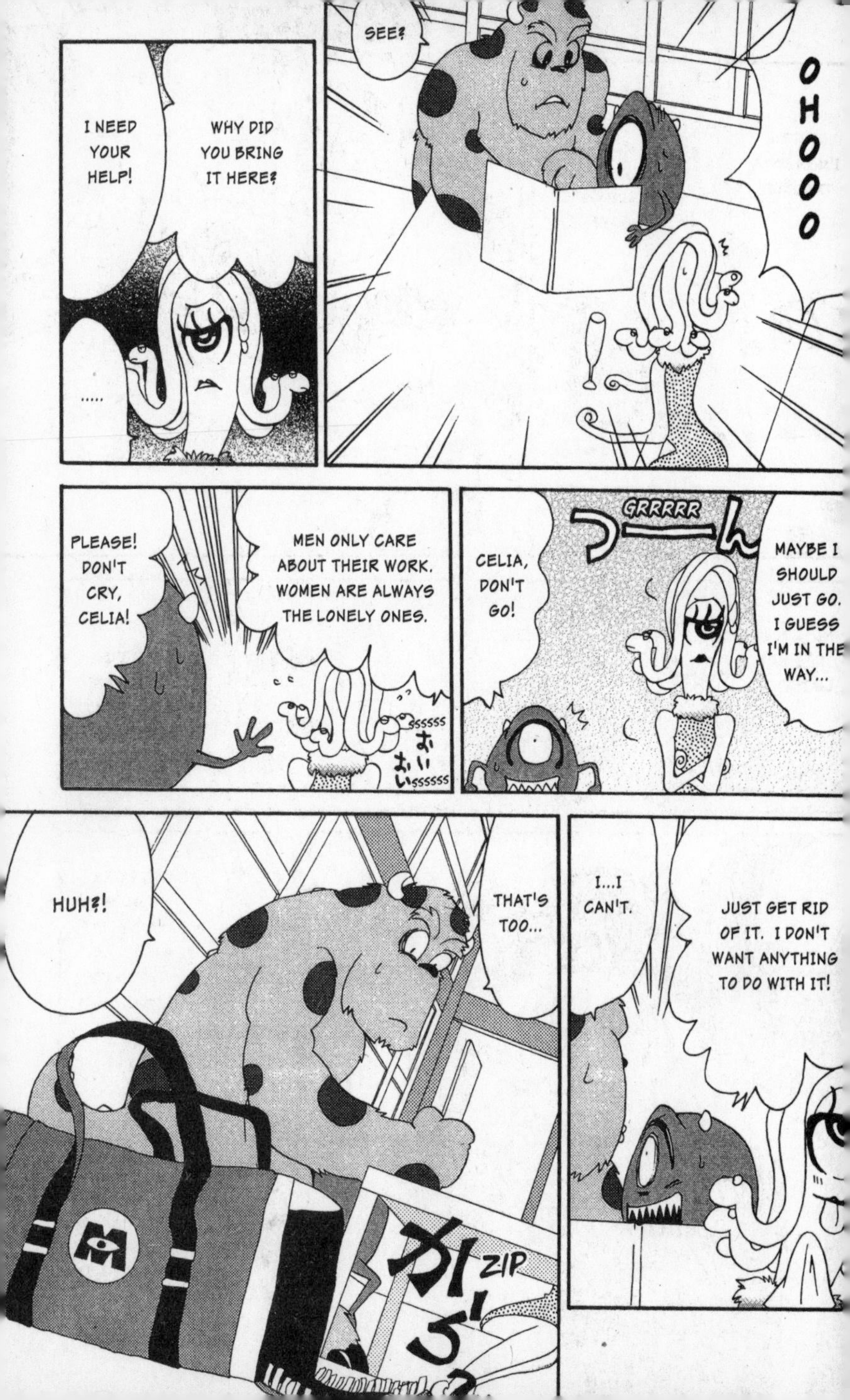
SEE?
OHOOOO
WHY DID YOU BRING IT HERE?
I NEED YOUR HELP!
.....
MAYBE I SHOULD JUST GO. I GUESS I'M IN THE WAY...
GRRRRR
つーん
CELIA, DON'T GO!
MEN ONLY CARE ABOUT THEIR WORK. WOMEN ARE ALWAYS THE LONELY ONES.
PLEASE! DON'T CRY, CELIA!
SSSSSS
おいおい
SSSSSS
JUST GET RID OF IT. I DON'T WANT ANYTHING TO DO WITH IT!
I...I CAN'T.
THAT'S TOO...
HUH?!
ZIP

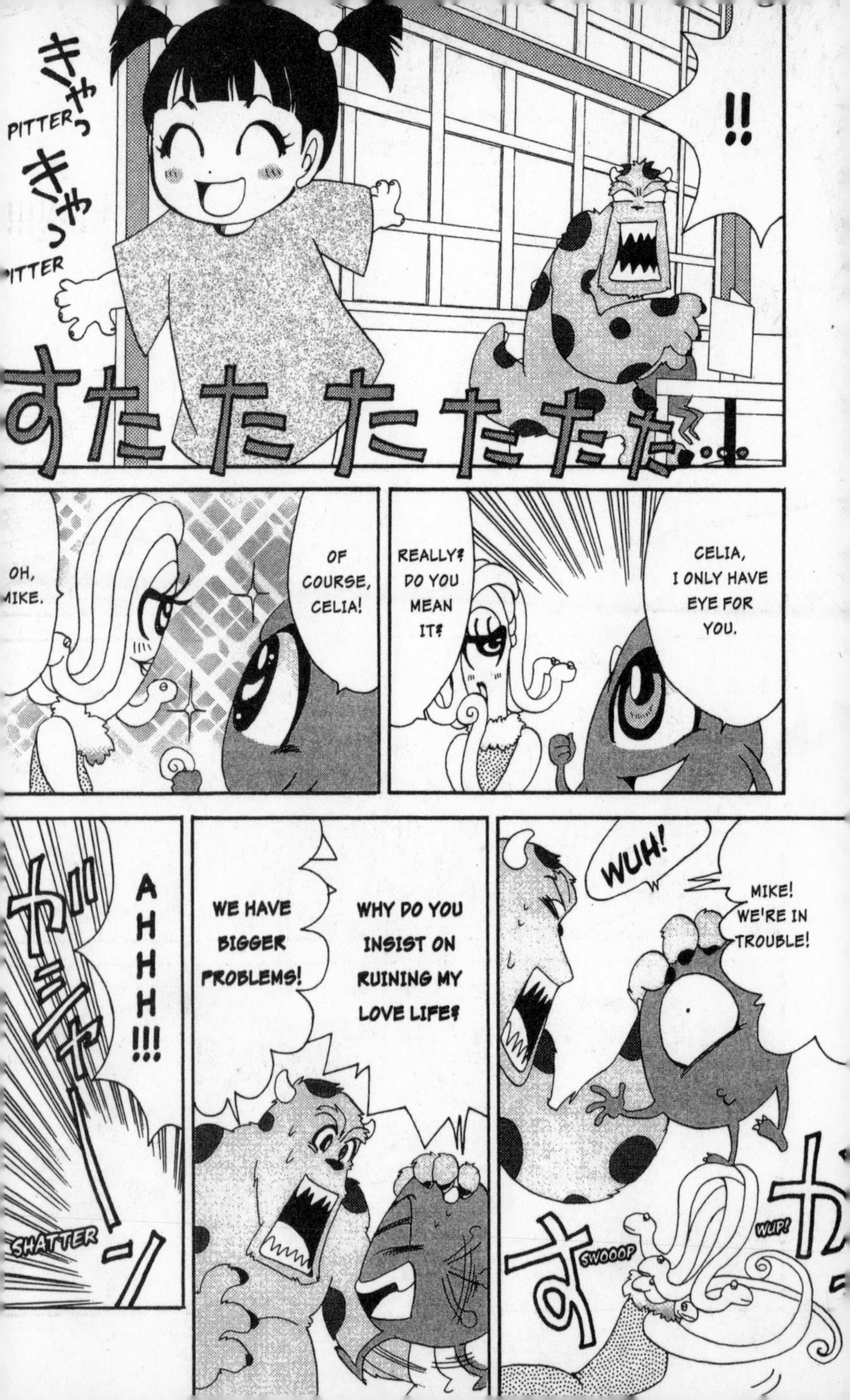

!!
きゃっ
PITTER
きゃっ
ITTER
すたたたたた…!
CELIA, I ONLY HAVE EYE FOR YOU.
REALLY? DO YOU MEAN IT?
OF COURSE, CELIA!
OH, MIKE.
WUH!
MIKE! WE'RE IN TROUBLE!
すっ
SWOOOP
WUP!
わっ
WHY DO YOU INSIST ON RUINING MY LOVE LIFE?
WE HAVE BIGGER PROBLEMS!
AHHH!!!
ガシャーン
SHATTER

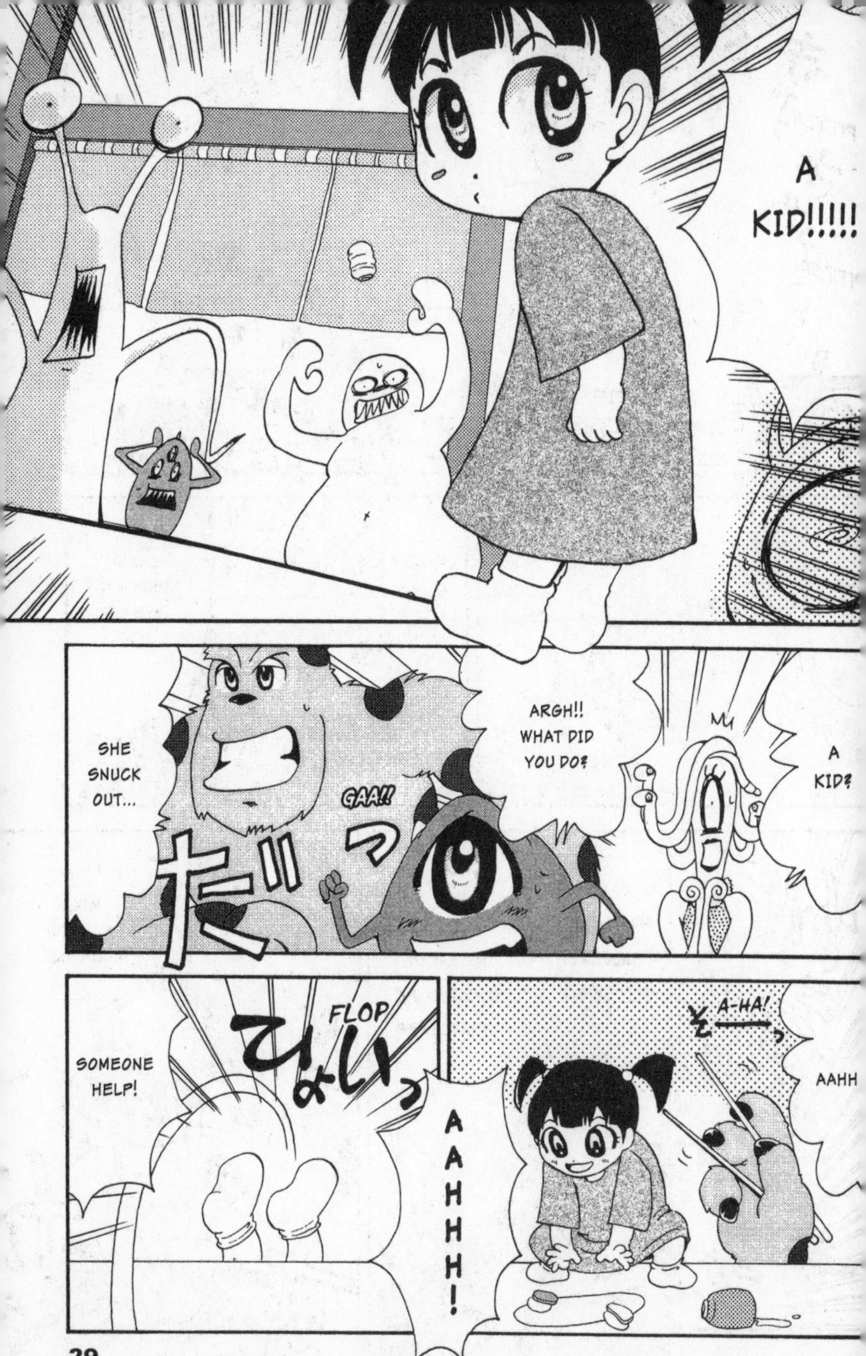
A KID!!!!!
A KID?
ARGH!! WHAT DID YOU DO?
GAA!!
SHE SNUCK OUT...
A-HA!
AAHH
FLOP
ひょいっ
SOMEONE HELP!
AAHHH!

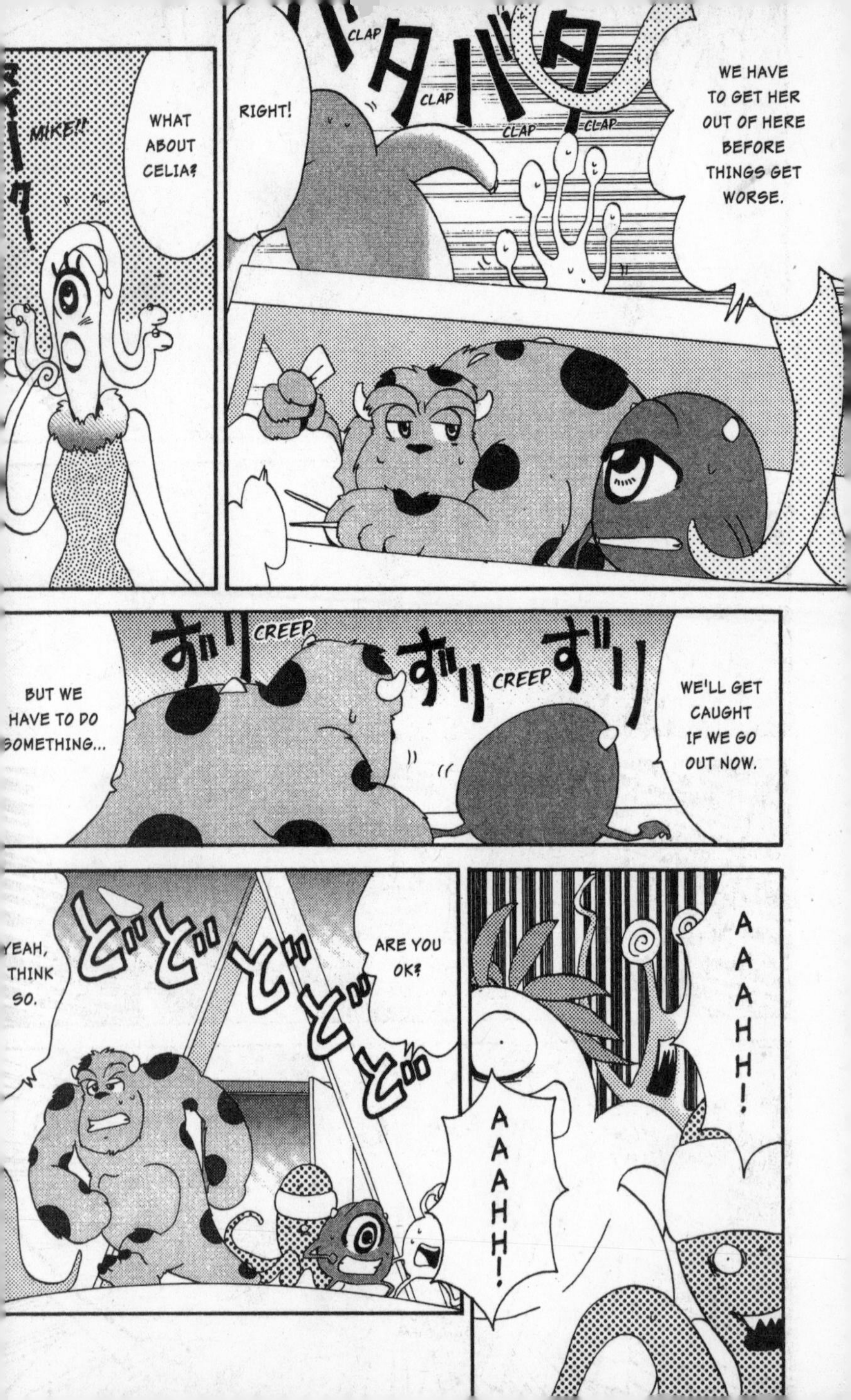
WE HAVE TO GET HER OUT OF HERE BEFORE THINGS GET WORSE.
バタバタ
CLAP
CLAP
CLAP
CLAP
RIGHT!
WHAT ABOUT CELIA?
MIKE!!
WE'LL GET CAUGHT IF WE GO OUT NOW.
ずり
CREEP
ずり
CREEP
ずり
CREEP
BUT WE HAVE TO DO SOMETHING...
AAAHH!
AAAHH!
ARE YOU OK?
YEAH, THINK SO.

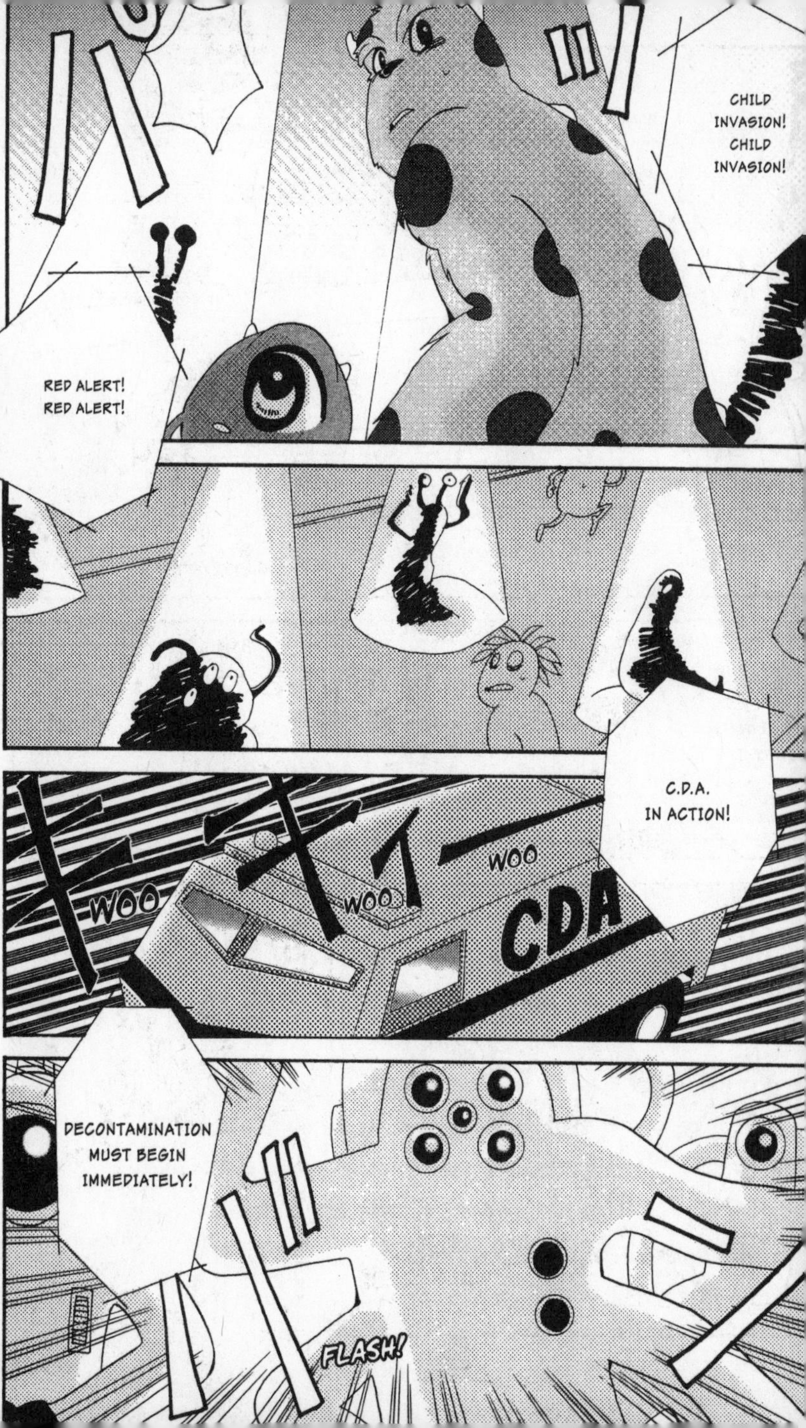
CHILD INVASION! CHILD INVASION!
RED ALERT! RED ALERT!
C.D.A. IN ACTION!
WOO
WOO
WOO
CDA
DECONTAMINATION MUST BEGIN IMMEDIATELY!
FLASH!

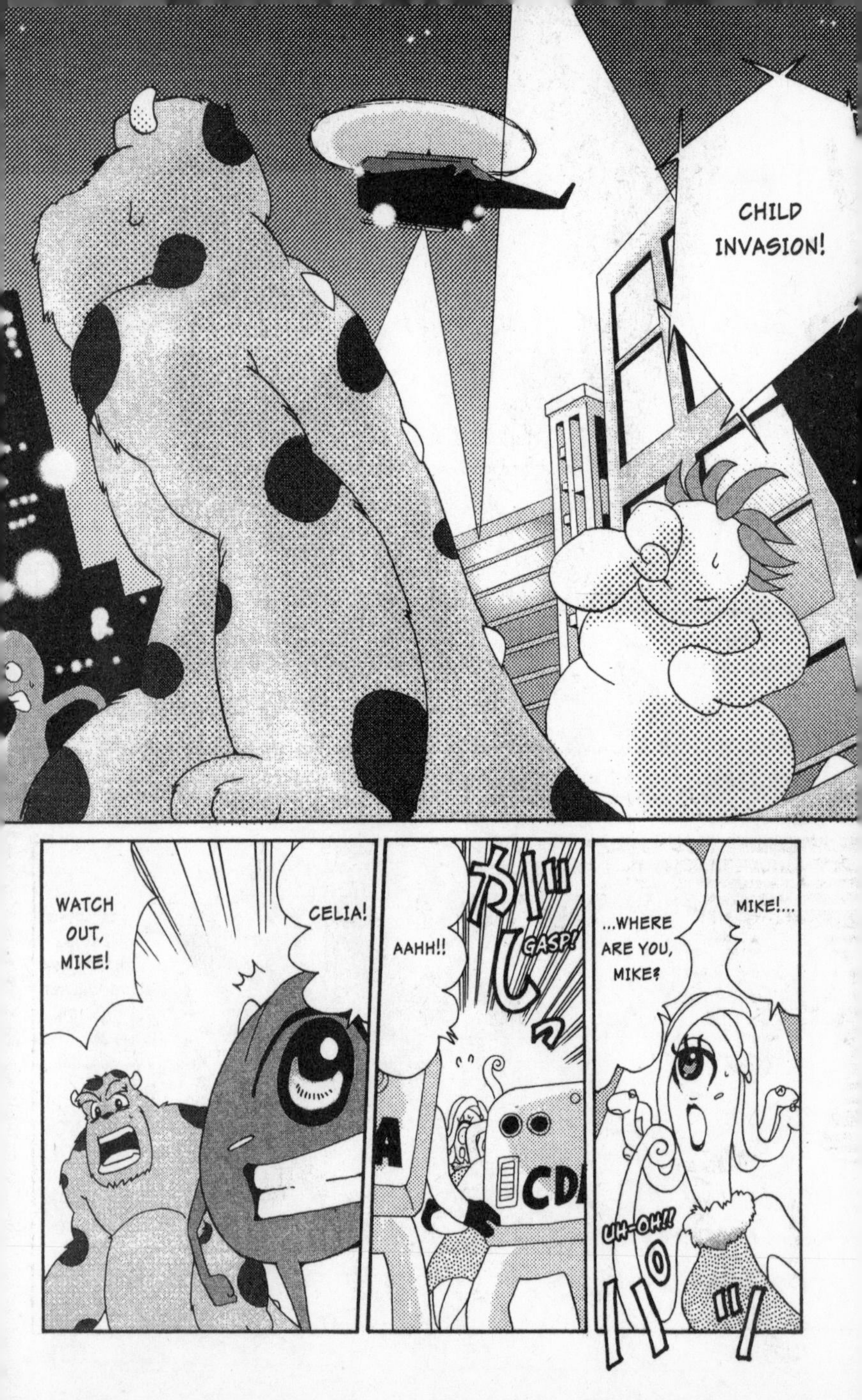
CHILD INVASION!
MIKE!...
...WHERE ARE YOU, MIKE?
UH-OH!!
GASP!
AAHH!!
CELIA!
WATCH OUT, MIKE!

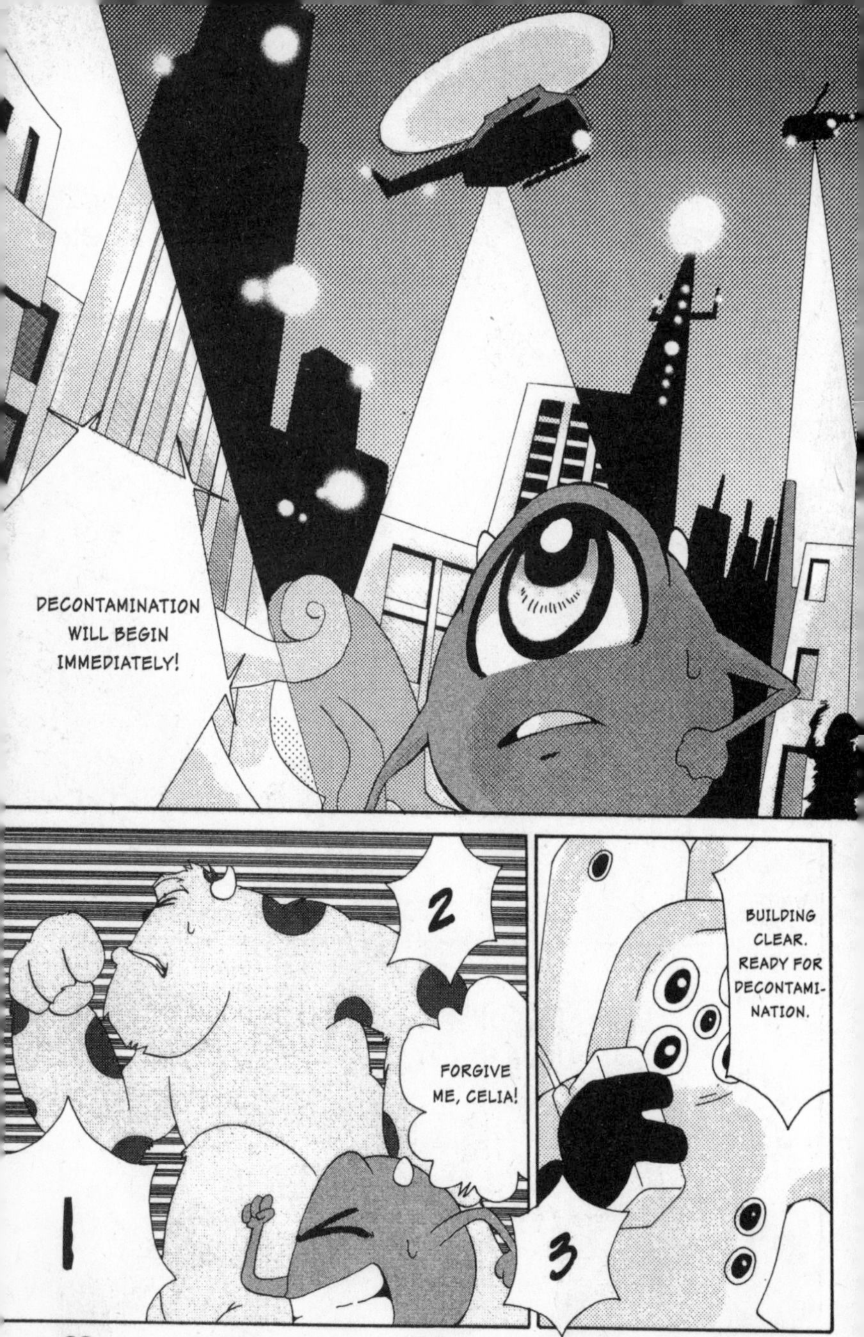
DECONTAMINATION WILL BEGIN IMMEDIATELY!
BUILDING CLEAR. READY FOR DECONTAMI-NATION.
2
FORGIVE ME, CELIA!
3
1

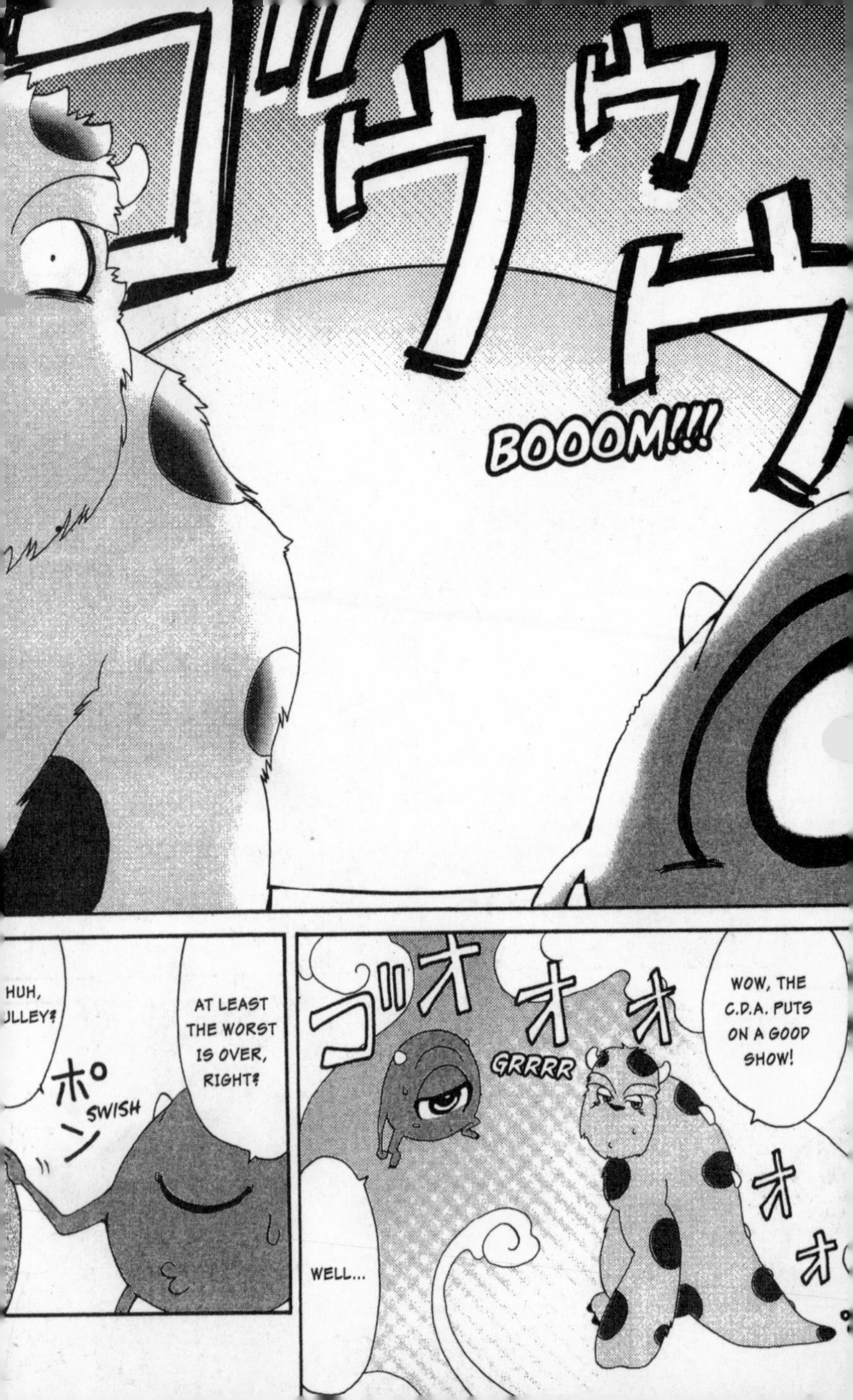
BOOOM!!!
WOW, THE C.D.A. PUTS ON A GOOD SHOW!
GRRRR
WELL...
AT LEAST THE WORST IS OVER, RIGHT?
HUH,
ULLEY?
ポン
SWISH

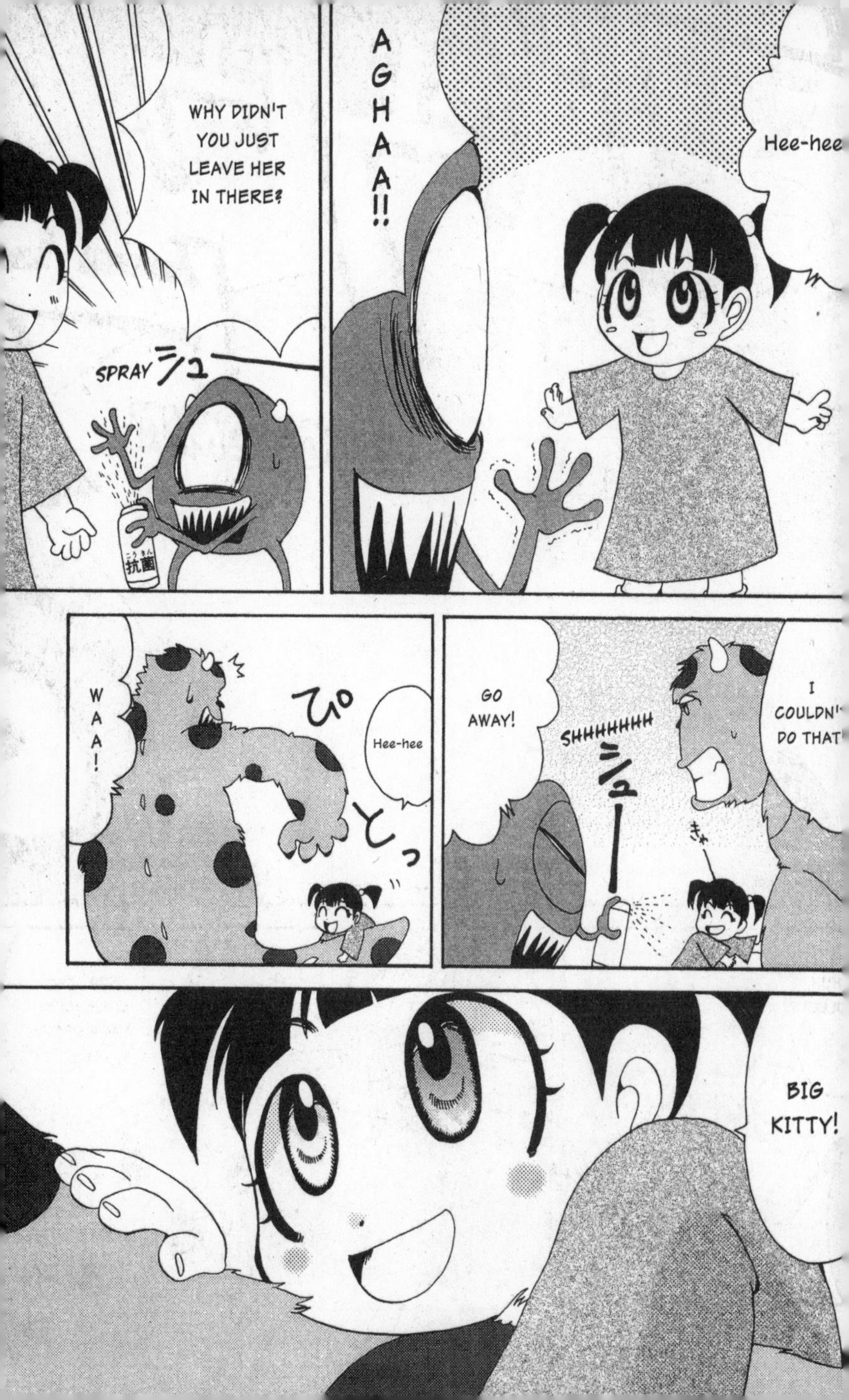
Hee-hee
AGHAA!!
WHY DIDN'T YOU JUST LEAVE HER IN THERE?
SPRAY シュ
抗菌
I COULDN' DO THAT
GO AWAY!
SHHHHHHH シュー
きゃ
Hee-hee
ぴ
WAAA!
とっ
BIG KITTY!

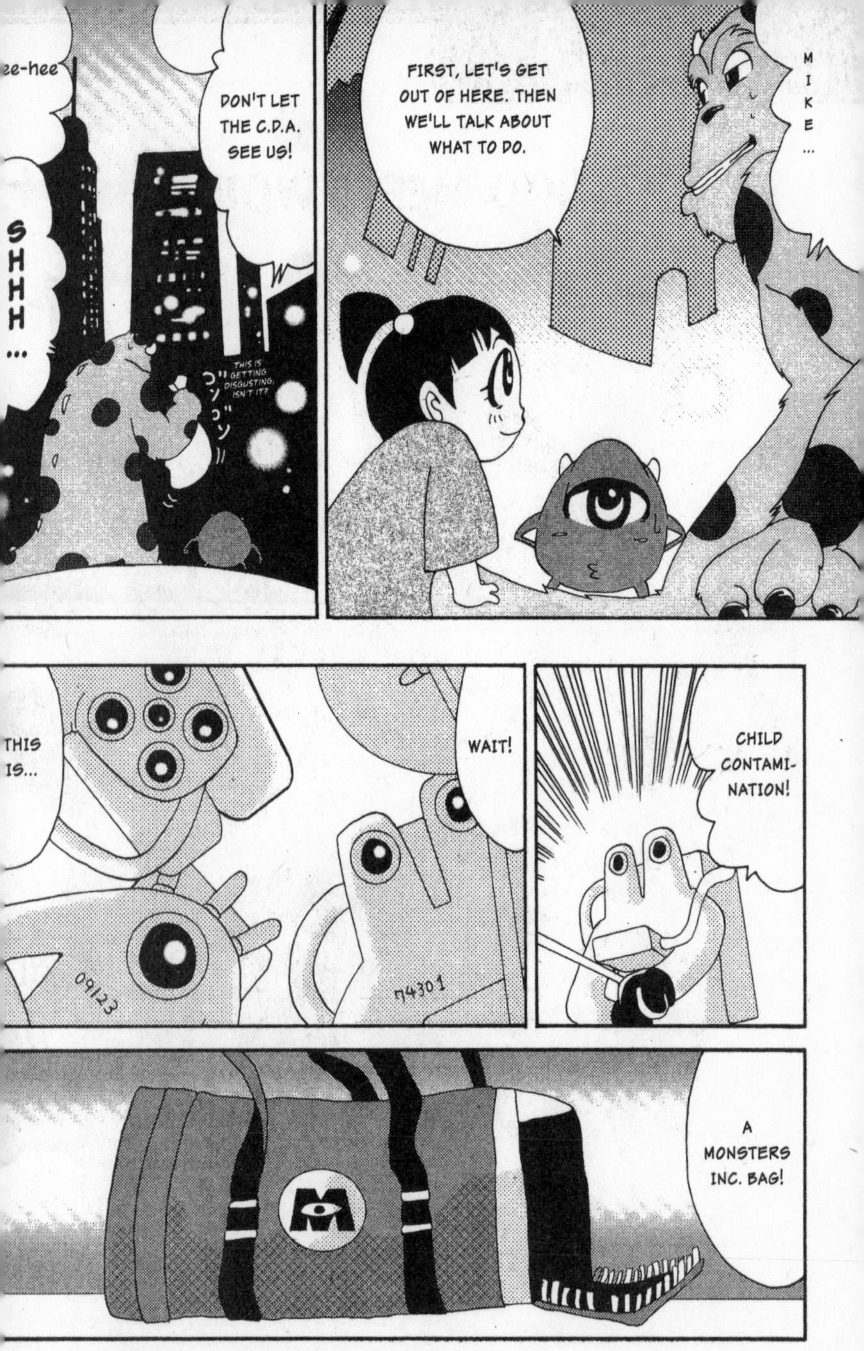
MIKE...
FIRST, LET'S GET OUT OF HERE. THEN WE'LL TALK ABOUT WHAT TO DO.
DON'T LET THE C.D.A. SEE US!
ee-hee
SHHH...
THIS IS GETTING DISGUSTING, ISN'T IT?
CHILD CONTAMI-NATION!
WAIT!
74301
THIS IS...
09123
A MONSTERS INC. BAG!

Chapter 2

BOO MEETS WORLD!

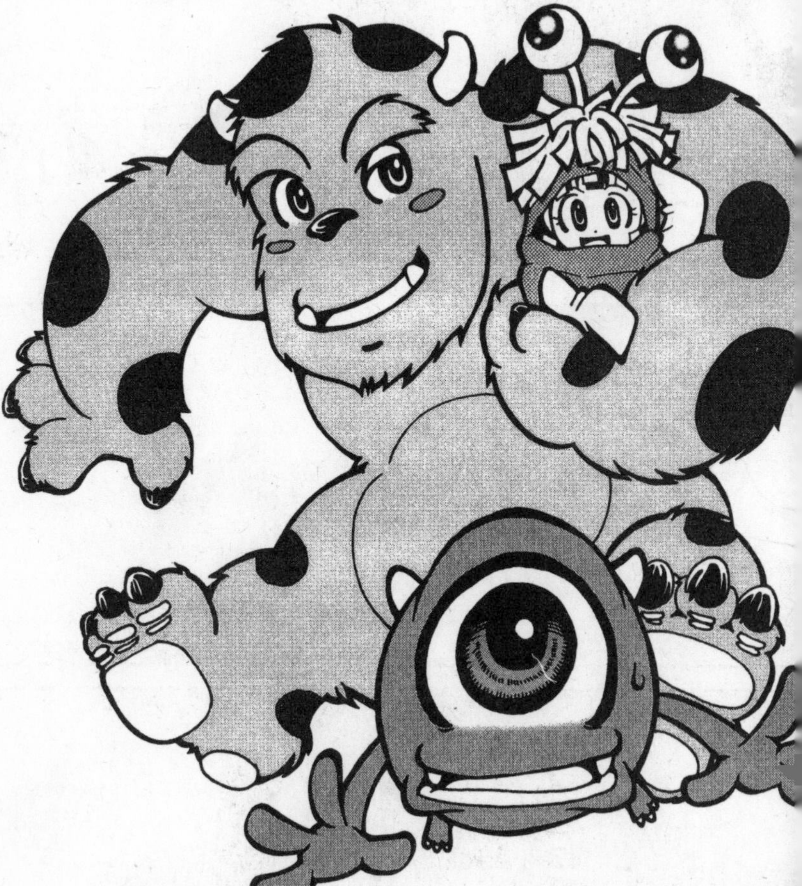

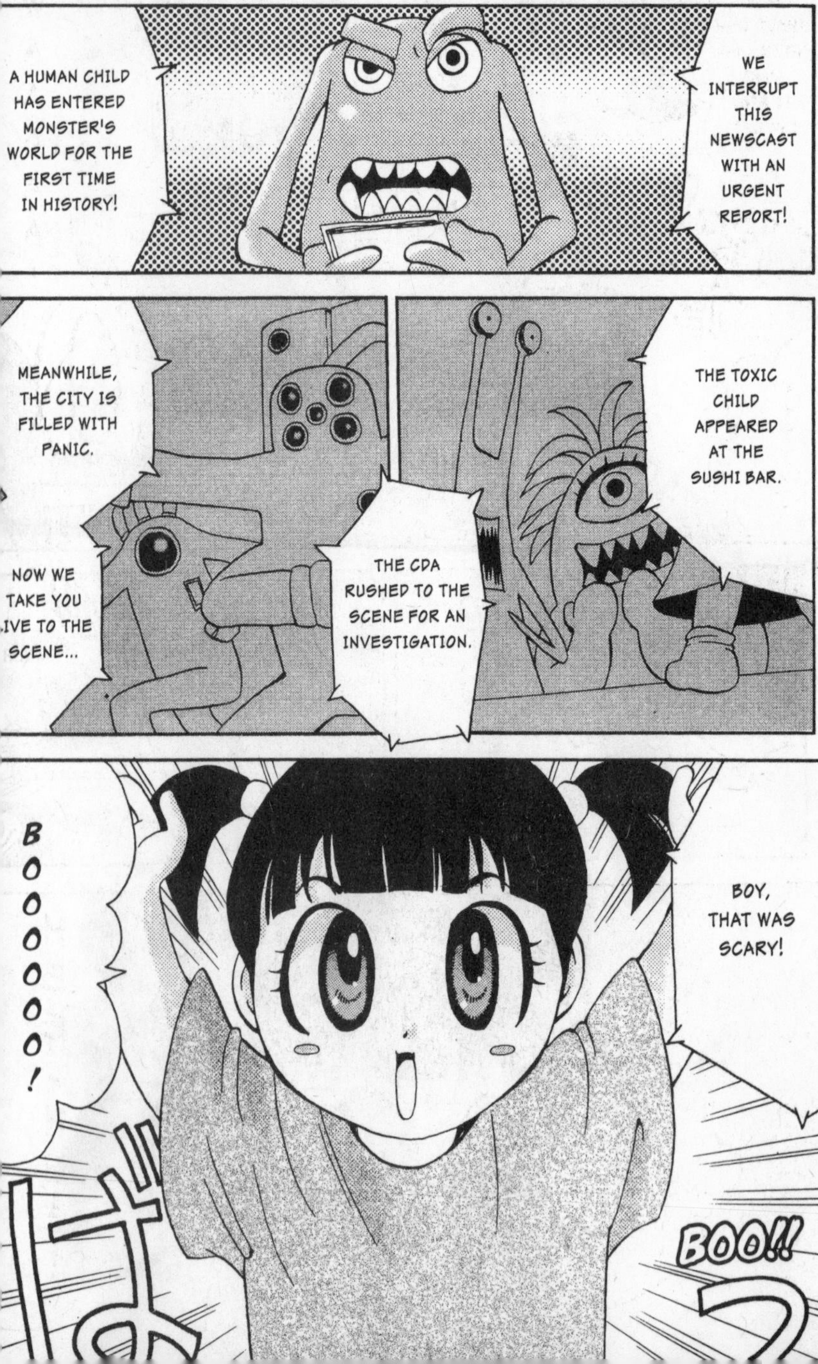
WE INTERRUPT THIS NEWSCAST WITH AN URGENT REPORT!
A HUMAN CHILD HAS ENTERED MONSTER'S WORLD FOR THE FIRST TIME IN HISTORY!
THE TOXIC CHILD APPEARED AT THE SUSHI BAR.
THE CDA RUSHED TO THE SCENE FOR AN INVESTIGATION.
MEANWHILE, THE CITY IS FILLED WITH PANIC.
NOW WE TAKE YOU IVE TO THE SCENE...
BOY, THAT WAS SCARY!
BOOOOOOOO!
BOO!!
ばっ

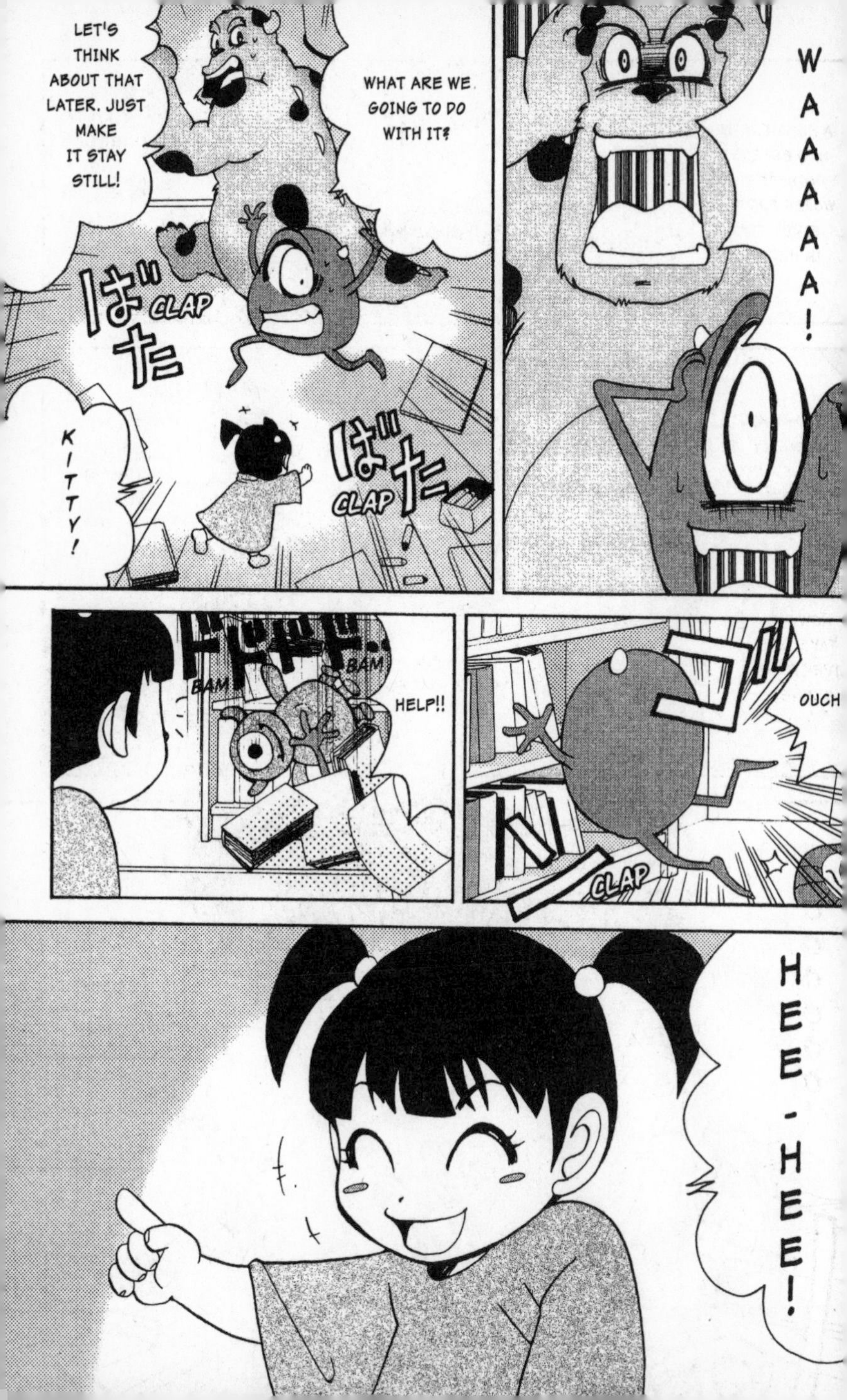
WAAAAA!
WHAT ARE WE GOING TO DO WITH IT?
LET'S THINK ABOUT THAT LATER. JUST MAKE IT STAY STILL!
ばた CLAP
ばたー CLAP
KITTY!
OUCH
CLAP
HELP!!
BAM
BAM
HEE-HEE!

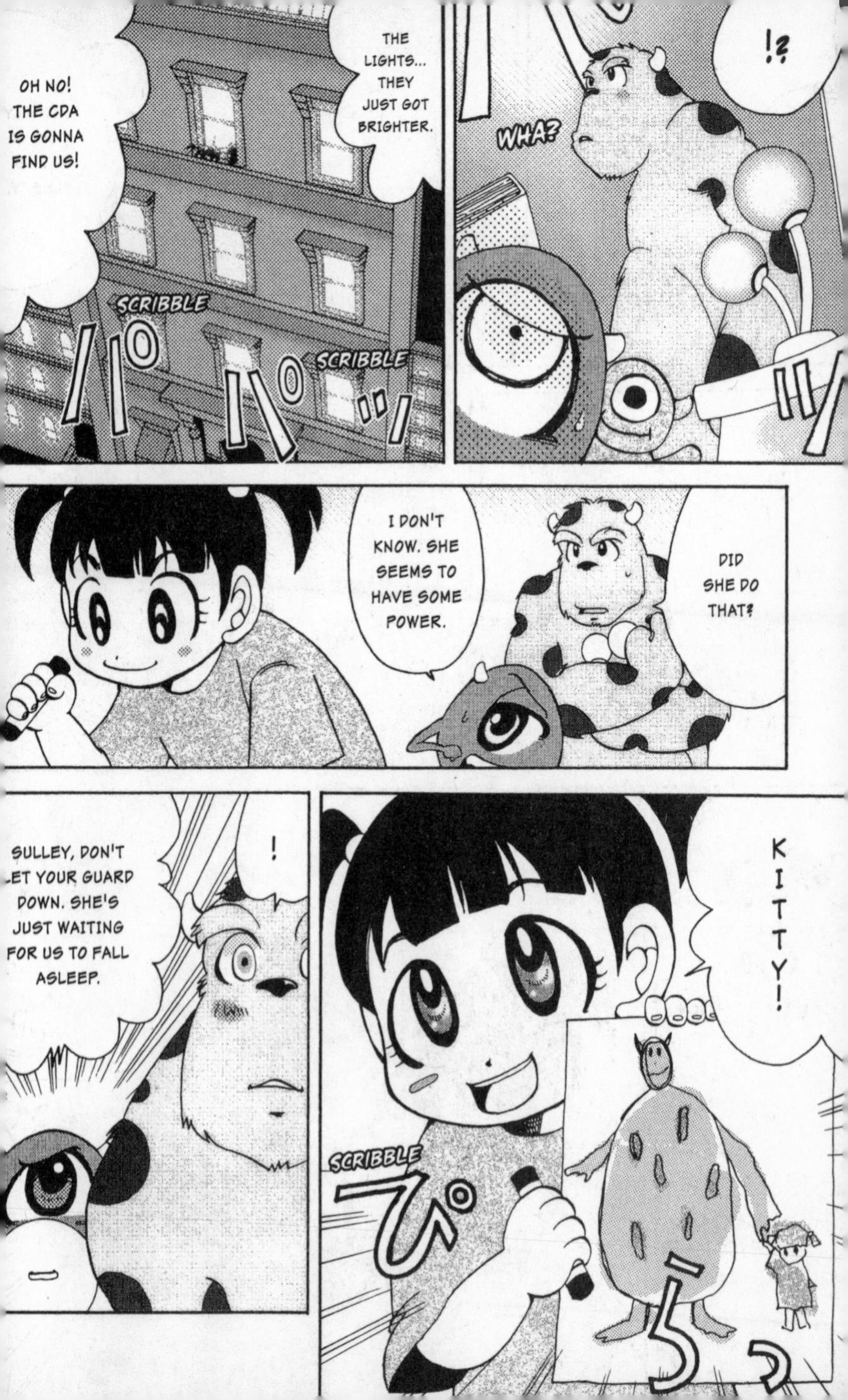
!?
WHA?
THE LIGHTS... THEY JUST GOT BRIGHTER.
OH NO! THE CDA IS GONNA FIND US!
SCRIBBLE
SCRIBBLE
DID SHE DO THAT?
I DON'T KNOW. SHE SEEMS TO HAVE SOME POWER.
KITTY!
SCRIBBLE
!
SULLEY, DON'T ET YOUR GUARD DOWN. SHE'S JUST WAITING FOR US TO FALL ASLEEP.

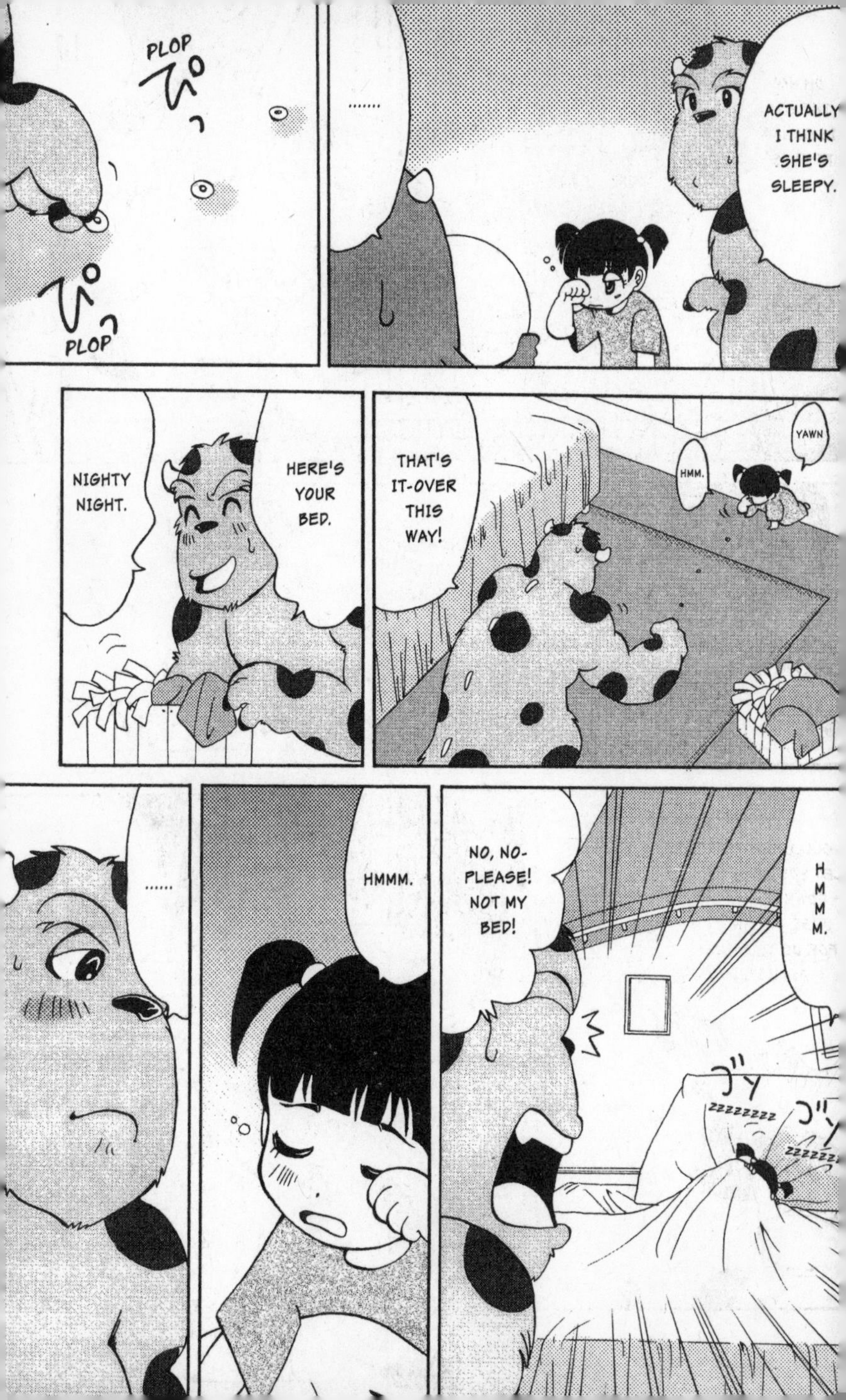
ACTUALLY I THINK SHE'S SLEEPY.
......
ぴっ
PLOP
ぴっ
PLOP
YAWN
HMM.
THAT'S IT-OVER THIS WAY!
HERE'S YOUR BED.
NIGHTY NIGHT.
HMMM.
NO, NO- PLEASE! NOT MY BED!
zzzzzzzz
zzzzzzz
HMMM.
......

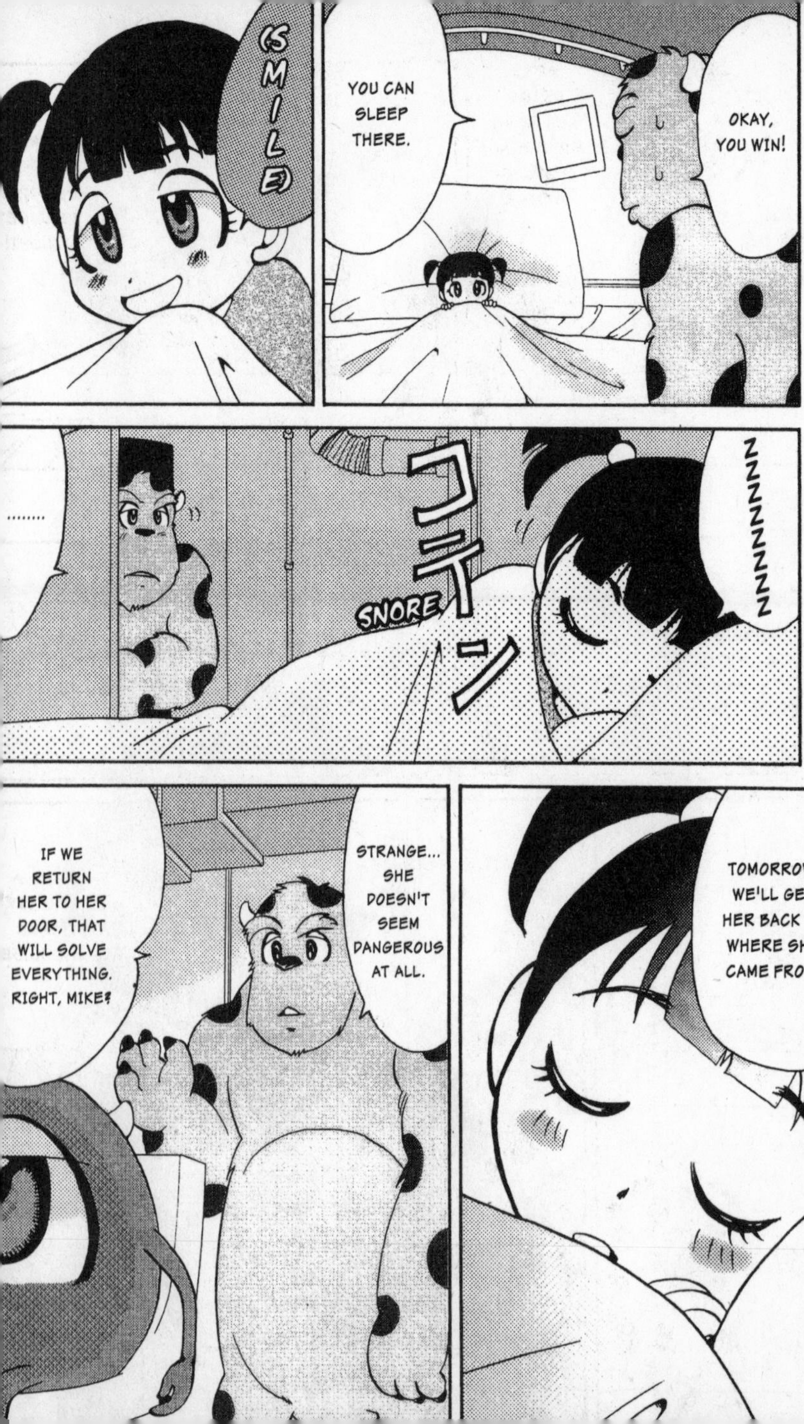
OKAY, YOU WIN!
YOU CAN SLEEP THERE.
(SMILE)
ZZZZZZZZ
コテン
SNORE
....
TOMORROW, WE'LL GET HER BACK TO WHERE SHE CAME FROM.
STRANGE... SHE DOESN'T SEEM DANGEROUS AT ALL.
IF WE RETURN HER TO HER DOOR, THAT WILL SOLVE EVERYTHING. RIGHT, MIKE?

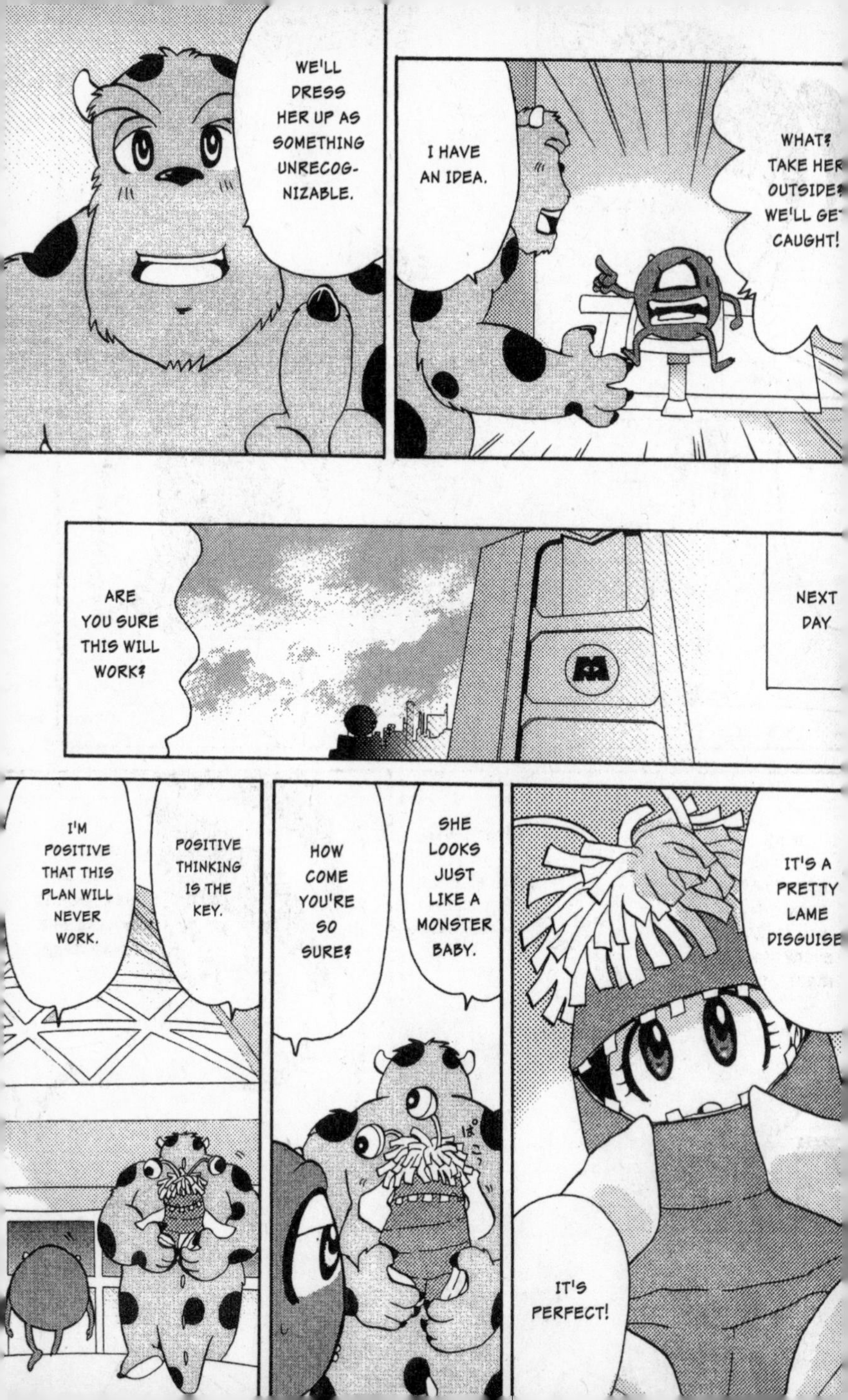
WHAT? TAKE HER OUTSIDE? WE'LL GE CAUGHT!
I HAVE AN IDEA.
WE'LL DRESS HER UP AS SOMETHING UNRECOG-NIZABLE.
NEXT DAY
ARE YOU SURE THIS WILL WORK?
IT'S A PRETTY LAME DISGUISE
IT'S PERFECT!
SHE LOOKS JUST LIKE A MONSTER BABY.
HOW COME YOU'RE SO SURE?
POSITIVE THINKING IS THE KEY.
I'M POSITIVE THAT THIS PLAN WILL NEVER WORK.

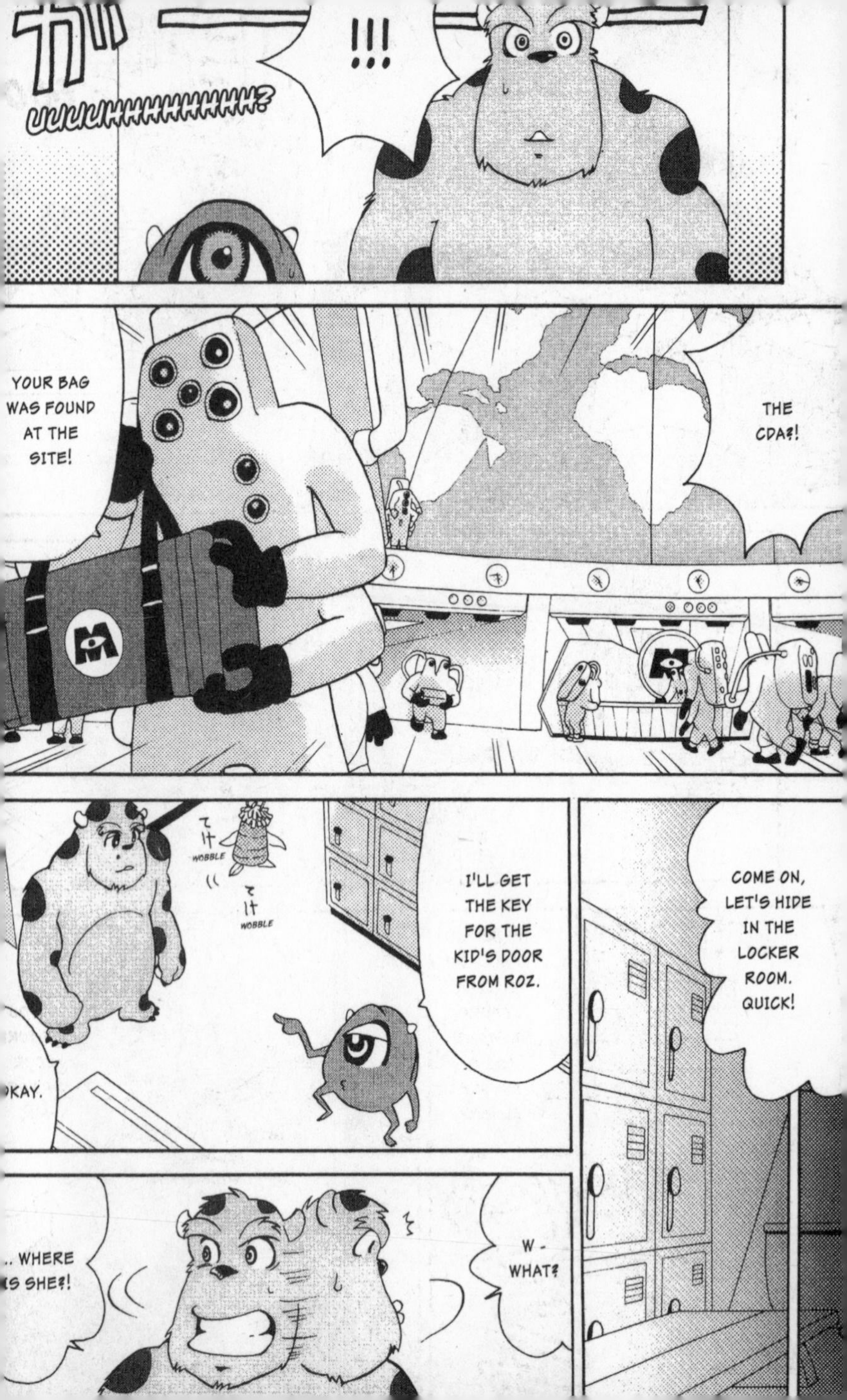

ガー!!!
UUUUHHHHHHHHH?
THE CDA?!
YOUR BAG WAS FOUND AT THE SITE!
COME ON, LET'S HIDE IN THE LOCKER ROOM. QUICK!
I'LL GET THE KEY FOR THE KID'S DOOR FROM ROZ.
てけ WOBBLE
てけ WOBBLE
...OKAY.
W-WHAT?
...WHERE IS SHE?!

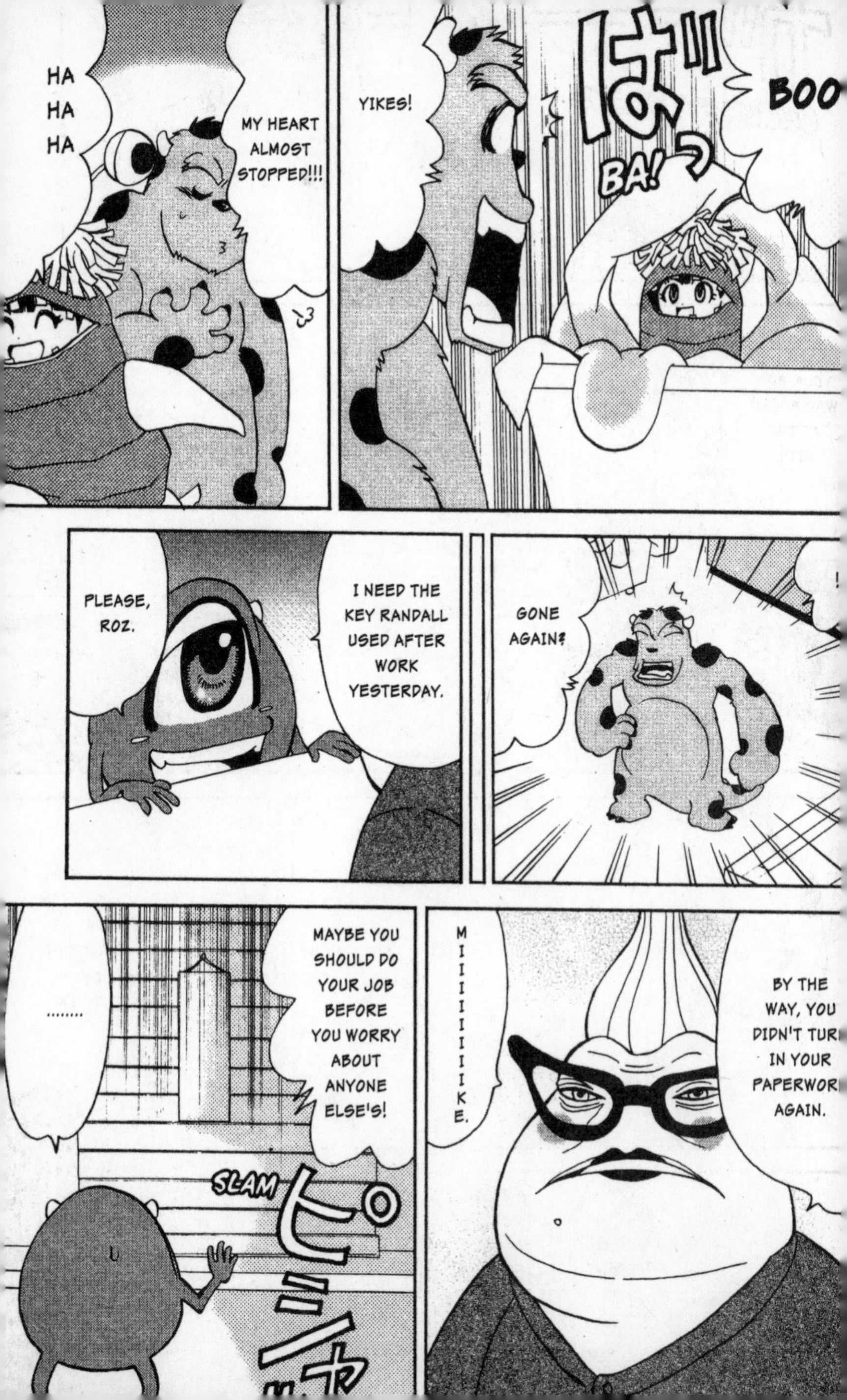
はっ
BOO
BA!
YIKES!
MY HEART ALMOST STOPPED!!!
HA HA HA
!
GONE AGAIN?
I NEED THE KEY RANDALL USED AFTER WORK YESTERDAY.
PLEASE, ROZ.
BY THE WAY, YOU DIDN'T TUR IN YOUR PAPERWOR AGAIN.
MIIIIIIIIKE.
MAYBE YOU SHOULD DO YOUR JOB BEFORE YOU WORRY ABOUT ANYONE ELSE'S!
SLAM
....

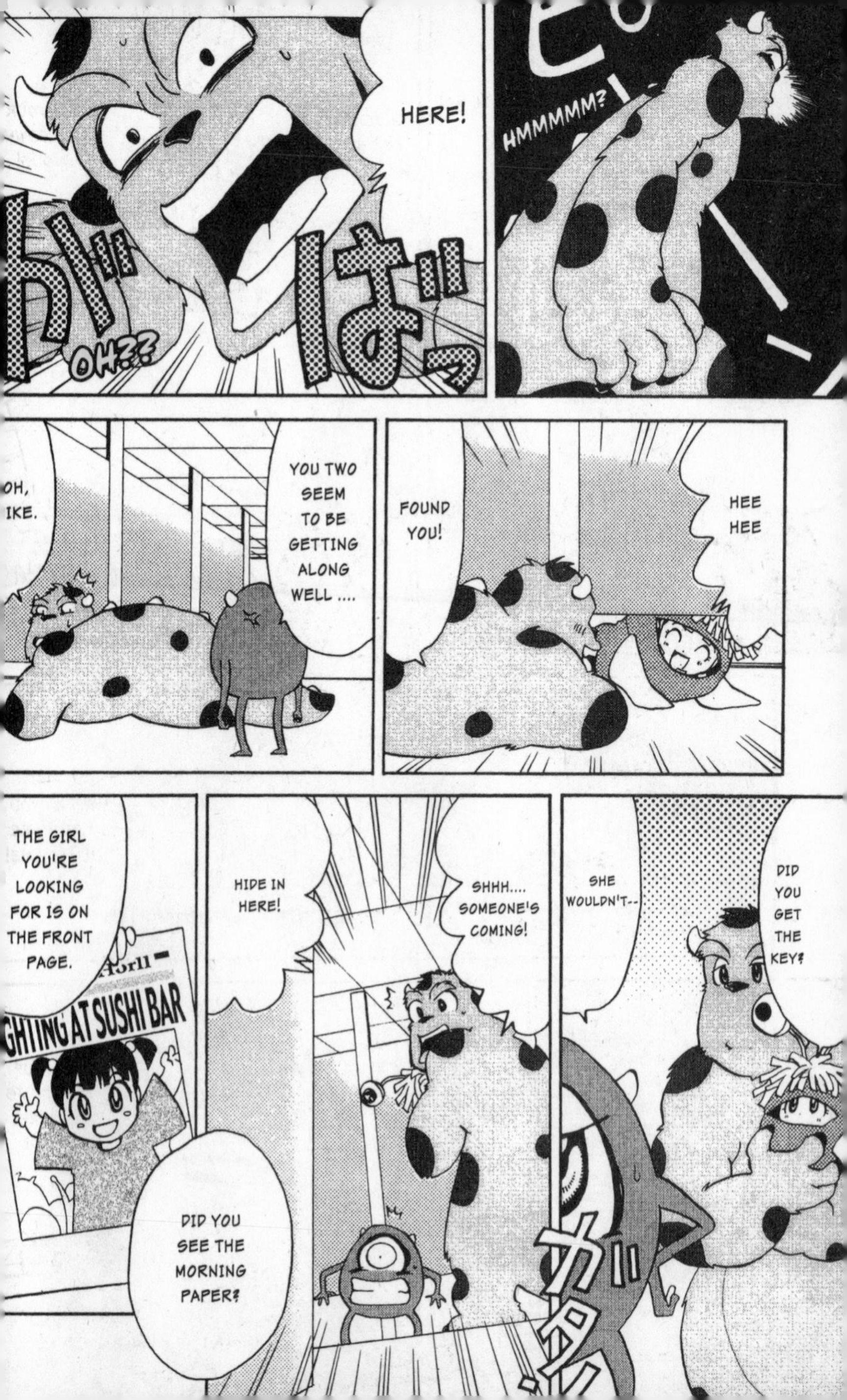
HMMMMM?
HERE!
がばっ
OH??
HEE HEE
FOUND YOU!
YOU TWO SEEM TO BE GETTING ALONG WELL ....
OH, IKE.
DID YOU GET THE KEY?
SHE WOULDN'T--
SHHH.... SOMEONE'S COMING!
HIDE IN HERE!
THE GIRL YOU'RE LOOKING FOR IS ON THE FRONT PAGE.
GHTING AT SUSHI BAR
DID YOU SEE THE MORNING PAPER?

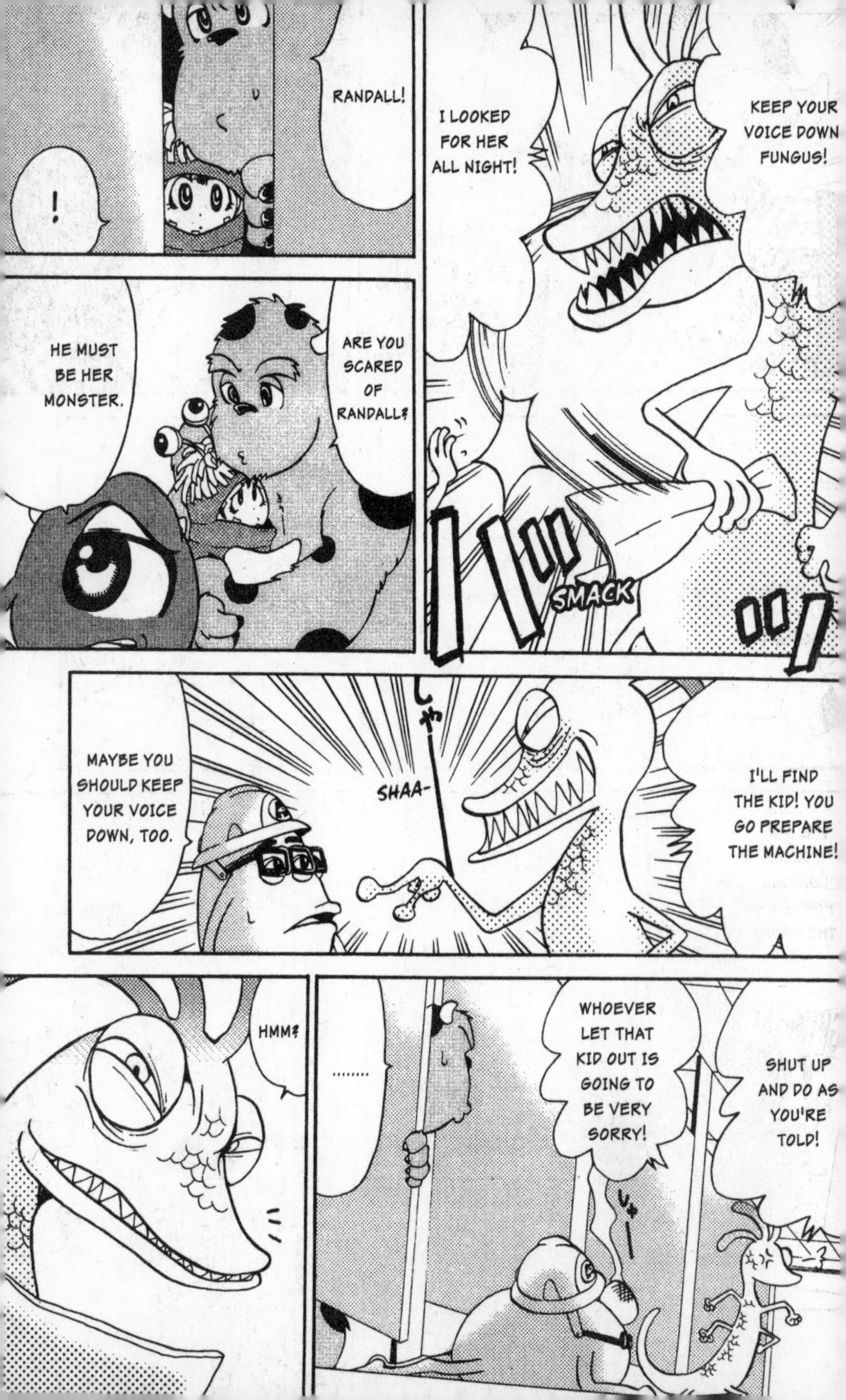
KEEP YOUR VOICE DOWN FUNGUS!
I LOOKED FOR HER ALL NIGHT!
SMACK
RANDALL!
!
ARE YOU SCARED OF RANDALL?
HE MUST BE HER MONSTER.
I'LL FIND THE KID! YOU GO PREPARE THE MACHINE!
SHAA-
MAYBE YOU SHOULD KEEP YOUR VOICE DOWN, TOO.
SHUT UP AND DO AS YOU'RE TOLD!
WHOEVER LET THAT KID OUT IS GOING TO BE VERY SORRY!
....
HMM?

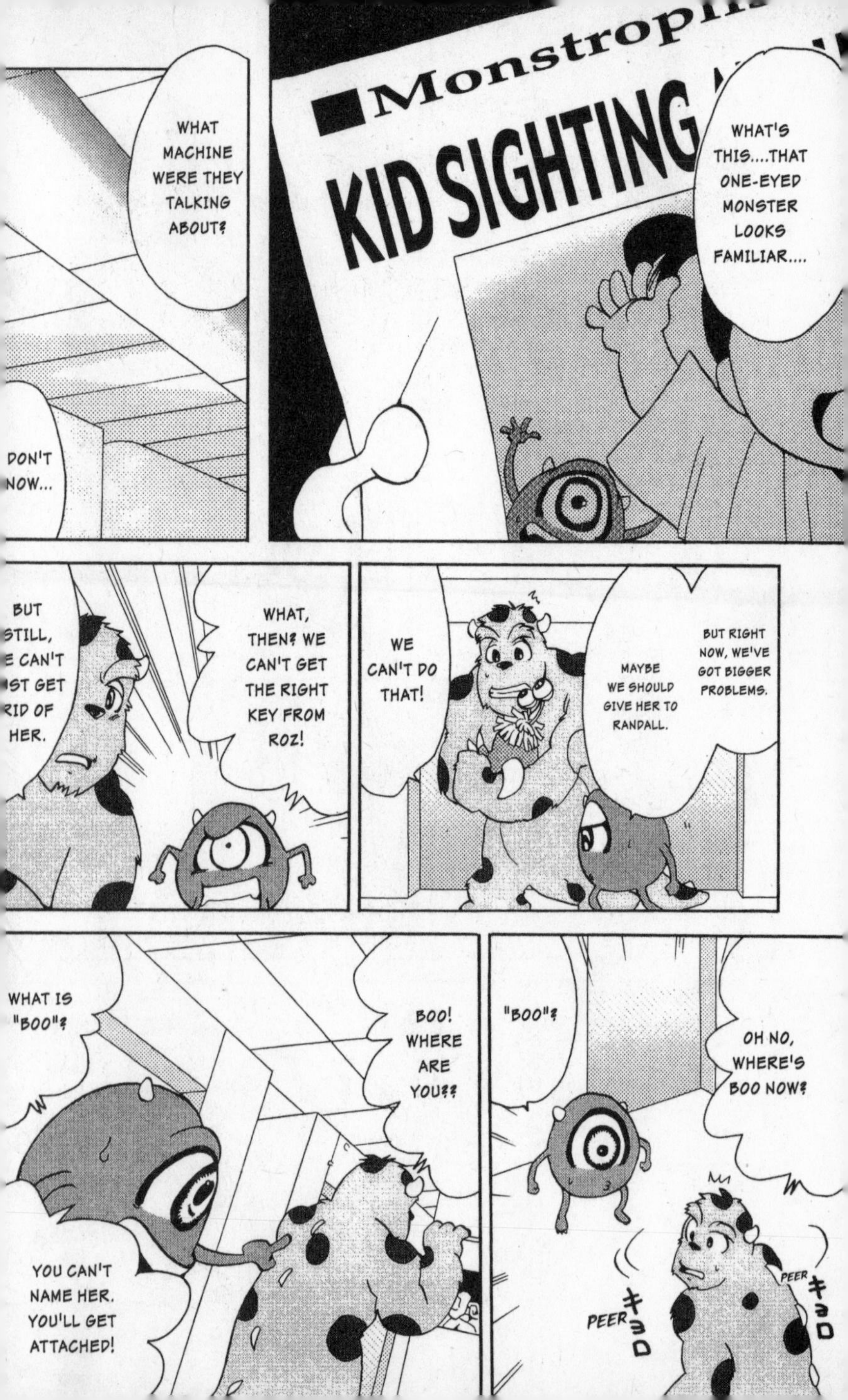
Monstropli
KID SIGHTING
WHAT'S THIS....THAT ONE-EYED MONSTER LOOKS FAMILIAR....
WHAT MACHINE WERE THEY TALKING ABOUT?
DON'T NOW...
BUT RIGHT NOW, WE'VE GOT BIGGER PROBLEMS.
MAYBE WE SHOULD GIVE HER TO RANDALL.
WE CAN'T DO THAT!
WHAT, THEN? WE CAN'T GET THE RIGHT KEY FROM ROZ!
BUT STILL, E CAN'T ST GET RID OF HER.
OH NO, WHERE'S BOO NOW?
"BOO"?
PEER キョロ
PEER キョロ
BOO! WHERE ARE YOU??
WHAT IS "BOO"?
YOU CAN'T NAME HER. YOU'LL GET ATTACHED!

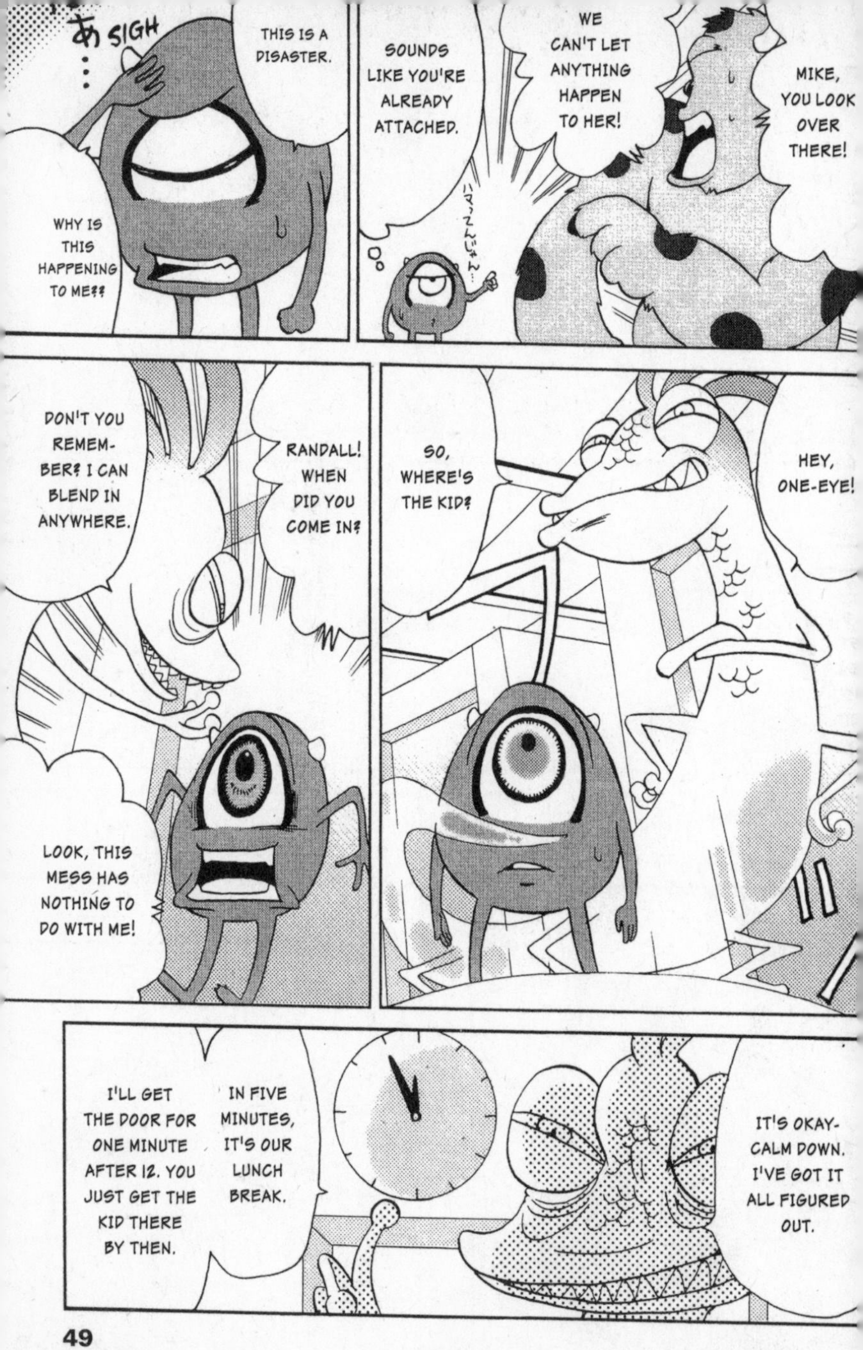
MIKE, YOU LOOK OVER THERE!
WE CAN'T LET ANYTHING HAPPEN TO HER!
SOUNDS LIKE YOU'RE ALREADY ATTACHED.
ハマってんじゃん…
あ SIGH …
THIS IS A DISASTER.
WHY IS THIS HAPPENING TO ME??
HEY, ONE-EYE!
SO, WHERE'S THE KID?
RANDALL! WHEN DID YOU COME IN?
DON'T YOU REMEMBER? I CAN BLEND IN ANYWHERE.
LOOK, THIS MESS HAS NOTHING TO DO WITH ME!
IT'S OKAY-CALM DOWN. I'VE GOT IT ALL FIGURED OUT.
IN FIVE MINUTES, IT'S OUR LUNCH BREAK.
I'LL GET THE DOOR FOR ONE MINUTE AFTER 12. YOU JUST GET THE KID THERE BY THEN.

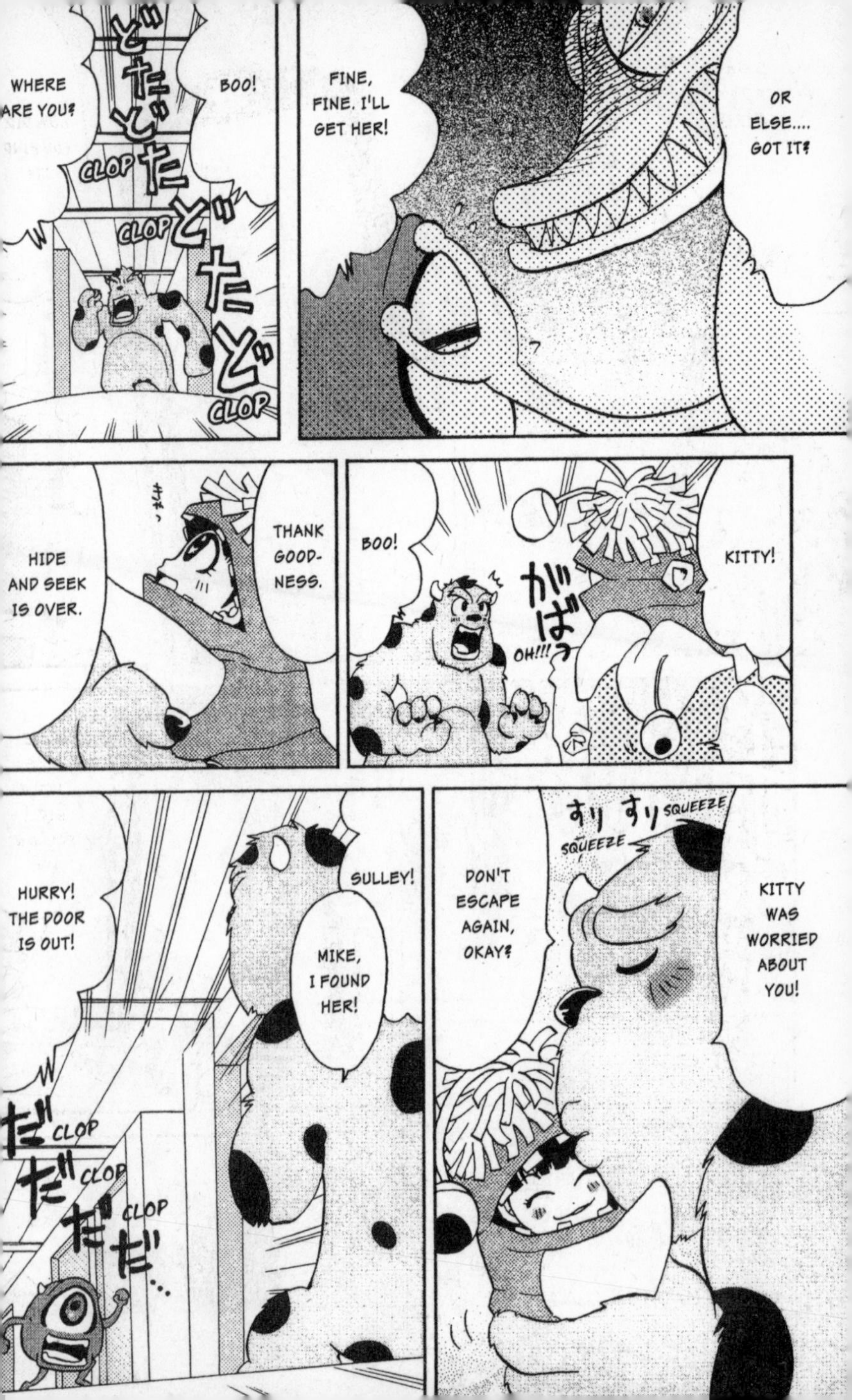

OR ELSE.... GOT IT?
FINE, FINE. I'LL GET HER!
BOO!
WHERE ARE YOU?
どたどたどたど
CLOP CLOP CLOP
KITTY!
がばっ
OH!!!
BOO!
THANK GOODNESS.
HIDE AND SEEK IS OVER.
KITTY WAS WORRIED ABOUT YOU!
すり すり
SQUEEZE SQUEEZE
DON'T ESCAPE AGAIN, OKAY?
SULLEY!
MIKE, I FOUND HER!
HURRY! THE DOOR IS OUT!
だだだだ...
CLOP CLOP CLOP

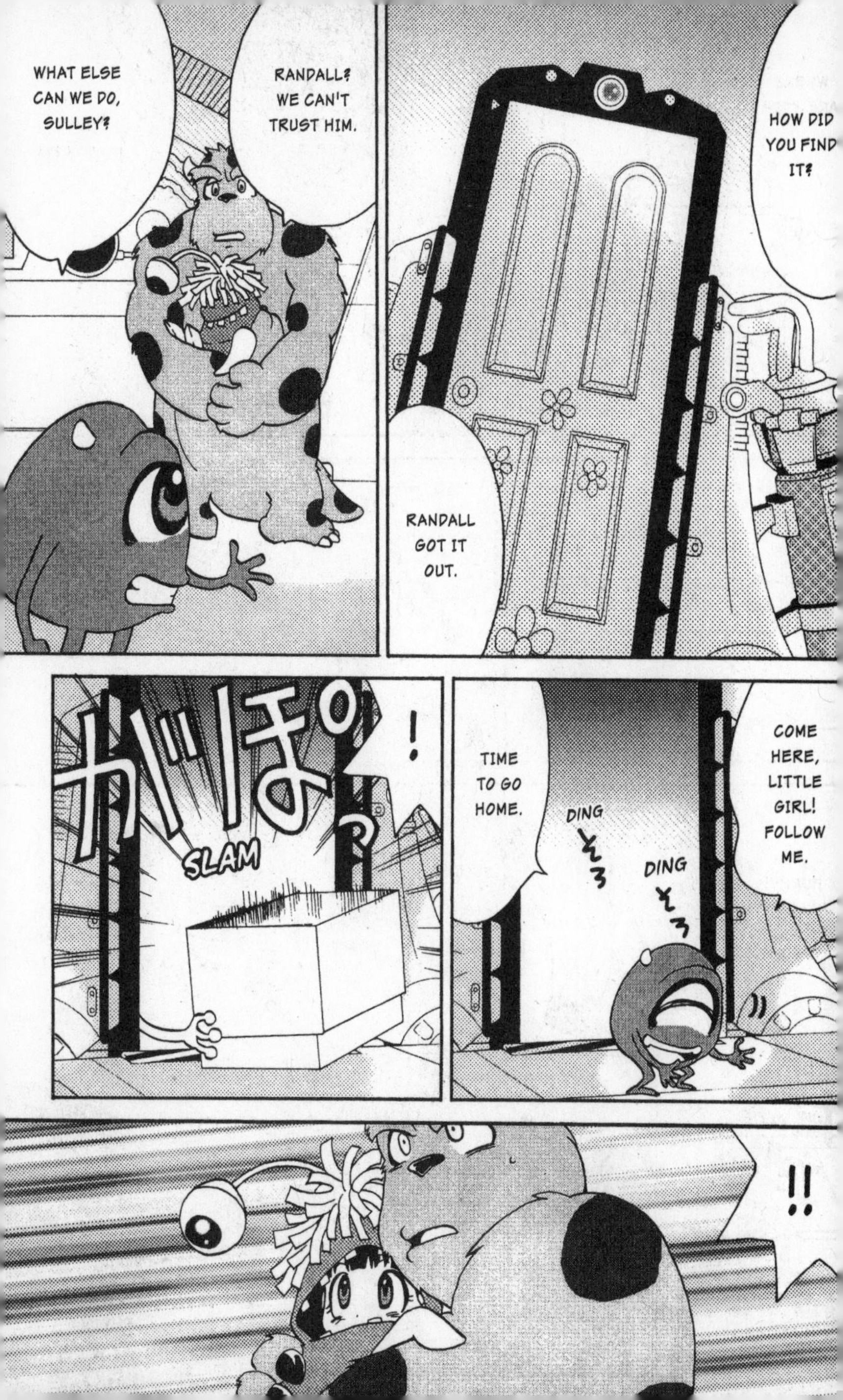
HOW DID YOU FIND IT?
RANDALL GOT IT OUT.
RANDALL? WE CAN'T TRUST HIM.
WHAT ELSE CAN WE DO, SULLEY?
COME HERE, LITTLE GIRL! FOLLOW ME.
DING
DING
TIME TO GO HOME.
!
がぽっ
SLAM
!!

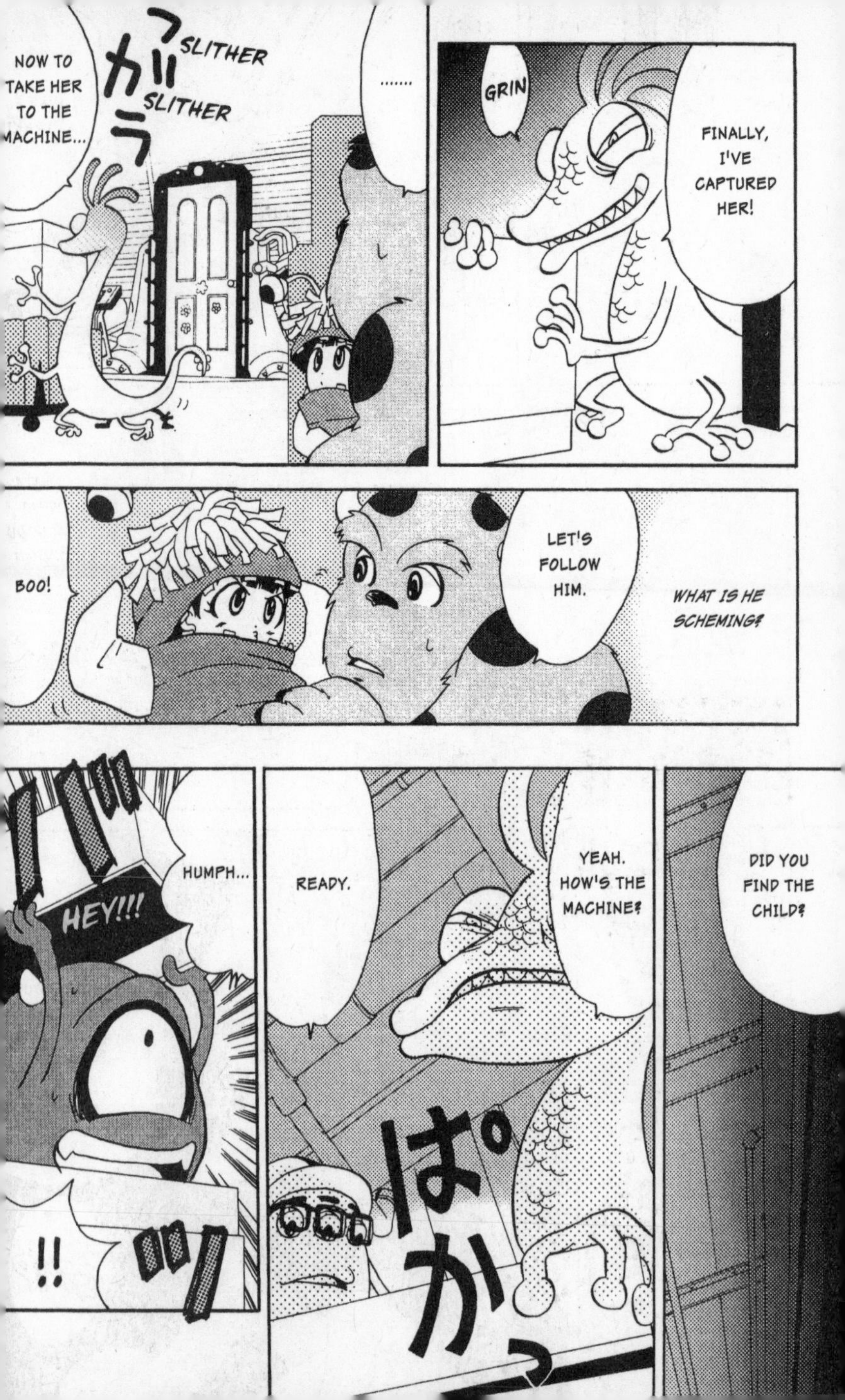
FINALLY, I'VE CAPTURED HER!
GRIN
......
SLITHER
SLITHER
NOW TO TAKE HER TO THE MACHINE...
WHAT IS HE SCHEMING?
LET'S FOLLOW HIM.
BOO!
DID YOU FIND THE CHILD?
YEAH. HOW'S THE MACHINE?
READY.
ぱかっ
HUMPH...
HEY!!!
バッ
!!

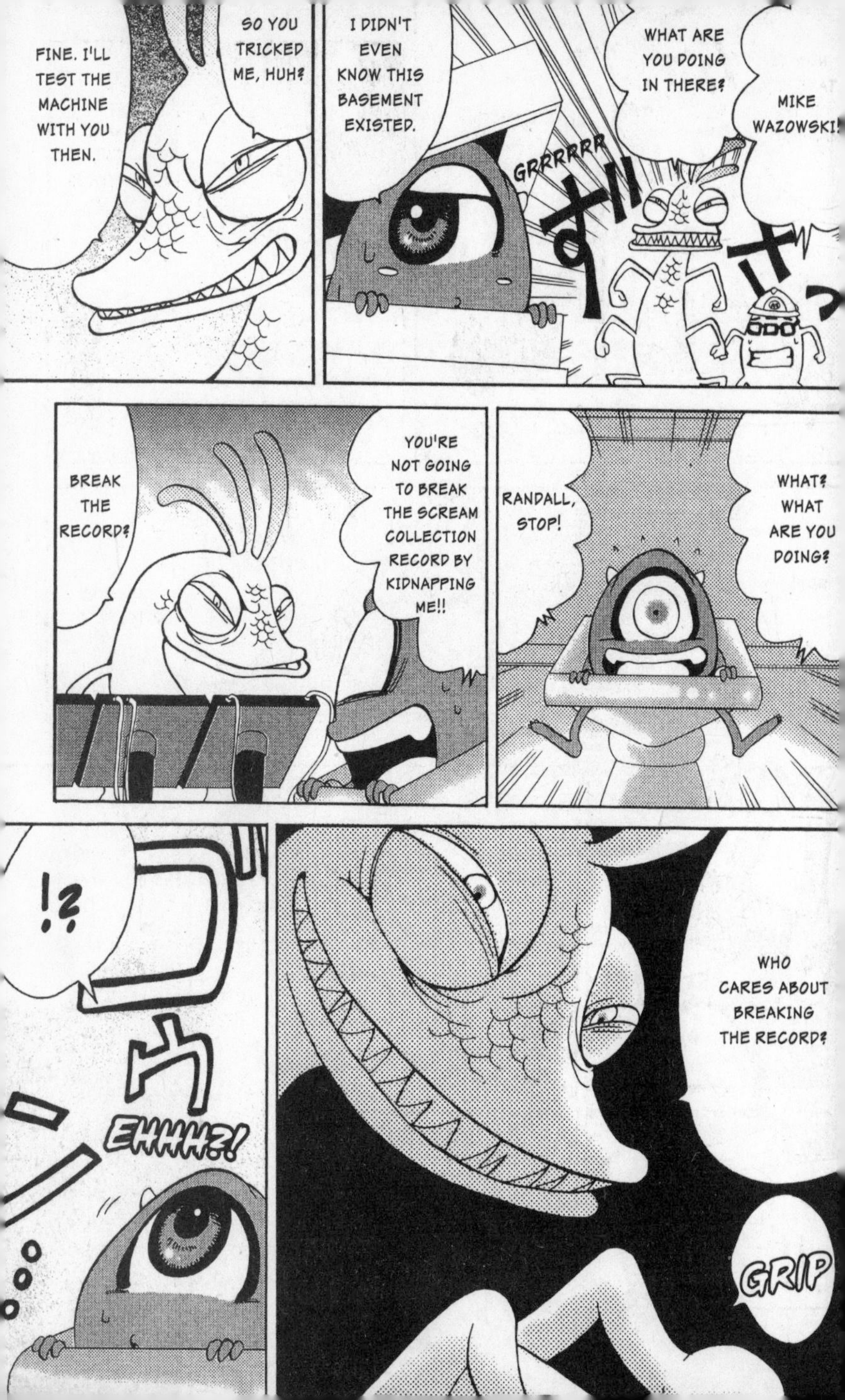
GRRRRRR
WHAT ARE YOU DOING IN THERE?
MIKE WAZOWSKI!
I DIDN'T EVEN KNOW THIS BASEMENT EXISTED.
SO YOU TRICKED ME, HUH?
FINE. I'LL TEST THE MACHINE WITH YOU THEN.
WHAT? WHAT ARE YOU DOING?
RANDALL, STOP!
YOU'RE NOT GOING TO BREAK THE SCREAM COLLECTION RECORD BY KIDNAPPING ME!!
BREAK THE RECORD?
WHO CARES ABOUT BREAKING THE RECORD?
GRIP
!?
EHHH?!

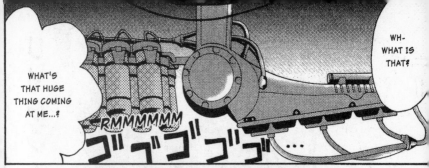

WH- WHAT IS THAT?
WHAT'S THAT HUGE THING COMING AT ME...?
RMMMMMM
ゴゴゴゴ...
IT'S A SCREAM MACHINE THAT I INVENTED.
A MONTH'S WORTH OF SCREAMS CAN BE COLLECTED IN A DAY.
IT IS GOING TO REVOLUTIONIZE THE SCREAM-COLLECTING BUSINESS.
SULLEY WON'T BE MY COMPETITION ANYMORE.
NO ONE WILL BE ABLE TO TOUCH ME!
...
WAIT! RANDALL!
LET'S TALK ABOUT THIS. I REALLY THINK YOU'RE MAKING A BIG MISTAKE!
ゴゴゴゴゴ
RMMMMMM
SWITCH...
... ON!

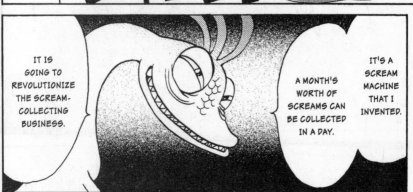

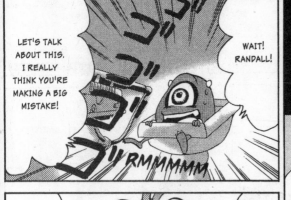

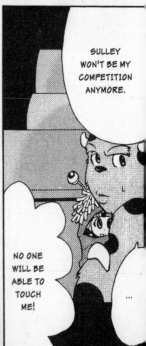

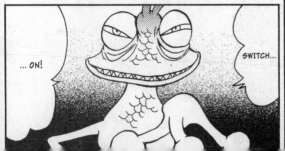

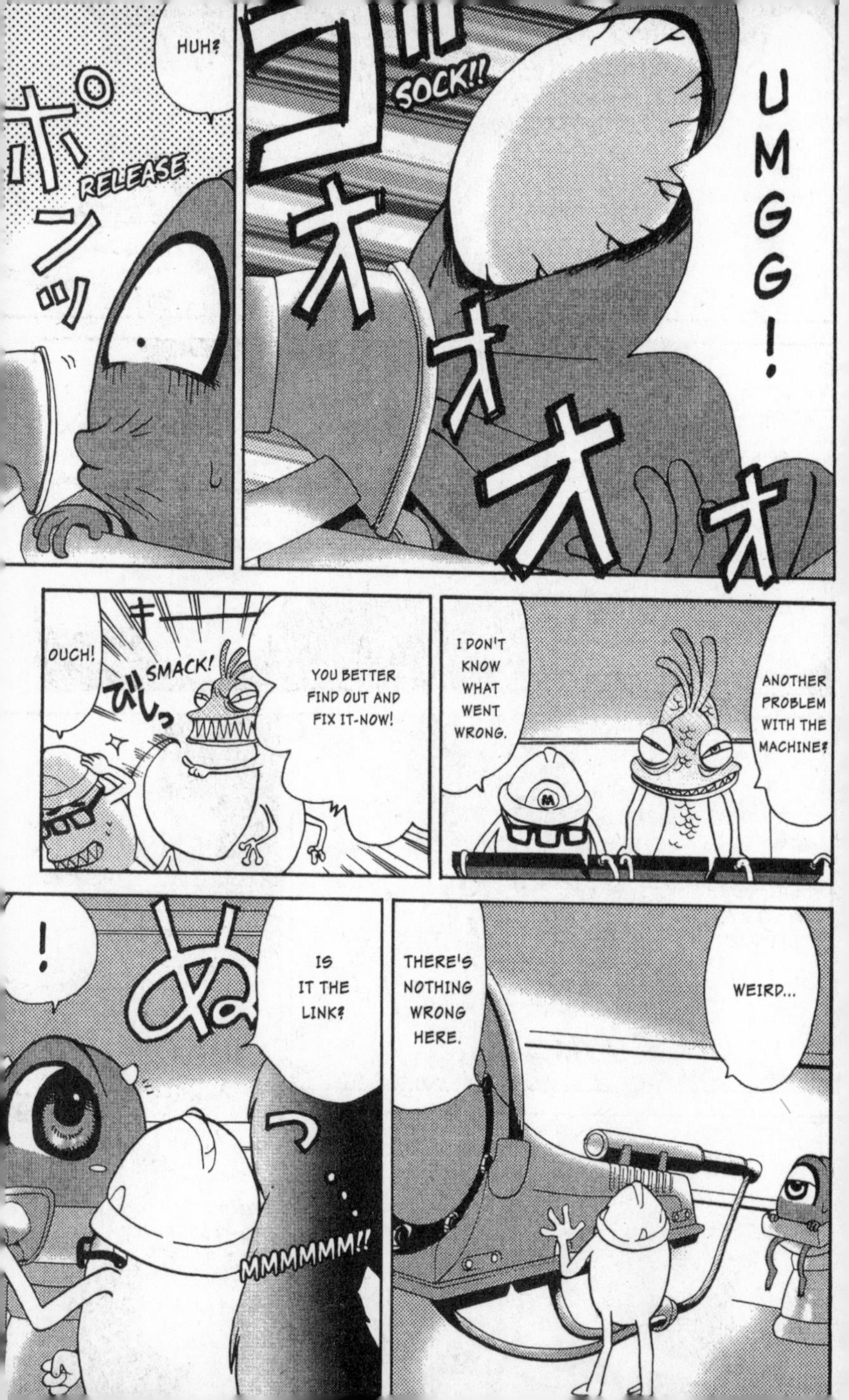
UMGG!
SOCK!!
HUH?
RELEASE
ANOTHER PROBLEM WITH THE MACHINE?
I DON'T KNOW WHAT WENT WRONG.
YOU BETTER FIND OUT AND FIX IT-NOW!
SMACK!
OUCH!
WEIRD...
THERE'S NOTHING WRONG HERE.
IS IT THE LINK?
!
MMMMMM!!

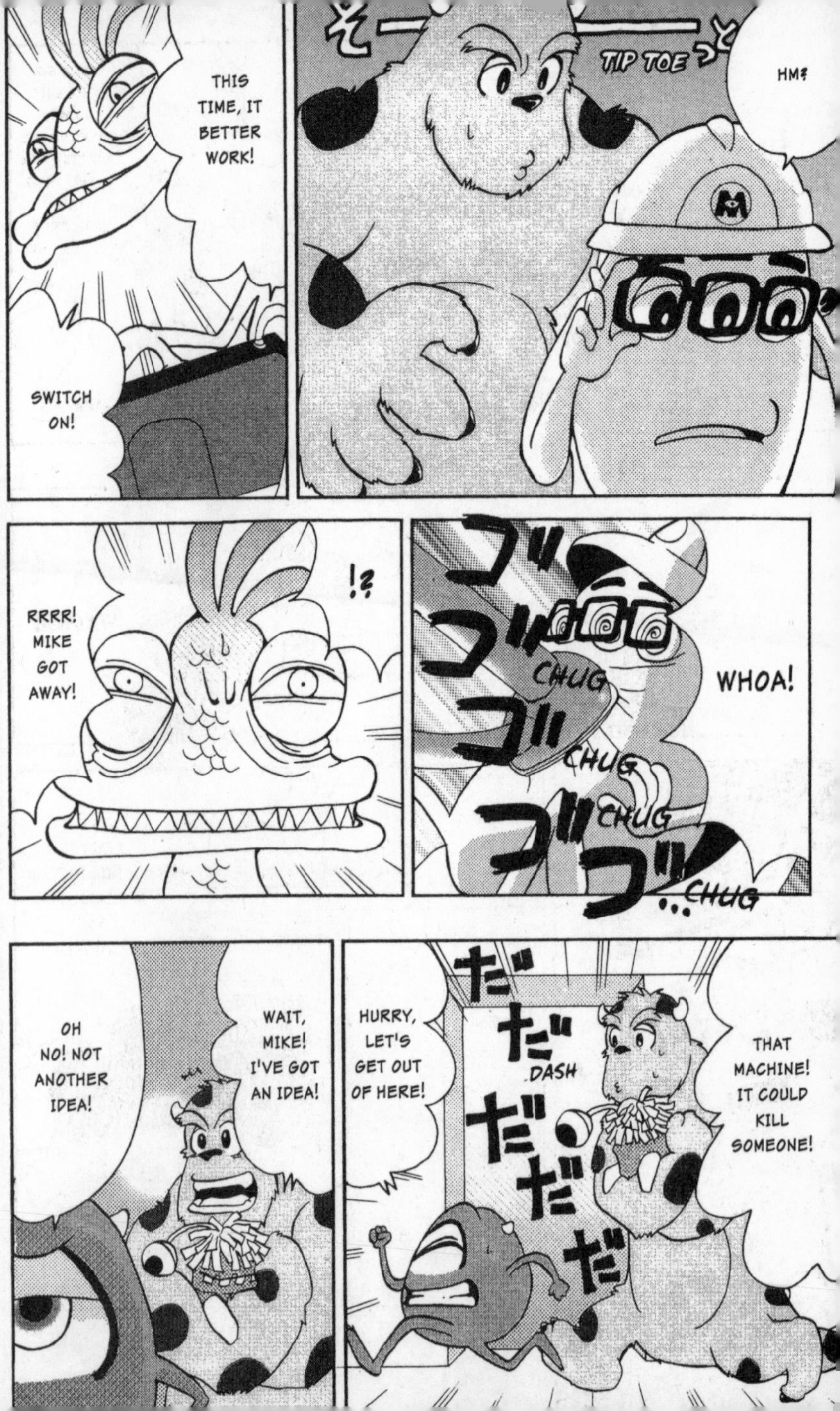

そー っと
TIP TOE
HM?
THIS TIME, IT BETTER WORK!
SWITCH ON!
ゴゴゴゴッ
CHUG CHUG CHUG CHUG
WHOA!
!?
RRRR! MIKE GOT AWAY!
THAT MACHINE! IT COULD KILL SOMEONE!
だだだだだ
DASH
HURRY, LET'S GET OUT OF HERE!
WAIT, MIKE! I'VE GOT AN IDEA!
OH NO! NOT ANOTHER IDEA!

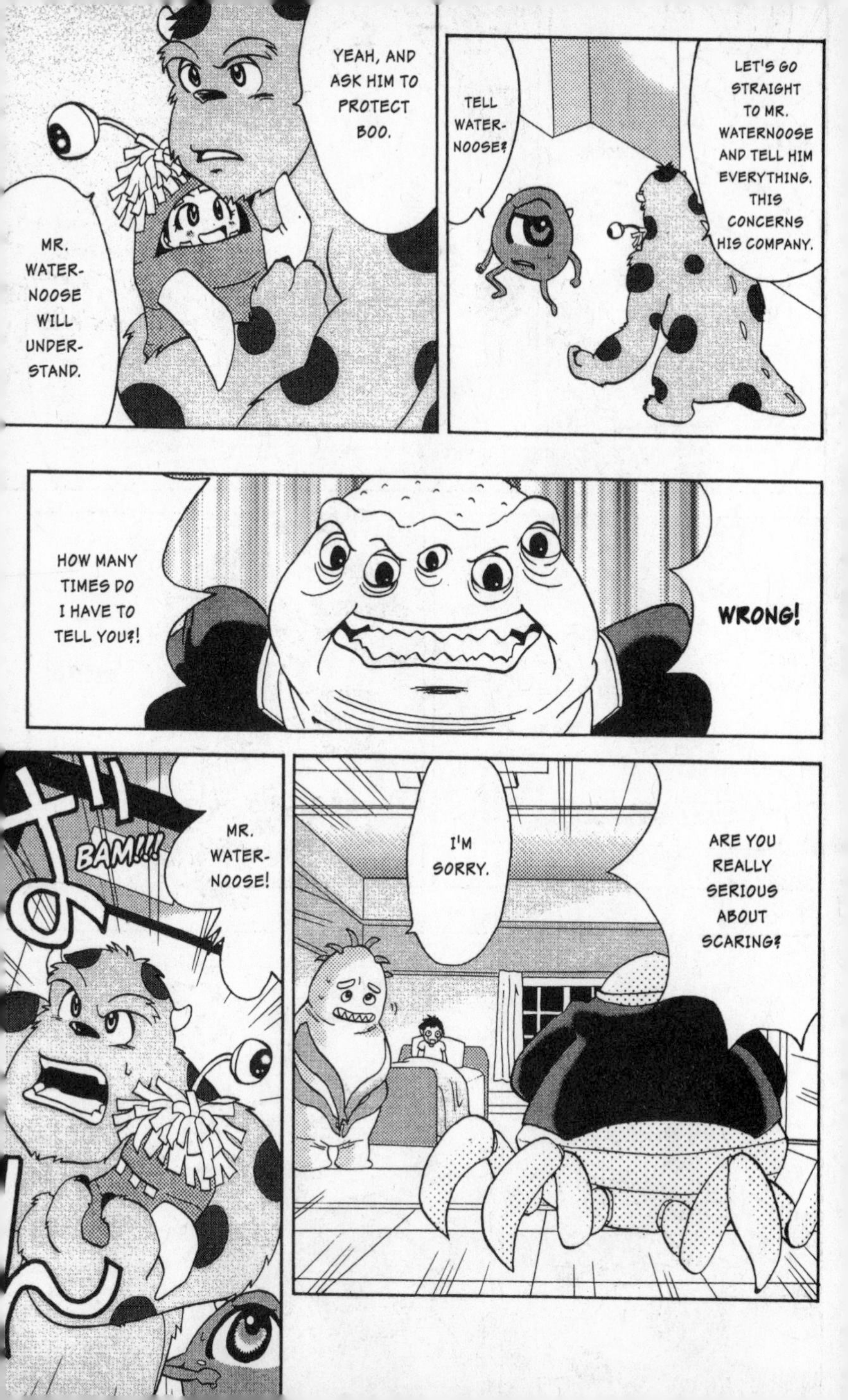
LET'S GO STRAIGHT TO MR. WATERNOOSE AND TELL HIM EVERYTHING. THIS CONCERNS HIS COMPANY.
TELL WATER-NOOSE?
YEAH, AND ASK HIM TO PROTECT BOO.
MR. WATER-NOOSE WILL UNDER-STAND.
WRONG!
HOW MANY TIMES DO I HAVE TO TELL YOU?!
ARE YOU REALLY SERIOUS ABOUT SCARING?
I'M SORRY.
MR. WATER-NOOSE!
BAM!!!

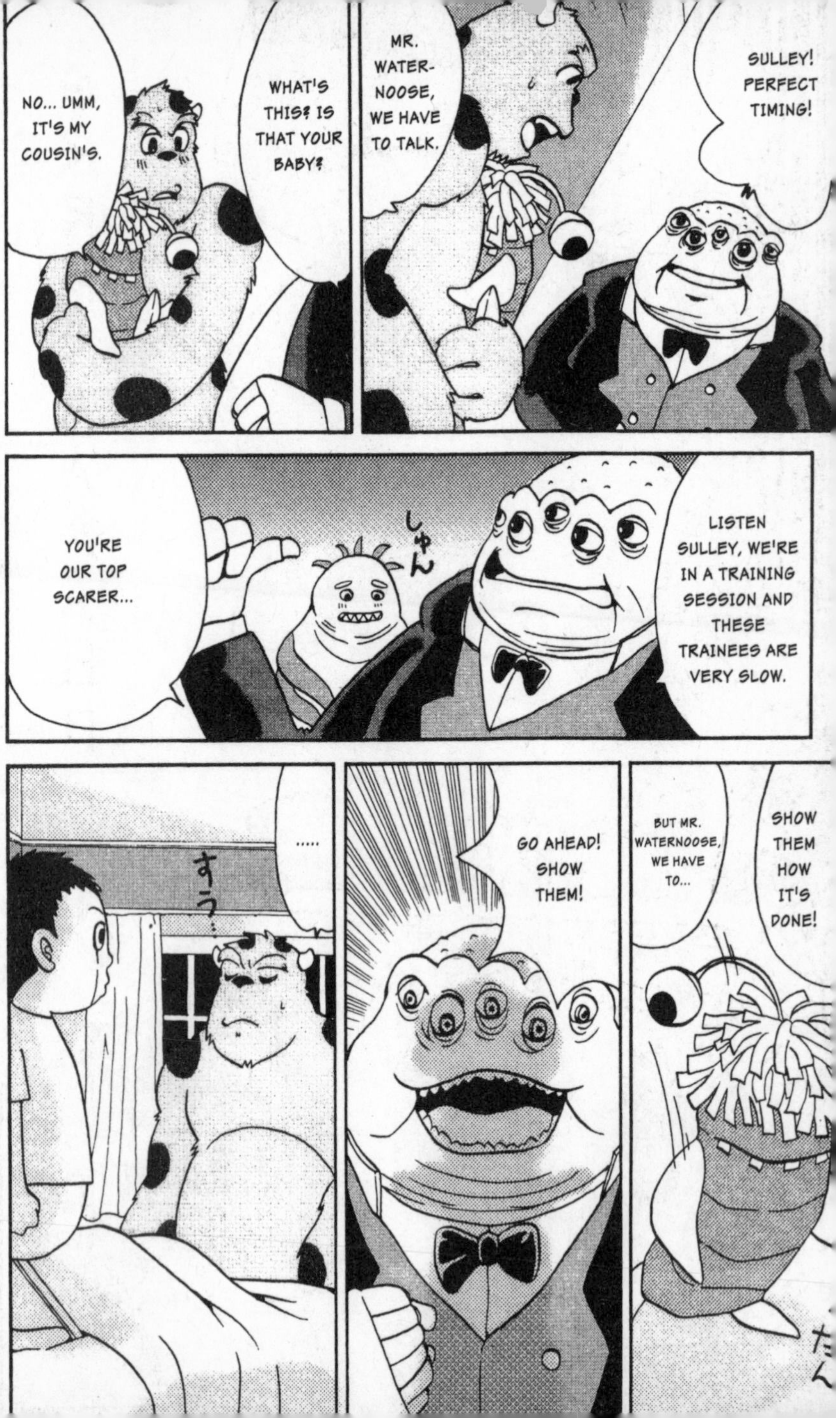
SULLEY! PERFECT TIMING!
MR. WATERNOOSE, WE HAVE TO TALK.
WHAT'S THIS? IS THAT YOUR BABY?
NO... UMM, IT'S MY COUSIN'S.
LISTEN SULLEY, WE'RE IN A TRAINING SESSION AND THESE TRAINEES ARE VERY SLOW.
しゅん
YOU'RE OUR TOP SCARER...
SHOW THEM HOW IT'S DONE!
BUT MR. WATERNOOSE, WE HAVE TO...
たん
GO AHEAD! SHOW THEM!
.....
すう...

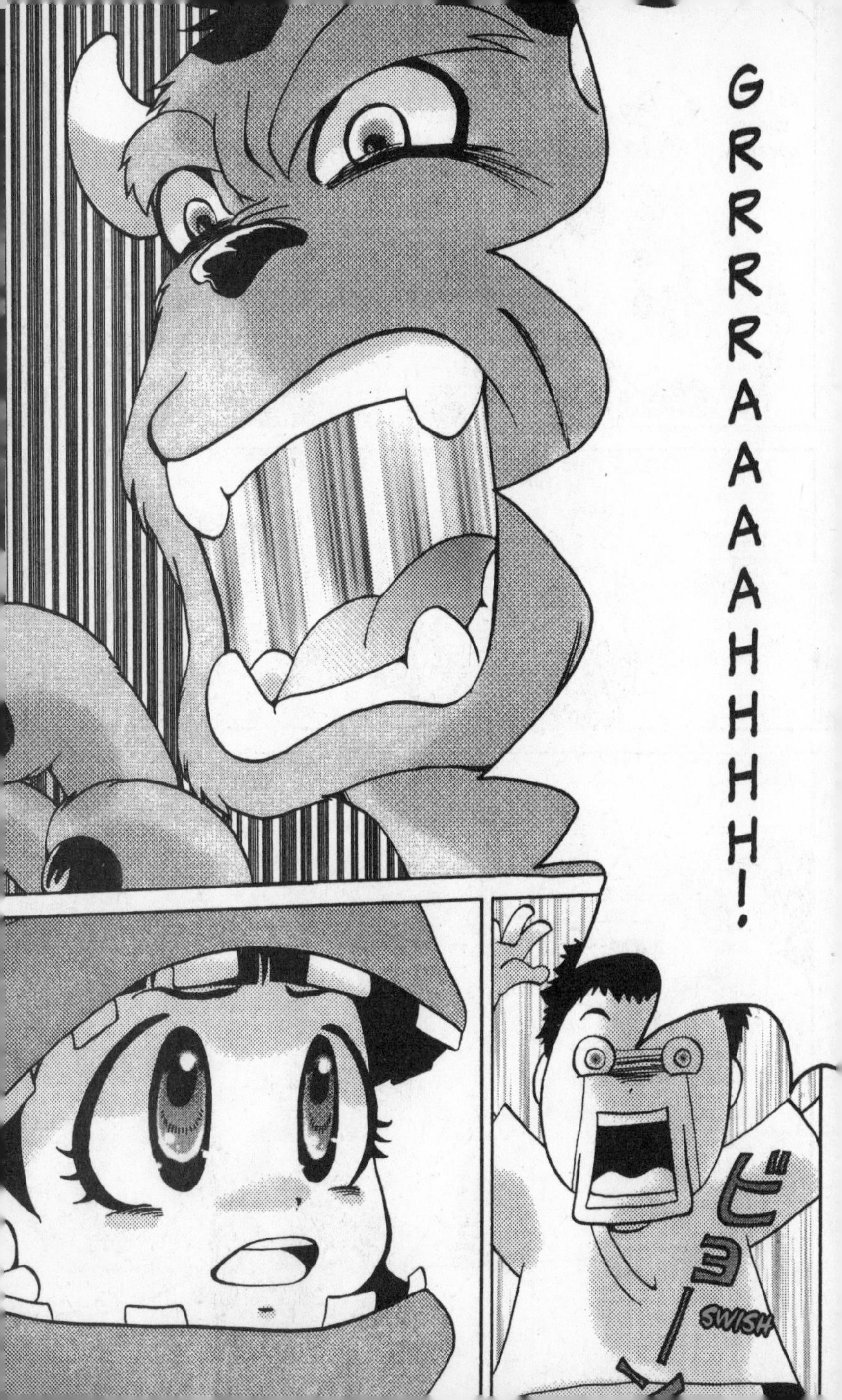
GRRRRAAAAHHHH!
ビョ
SWISH

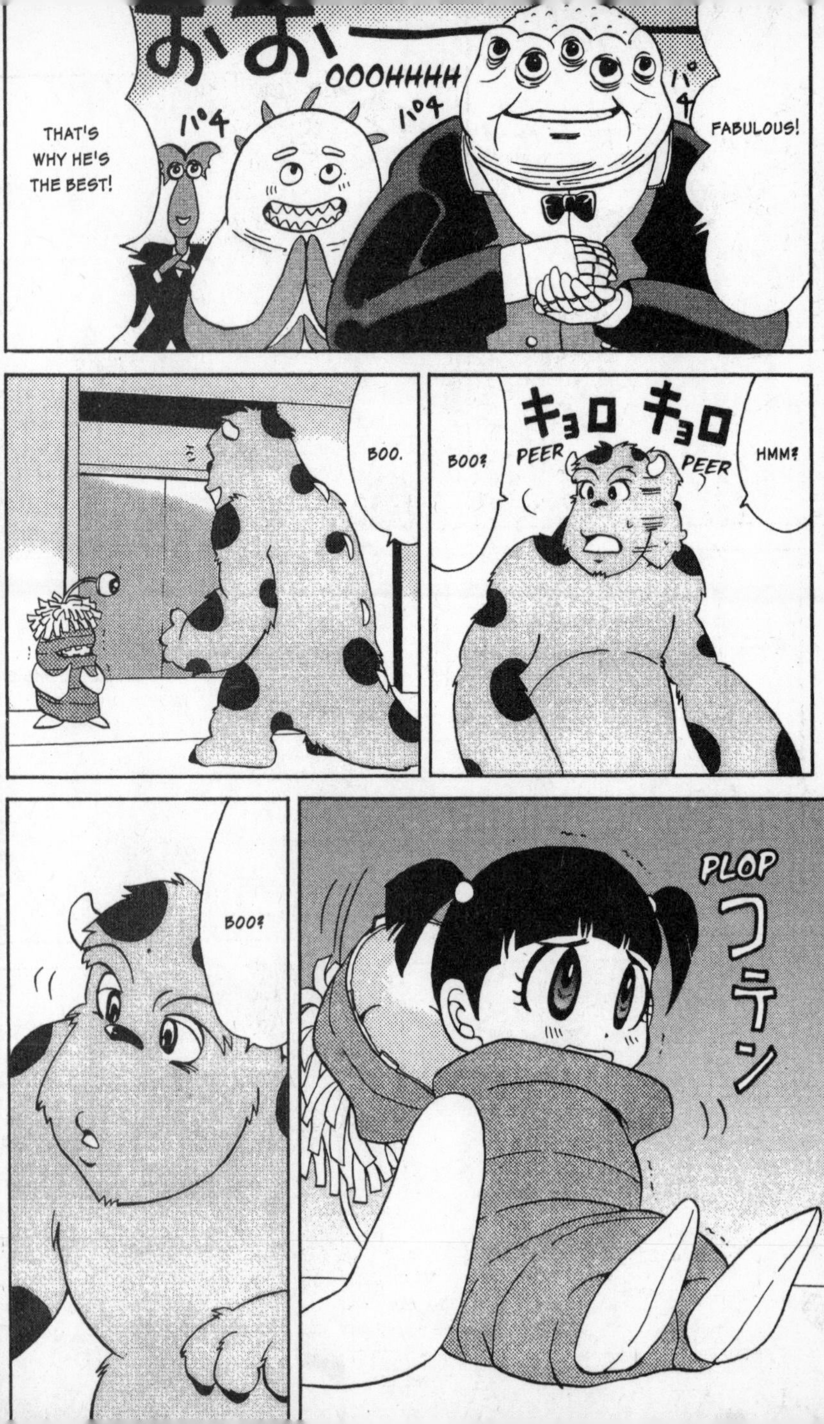

パチ
FABULOUS!
おおー
OOOHHHH
パチ
パチ
THAT'S WHY HE'S THE BEST!
HMM?
キョロ キョロ
PEER PEER
BOO?
BOO.
PLOP
コテン
BOO?

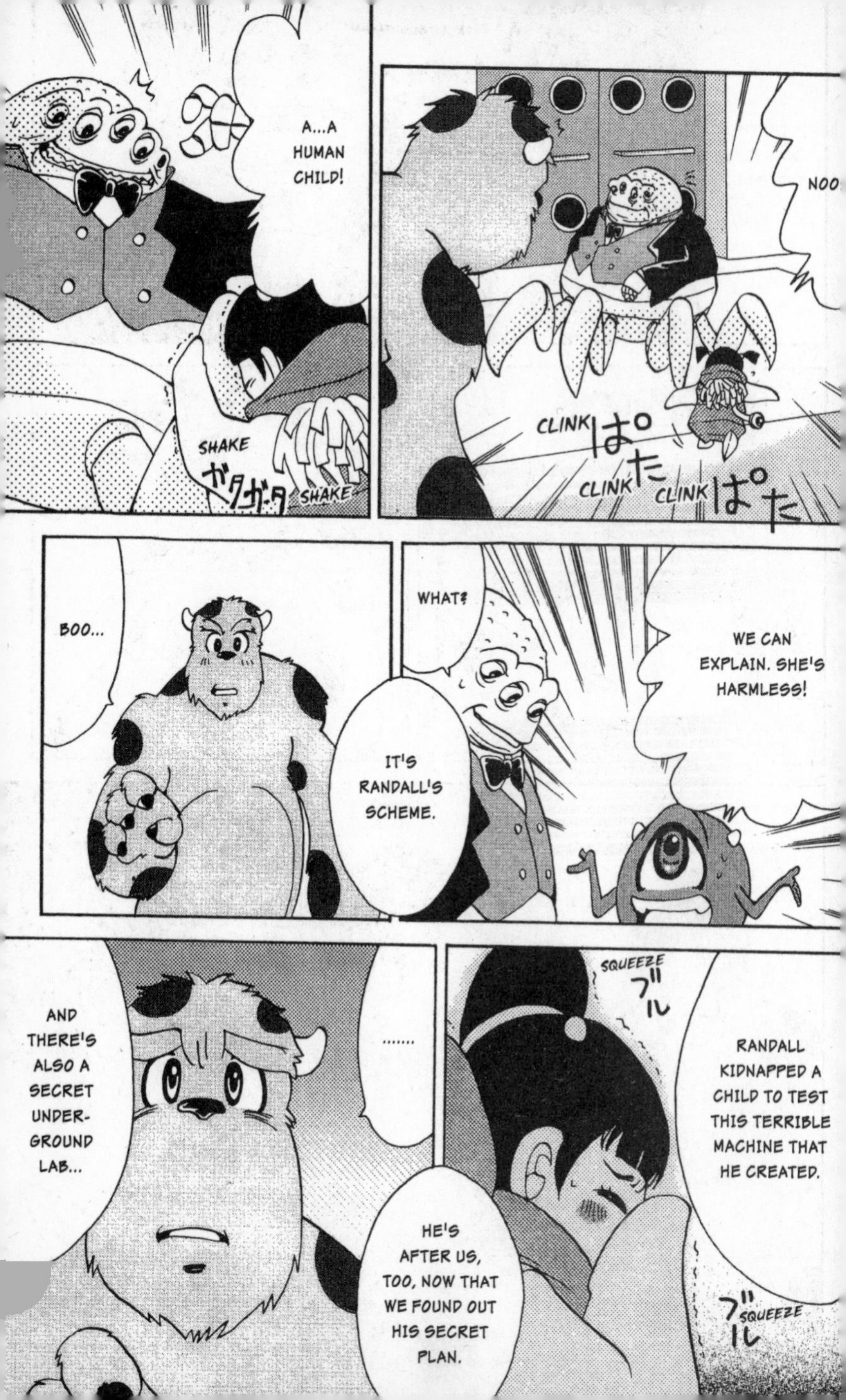
NOO
CLINK ぱた
CLINK
CLINK ぱた
A...A HUMAN CHILD!
SHAKE
ガタガタ
SHAKE
WE CAN EXPLAIN. SHE'S HARMLESS!
WHAT?
IT'S RANDALL'S SCHEME.
BOO...
SQUEEZE
ブル
RANDALL KIDNAPPED A CHILD TO TEST THIS TERRIBLE MACHINE THAT HE CREATED.
ブル
SQUEEZE
HE'S AFTER US, TOO, NOW THAT WE FOUND OUT HIS SECRET PLAN.
....
AND THERE'S ALSO A SECRET UNDER-GROUND LAB...

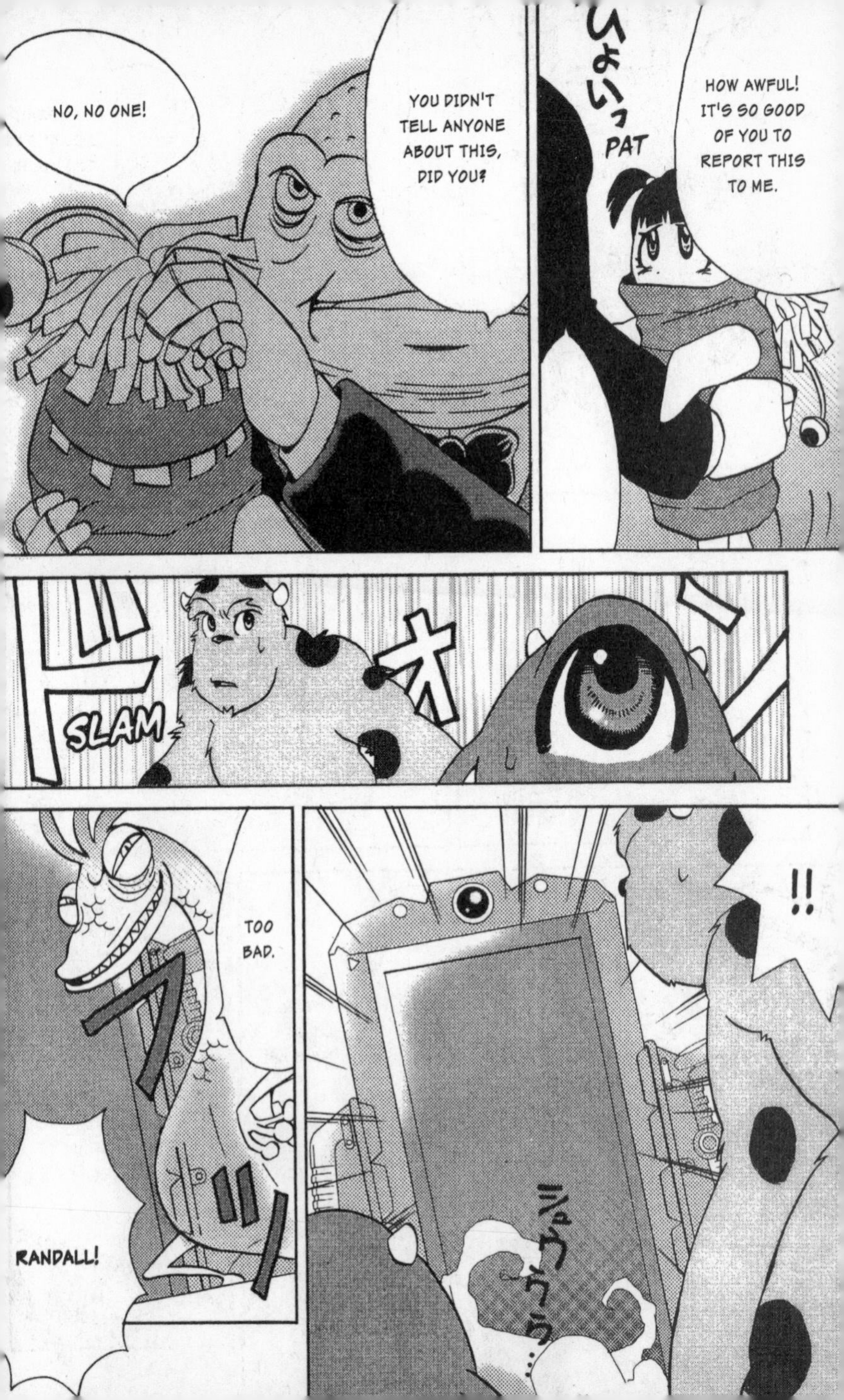
ひょいっ
PAT
HOW AWFUL! IT'S SO GOOD OF YOU TO REPORT THIS TO ME.
YOU DIDN'T TELL ANYONE ABOUT THIS, DID YOU?
NO, NO ONE!
SLAM
!!
TOO BAD.
RANDALL!

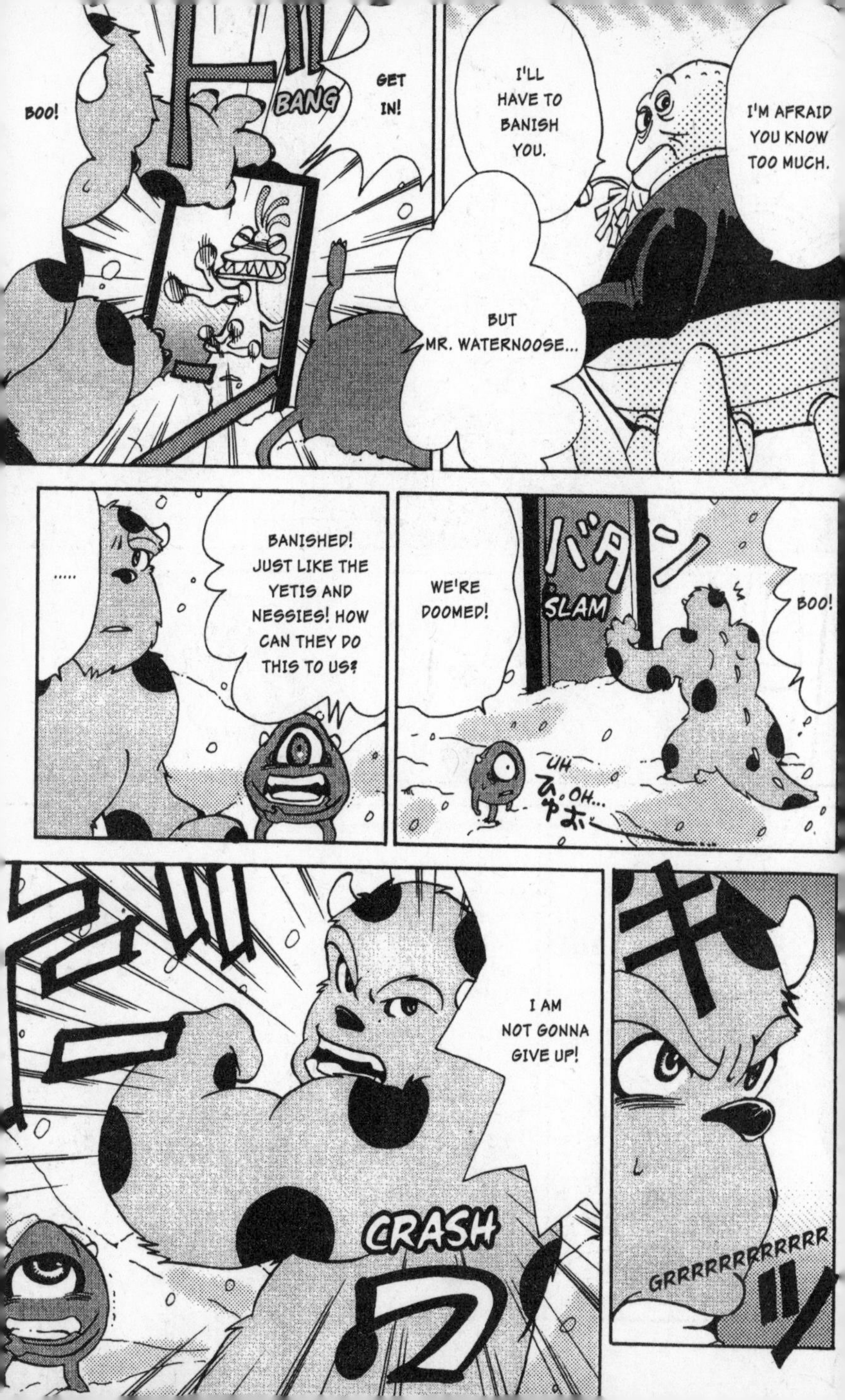
I'M AFRAID YOU KNOW TOO MUCH.
I'LL HAVE TO BANISH YOU.
BUT MR. WATERNOOSE...
GET IN!
BANG
BOO!
BOO!
バタン
SLAM
WE'RE DOOMED!
UH OH...
BANISHED! JUST LIKE THE YETIS AND NESSIES! HOW CAN THEY DO THIS TO US?
.....
GRRRRRRRRRRR
I AM NOT GONNA GIVE UP!
CRASH

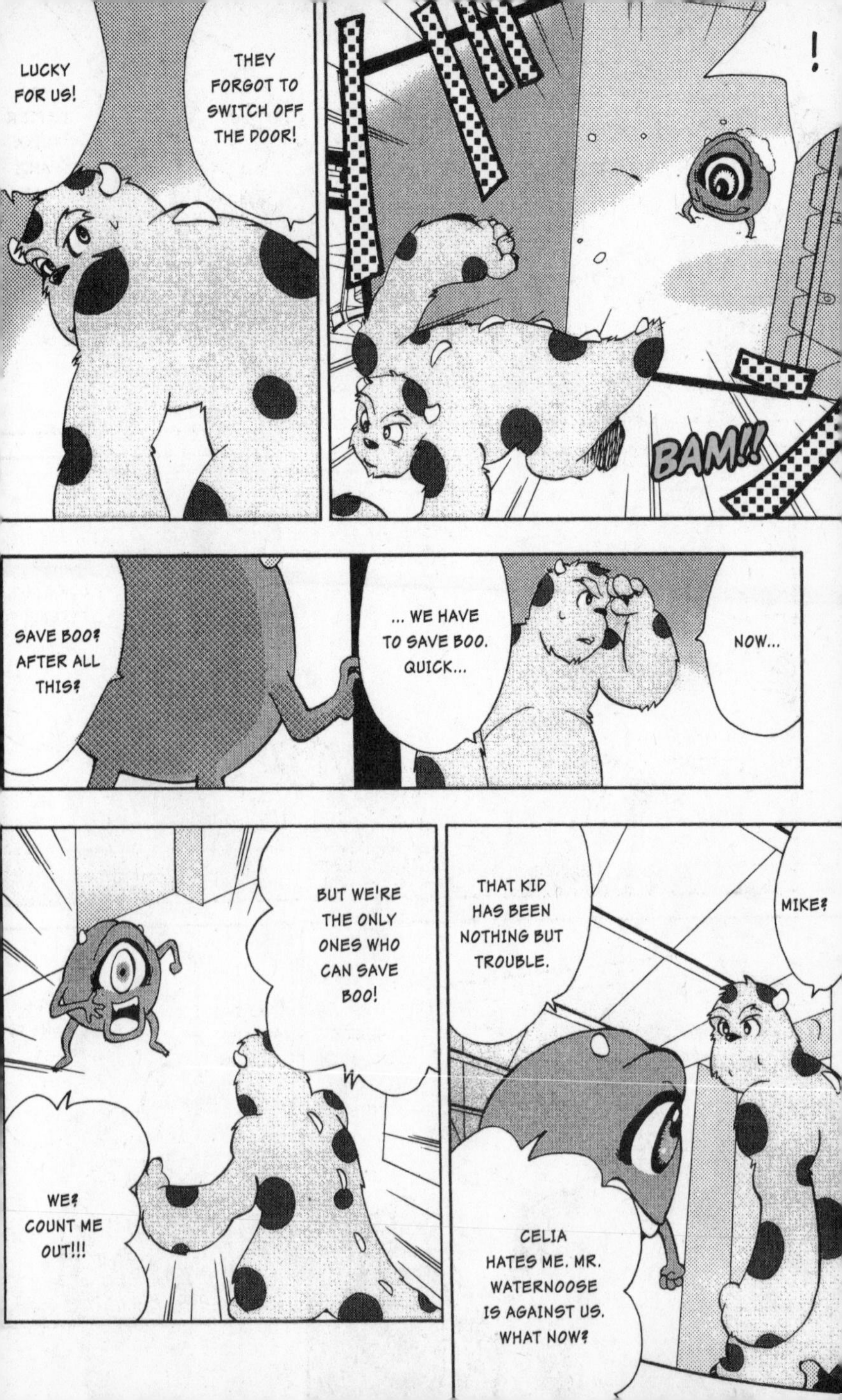
!
BAM!!
THEY FORGOT TO SWITCH OFF THE DOOR!
LUCKY FOR US!
NOW...
... WE HAVE TO SAVE BOO. QUICK...
SAVE BOO? AFTER ALL THIS?
MIKE?
THAT KID HAS BEEN NOTHING BUT TROUBLE.
CELIA HATES ME. MR. WATERNOOSE IS AGAINST US. WHAT NOW?
BUT WE'RE THE ONLY ONES WHO CAN SAVE BOO!
WE? COUNT ME OUT!!!

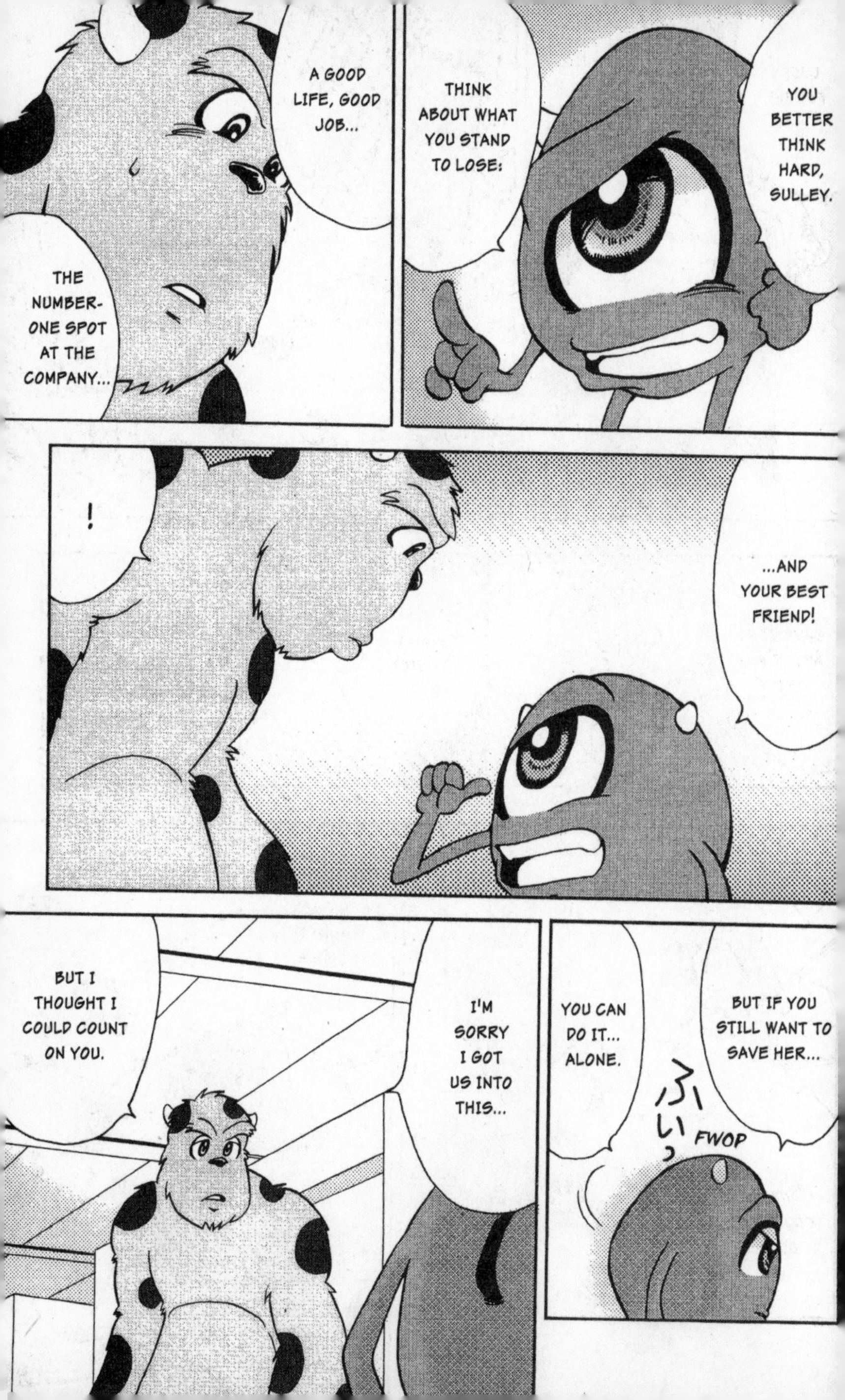
YOU BETTER THINK HARD, SULLEY.
THINK ABOUT WHAT YOU STAND TO LOSE:
A GOOD LIFE, GOOD JOB...
THE NUMBER-ONE SPOT AT THE COMPANY...
...AND YOUR BEST FRIEND!
!
BUT IF YOU STILL WANT TO SAVE HER...
YOU CAN DO IT... ALONE.
ふい
FWOP
I'M SORRY I GOT US INTO THIS...
BUT I THOUGHT I COULD COUNT ON YOU.

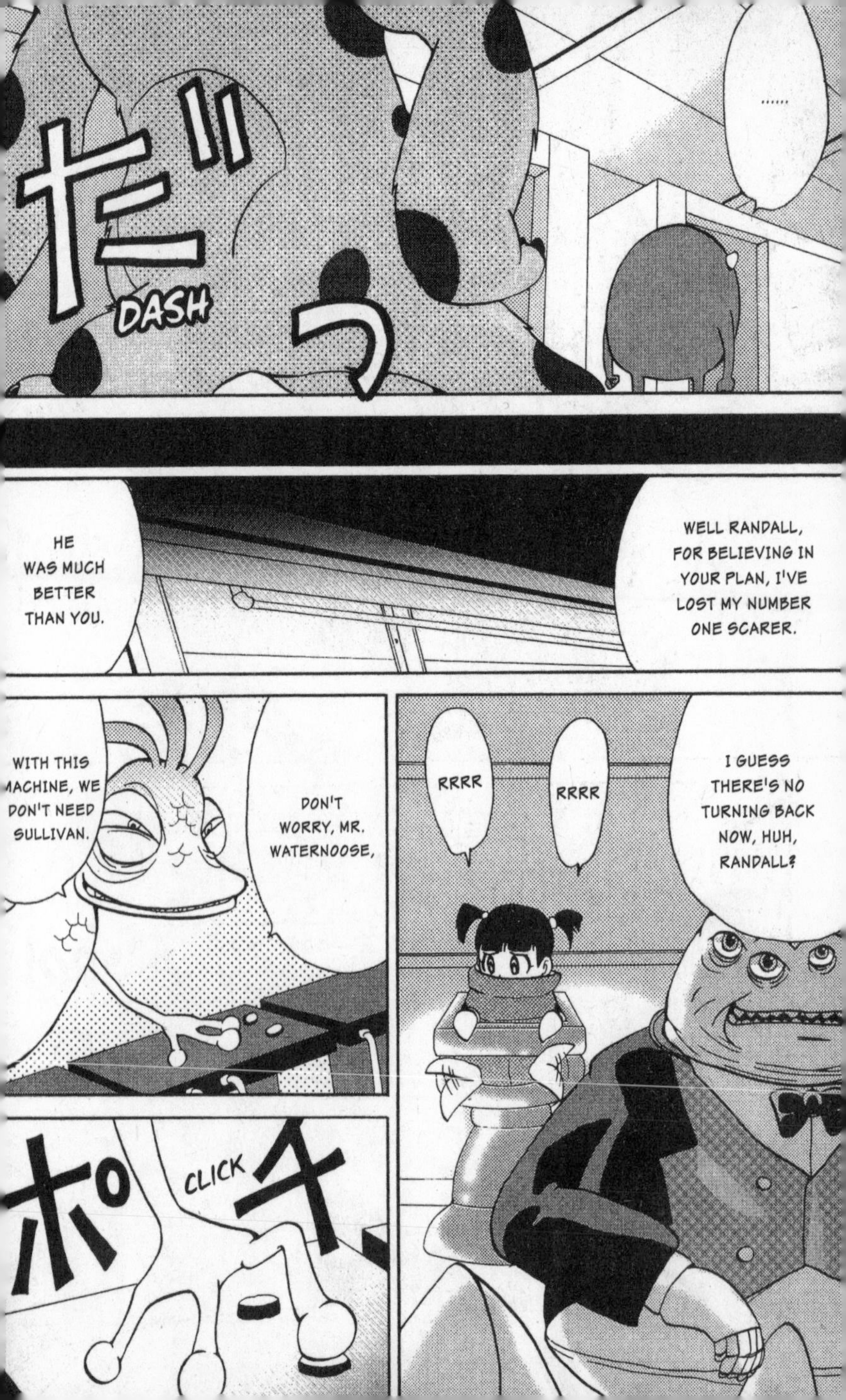
......
DASH
WELL RANDALL, FOR BELIEVING IN YOUR PLAN, I'VE LOST MY NUMBER ONE SCARER.
HE WAS MUCH BETTER THAN YOU.
I GUESS THERE'S NO TURNING BACK NOW, HUH, RANDALL?
RRRR
RRRR
DON'T WORRY, MR. WATERNOOSE,
WITH THIS MACHINE, WE DON'T NEED SULLIVAN.
CLICK

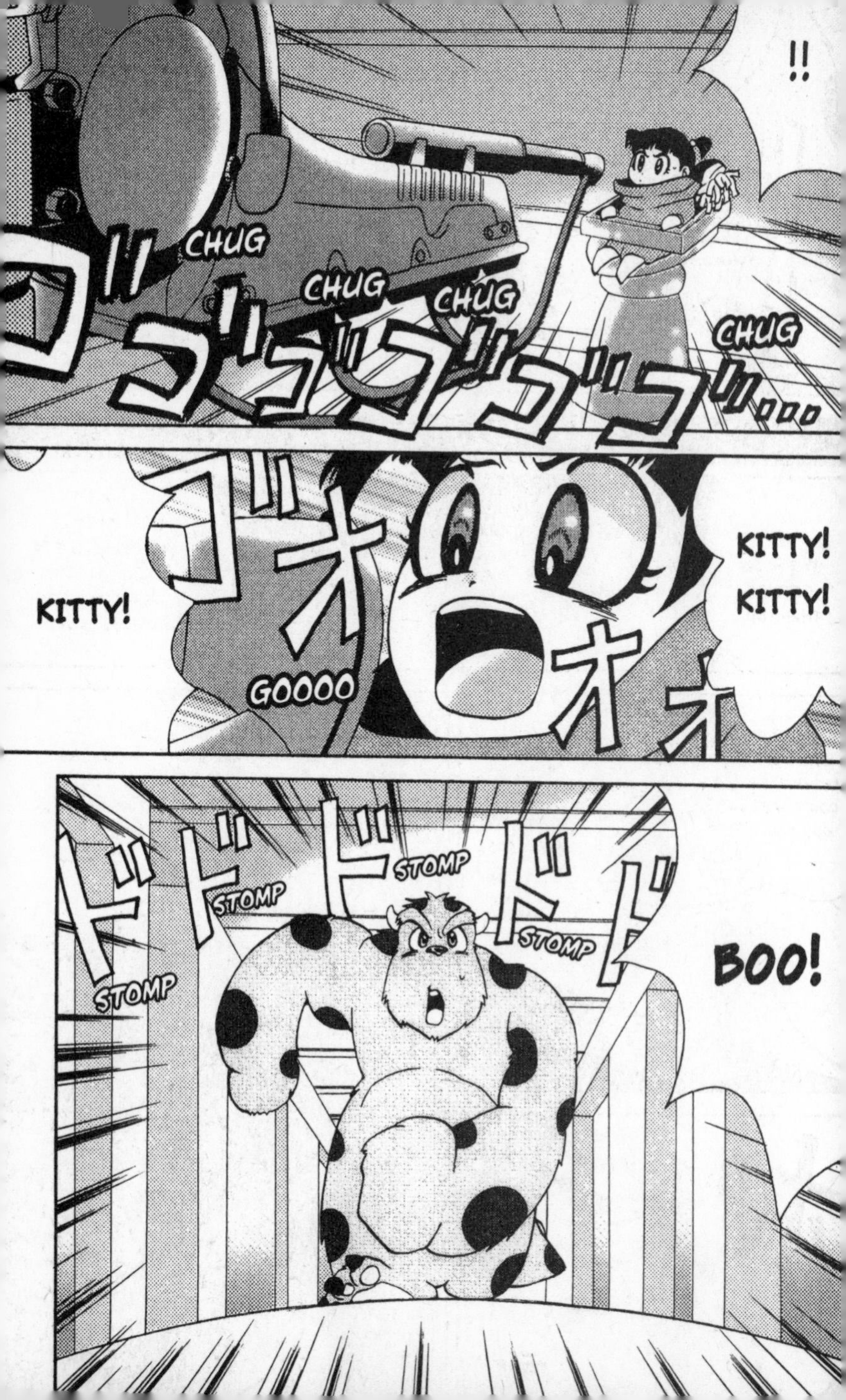
!!
CHUG
CHUG
CHUG
CHUG
KITTY! KITTY!
GOOOO
KITTY!
BOO!
STOMP
STOMP
STOMP
STOMP

Chapter 3

A MONSTER PLAN!

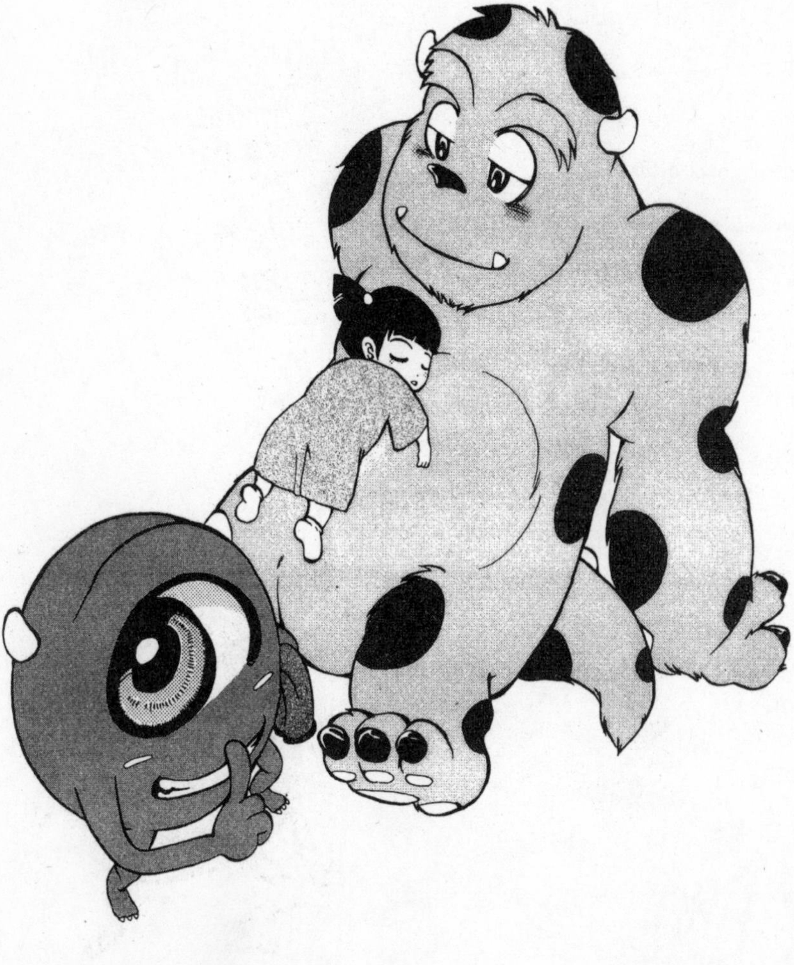

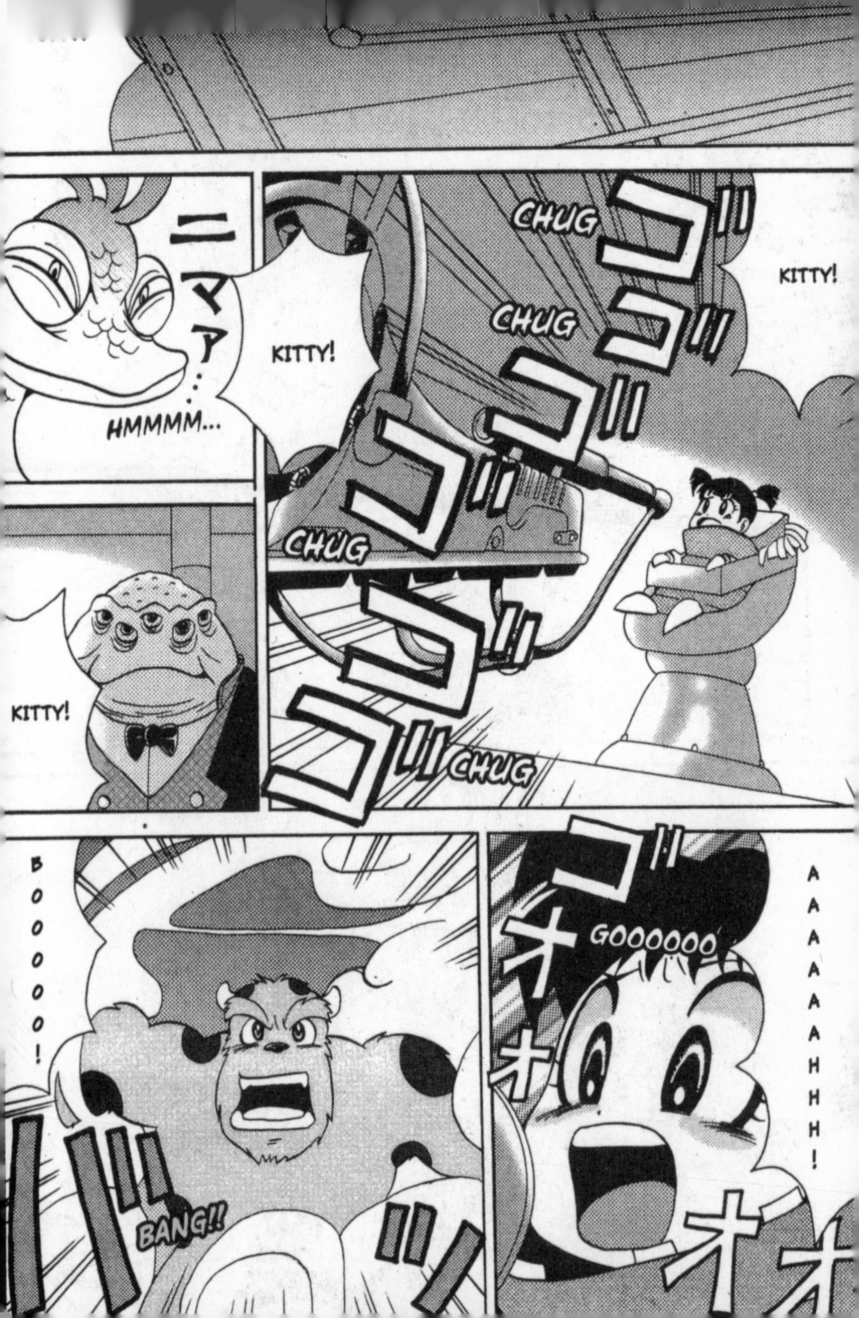
KITTY!
CHUG
CHUG
CHUG
CHUG
ニマア…
HMMMM...
KITTY!
KITTY!
GOOOOOO
AAAAAAAAHHHH!
BOOOOOO!
BANG!!

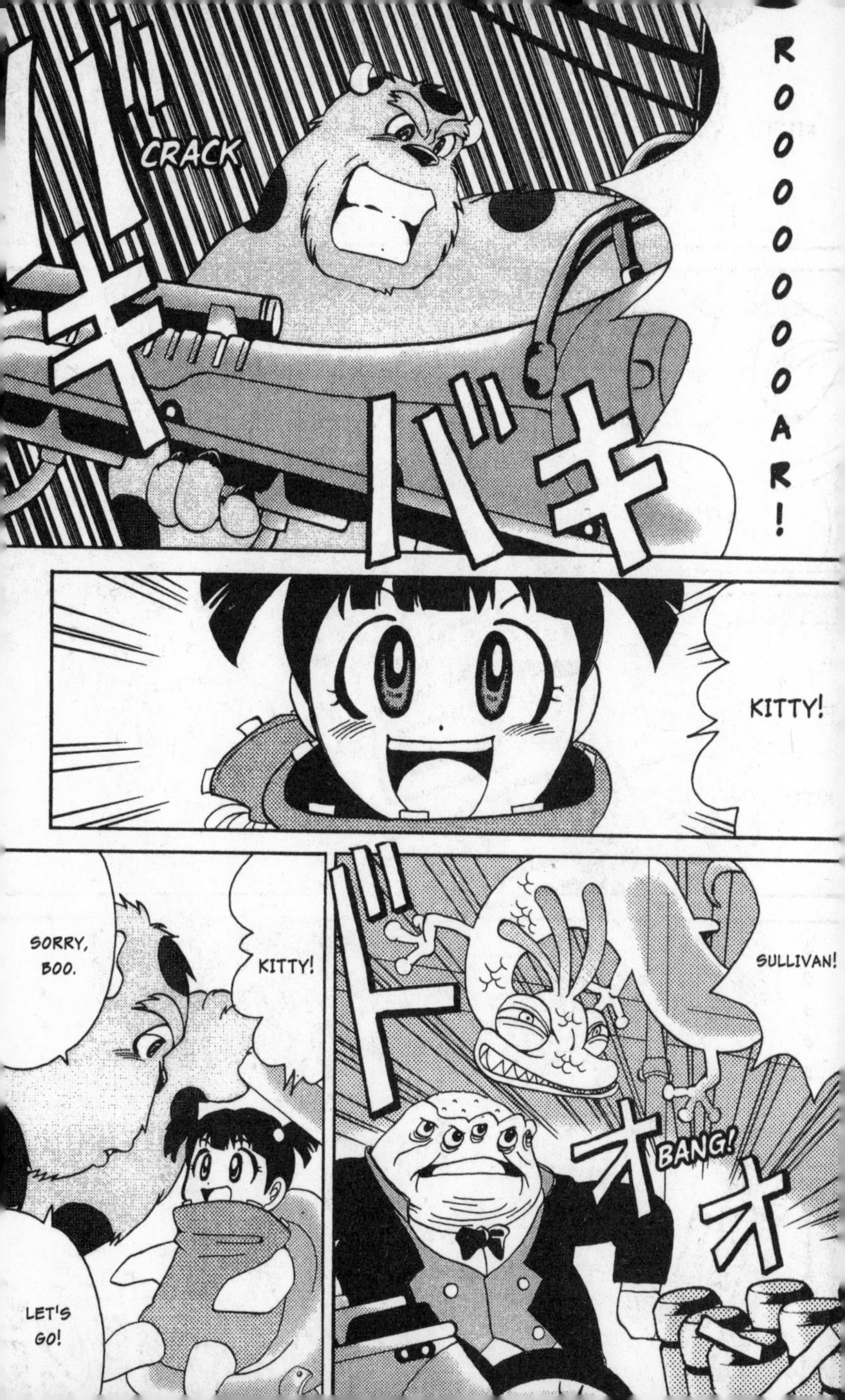
ROOOOOOOOAR!
CRACK
KITTY!
SULLIVAN!
BANG!
KITTY!
SORRY, BOO.
LET'S GO!

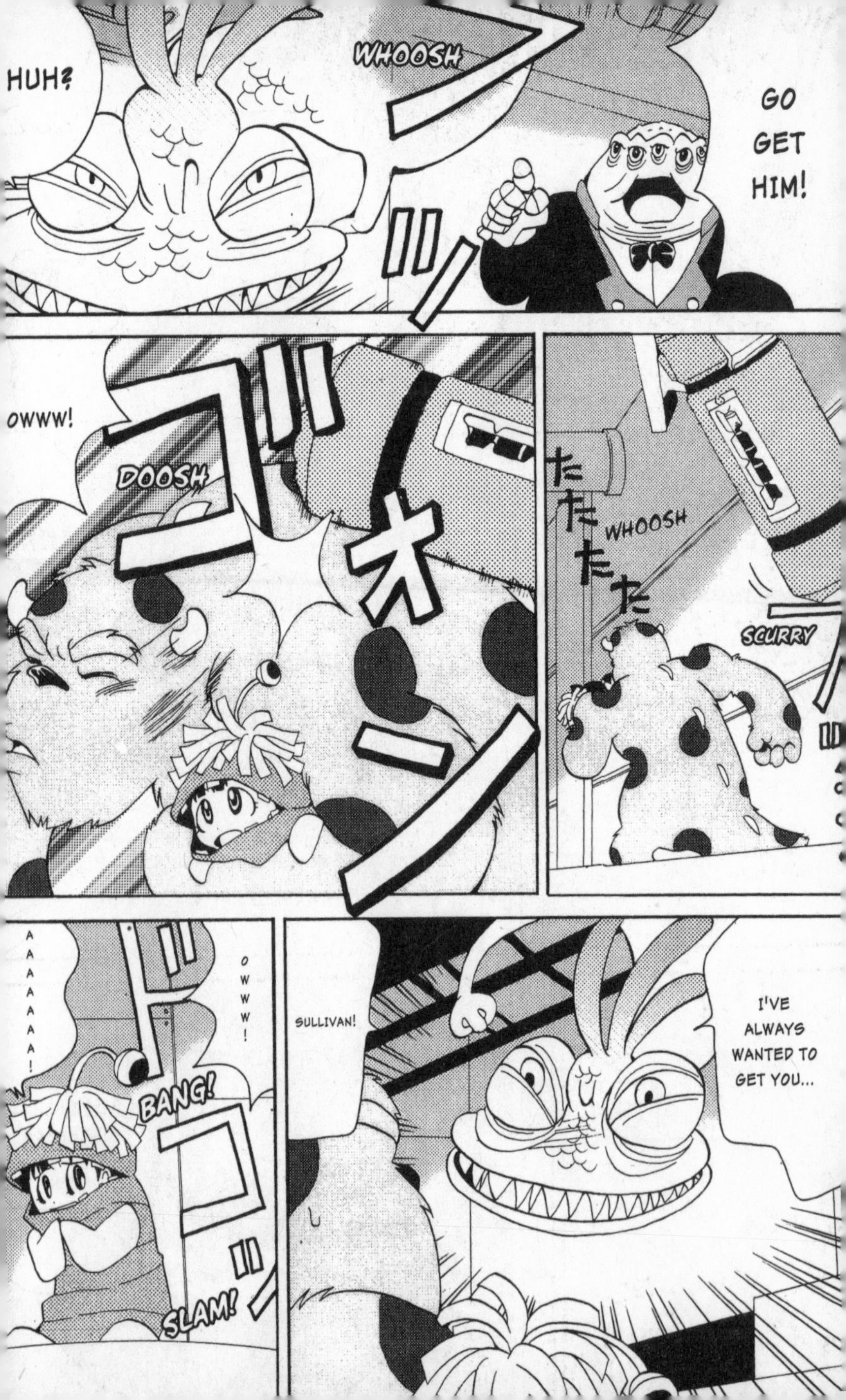
GO GET HIM!
WHOOSH
HUH?
たたた
WHOOSH
SCURRY
DOOSH
OWWW!
I'VE ALWAYS WANTED TO GET YOU...
SULLIVAN!
OWWW!
BANG!
SLAM!
AAAAAAA!

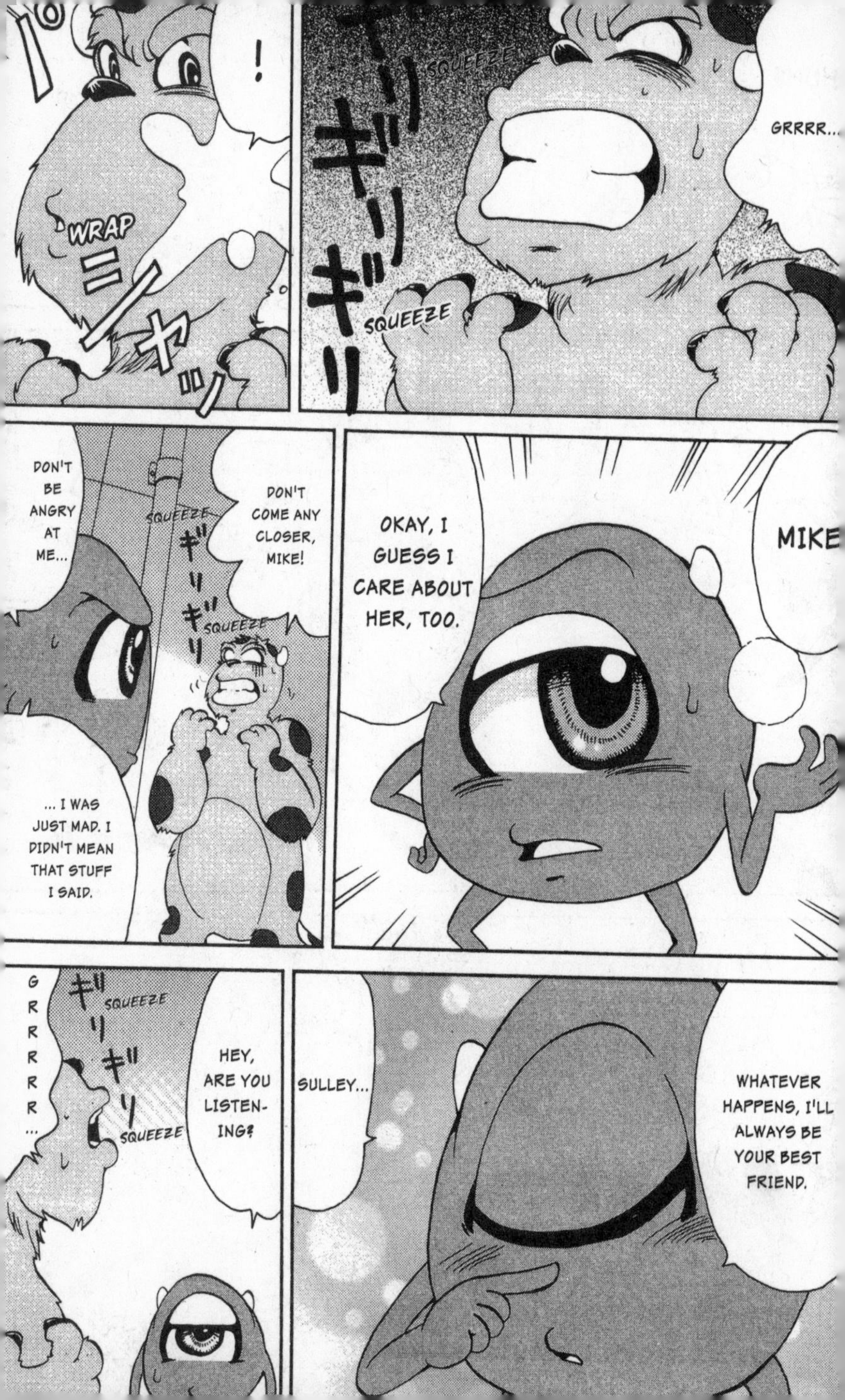
SQUEEZE
GRRRR...
ギリギリ
SQUEEZE
!
WRAP
MIKE
OKAY, I GUESS I CARE ABOUT HER, TOO.
DON'T COME ANY CLOSER, MIKE!
SQUEEZE
SQUEEZE
DON'T BE ANGRY AT ME...
... I WAS JUST MAD. I DIDN'T MEAN THAT STUFF I SAID.
WHATEVER HAPPENS, I'LL ALWAYS BE YOUR BEST FRIEND.
SULLEY...
HEY, ARE YOU LISTENING?
SQUEEZE
SQUEEZE
GRRRRR...

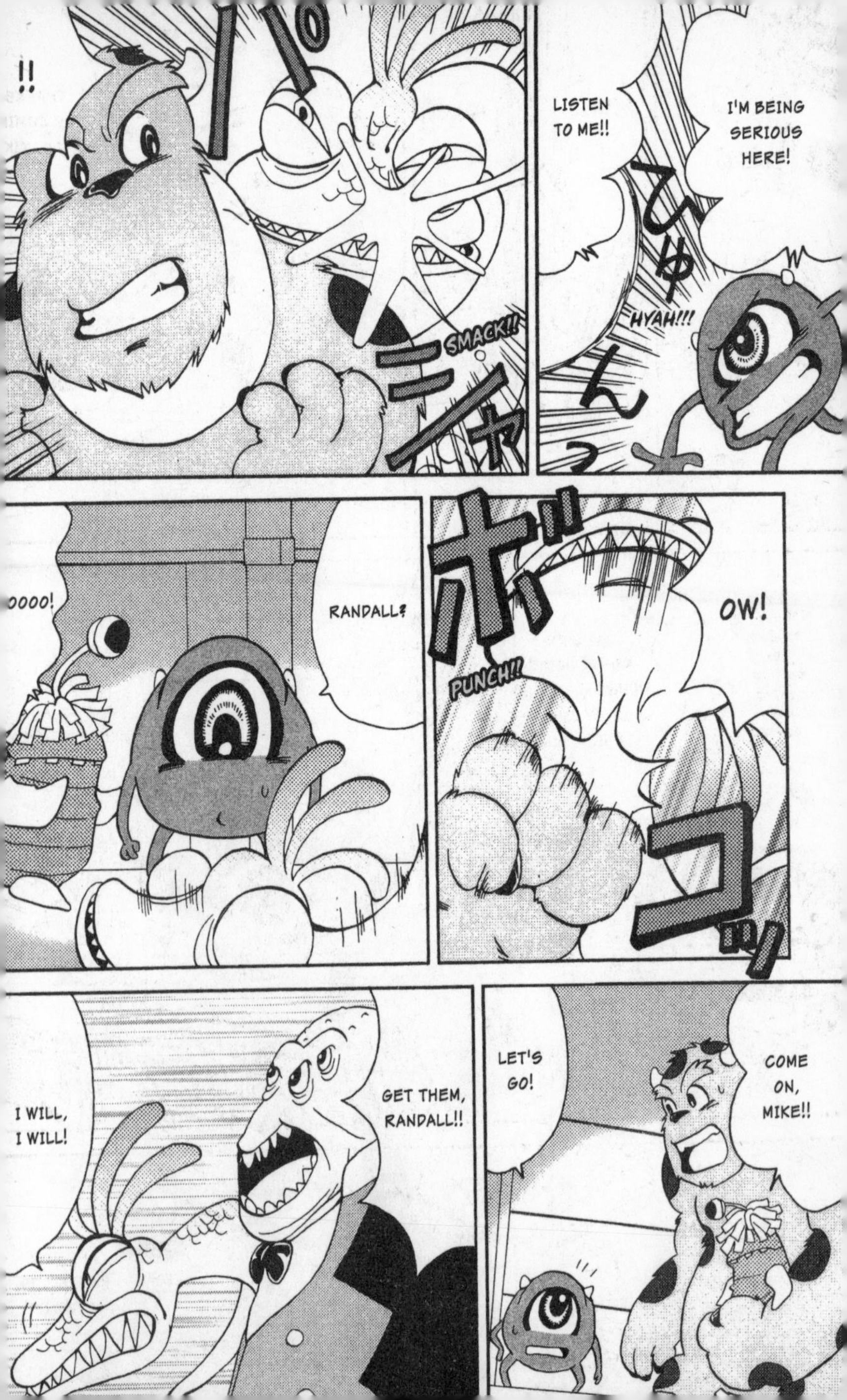

I'M BEING SERIOUS HERE!
LISTEN TO ME!!
ひゅんっ
HYAH!!!
!!
SMACK!!
OW!
ボゴッ
PUNCH!!
RANDALL?
OOOO!
COME ON, MIKE!!
LET'S GO!
GET THEM, RANDALL!!
I WILL, I WILL!

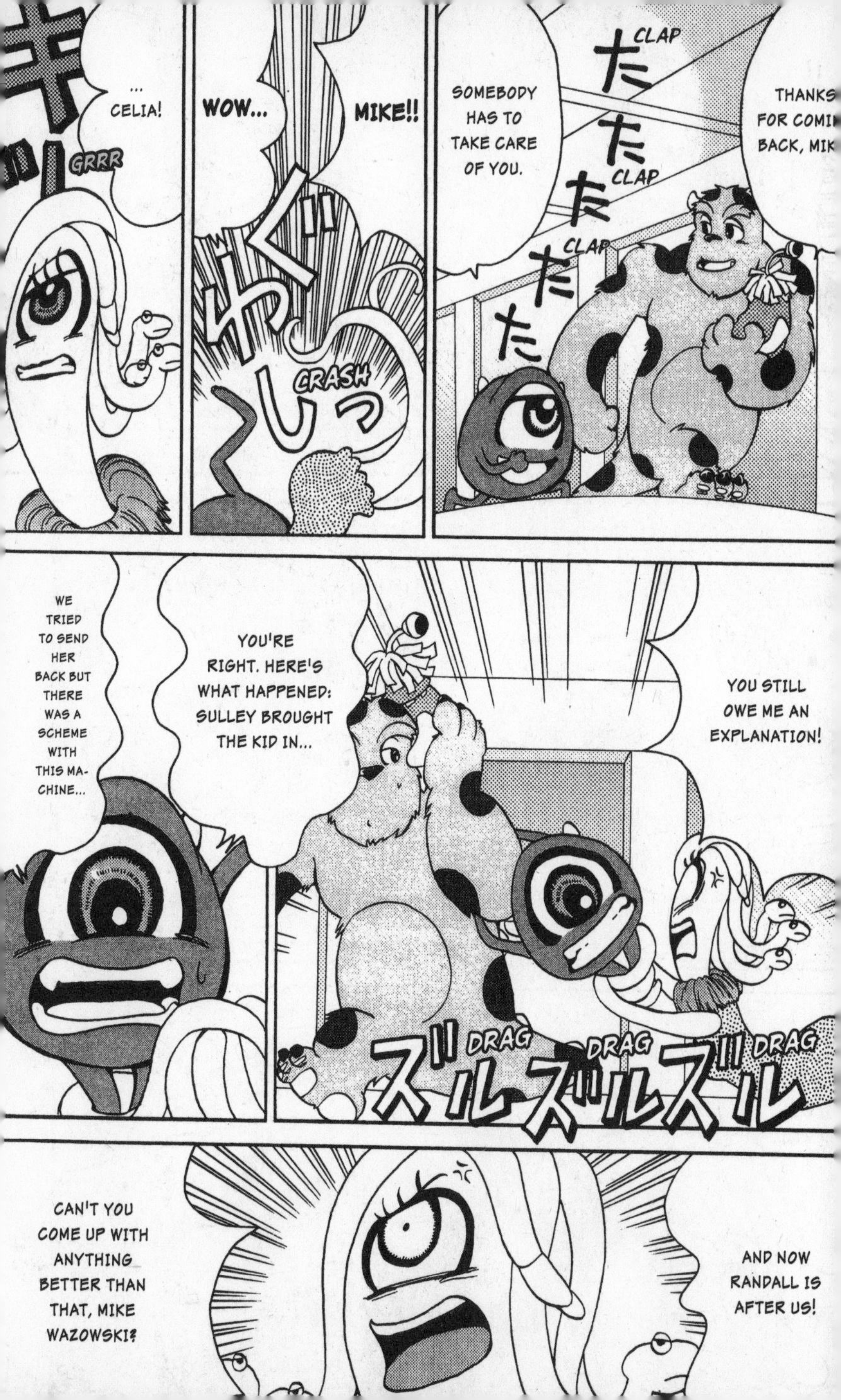
THANKS FOR COMI BACK, MIK
SOMEBODY HAS TO TAKE CARE OF YOU.
たたたたた
CLAP CLAP CLAP
MIKE!!
WOW...
CRASH
... CELIA!
GRRR
YOU STILL OWE ME AN EXPLANATION!
YOU'RE RIGHT. HERE'S WHAT HAPPENED: SULLEY BROUGHT THE KID IN...
WE TRIED TO SEND HER BACK BUT THERE WAS A SCHEME WITH THIS MA-CHINE...
ズルズルズル
DRAG DRAG DRAG
AND NOW RANDALL IS AFTER US!
CAN'T YOU COME UP WITH ANYTHING BETTER THAN THAT, MIKE WAZOWSKI?

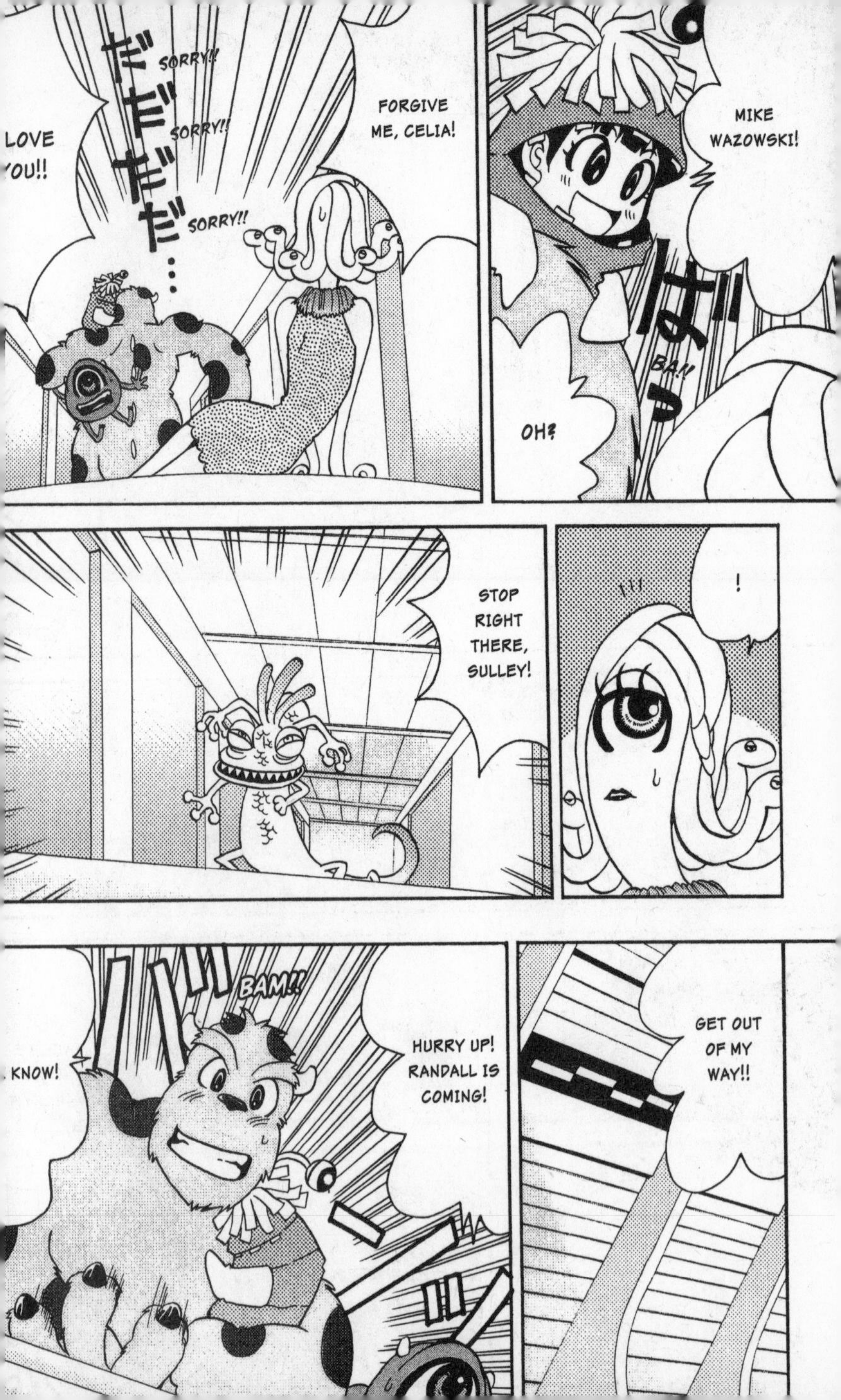
MIKE WAZOWSKI!
はっ
BA!!
OH?
FORGIVE ME, CELIA!
だだだだ…
SORRY!!
SORRY!!
SORRY!!
LOVE
!
STOP RIGHT THERE, SULLEY!
GET OUT OF MY WAY!!
HURRY UP! RANDALL IS COMING!
BAM!!
KNOW!

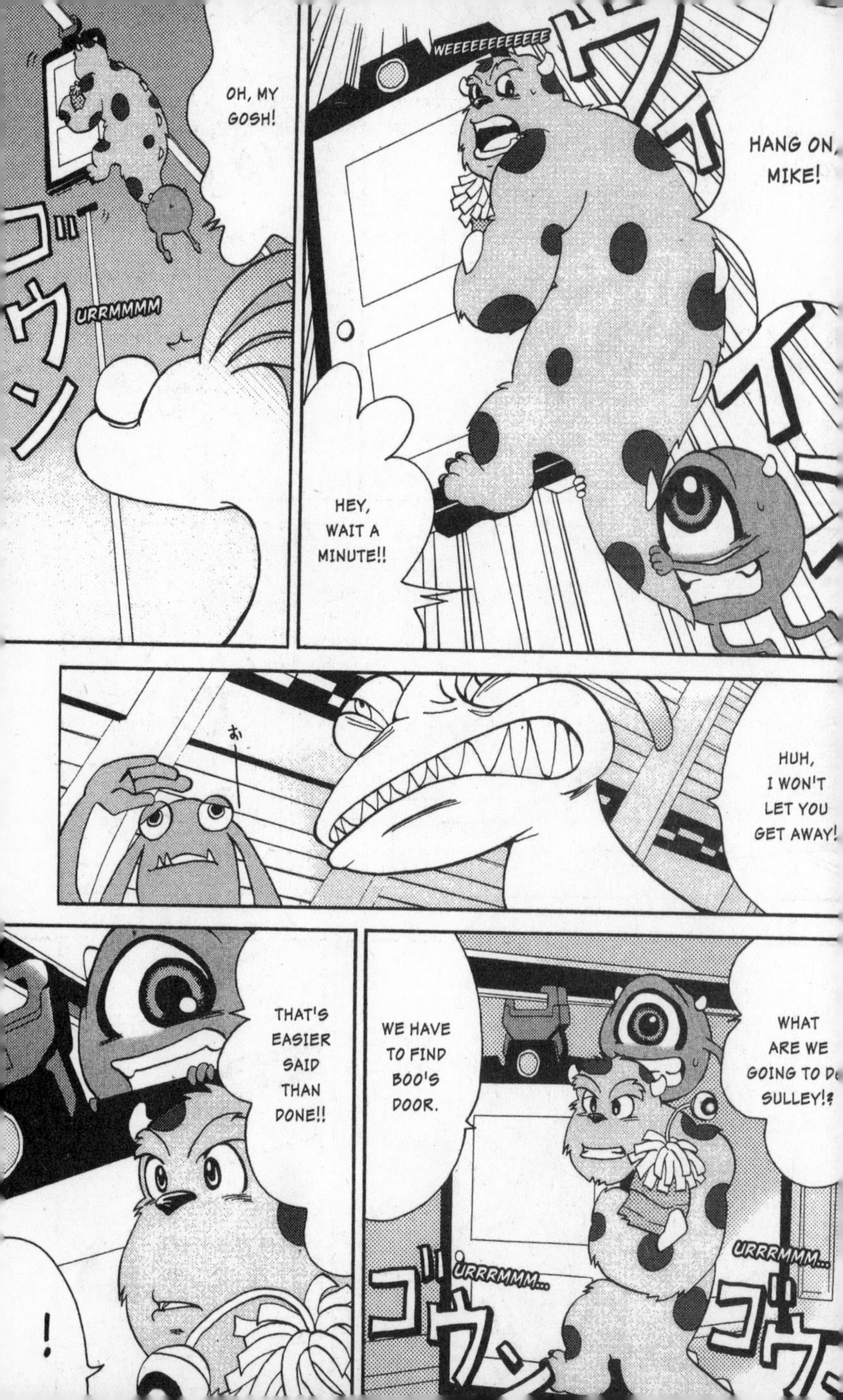
WEEEEEEEEEEE
HANG ON, MIKE!
HEY, WAIT A MINUTE!!
OH, MY GOSH!
URRMMMM
HUH, I WON'T LET YOU GET AWAY!
WHAT ARE WE GOING TO D SULLEY!?
URRRMMM...
WE HAVE TO FIND BOO'S DOOR.
URRRMMM...
THAT'S EASIER SAID THAN DONE!!
!

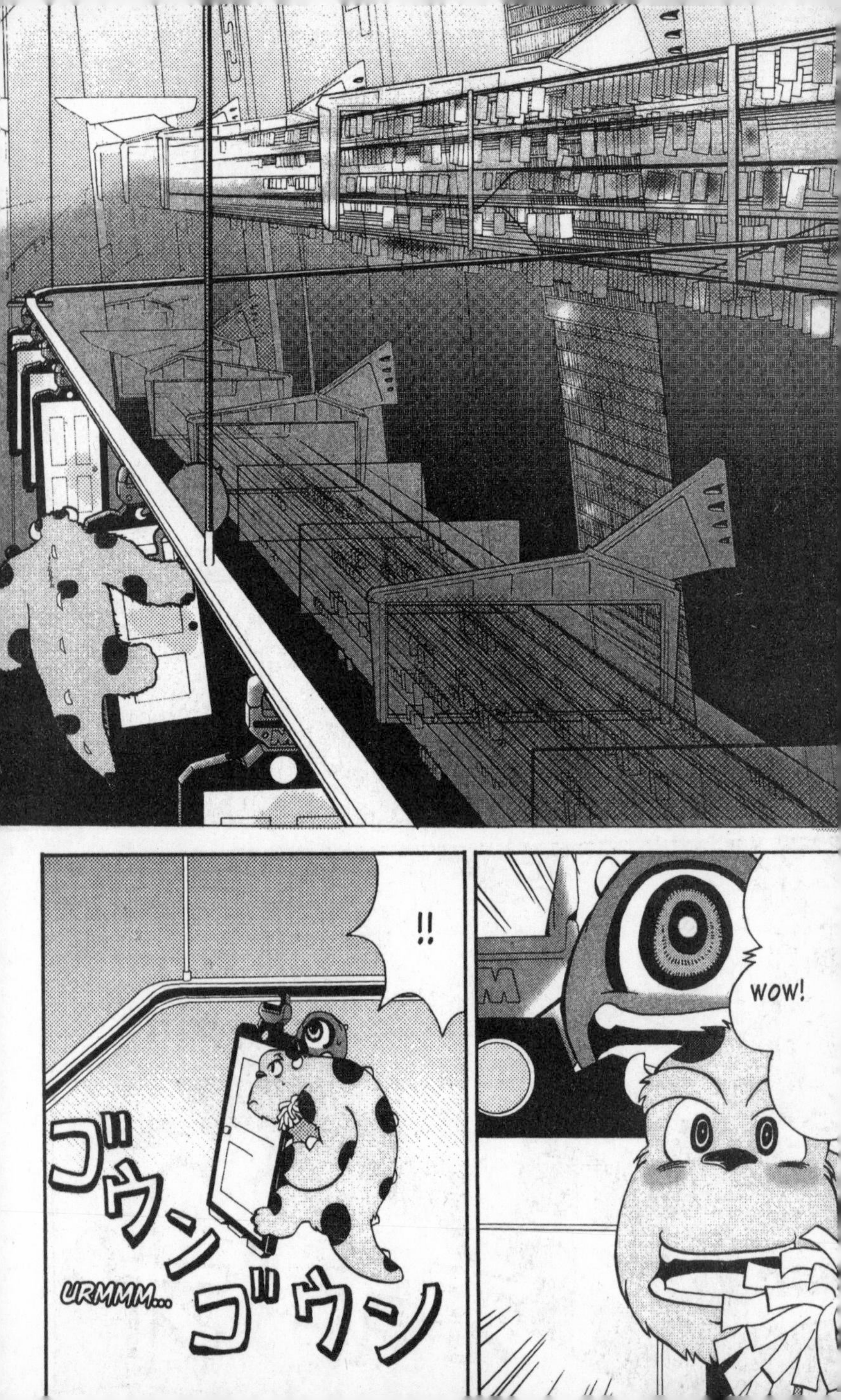
WOW!
!!
ゴウーン
URMMM...
ゴウーン

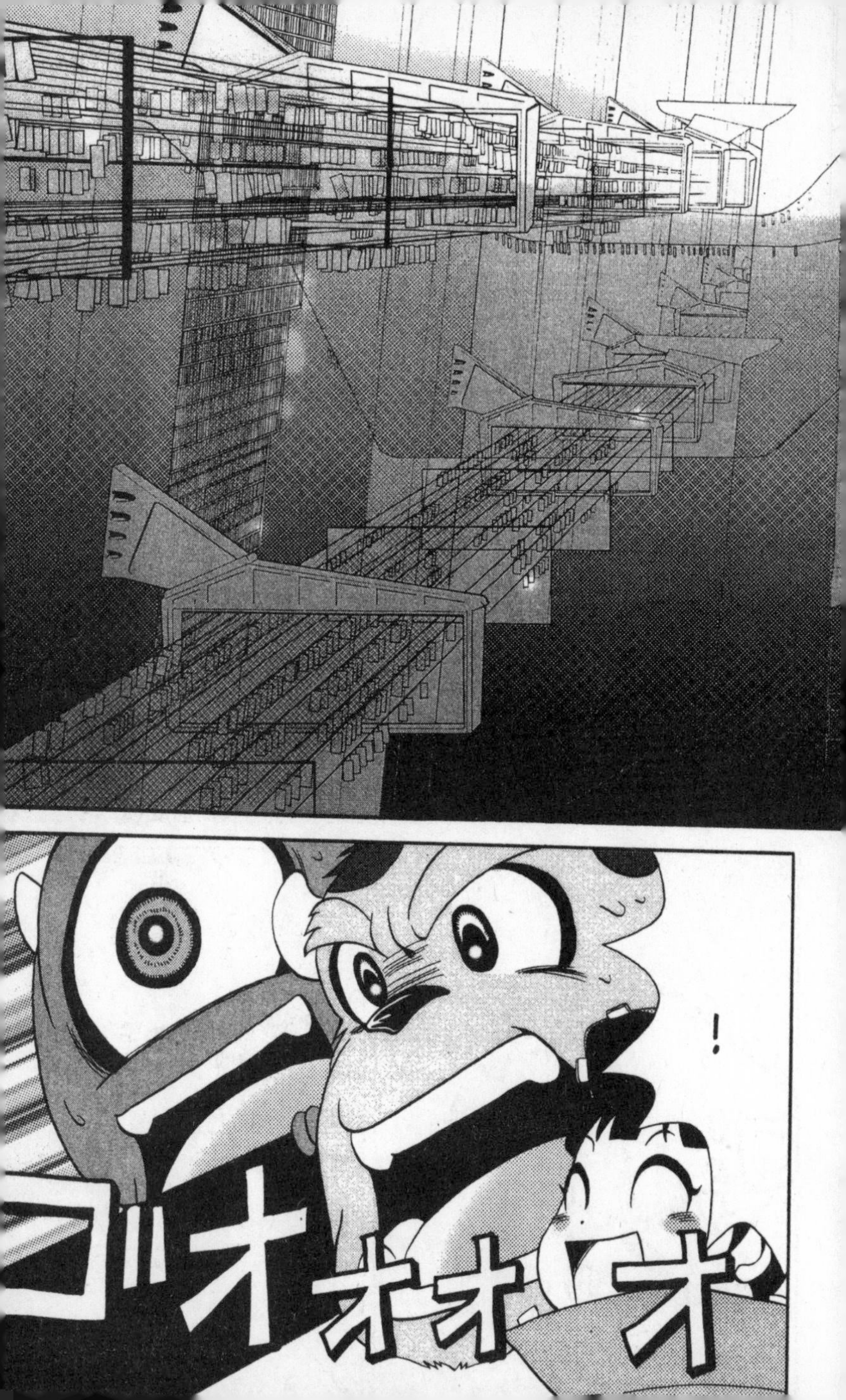
!
ゴオオオオ

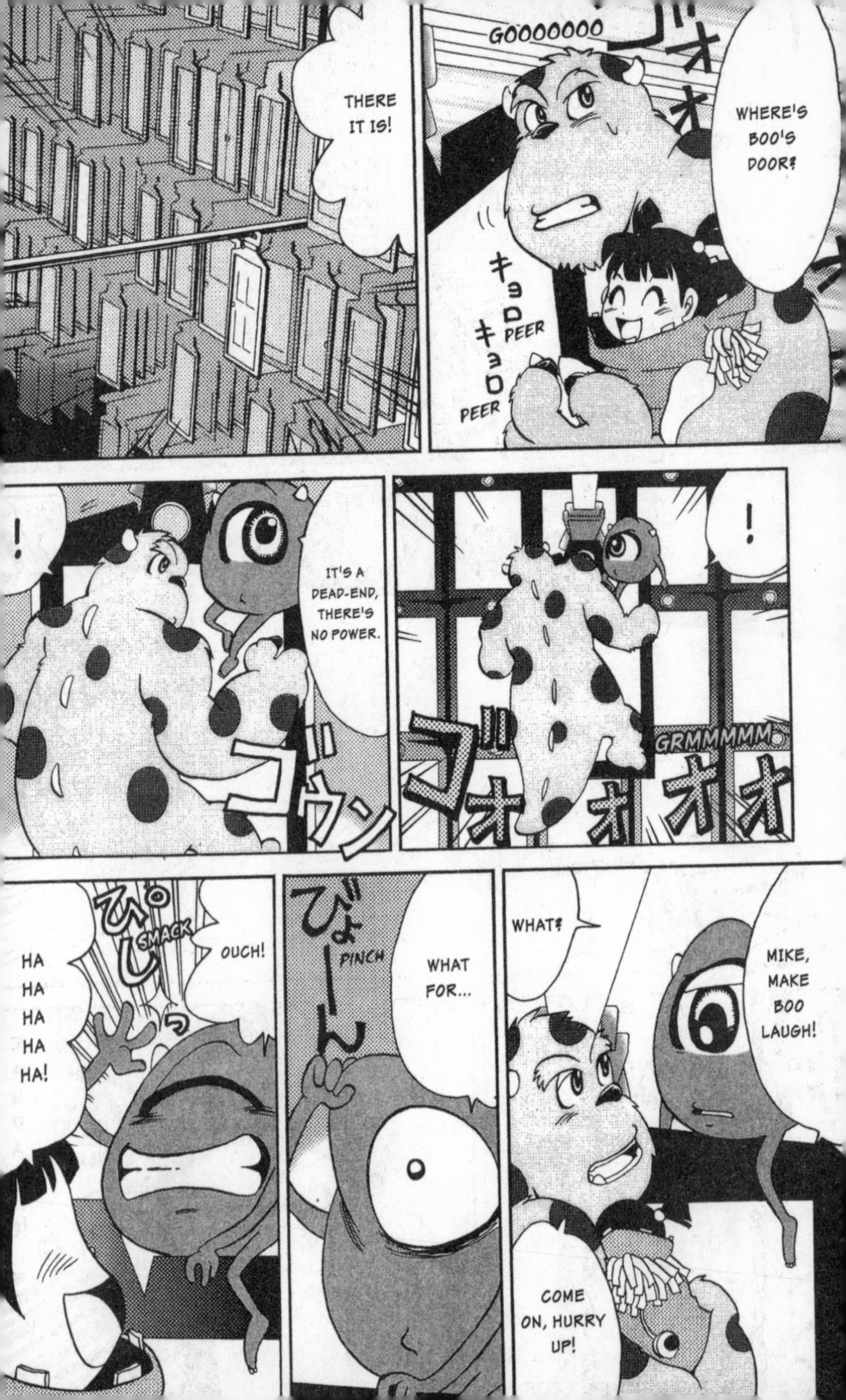
GOOOOOOO
WHERE'S BOO'S DOOR?
キョロ PEER
キョロ PEER
THERE IT IS!
!
GRMMMMM
ブオオオオ
!
IT'S A DEAD-END, THERE'S NO POWER.
ゴウン
MIKE, MAKE BOO LAUGH!
WHAT?
COME ON, HURRY UP!
WHAT FOR...
びょーん
PINCH
OUCH!
ぴしっ
SMACK
HA HA HA HA HA!

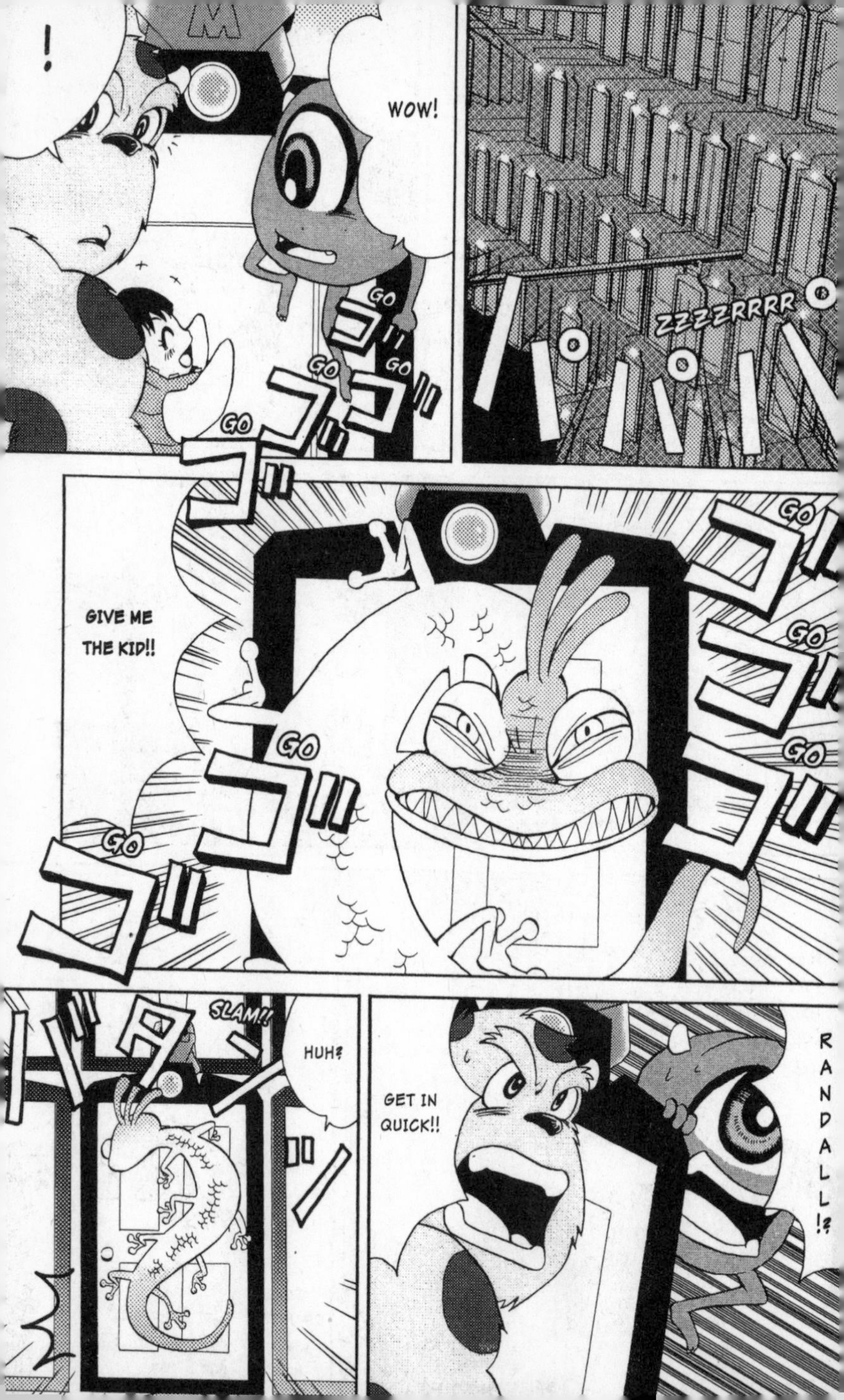
ZZZZRRRR
WOW!
!
GO
GO
GO
GO
GO
GO
GO
GIVE ME THE KID!!
GO
GO
RANDALL!?
GET IN QUICK!!
SLAM!!
HUH?

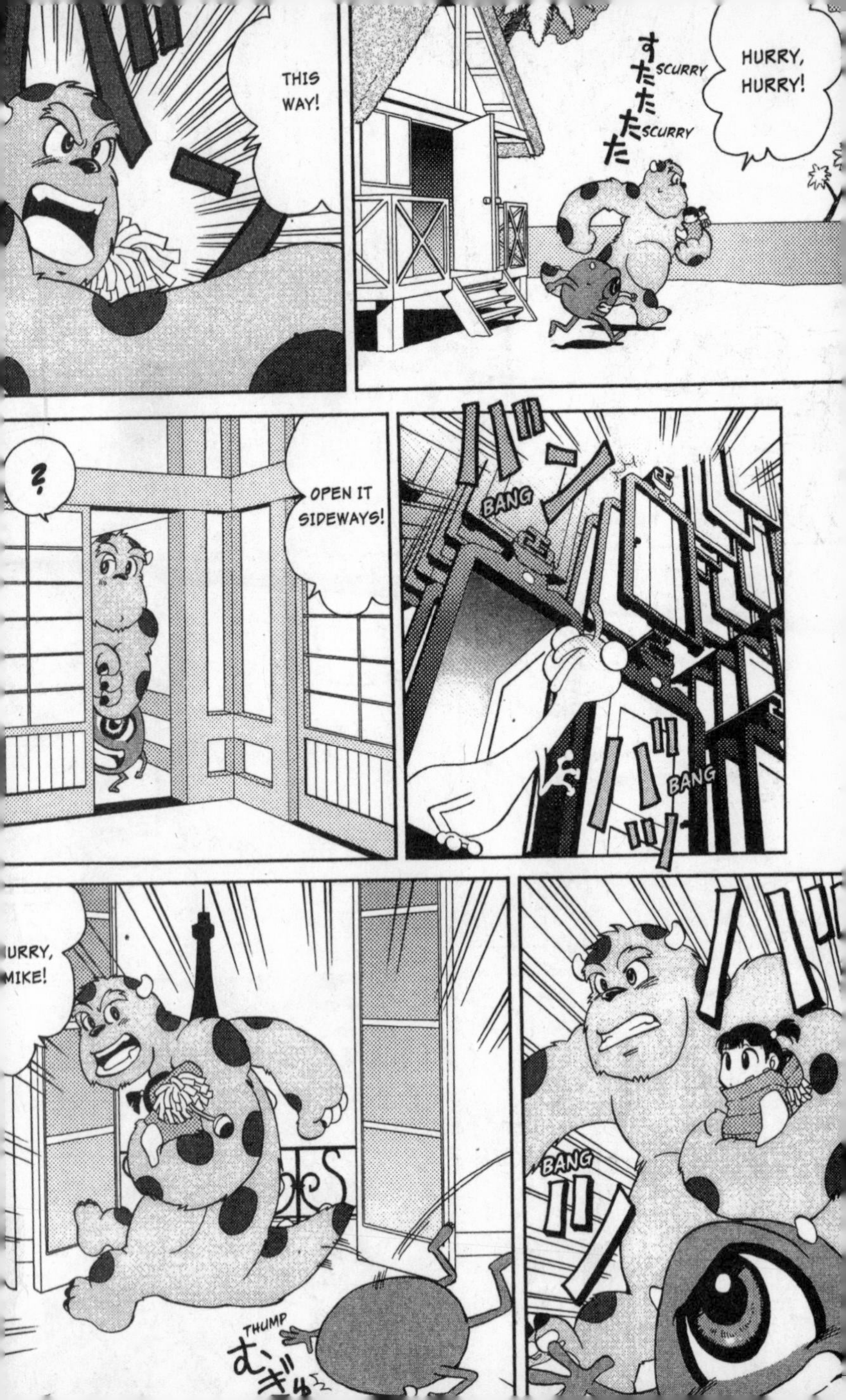
HURRY, HURRY!
すたたたた
SCURRY
SCURRY
THIS WAY!
BANG
BANG
OPEN IT SIDEWAYS!
?
BANG
URRY, MIKE!
THUMP

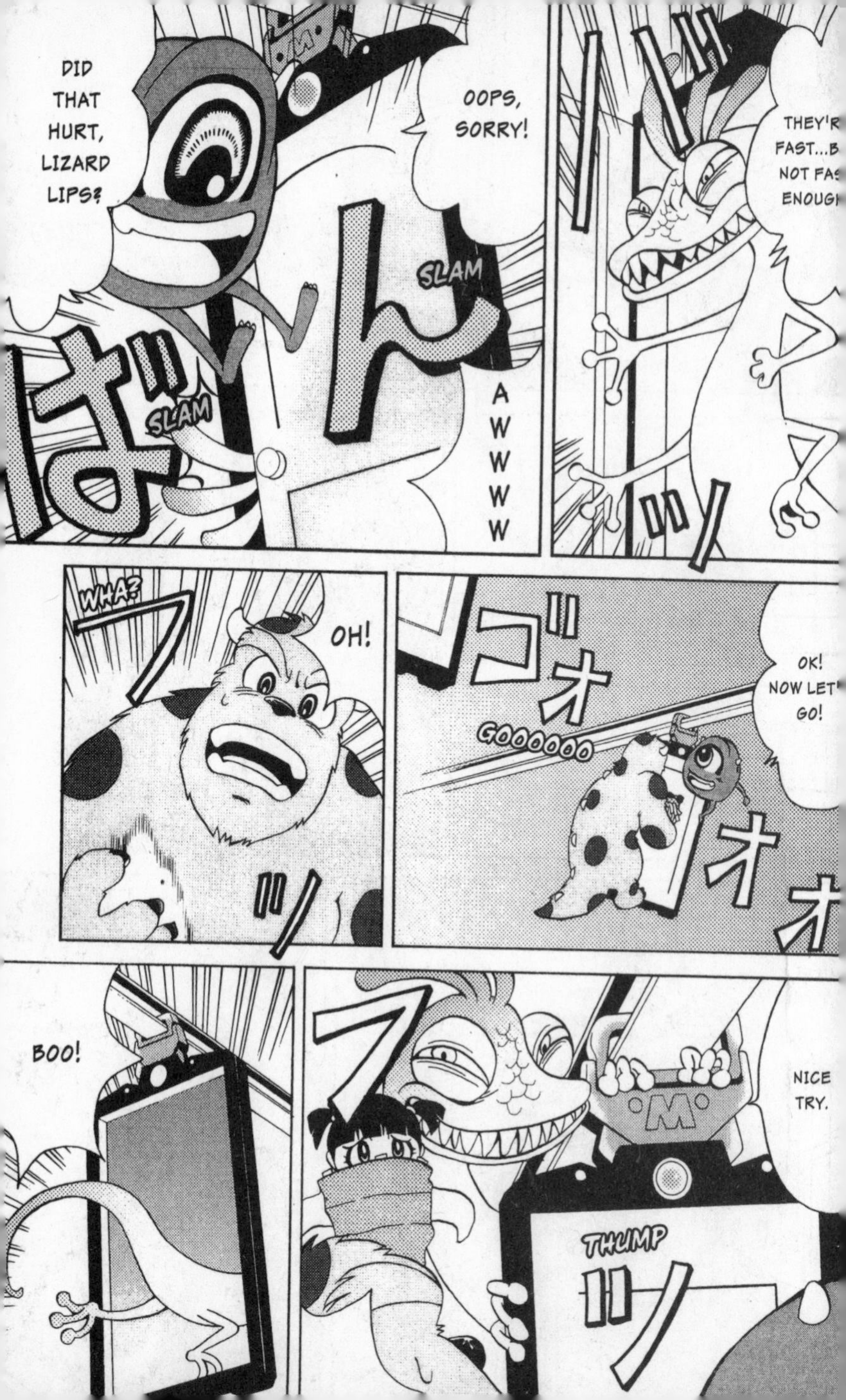
THEY'R
FAST...B
NOT FAS
ENOUG
OOPS, SORRY!
DID THAT HURT, LIZARD LIPS?
SLAM
AWWWWW
SLAM
OK! NOW LET
GO!
GOOOOOO
OH!
WHA?
NICE TRY.
THUMP
BOO!

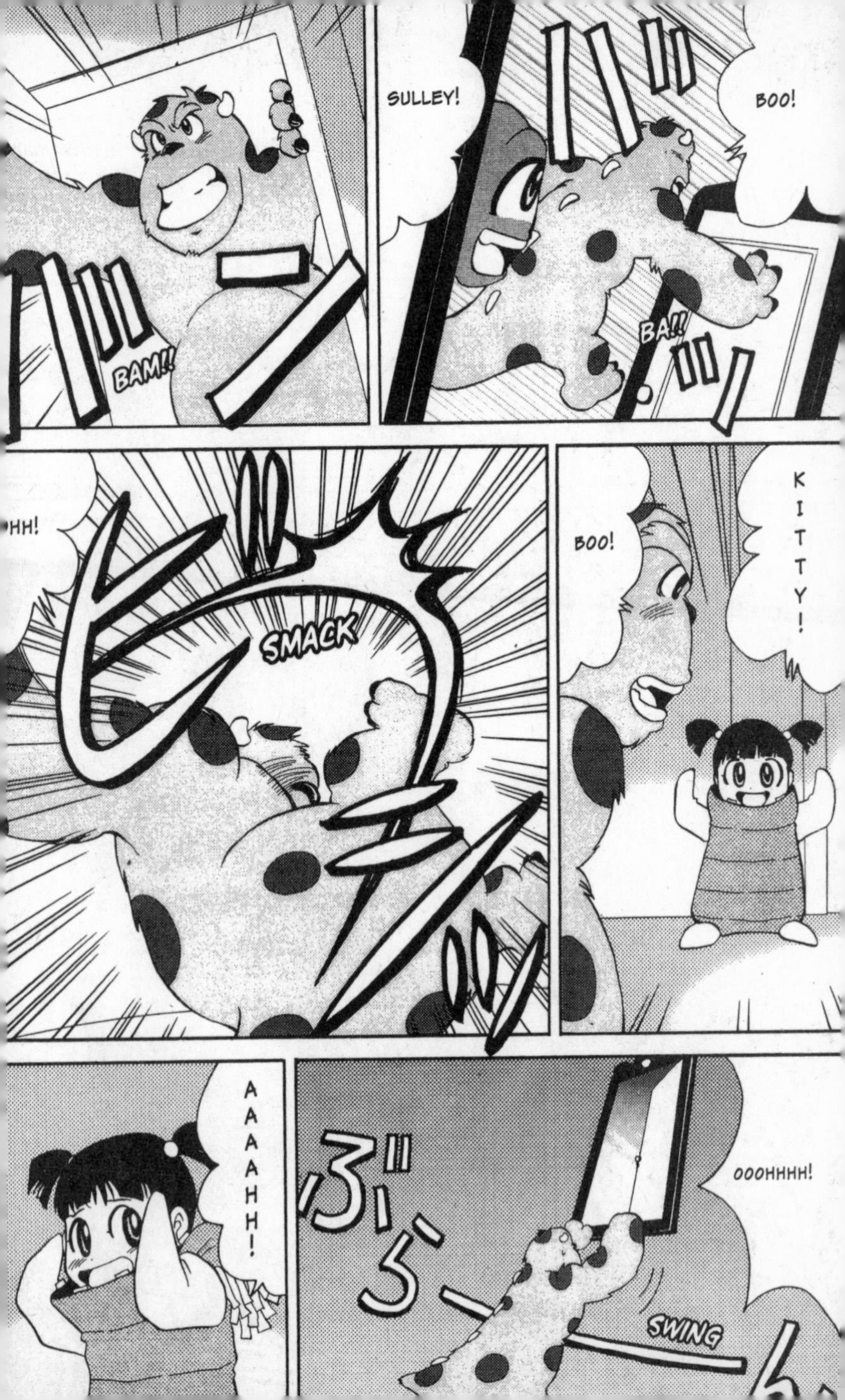
BOO!
SULLEY!
BA!!
BAM!!
KITTY!
BOO!
HH!
SMACK
OOOHHHH!
SWING
AAAAHH!

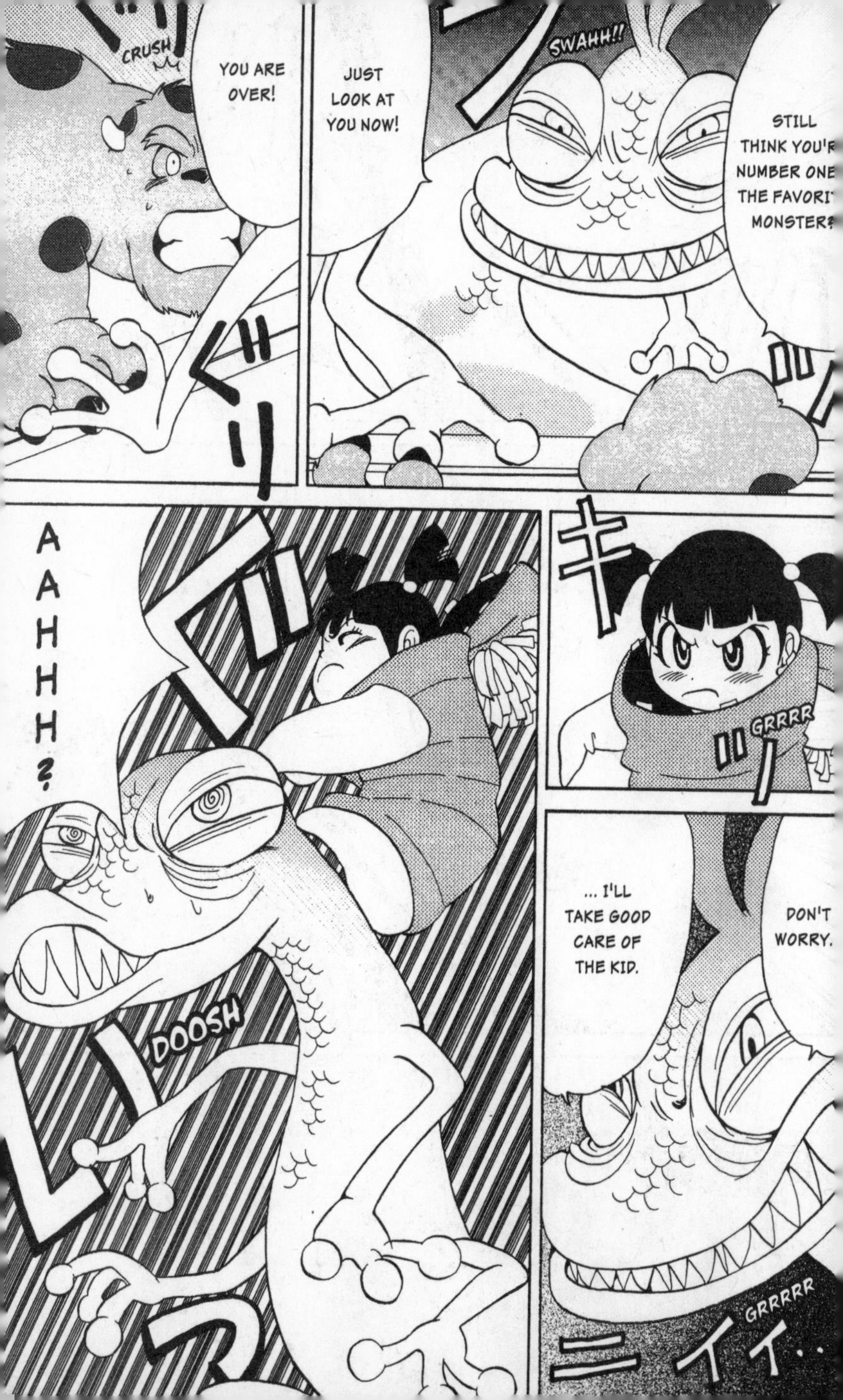
SWAHH!!
STILL THINK YOU'R NUMBER ONE THE FAVORI MONSTER?
JUST LOOK AT YOU NOW!
CRUSH
YOU ARE OVER!
GRRRR
DON'T WORRY.
... I'LL TAKE GOOD CARE OF THE KID.
GRRRRR
AAHHH?
DOOSH

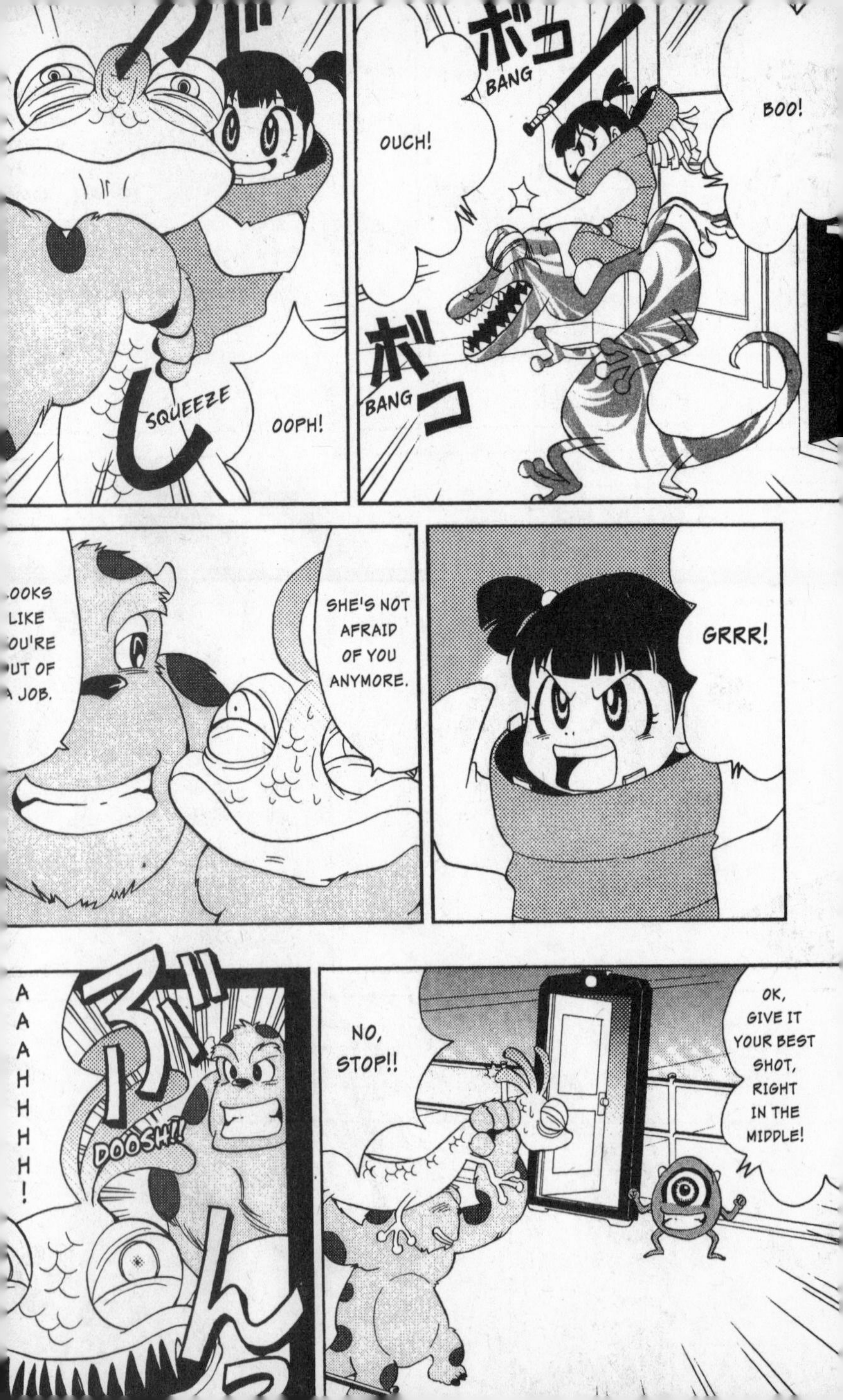
BOO!
ボッ BANG
OUCH!
ボッ BANG
し SQUEEZE
OOPH!
GRRR!
SHE'S NOT AFRAID OF YOU ANYMORE.
OOKS LIKE OU'RE UT OF A JOB.
OK, GIVE IT YOUR BEST SHOT, RIGHT IN THE MIDDLE!
NO, STOP!!
AAAHHHHH!
DOOSH!!

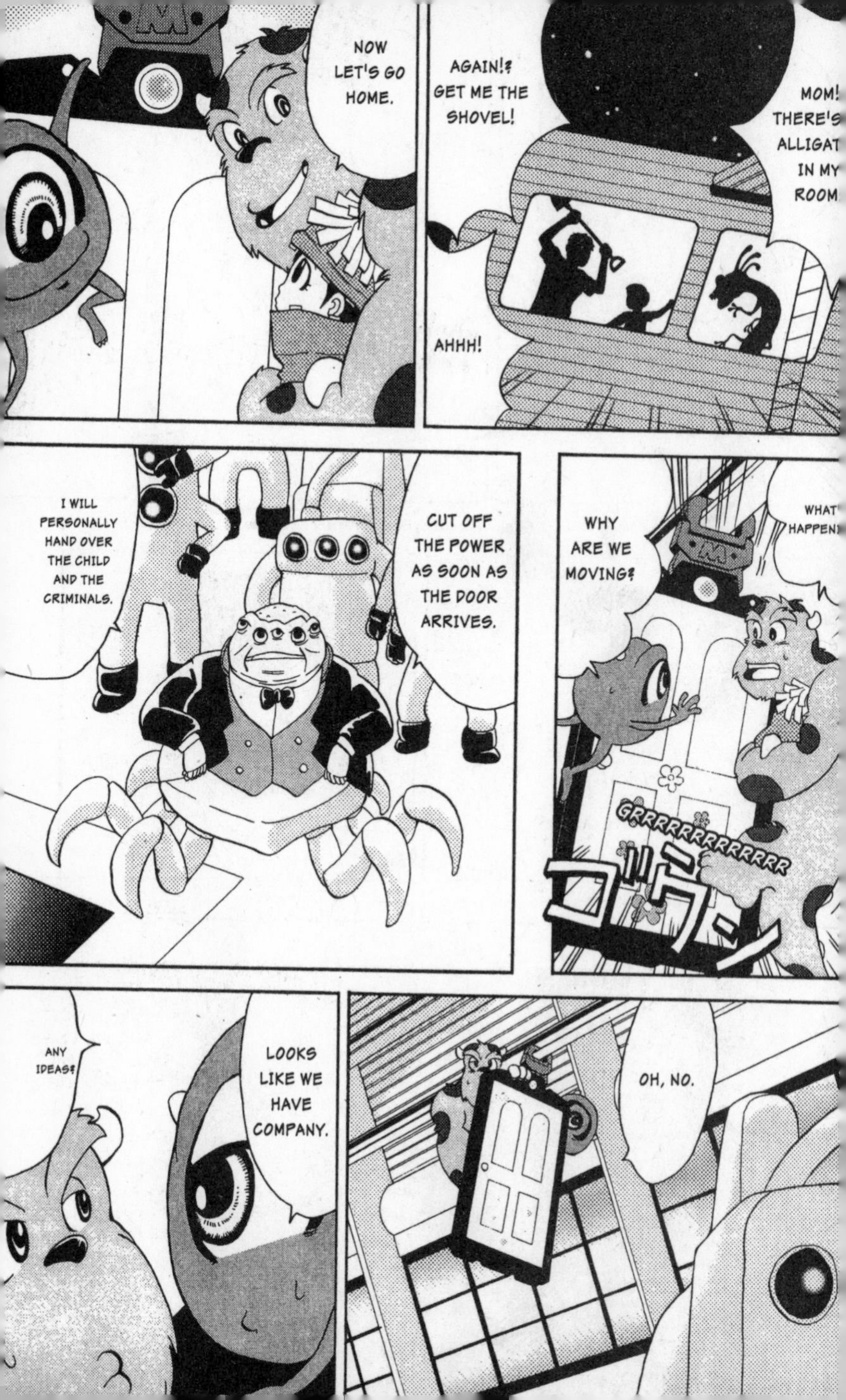
MOM! THERE'S ALLIGAT IN MY ROOM
AGAIN!? GET ME THE SHOVEL!
AHHH!
NOW LET'S GO HOME.
WHAT HAPPEN
WHY ARE WE MOVING?
GRRRRRRRRRRRRR
CUT OFF THE POWER AS SOON AS THE DOOR ARRIVES.
I WILL PERSONALLY HAND OVER THE CHILD AND THE CRIMINALS.
OH, NO.
LOOKS LIKE WE HAVE COMPANY.
ANY IDEAS?

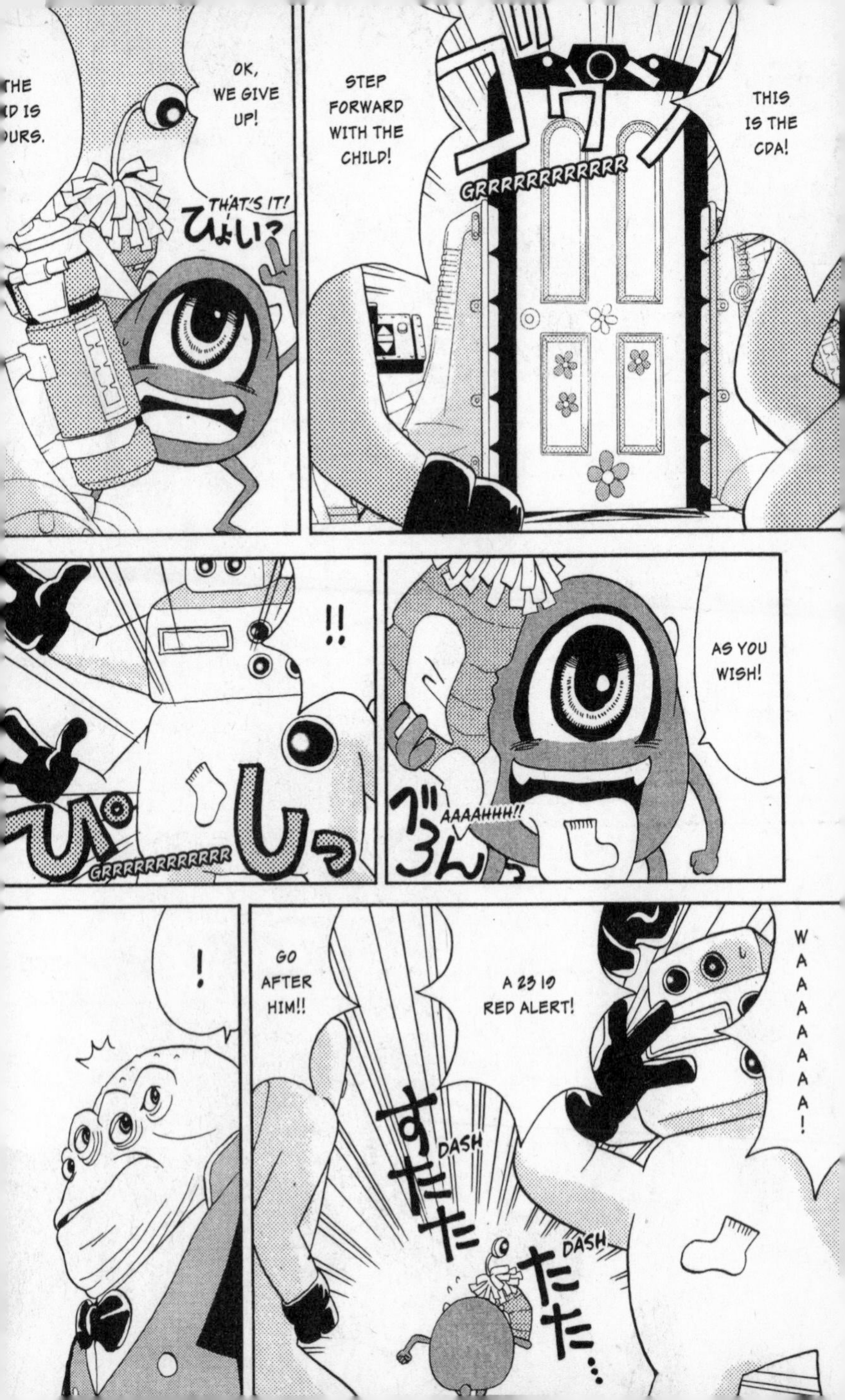

THIS IS THE CDA!
STEP FORWARD WITH THE CHILD!
GRRRRRRRRRRRR
OK, WE GIVE UP!
THAT'S IT!
ひょい？
AS YOU WISH!
AAAAHHH!!
ぶるんっ
!!
ぴしっ
GRRRRRRRRRRRR
WAAAAAAAA!
A 23 19 RED ALERT!
GO AFTER HIM!!
すたた
DASH
たた…
DASH
!

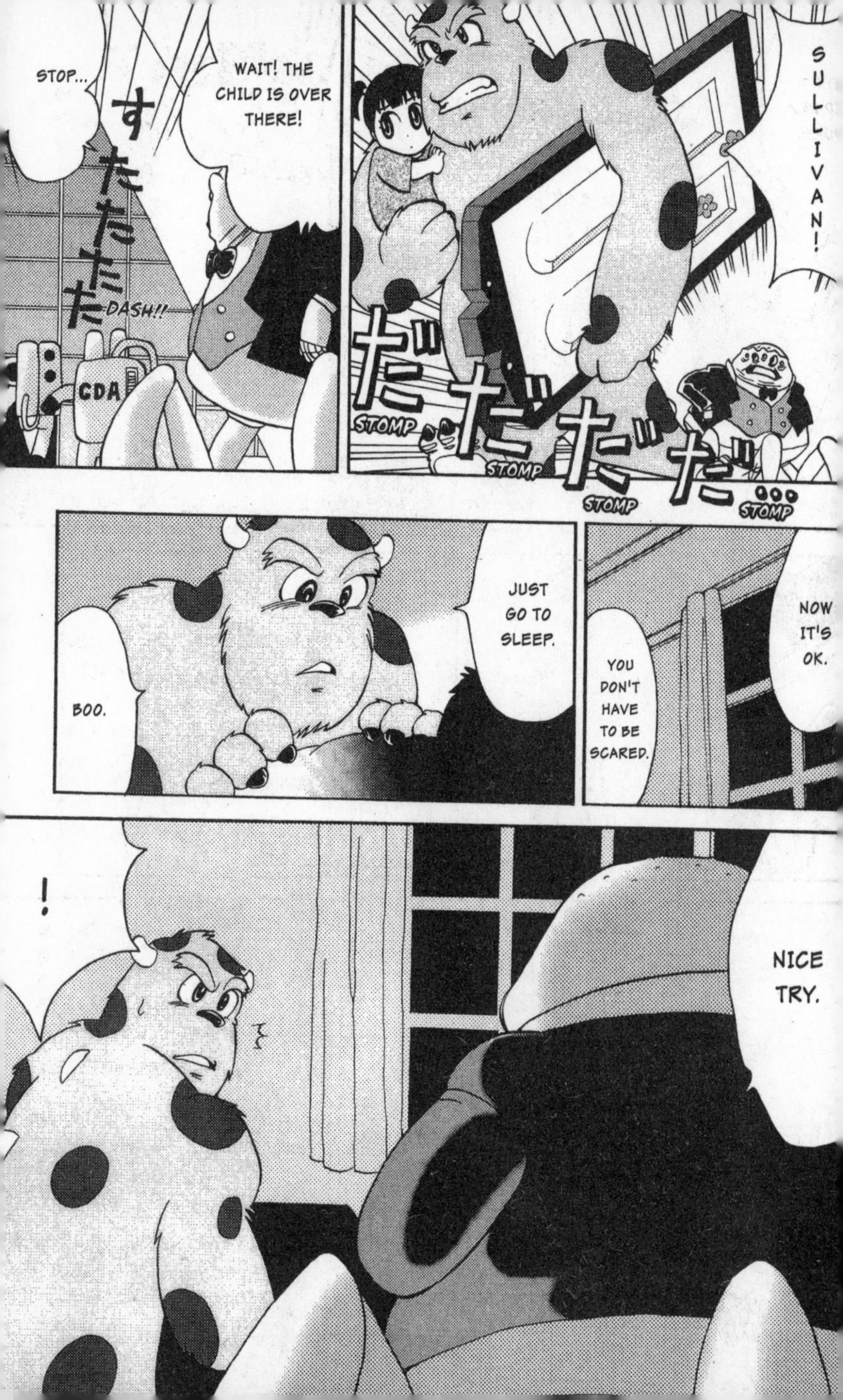
SULLIVAN!
だだだだ
STOMP STOMP STOMP STOMP
WAIT! THE CHILD IS OVER THERE!
STOP...
すたたた
DASH!!
CDA
NOW IT'S OK.
YOU DON'T HAVE TO BE SCARED.
JUST GO TO SLEEP.
BOO.
NICE TRY.
!

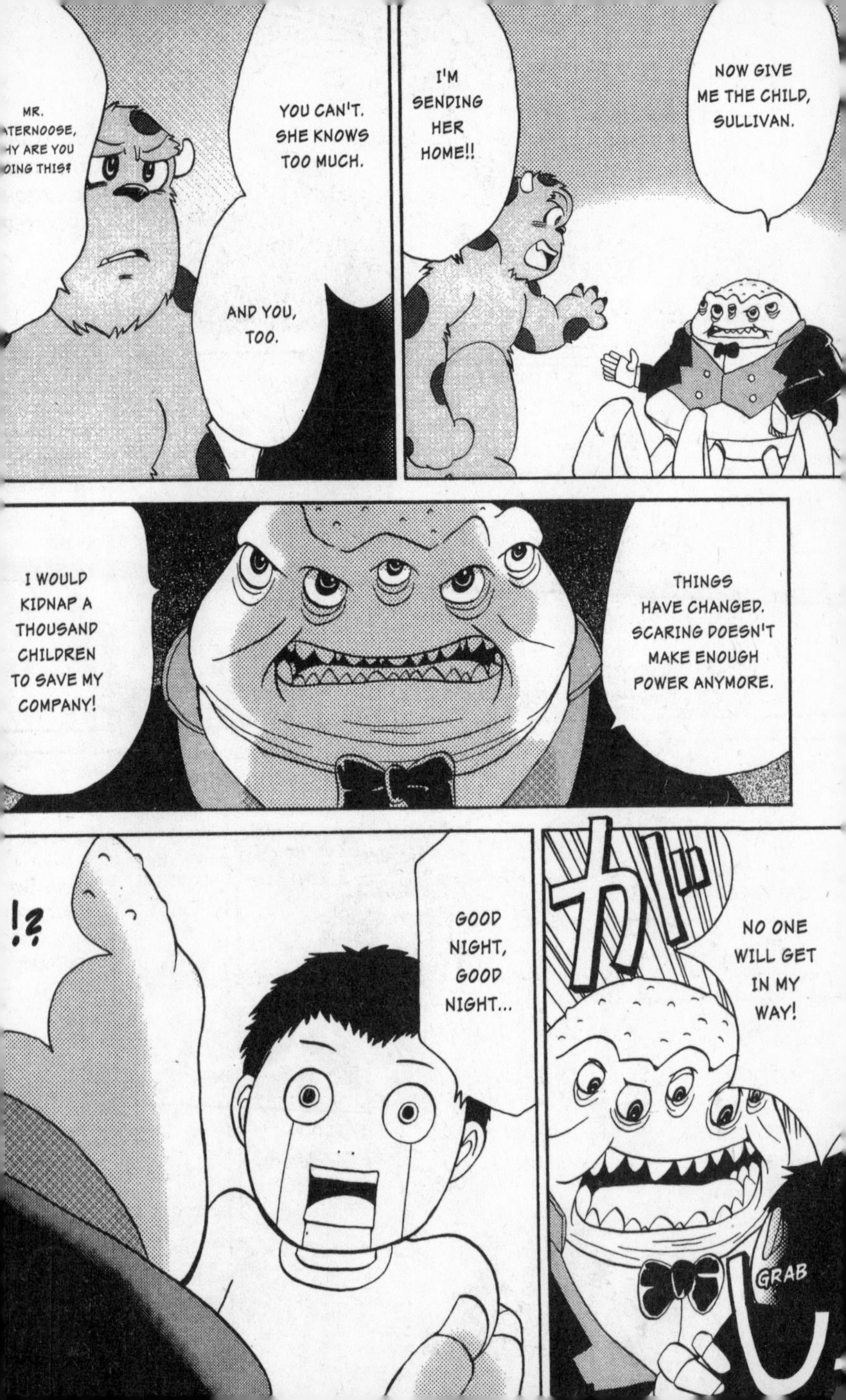
NOW GIVE ME THE CHILD, SULLIVAN.
I'M SENDING HER HOME!!
YOU CAN'T. SHE KNOWS TOO MUCH.
AND YOU, TOO.
MR. ATERNOOSE, HY ARE YOU OING THIS?
THINGS HAVE CHANGED. SCARING DOESN'T MAKE ENOUGH POWER ANYMORE.
I WOULD KIDNAP A THOUSAND CHILDREN TO SAVE MY COMPANY!
カッ
NO ONE WILL GET IN MY WAY!
GRAB
GOOD NIGHT, GOOD NIGHT...
!?

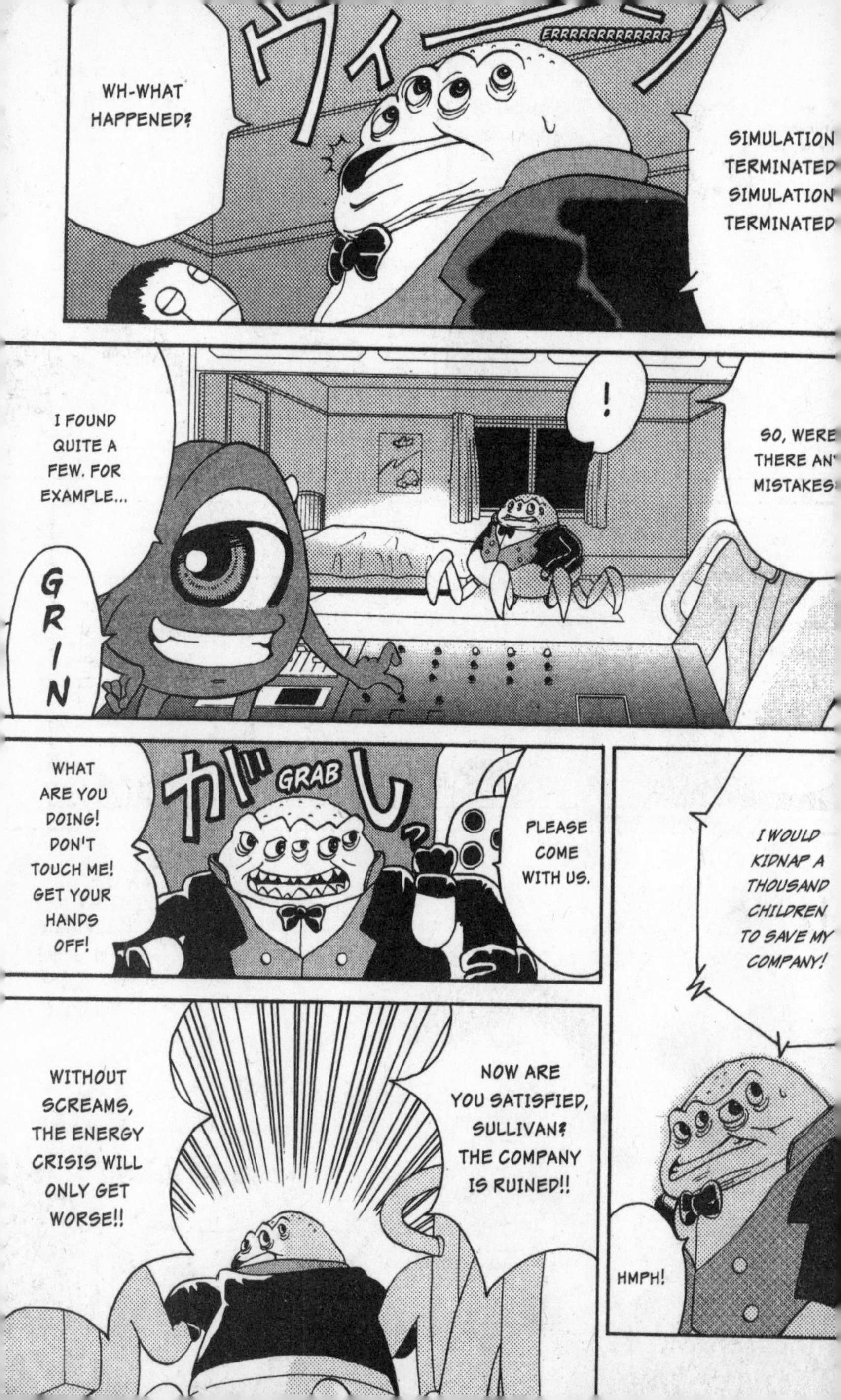
ERRRRRRRRRRRRR
SIMULATION TERMINATED SIMULATION TERMINATED
WH-WHAT HAPPENED?
SO, WERE THERE AN MISTAKES
!
I FOUND QUITE A FEW. FOR EXAMPLE...
GRIN
I WOULD KIDNAP A THOUSAND CHILDREN TO SAVE MY COMPANY!
HMPH!
PLEASE COME WITH US.
GRAB
WHAT ARE YOU DOING! DON'T TOUCH ME! GET YOUR HANDS OFF!
NOW ARE YOU SATISFIED, SULLIVAN? THE COMPANY IS RUINED!!
WITHOUT SCREAMS, THE ENERGY CRISIS WILL ONLY GET WORSE!!

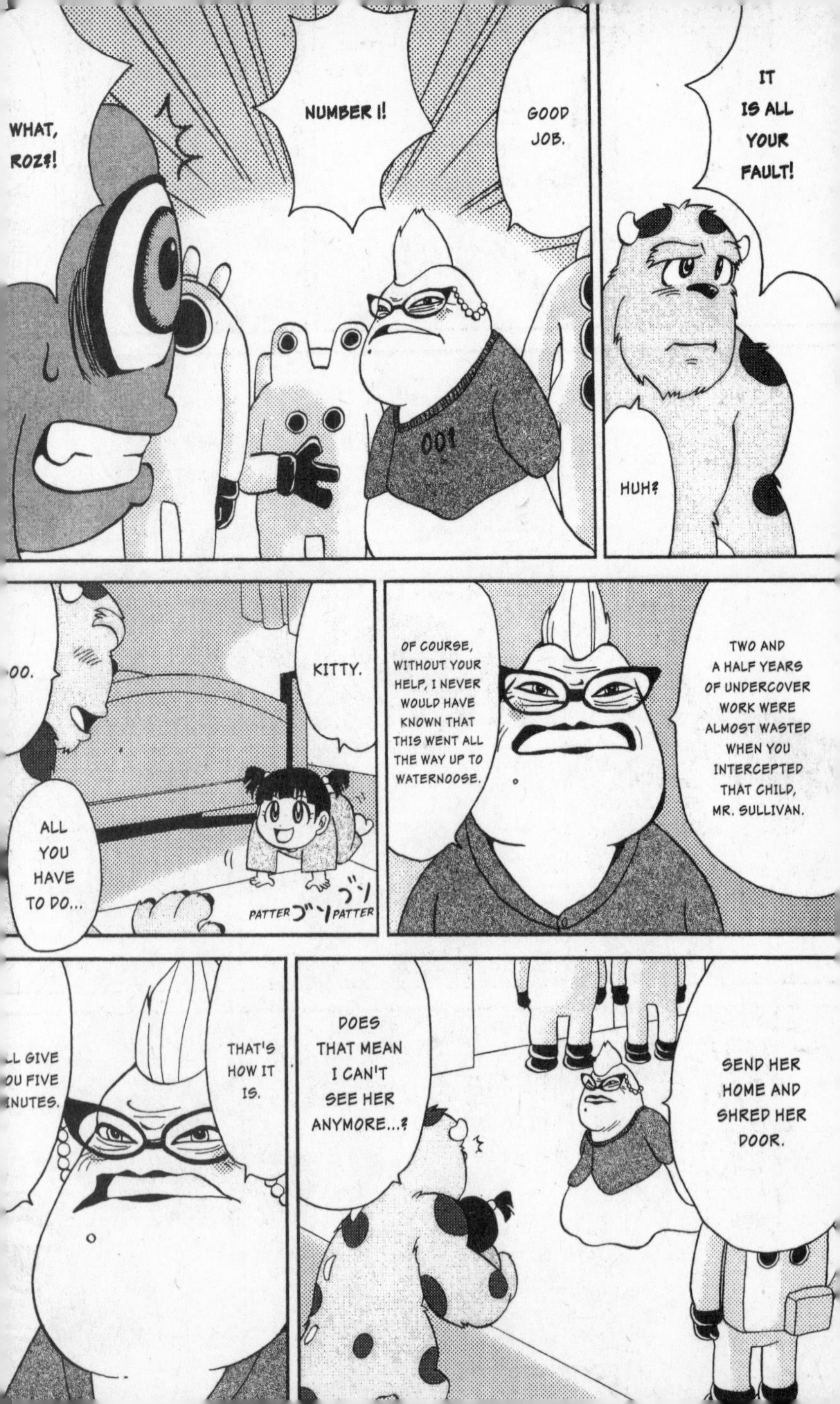
IT IS ALL YOUR FAULT!
HUH?
GOOD JOB.
NUMBER 1!
WHAT, ROZ?!
TWO AND A HALF YEARS OF UNDERCOVER WORK WERE ALMOST WASTED WHEN YOU INTERCEPTED THAT CHILD, MR. SULLIVAN.
OF COURSE, WITHOUT YOUR HELP, I NEVER WOULD HAVE KNOWN THAT THIS WENT ALL THE WAY UP TO WATERNOOSE.
KITTY.
OO.
ALL YOU HAVE TO DO...
PATTER PATTER
SEND HER HOME AND SHRED HER DOOR.
DOES THAT MEAN I CAN'T SEE HER ANYMORE...?
THAT'S HOW IT IS.
LL GIVE OU FIVE INUTES.

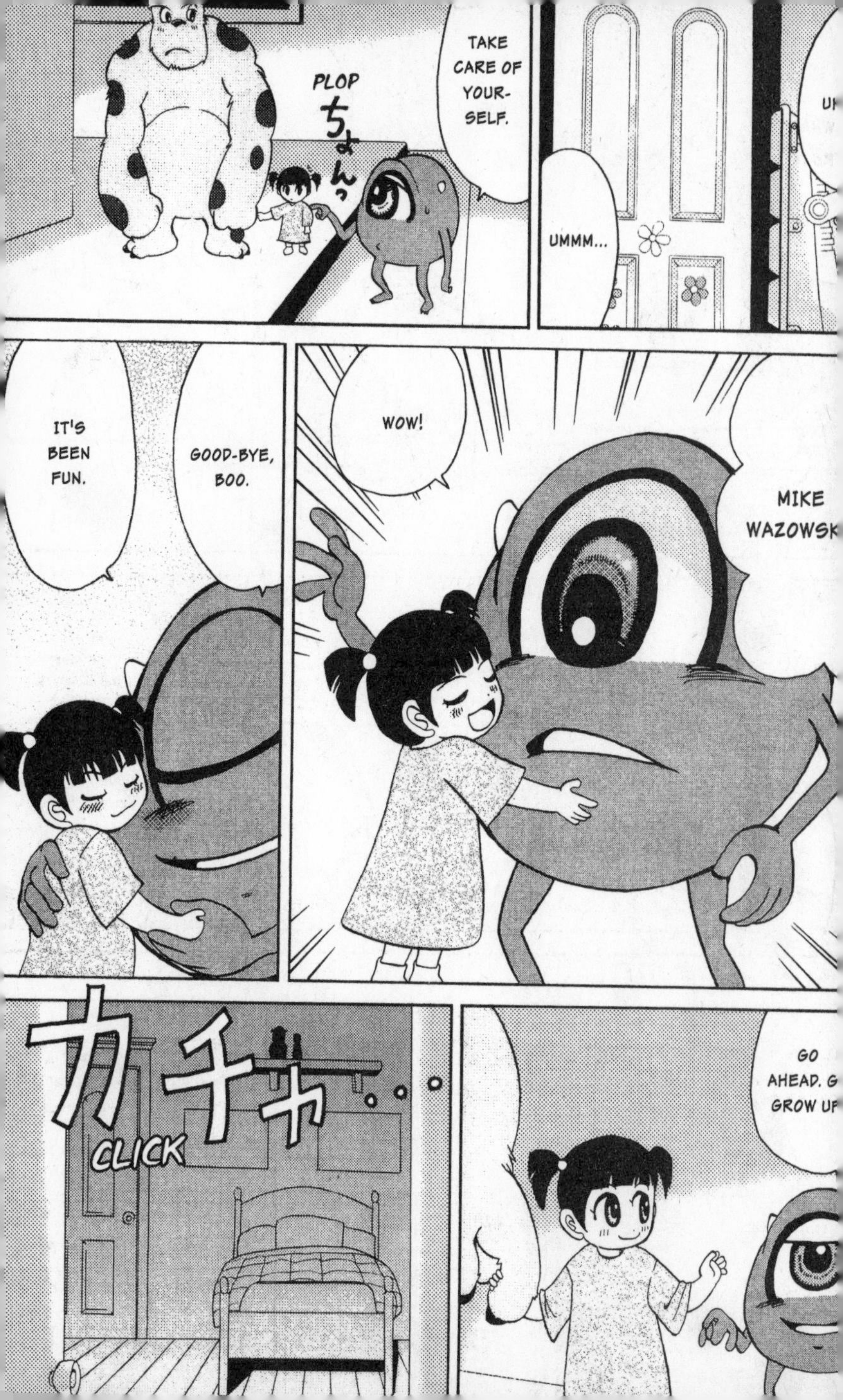
UMMM...
TAKE CARE OF YOUR-SELF.
PLOP
ちょんっ
MIKE WAZOWSK
WOW!
GOOD-BYE, BOO.
IT'S BEEN FUN.
GO AHEAD. G
GROW UP
カチャ
CLICK

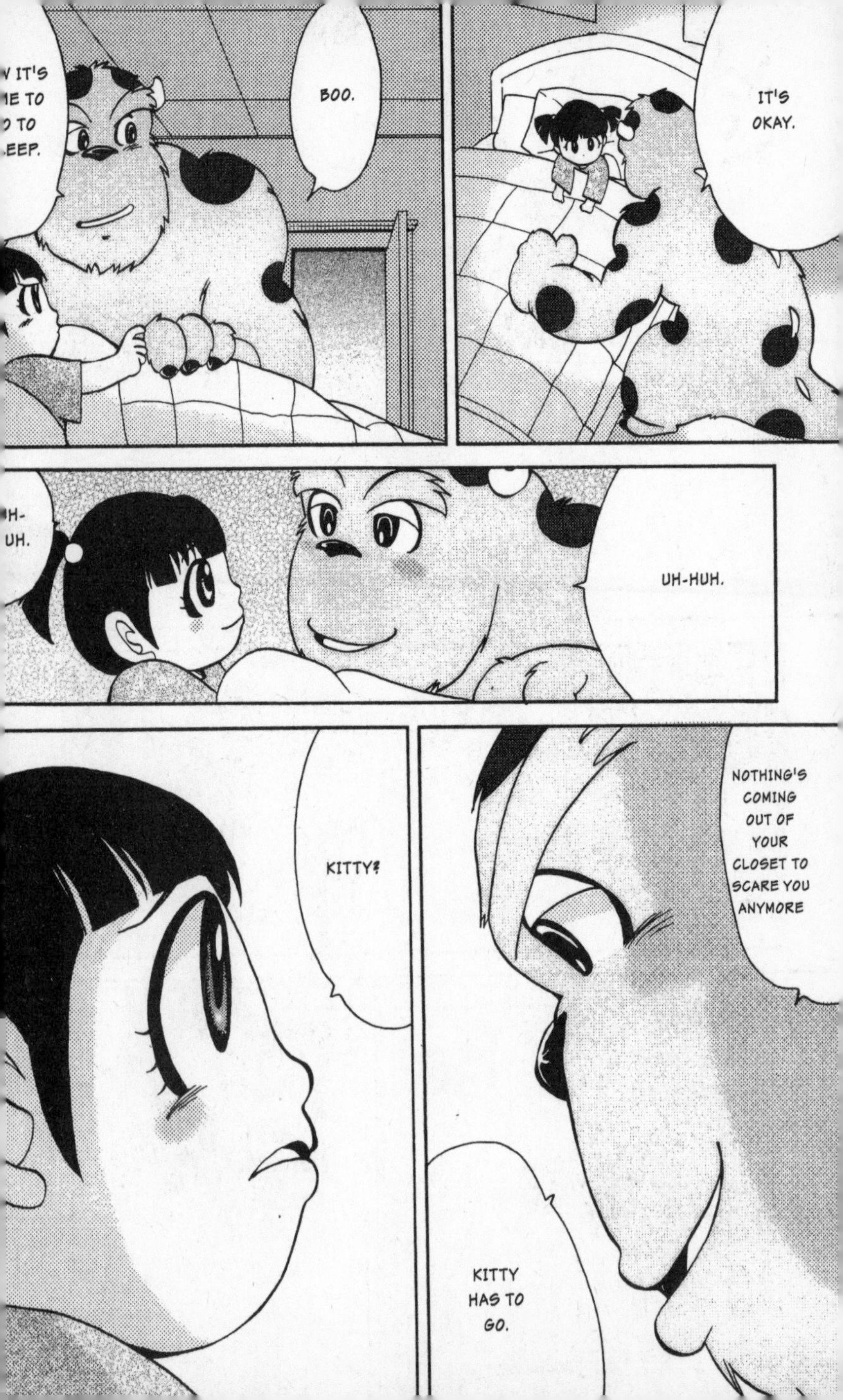
IT'S OKAY.
BOO.
W IT'S ME TO O TO EEP.
UH-HUH.
H- UH.
NOTHING'S COMING OUT OF YOUR CLOSET TO SCARE YOU ANYMORE
KITTY HAS TO GO.
KITTY?

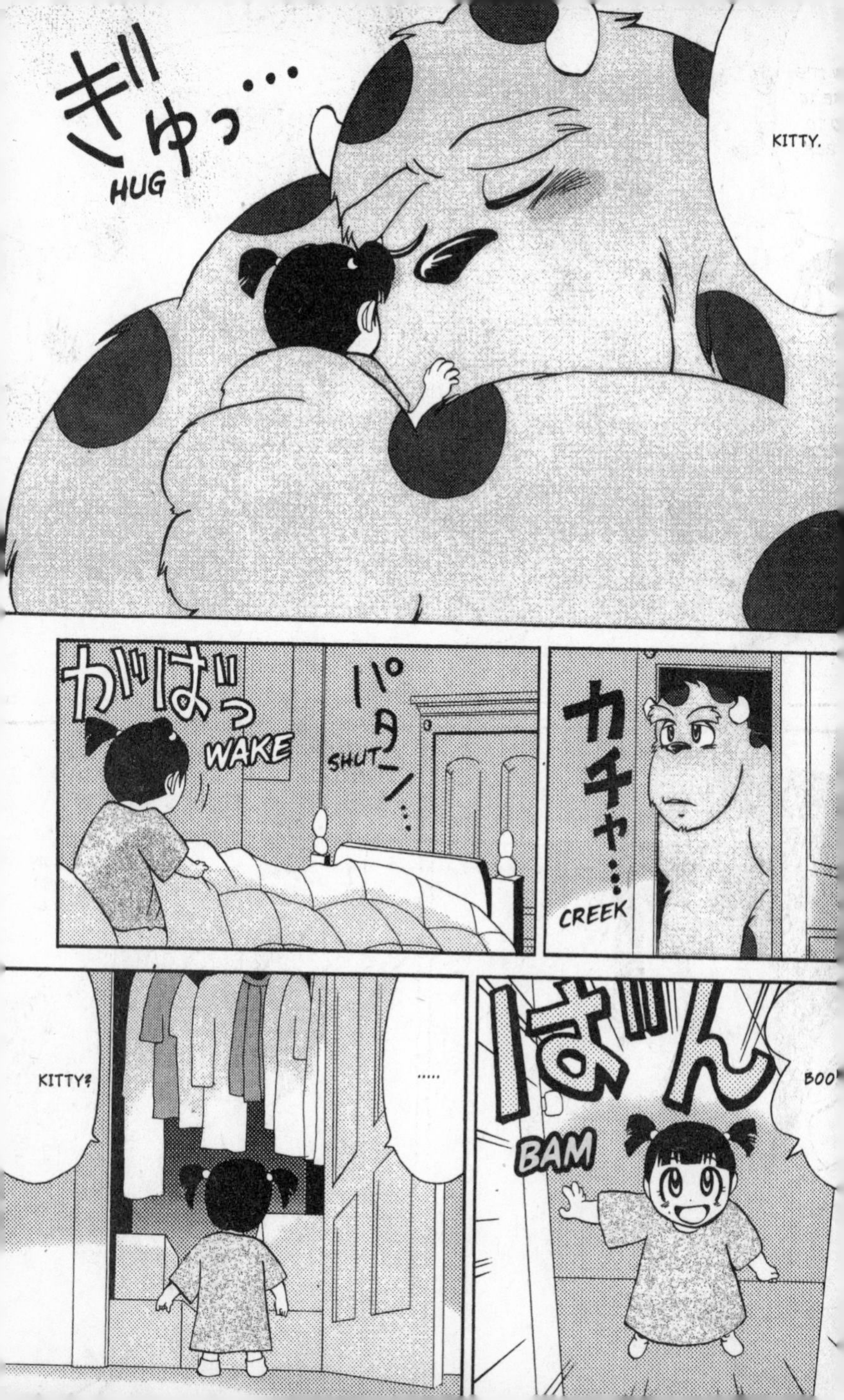
KITTY.
ぎゅっ…
HUG
カチャ…
CREEK
パタン…
SHUT
がばっ
WAKE
ばん
BAM
BOO
......
KITTY?

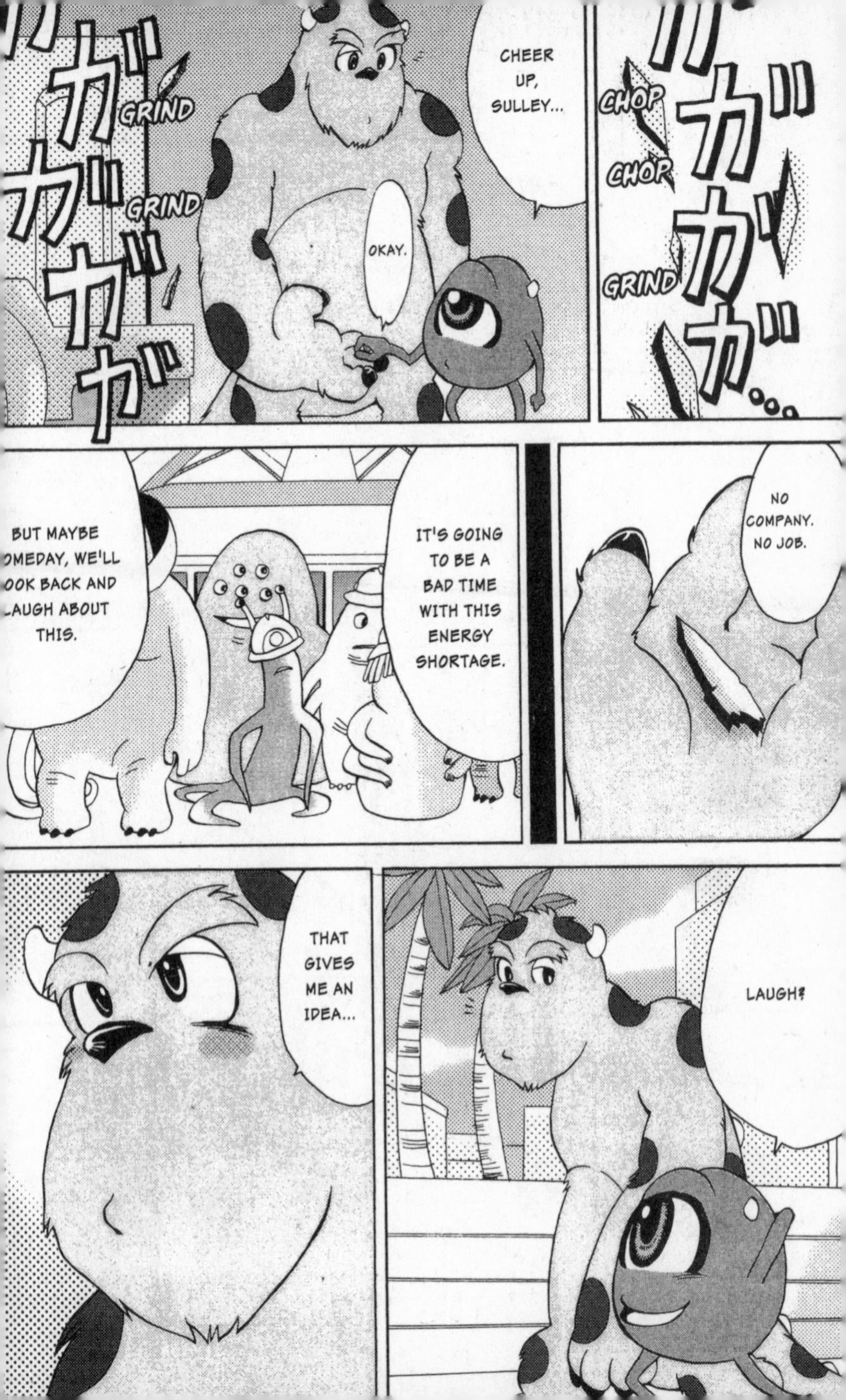

CHOP
CHOP
GRIND
ガガガ...
CHEER UP, SULLEY...
OKAY.
ガガガガ
GRIND
GRIND
NO COMPANY. NO JOB.
IT'S GOING TO BE A BAD TIME WITH THIS ENERGY SHORTAGE.
BUT MAYBE OMEDAY, WE'LL OOK BACK AND AUGH ABOUT THIS.
LAUGH?
THAT GIVES ME AN IDEA...

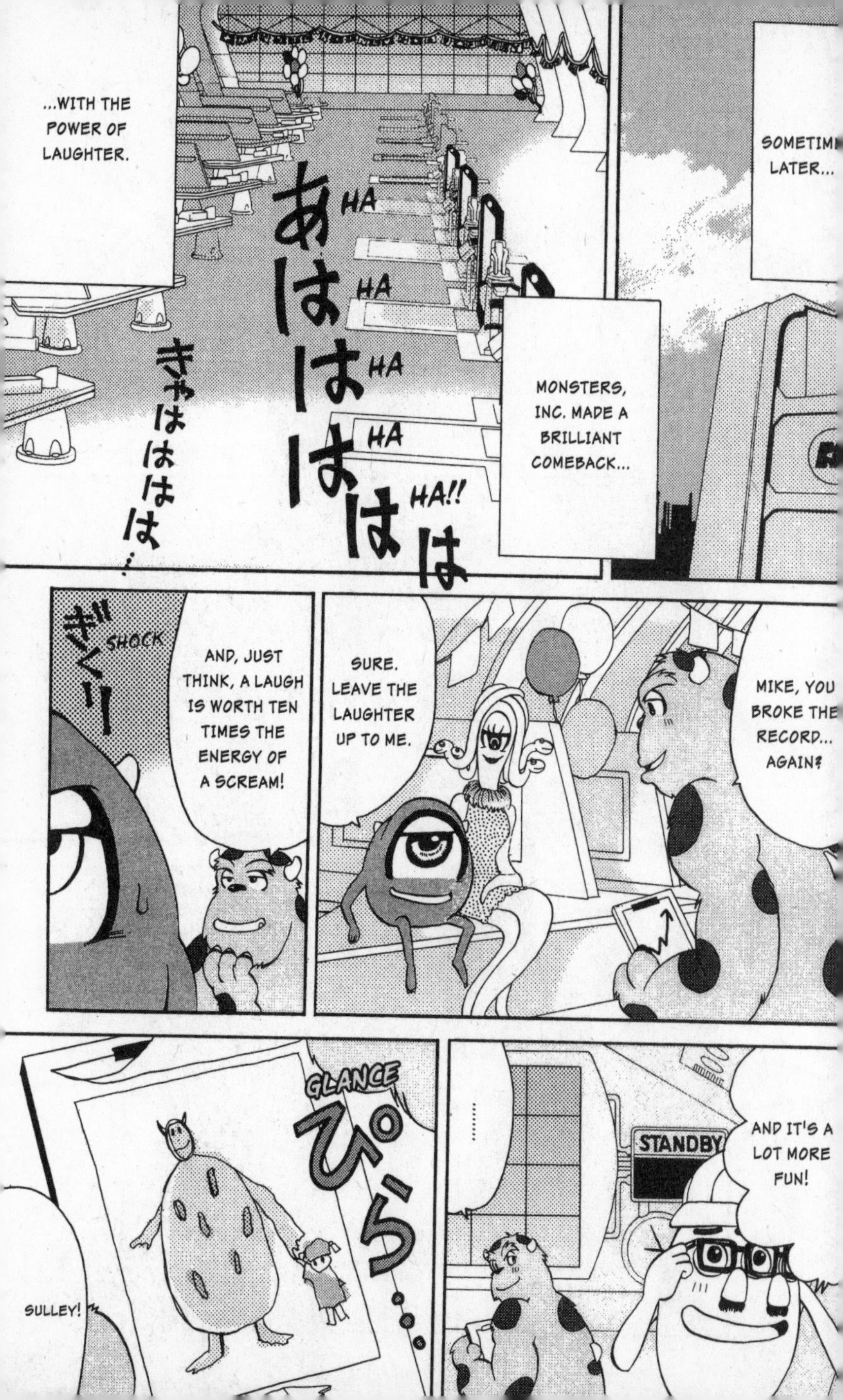
SOMETIM
LATER...
MONSTERS, INC. MADE A BRILLIANT COMEBACK...
...WITH THE POWER OF LAUGHTER.
あははーはは
HA HA HA HA HA!!
きゃはははは…
MIKE, YOU BROKE THE RECORD... AGAIN?
SURE. LEAVE THE LAUGHTER UP TO ME.
AND, JUST THINK, A LAUGH IS WORTH TEN TIMES THE ENERGY OF A SCREAM!
ぎくーっ
SHOCK
AND IT'S A LOT MORE FUN!
STANDBY
......
ぴら
GLANCE
SULLEY!

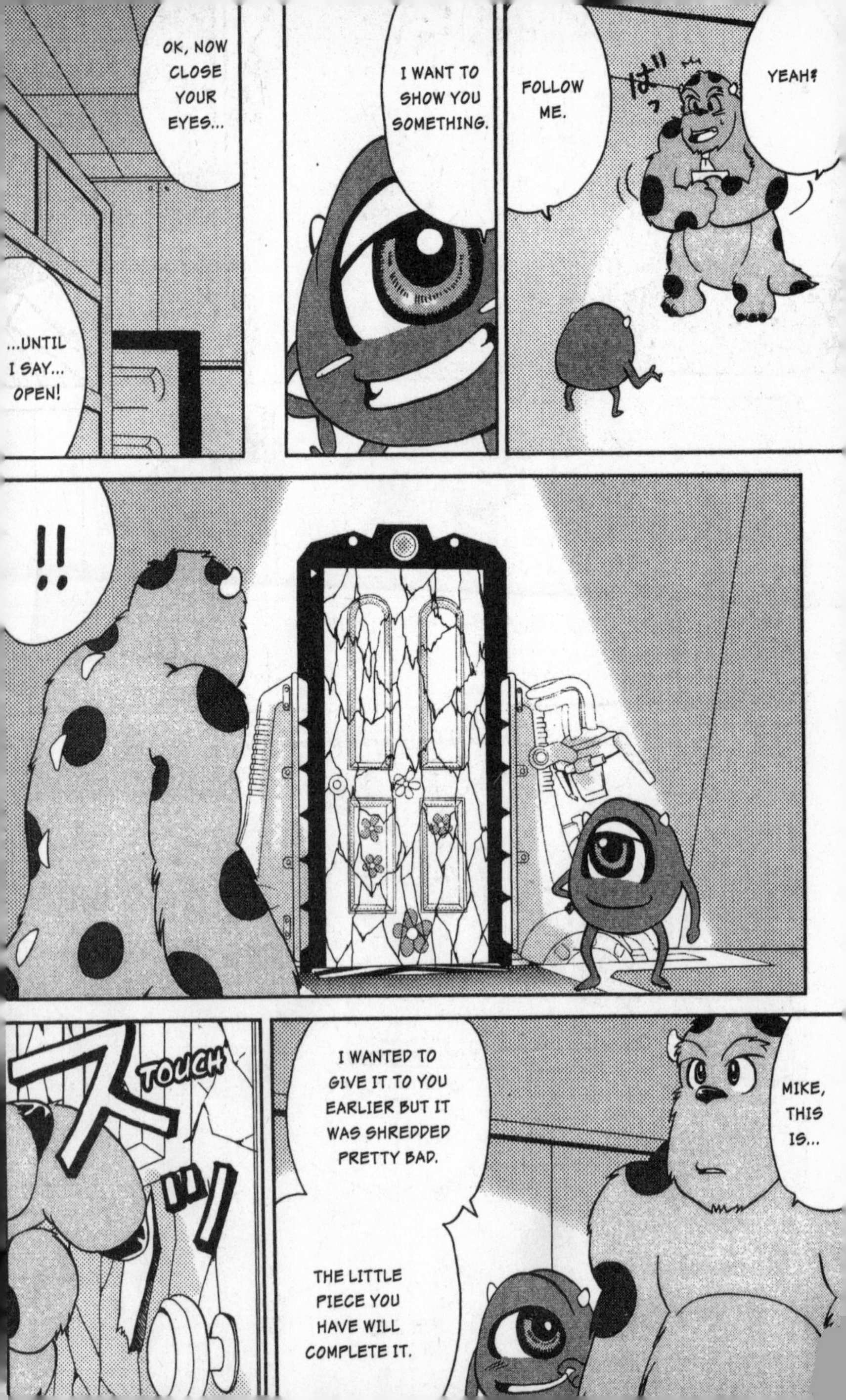
YEAH?
FOLLOW ME.
I WANT TO SHOW YOU SOMETHING.
OK, NOW CLOSE YOUR EYES...
...UNTIL I SAY... OPEN!
!!
MIKE, THIS IS...
I WANTED TO GIVE IT TO YOU EARLIER BUT IT WAS SHREDDED PRETTY BAD.
THE LITTLE PIECE YOU HAVE WILL COMPLETE IT.
TOUCH

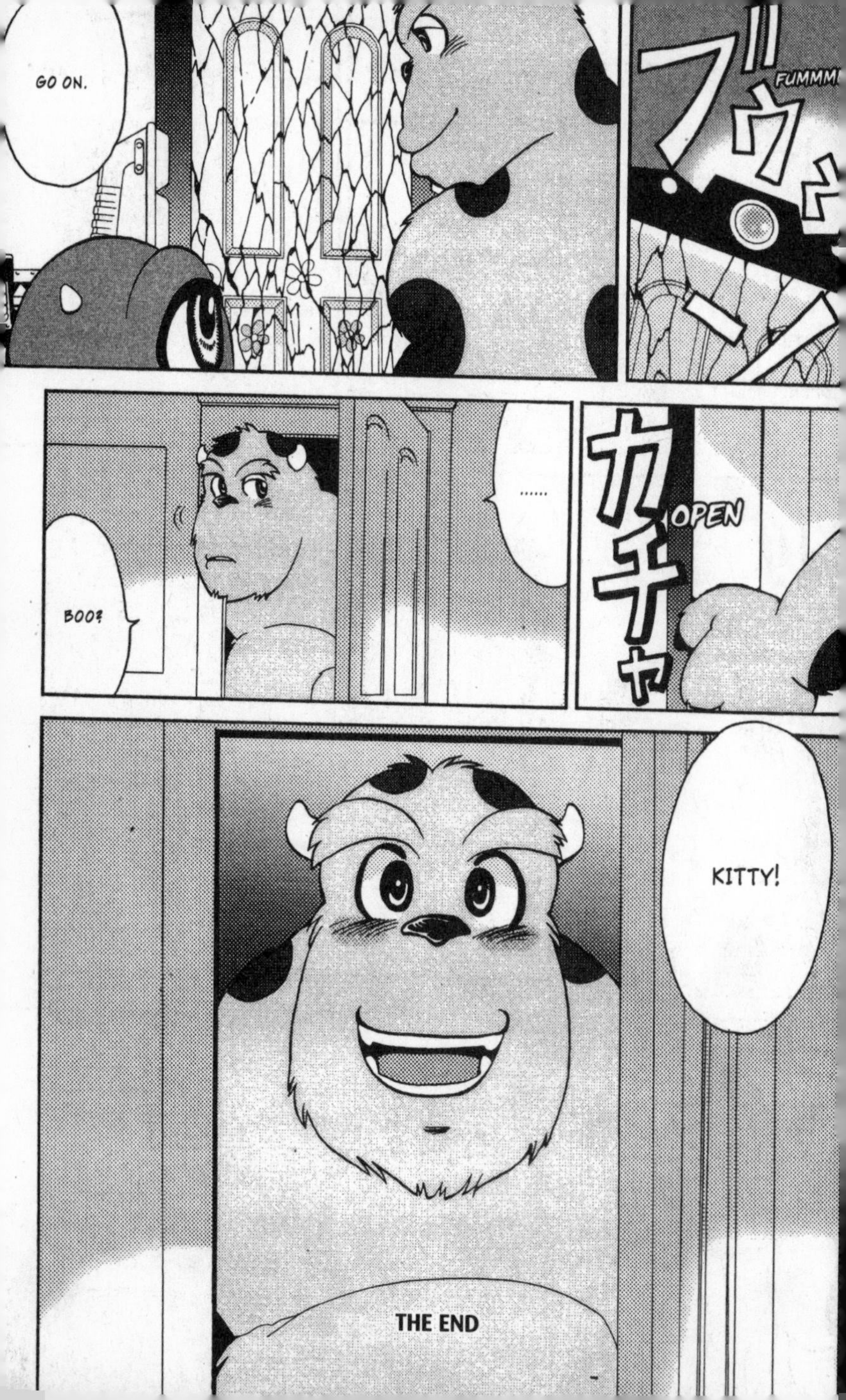
FUMMM
GO ON.
カチャ
OPEN
......
BOO?
KITTY!
THE END

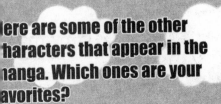

MONSTERS, INC. CHARACTERS

DISNEY·PIXAR

PART 2

Here are some of the other characters that appear in the manga. Which ones are your favorites?

▲ GEORGE

▲ One of the workers at Monsters, Inc., who makes contact with a human child's sock.

▲ NEWSCASTER

▲ This reporter tells everyone in Monstropolis about the incident at Harryhausen's restaurant.

▲ CDA (CHILD DETECTION AGENCY)

▲ A group of monsters that protect the monsters in Monstropolis from anything toxic... including human children.

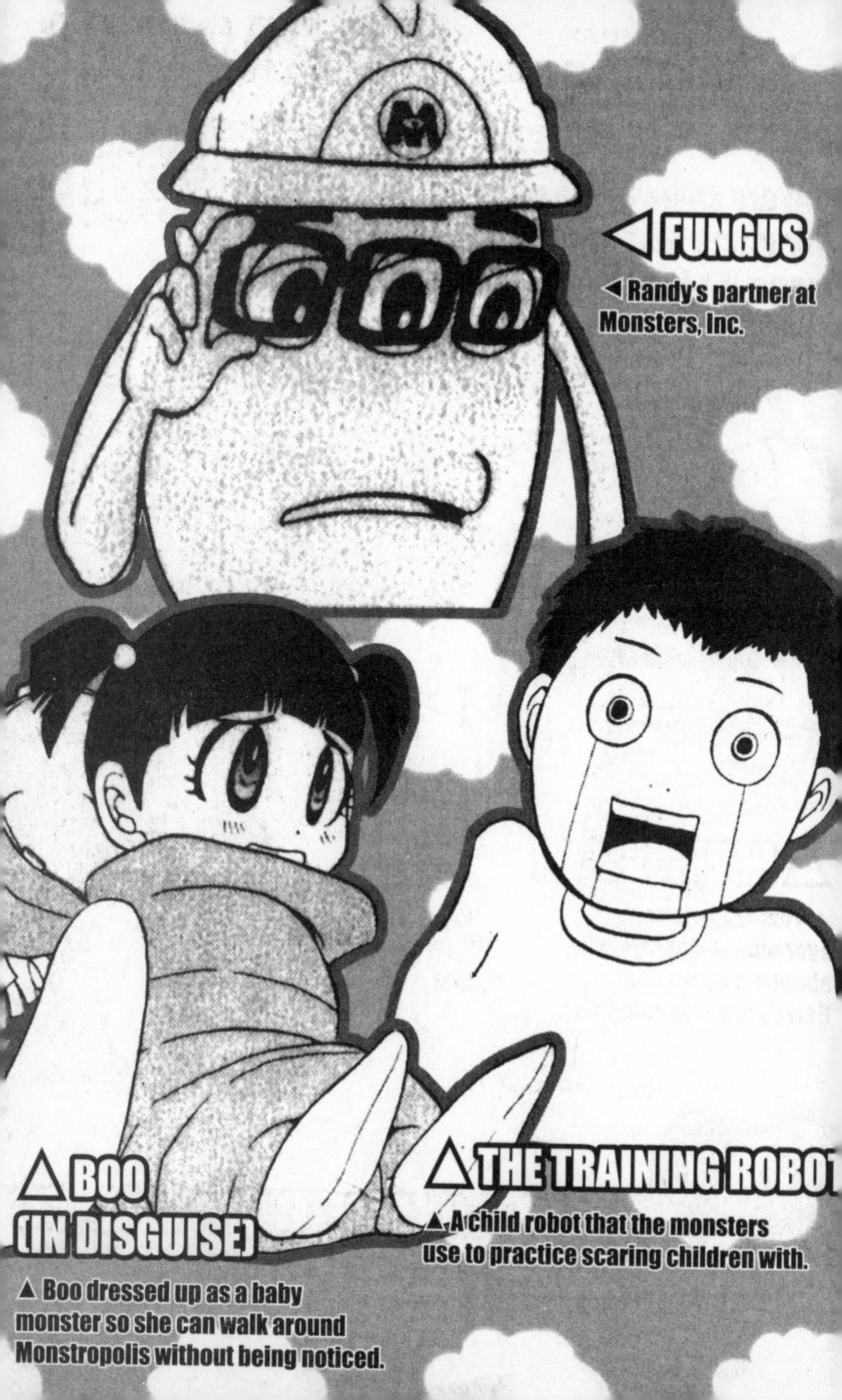
◀ FUNGUS
◀ Randy's partner at Monsters, Inc.
△ BOO (IN DISGUISE)
▲ Boo dressed up as a baby monster so she can walk around Monstropolis without being noticed.
△ THE TRAINING ROBOT
▲ A child robot that the monsters use to practice scaring children with.

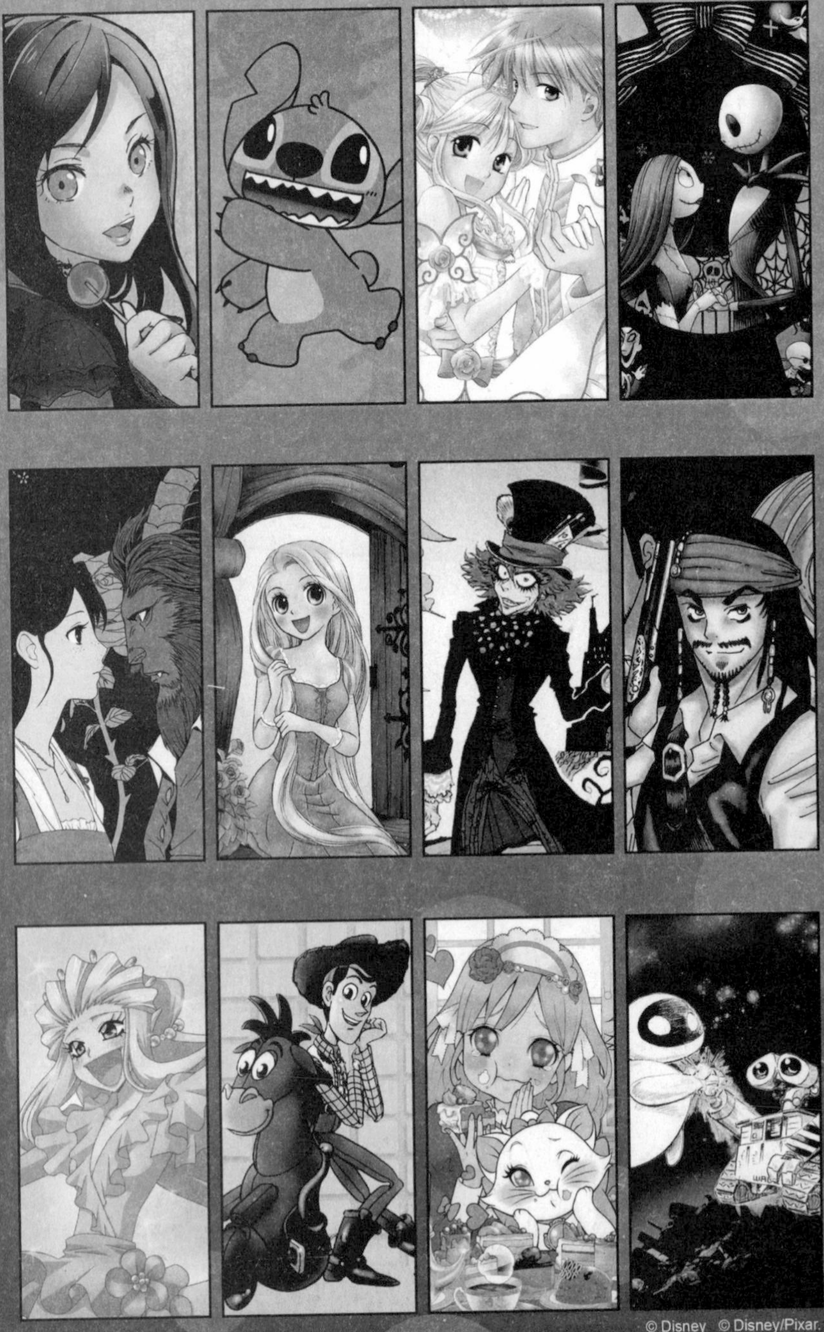

Add These Disney Manga to Your Collection Today!

A SNEAK PEEK OF NEW DISNEY · PIXAR TITLE

Woody the cowboy doll is Andy's favorite toy, and he can't control his jealousy when Andy gets a brand new toy for his birthday: the spaceman Buzz Lightyear. After a fight leaves them stranded far away from their home, they must learn to get along in order to get back to the toybox. And when Woody is stolen by a greedy toy collector, Buzz and the rest of Andy's toys mount a rescue mission to get him back... and bring Woody's new friends back with them!

Find out what kinds of mischief Andy's toys get up to when he's not playing with them in this special collectors edition manga version of the hit Disney Pixar movies, *Toy Story* and *Toy Story 2*.

COMING SOON!

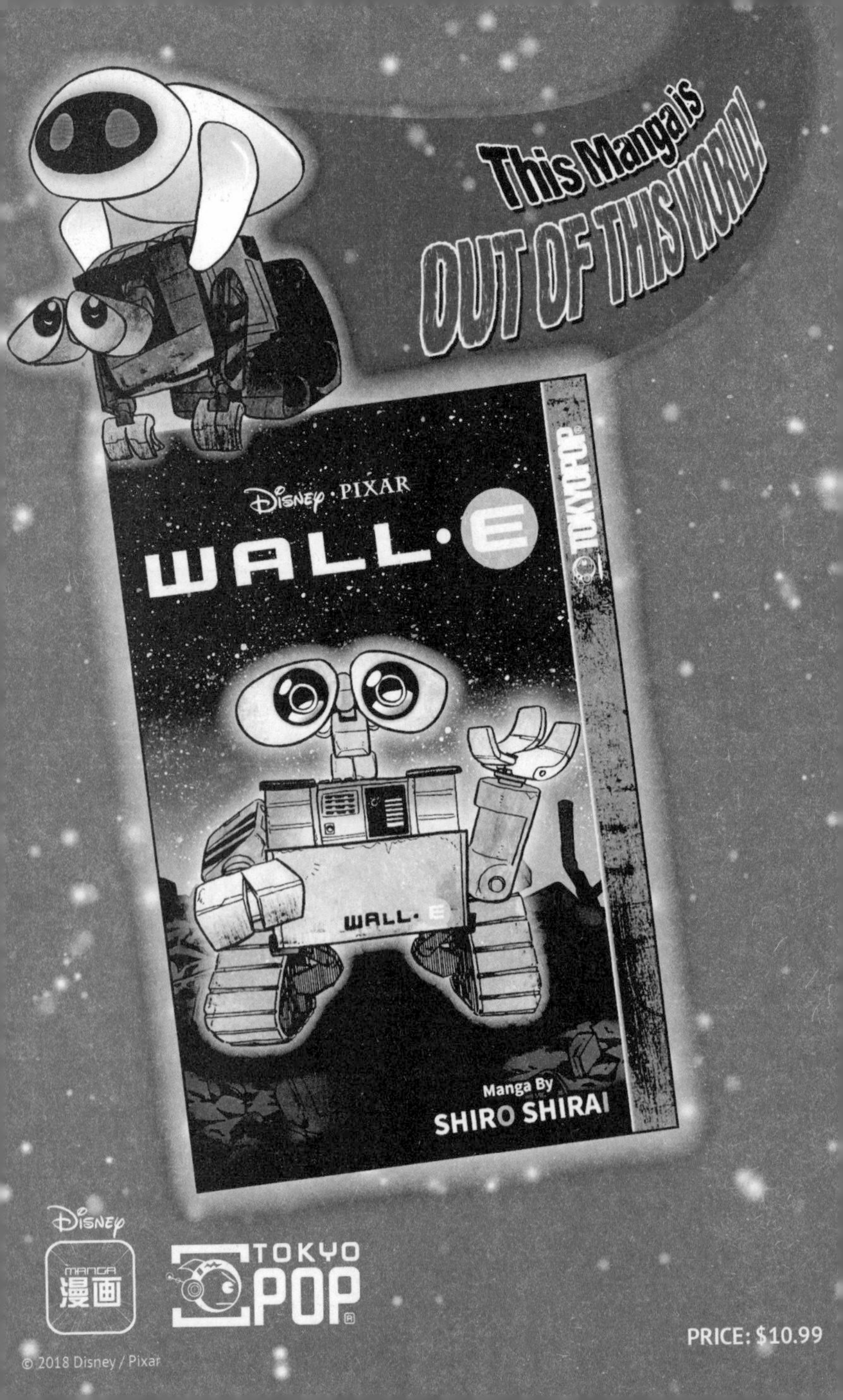
This Manga is
OUT OF THIS WORLD!
Disney · PIXAR
WALL·E
TOKYOPOP
WALL·E
Manga By
SHIRO SHIRAI
Disney
MANGA
漫画
TOKYO
POP
PRICE: $10.99
© 2018 Disney / Pixar

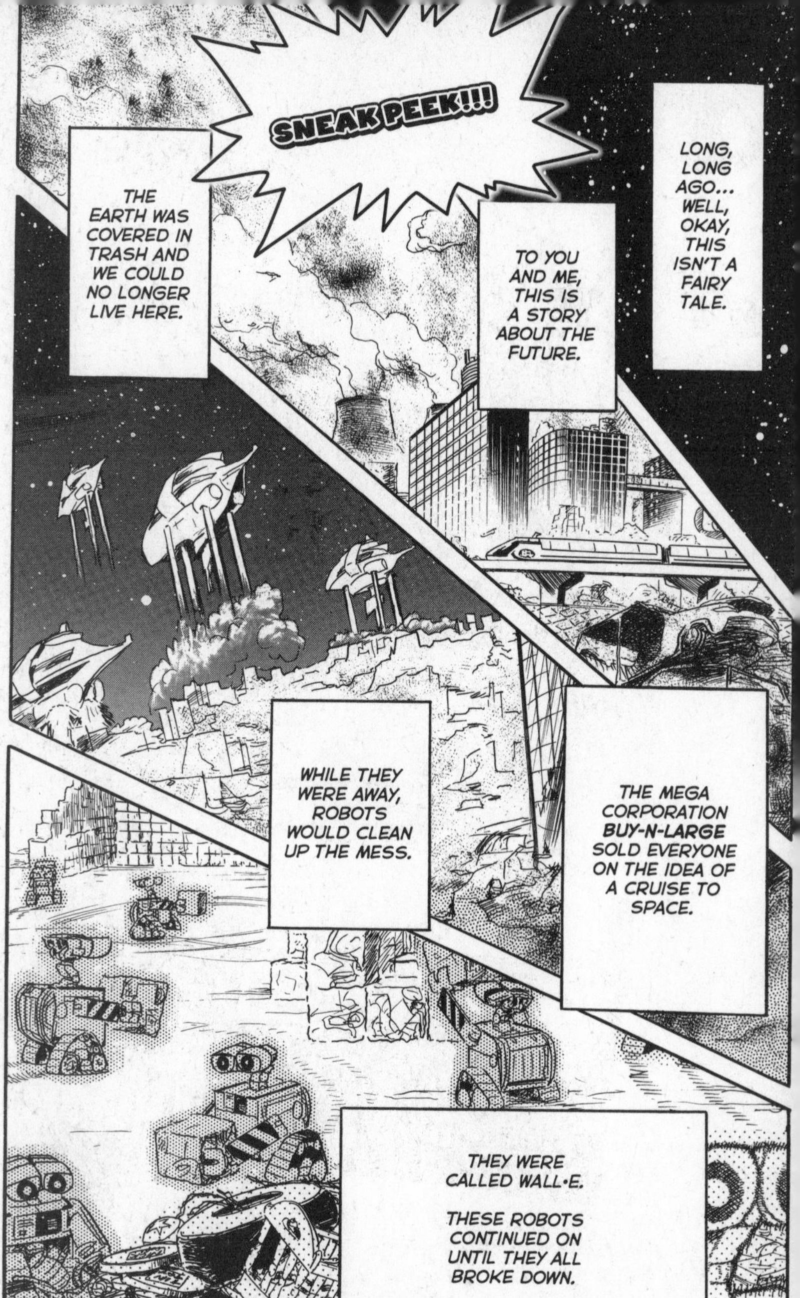
SNEAK PEEK!!!
LONG, LONG AGO... WELL, OKAY, THIS ISN'T A FAIRY TALE.
TO YOU AND ME, THIS IS A STORY ABOUT THE FUTURE.
THE EARTH WAS COVERED IN TRASH AND WE COULD NO LONGER LIVE HERE.
THE MEGA CORPORATION BUY-N-LARGE SOLD EVERYONE ON THE IDEA OF A CRUISE TO SPACE.
WHILE THEY WERE AWAY, ROBOTS WOULD CLEAN UP THE MESS.
THEY WERE CALLED WALL·E.
THESE ROBOTS CONTINUED ON UNTIL THEY ALL BROKE DOWN.

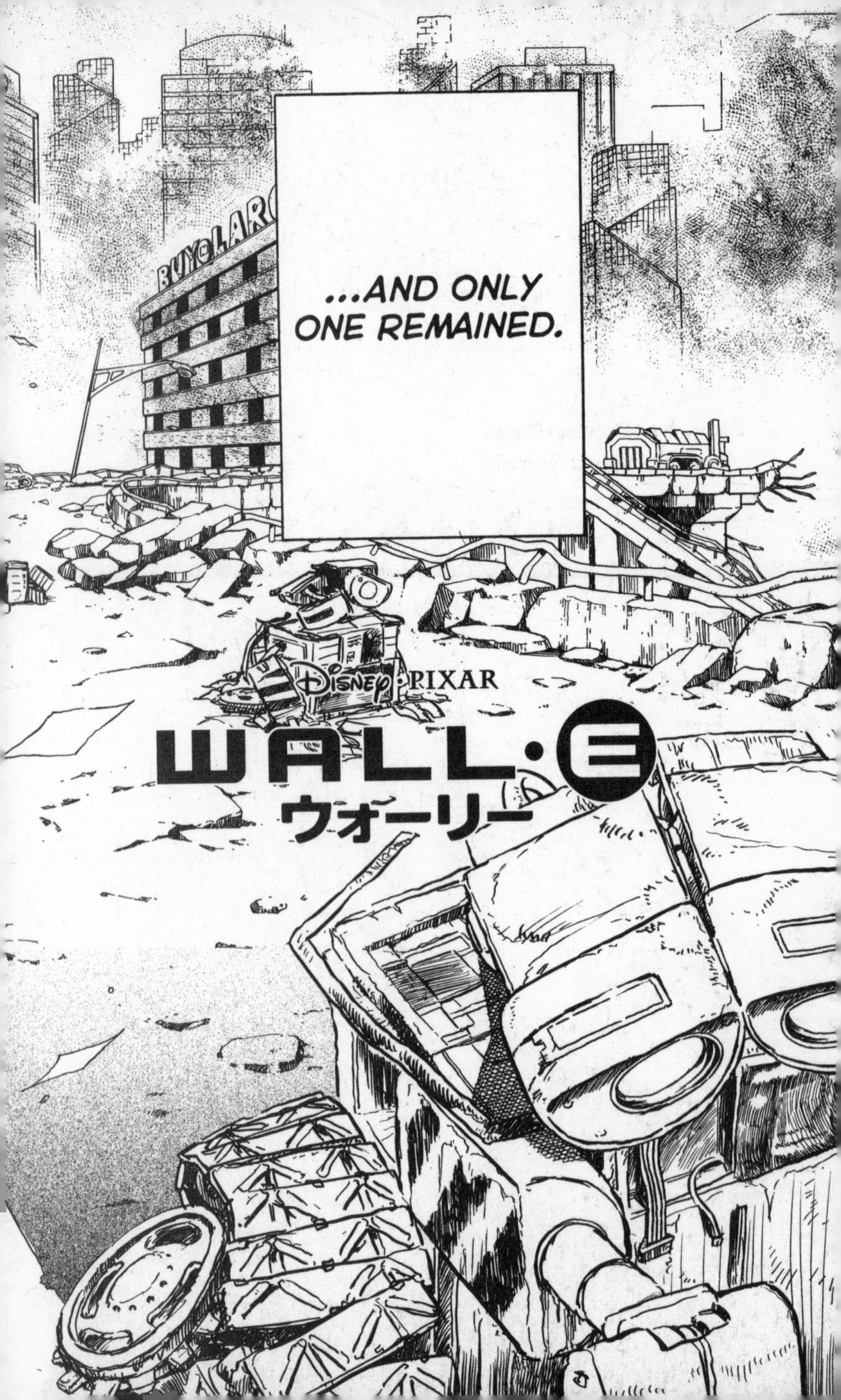
...AND ONLY ONE REMAINED.
BUY n LARG
DISNEY·PIXAR
WALL·E
ウォーリー

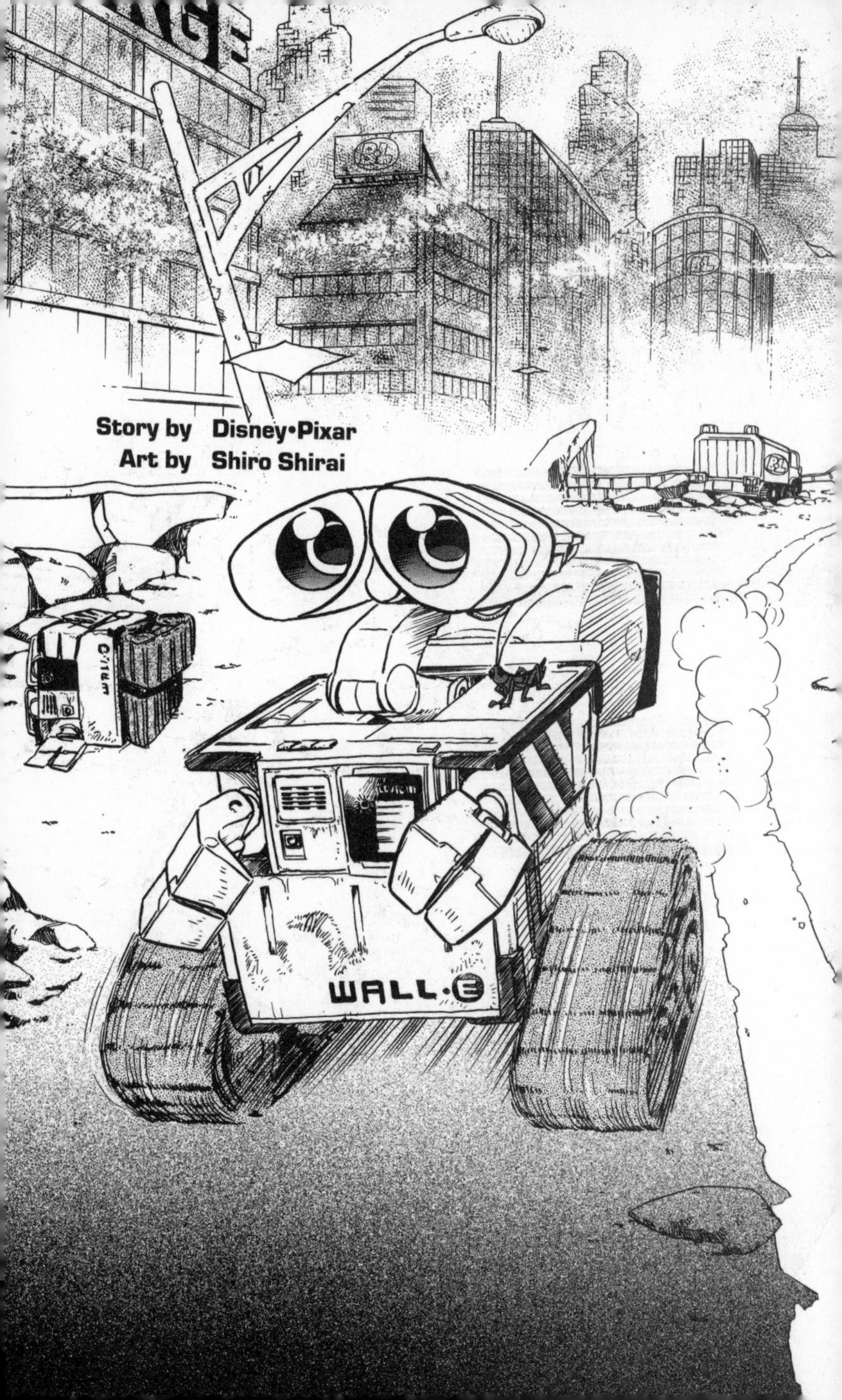
Story by Disney•Pixar
Art by Shiro Shirai
WALL·E

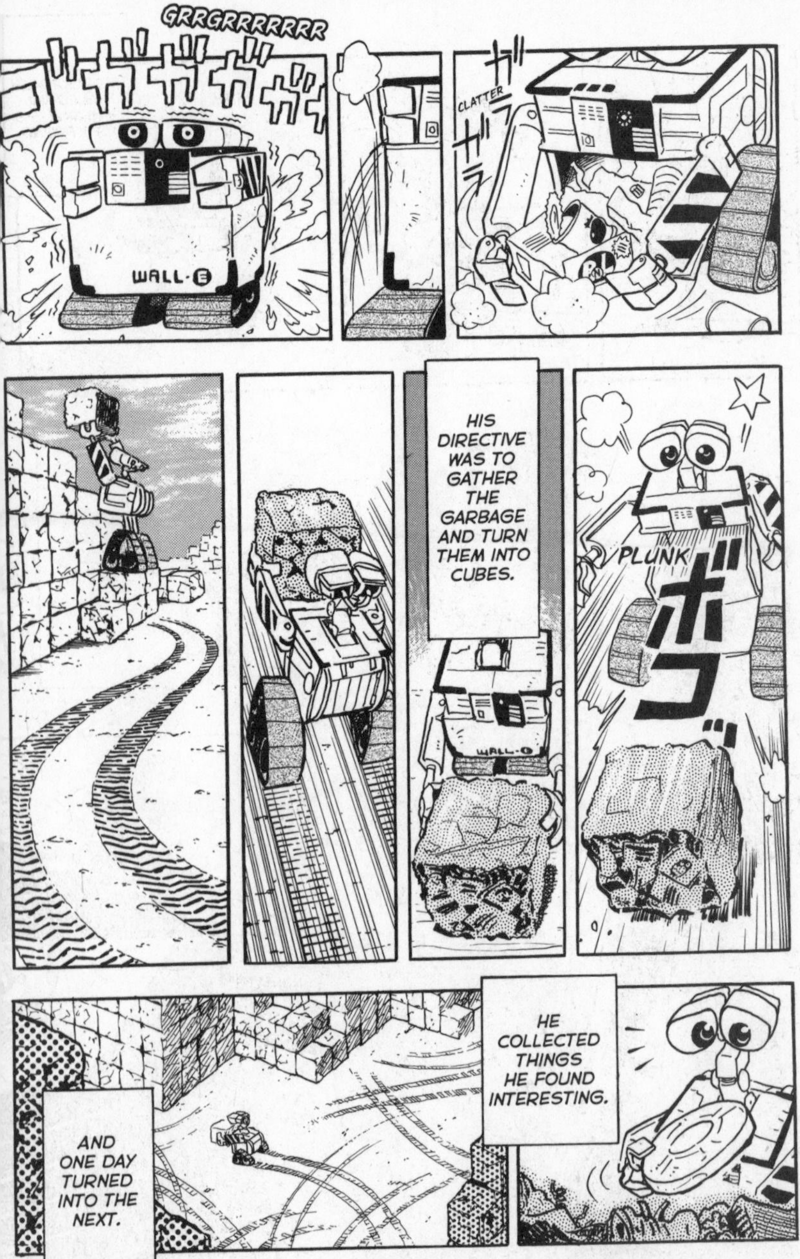
CLATTER
GRRGRRRRRRR
WALL·E
PLUNK
HIS DIRECTIVE WAS TO GATHER THE GARBAGE AND TURN THEM INTO CUBES.
WALL·E
HE COLLECTED THINGS HE FOUND INTERESTING.
AND ONE DAY TURNED INTO THE NEXT.

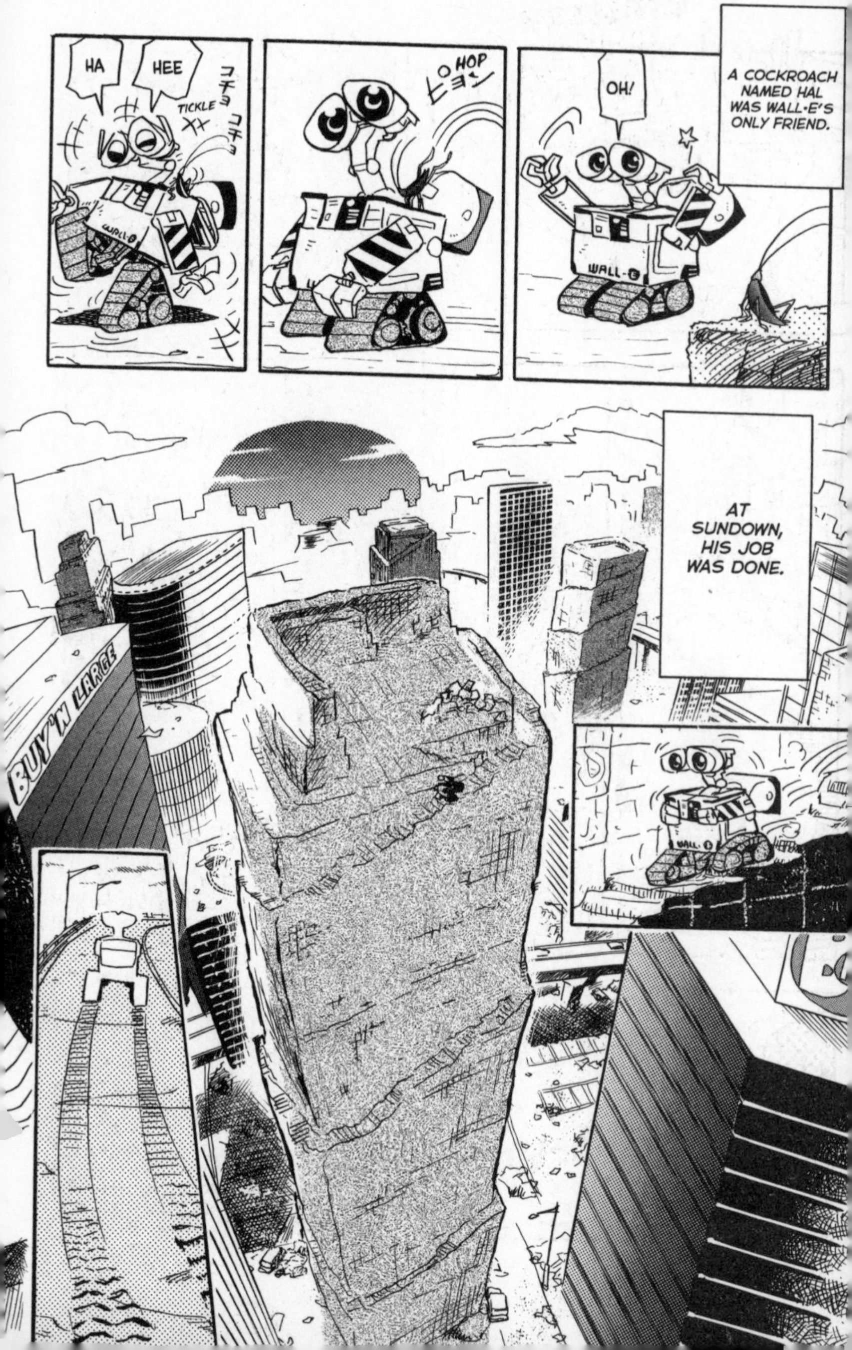
A COCKROACH NAMED HAL WAS WALL·E'S ONLY FRIEND.
OH!
WALL-E
HOP
ピョン
HA
HEE
TICKLE
コチョ
コチョ
WALL-E
AT SUNDOWN, HIS JOB WAS DONE.
BUY'N LARGE
WALL-E

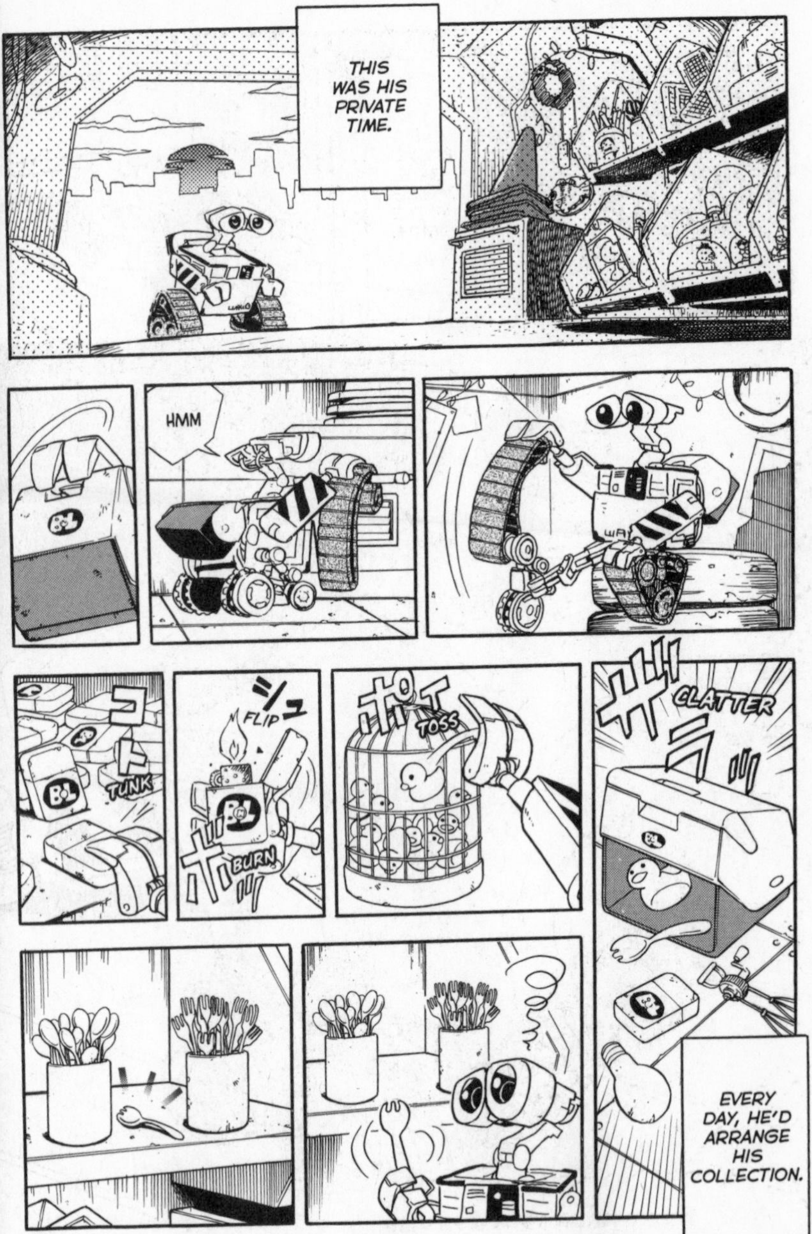
THIS WAS HIS PRIVATE TIME.
HMM
CLATTER
EVERY DAY, HE'D ARRANGE HIS COLLECTION.
ポイ
TOSS
シュ
FLIP
ボッ
BURN
コト
TUNK

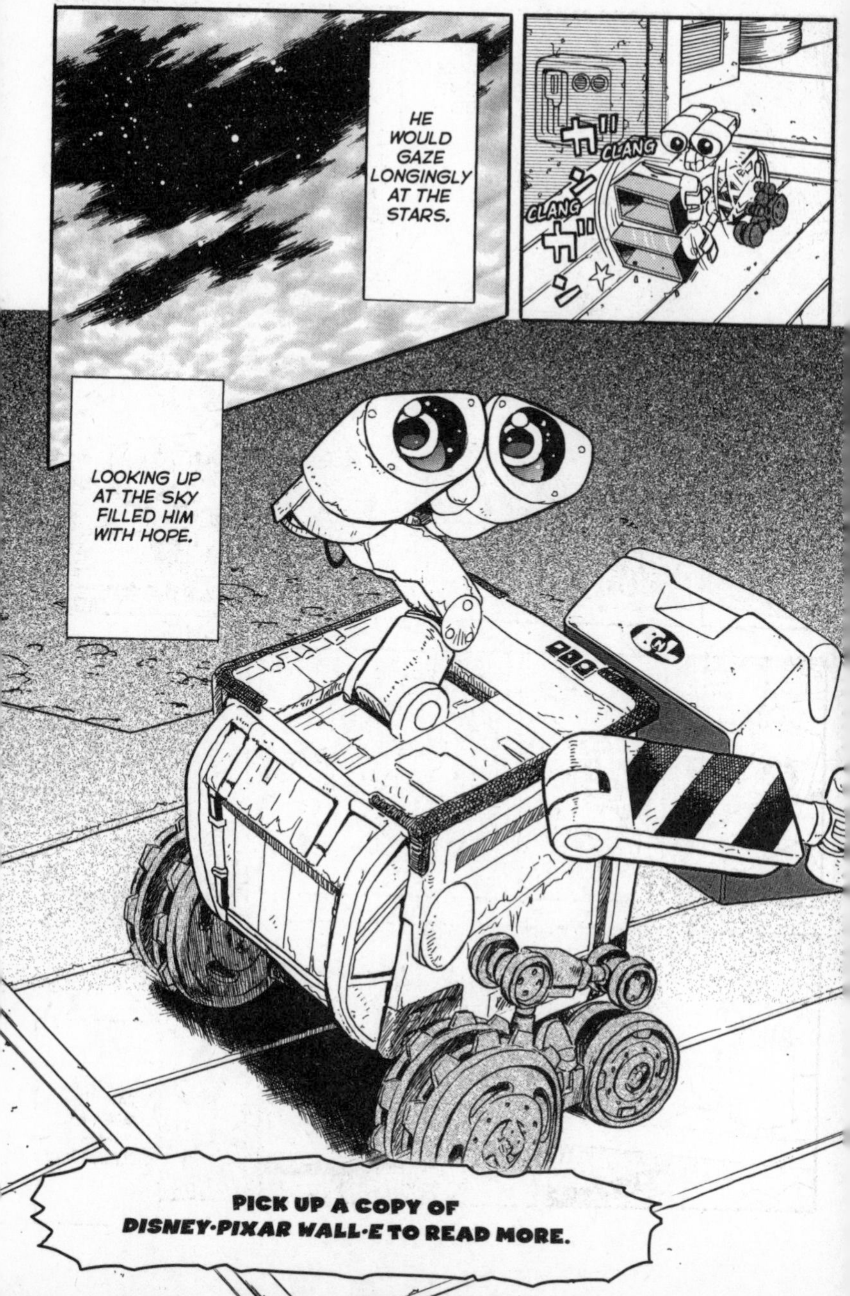
CLANG
CLANG
HE WOULD GAZE LONGINGLY AT THE STARS.
LOOKING UP AT THE SKY FILLED HIM WITH HOPE.
PICK UP A COPY OF DISNEY·PIXAR WALL·E TO READ MORE.

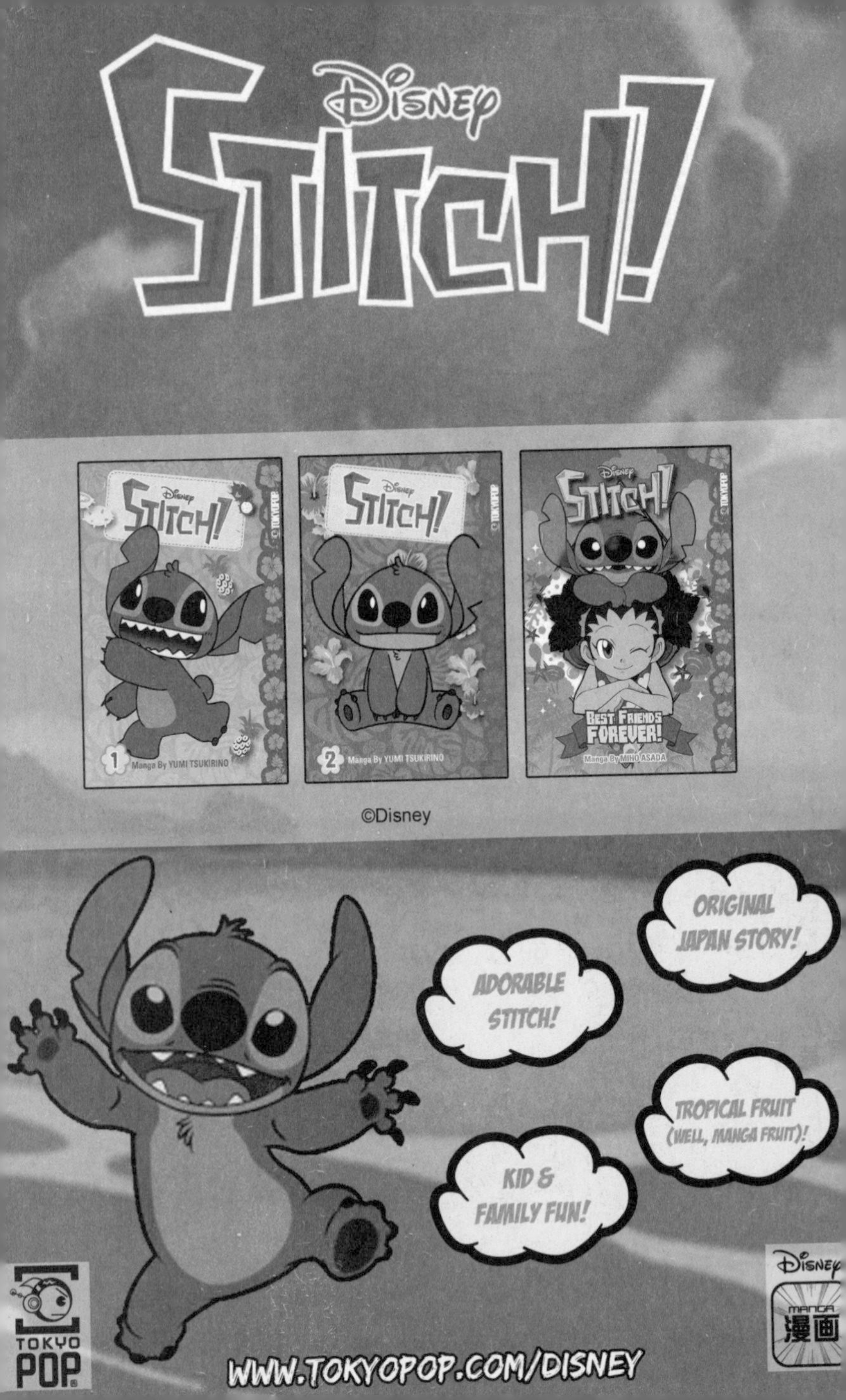

DISNEY
STITCH!
Manga By YUMI TSUKIRINO
Manga By YUMI TSUKIRINO
BEST FRIENDS FOREVER!
Manga By MIHO ASADA
©Disney
ORIGINAL JAPAN STORY!
ADORABLE STITCH!
TROPICAL FRUIT (WELL, MANGA FRUIT)!
KID & FAMILY FUN!
TOKYOPOP
DISNEY MANGA 漫画
WWW.TOKYOPOP.COM/DISNEY

KIJIMUNAA AND THE FOREST

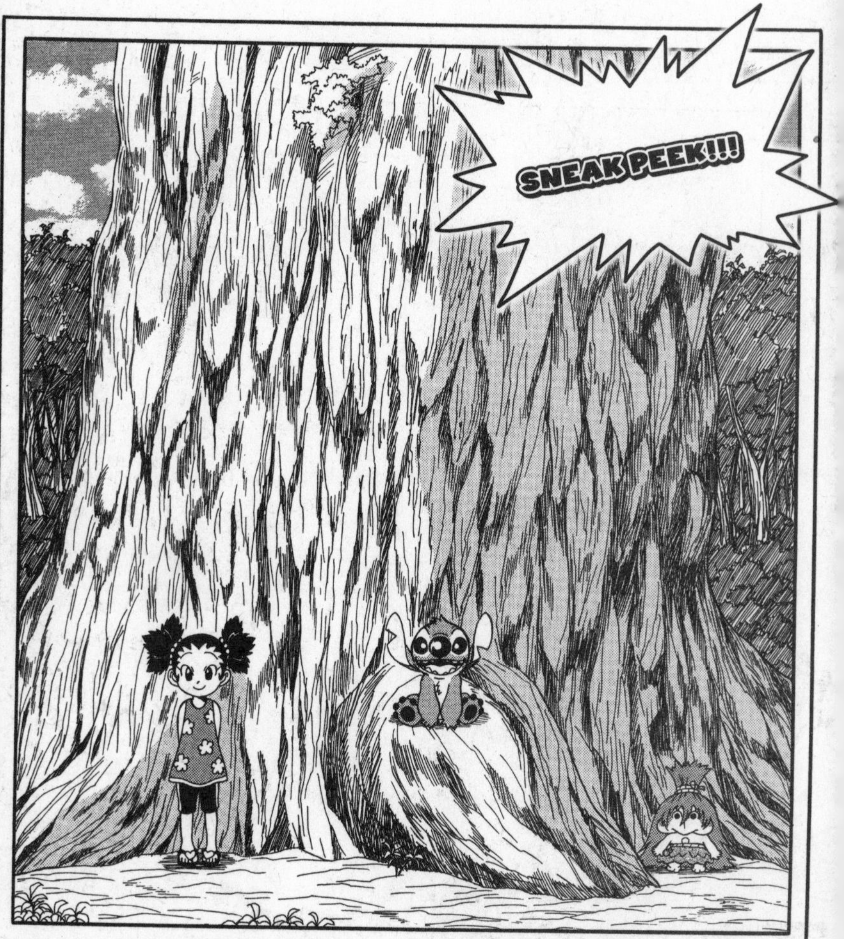
SNEAK PEEK!!!

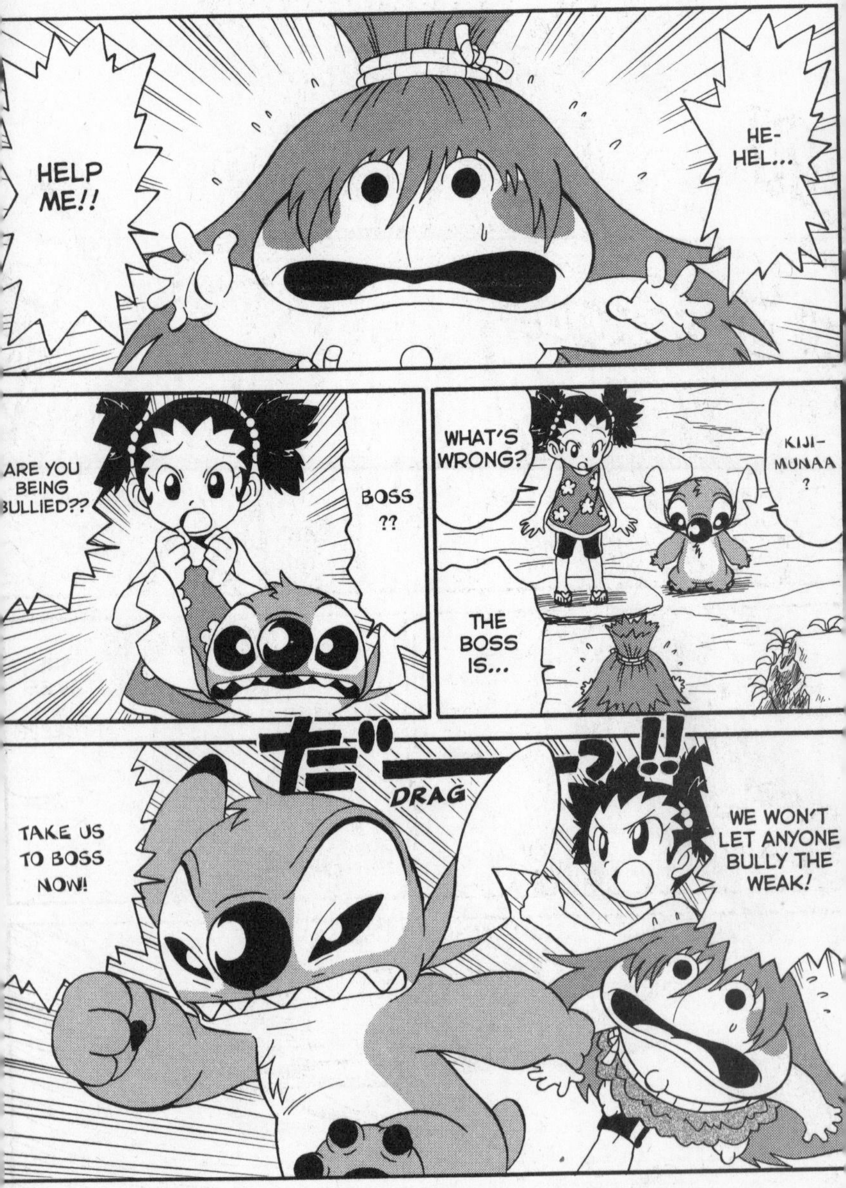
HE- HEL...
HELP ME!!
KIJI- MUNAA ?
WHAT'S WRONG?
THE BOSS IS...
BOSS ??
ARE YOU BEING BULLIED??
だーーーっ!!
DRAG
WE WON'T LET ANYONE BULLY THE WEAK!
TAKE US TO BOSS NOW!

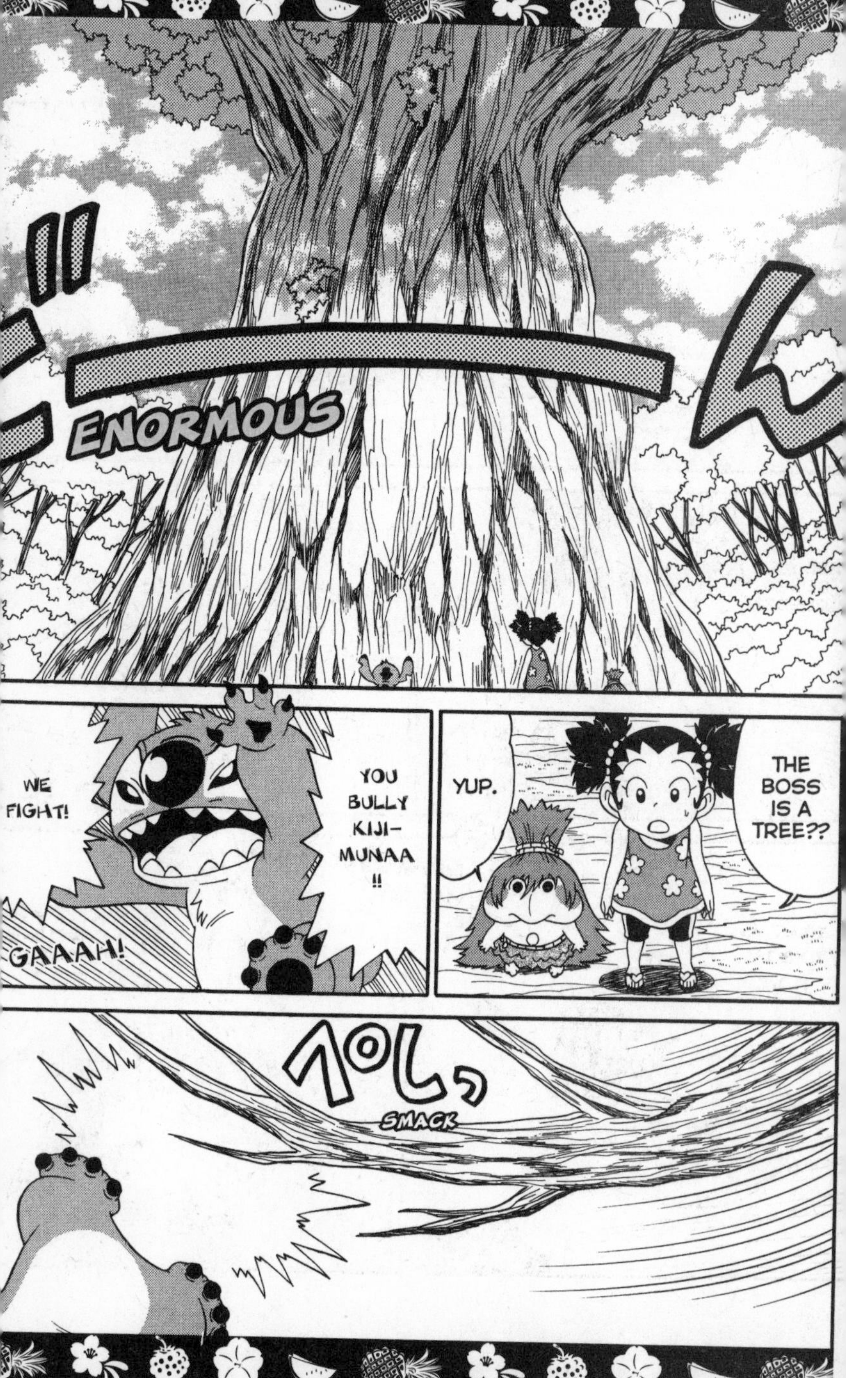
ENORMOUS
THE BOSS IS A TREE??
YUP.
YOU BULLY KIJI-MUNAA!!
WE FIGHT!
GAAAH!
SMACK

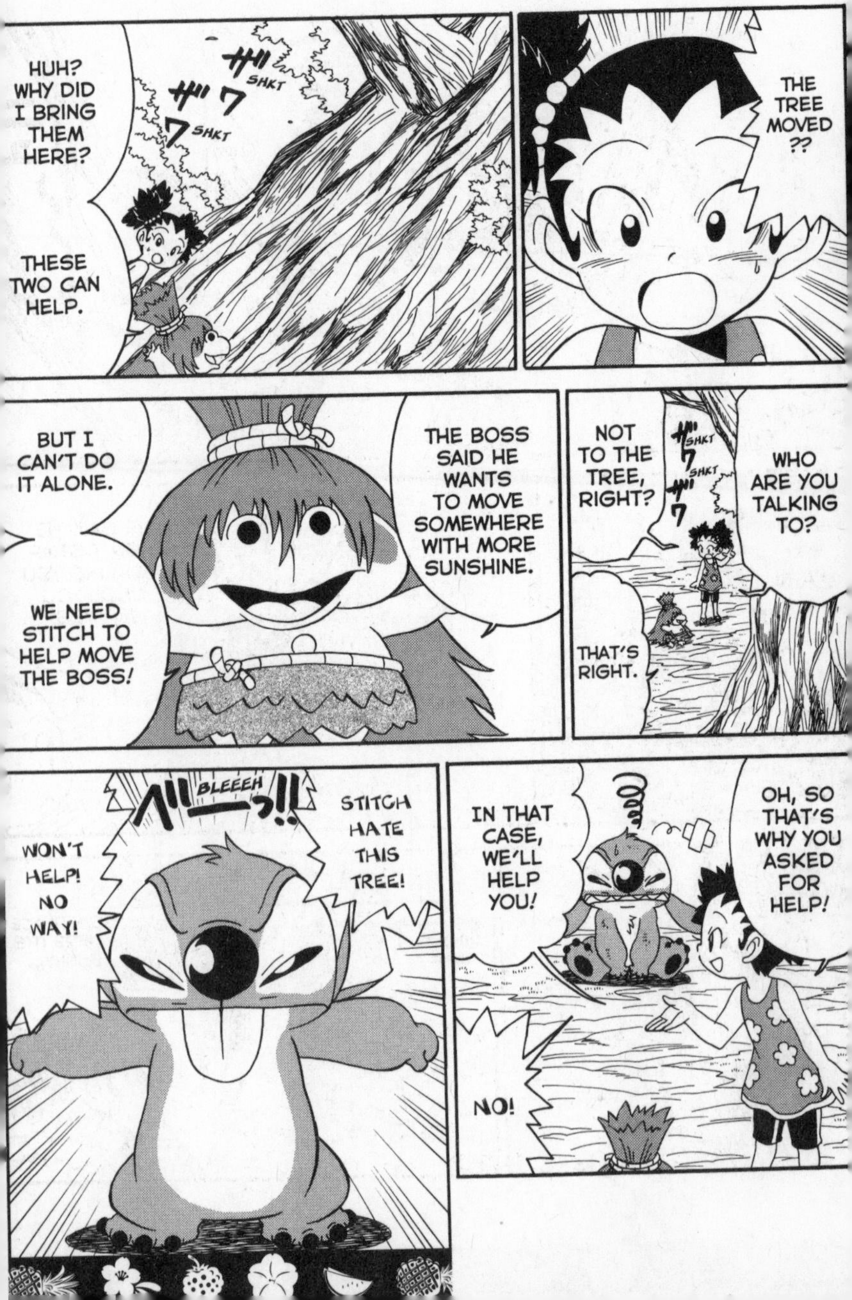
THE TREE MOVED ??
ザワ SHKT
ザワ SHKT
HUH? WHY DID I BRING THEM HERE?
THESE TWO CAN HELP.
WHO ARE YOU TALKING TO?
ザワ SHKT
ザワ SHKT
NOT TO THE TREE, RIGHT?
THAT'S RIGHT.
THE BOSS SAID HE WANTS TO MOVE SOMEWHERE WITH MORE SUNSHINE.
BUT I CAN'T DO IT ALONE.
WE NEED STITCH TO HELP MOVE THE BOSS!
OH, SO THAT'S WHY YOU ASKED FOR HELP!
IN THAT CASE, WE'LL HELP YOU!
NO!
ベーっ!! BLEEEH
STITCH HATE THIS TREE!
WON'T HELP! NO WAY!

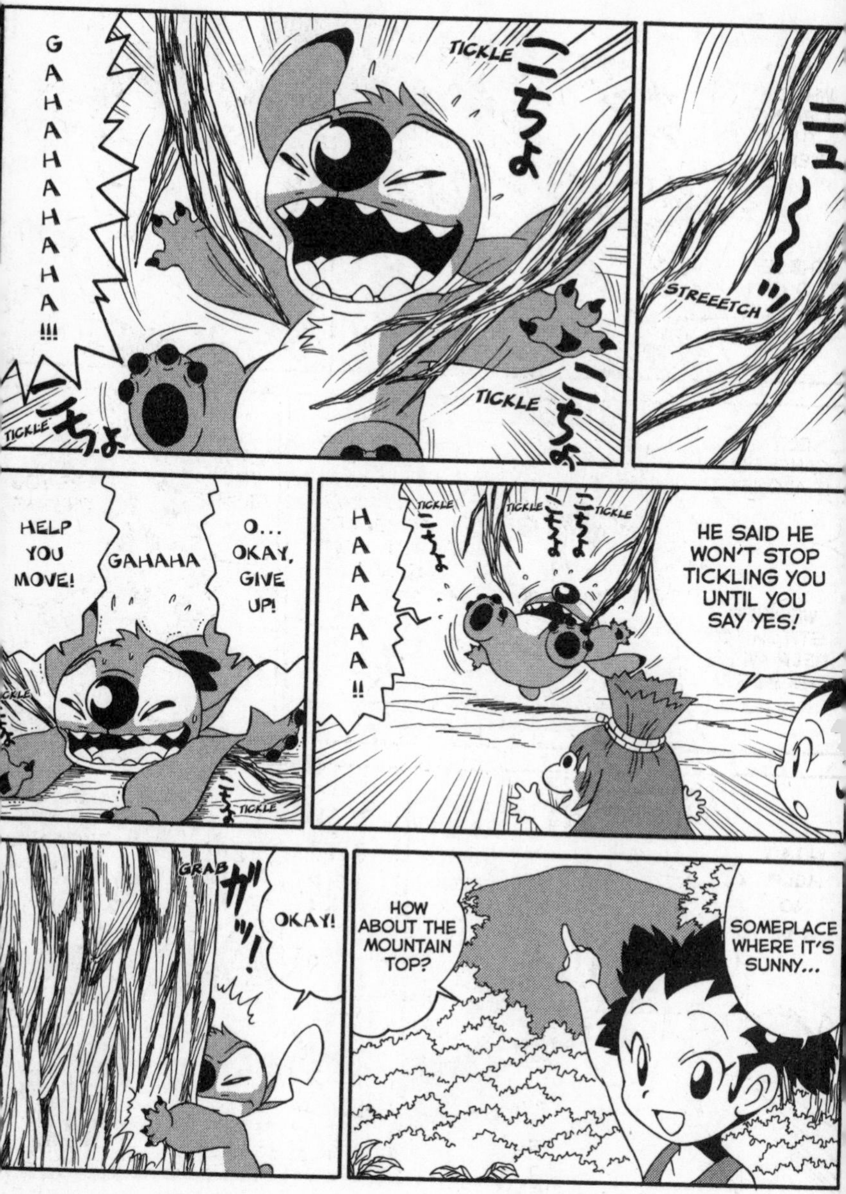

ニュ~~ッ
STREEETCH
TICKLE
こちょ
GAHAHAHAHAHA!!!
TICKLE
こちょ
TICKLE
こちょ
HE SAID HE WON'T STOP TICKLING YOU UNTIL YOU SAY YES!
TICKLE
こちょ
TICKLE
TICKLE
こちょ
HAAAAAA!!
O... OKAY, GIVE UP!
GAHAHA
HELP YOU MOVE!
TICKLE
SOMEPLACE WHERE IT'S SUNNY...
HOW ABOUT THE MOUNTAIN TOP?
OKAY!
GRAB
ガッ!

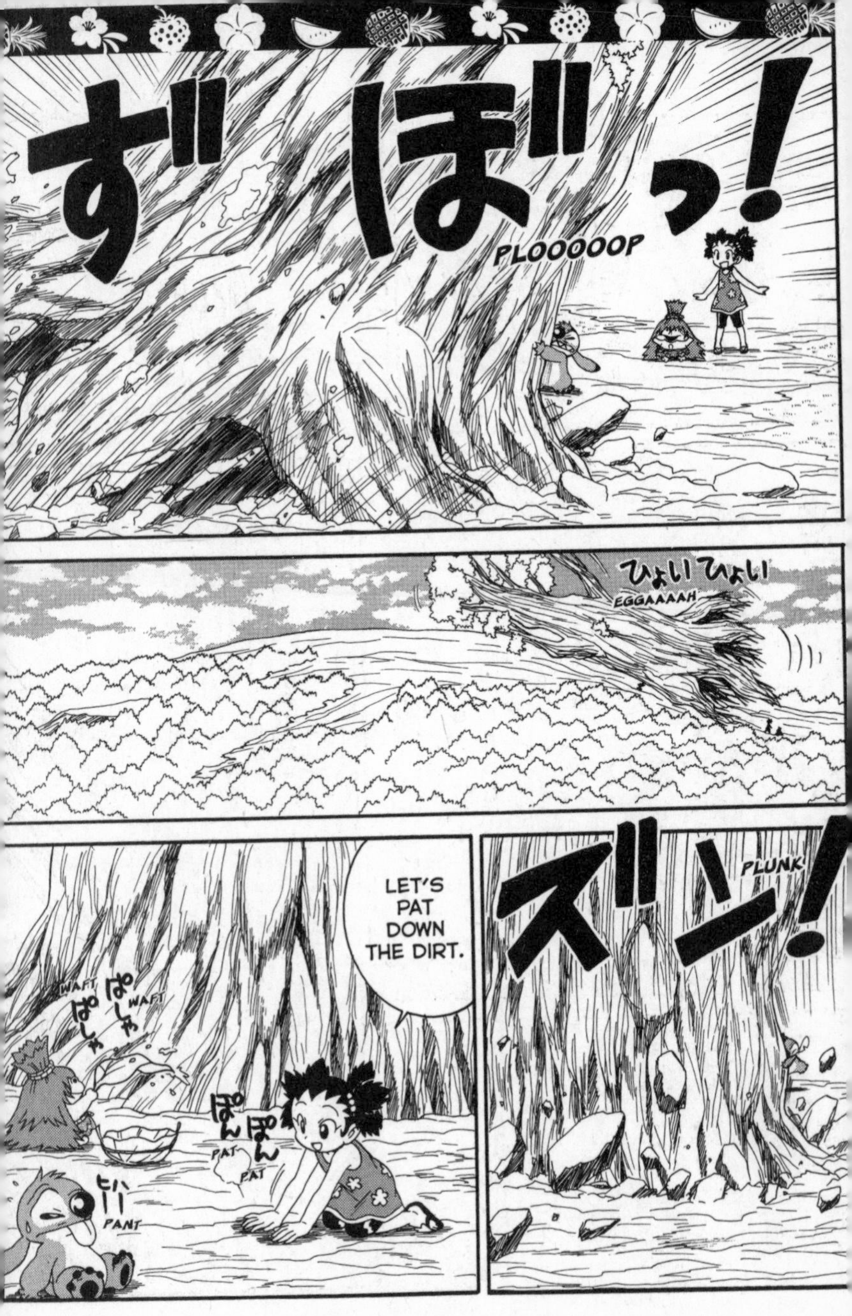
ずぼっ!
PLOOOOOP
ひょいひょい
EGGAAAAH
ズン!
PLUNK
LET'S PAT DOWN THE DIRT.
ぱしゃぱしゃ
WAFT WAFT
ぽんぽん
PAT PAT
ハーヒー
PANT

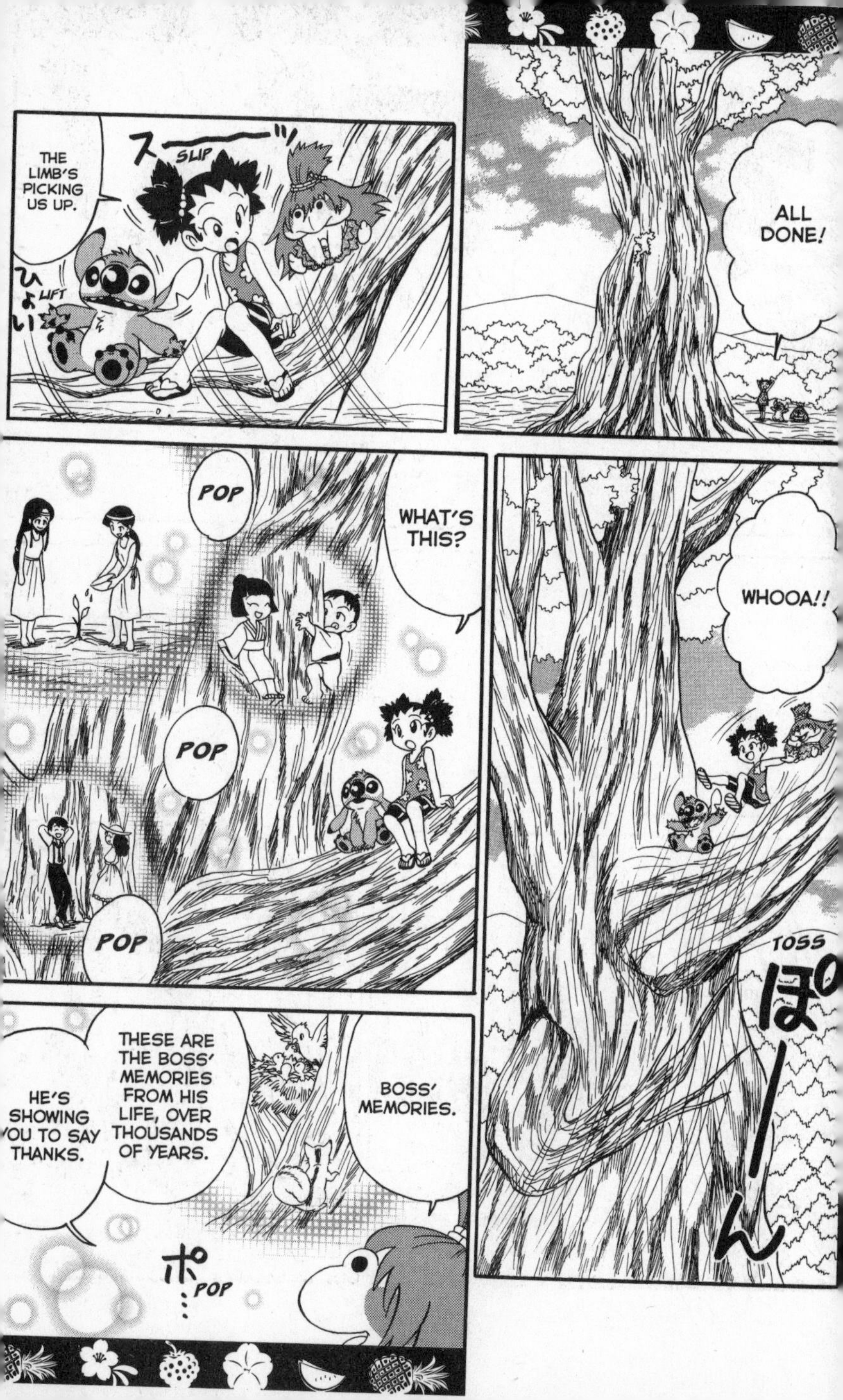
ALL DONE!
スーッ SLIP
THE LIMB'S PICKING US UP.
ひょい LIFT
WHOOA!!
TOSS
ぽーん
WHAT'S THIS?
POP
POP
POP
BOSS' MEMORIES.
THESE ARE THE BOSS' MEMORIES FROM HIS LIFE, OVER THOUSANDS OF YEARS.
HE'S SHOWING YOU TO SAY THANKS.
ポ POP

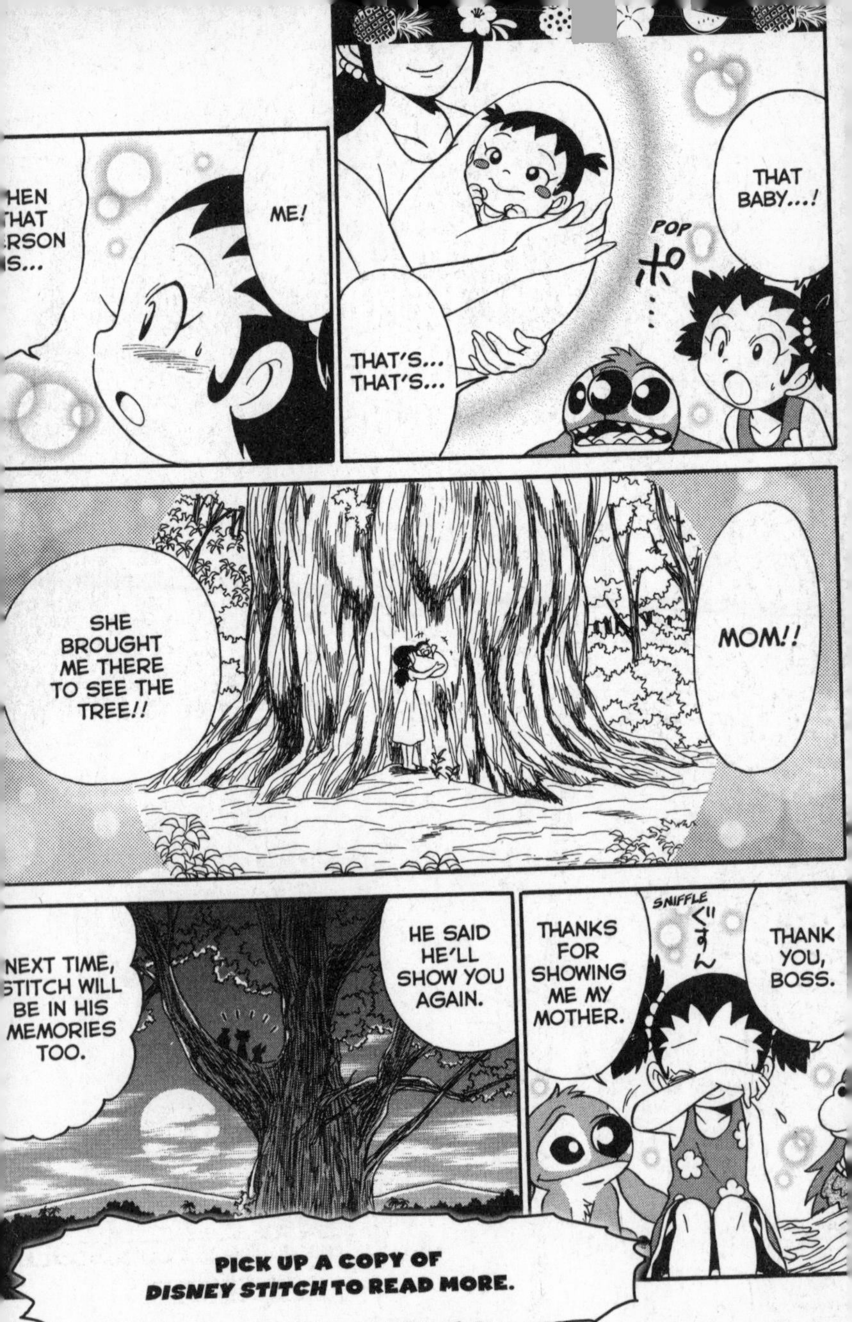
THAT BABY...!
POP ポ...
THAT'S... THAT'S...
ME!
HEN THAT RSON S...
MOM!!
SHE BROUGHT ME THERE TO SEE THE TREE!!
THANK YOU, BOSS.
SNIFFLE ぐすん
THANKS FOR SHOWING ME MY MOTHER.
HE SAID HE'LL SHOW YOU AGAIN.
NEXT TIME, STITCH WILL BE IN HIS MEMORIES TOO.
PICK UP A COPY OF *DISNEY STITCH* TO READ MORE.

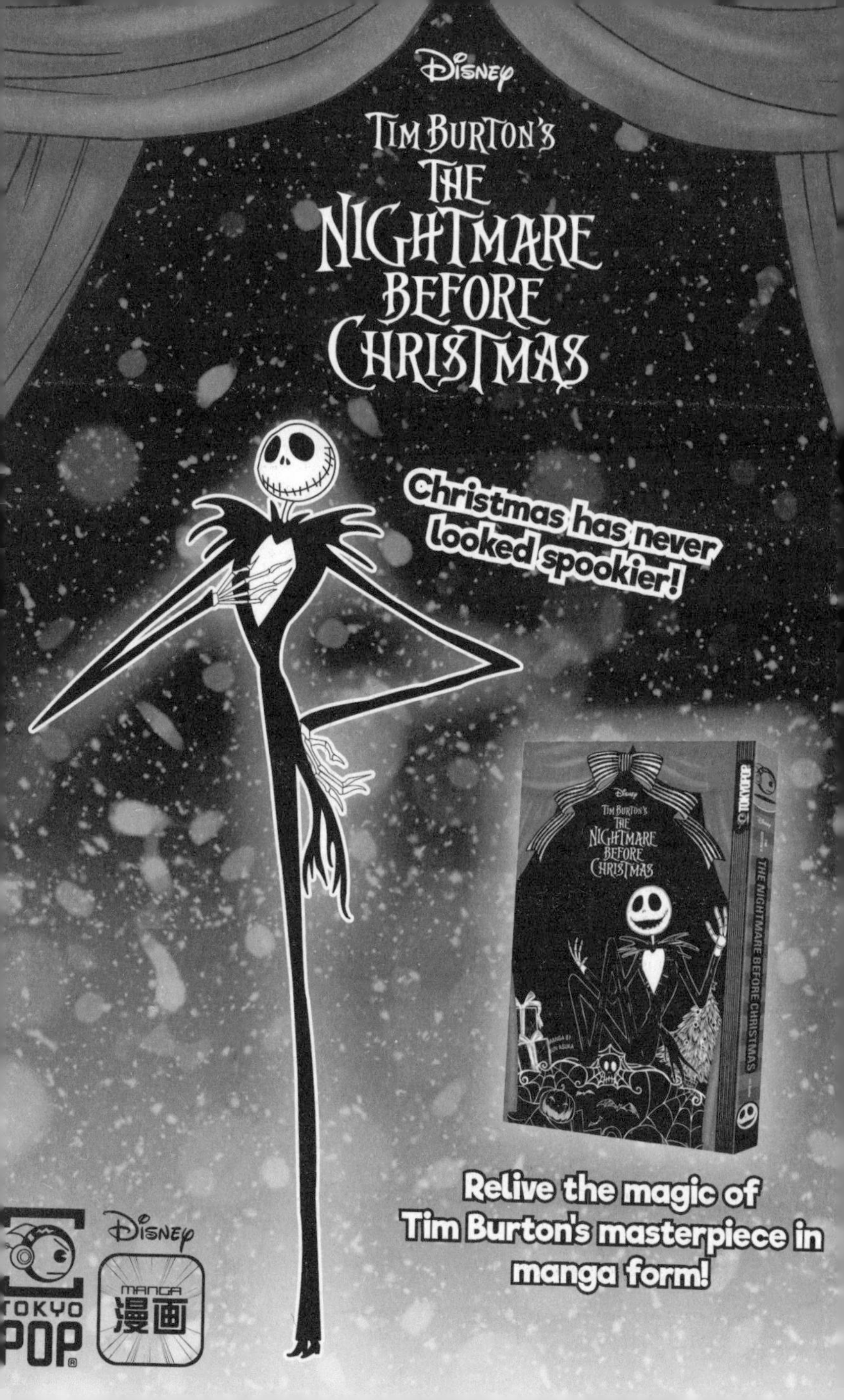
Disney
Tim Burton's
The Nightmare Before Christmas
Christmas has never looked spookier!
Disney
Tim Burton's
The Nightmare Before Christmas
TOKYOPOP
THE NIGHTMARE BEFORE CHRISTMAS
Relive the magic of Tim Burton's masterpiece in manga form!
TOKYO POP
Disney
MANGA
漫画

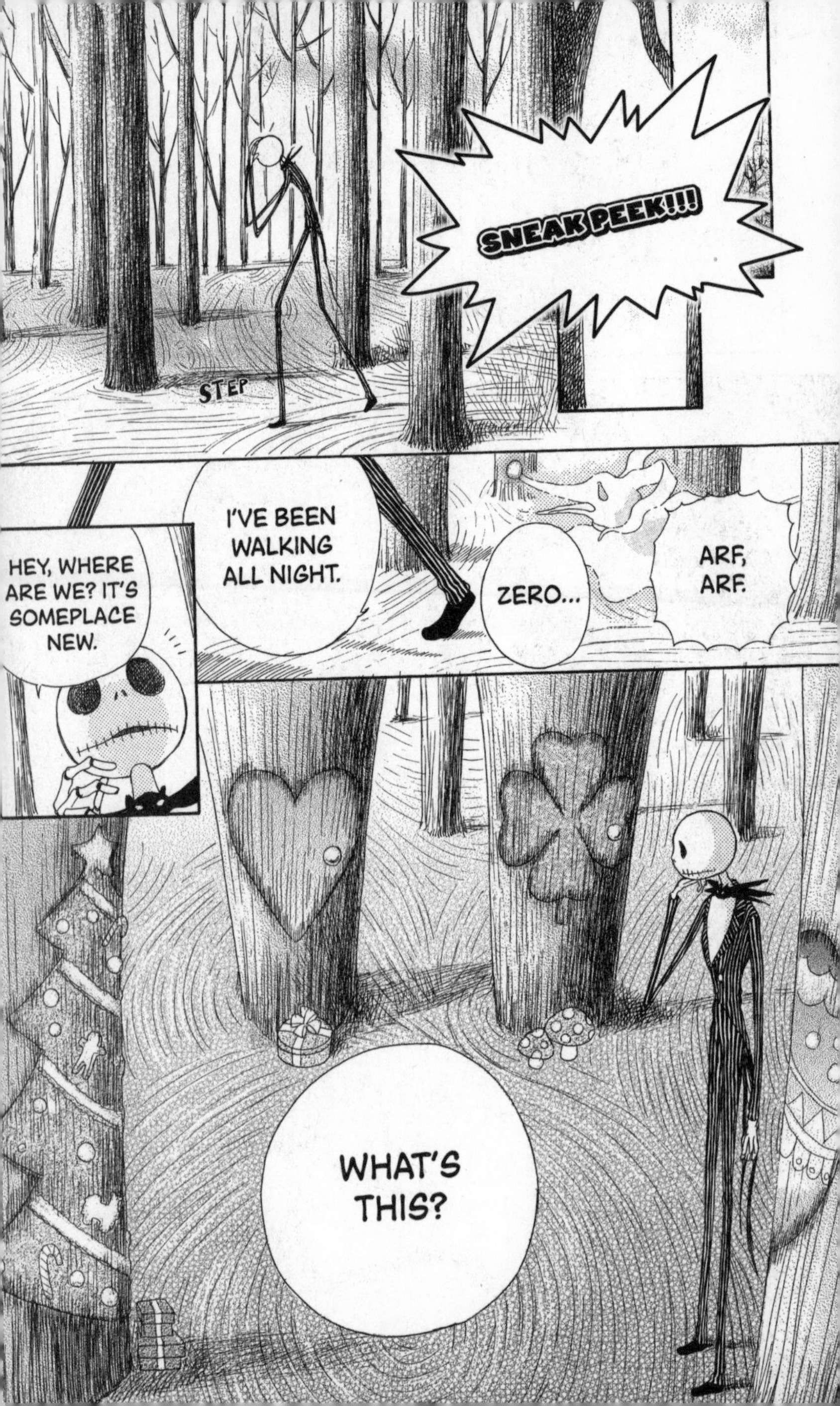
SNEAK PEEK!!!
STEP
ARF, ARF.
ZERO...
I'VE BEEN WALKING ALL NIGHT.
HEY, WHERE ARE WE? IT'S SOMEPLACE NEW.
WHAT'S THIS?

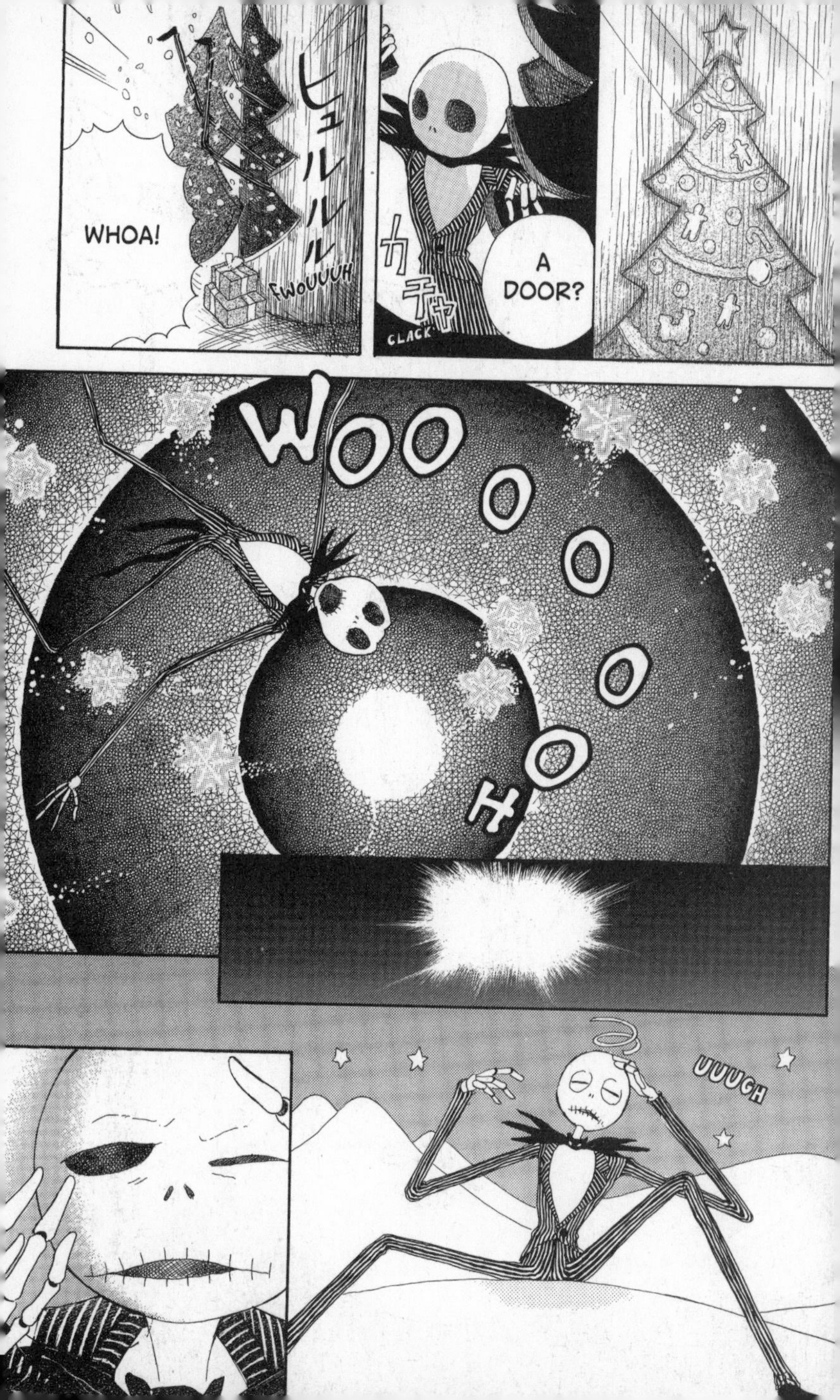

A DOOR?
カチャ
CLACK
ヒュルルルル
FWOUUUH
WHOA!
WOOOOOOH
UUUGH

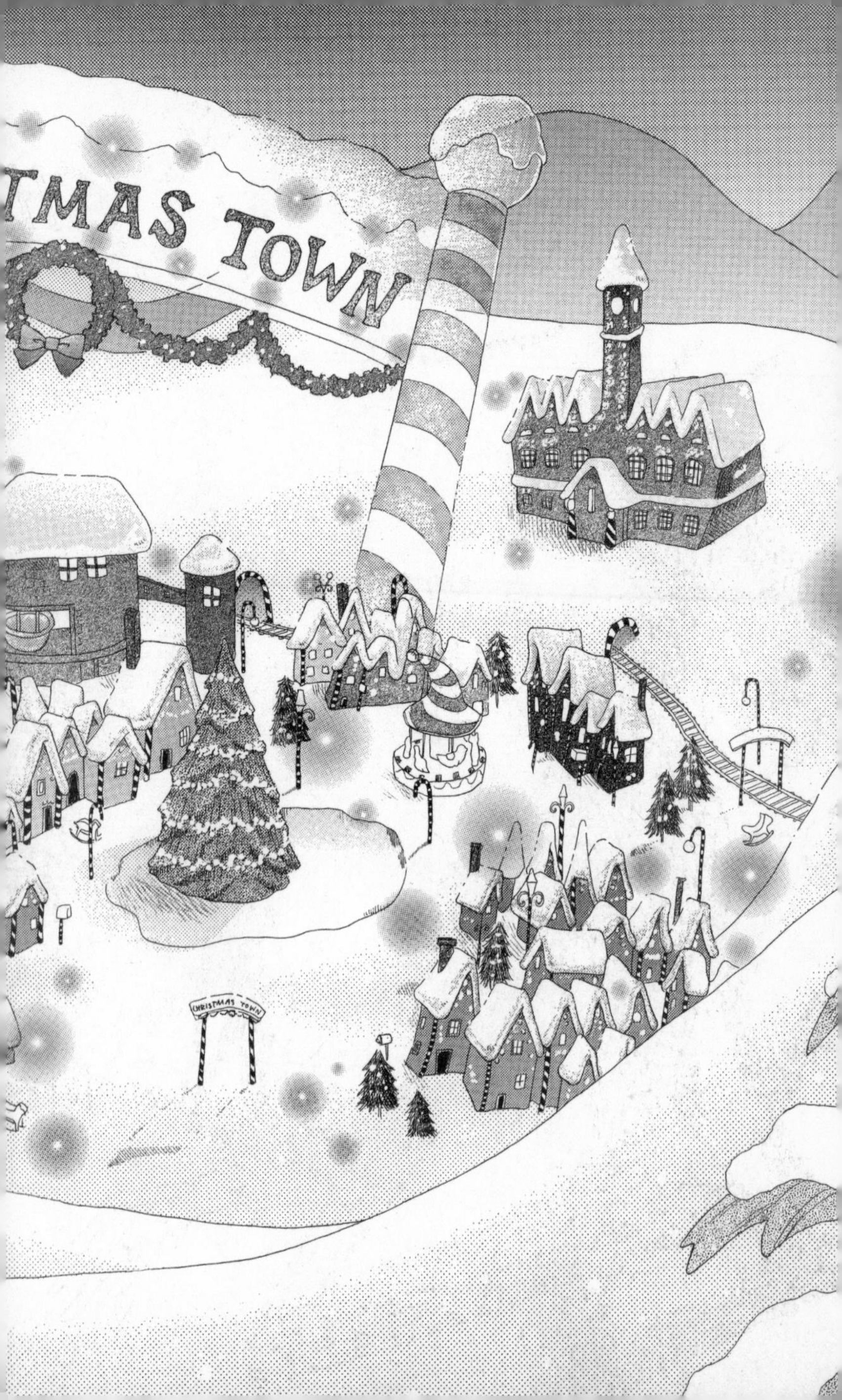
TMAS TOWN
CHRISTMAS TOWN

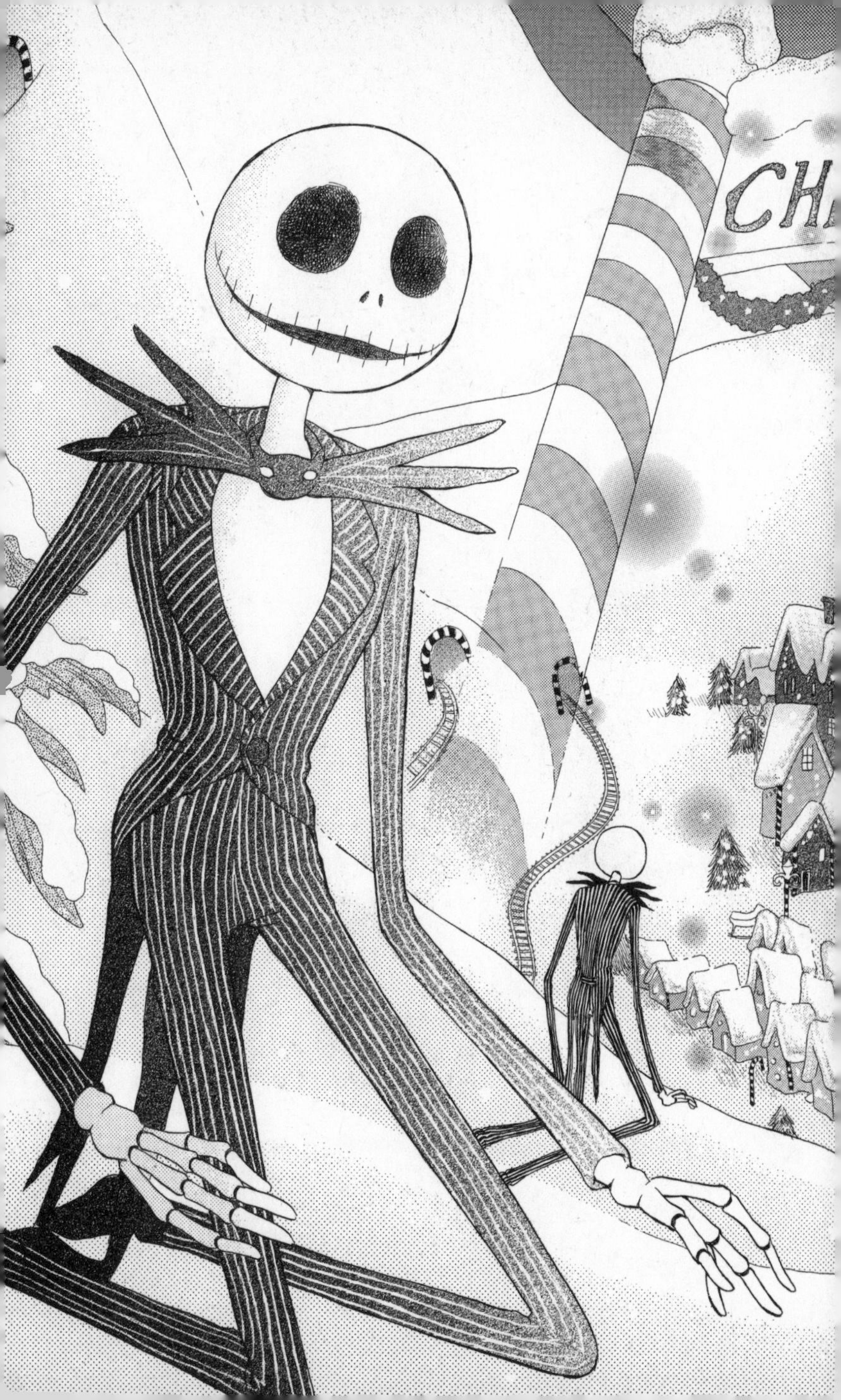
CH

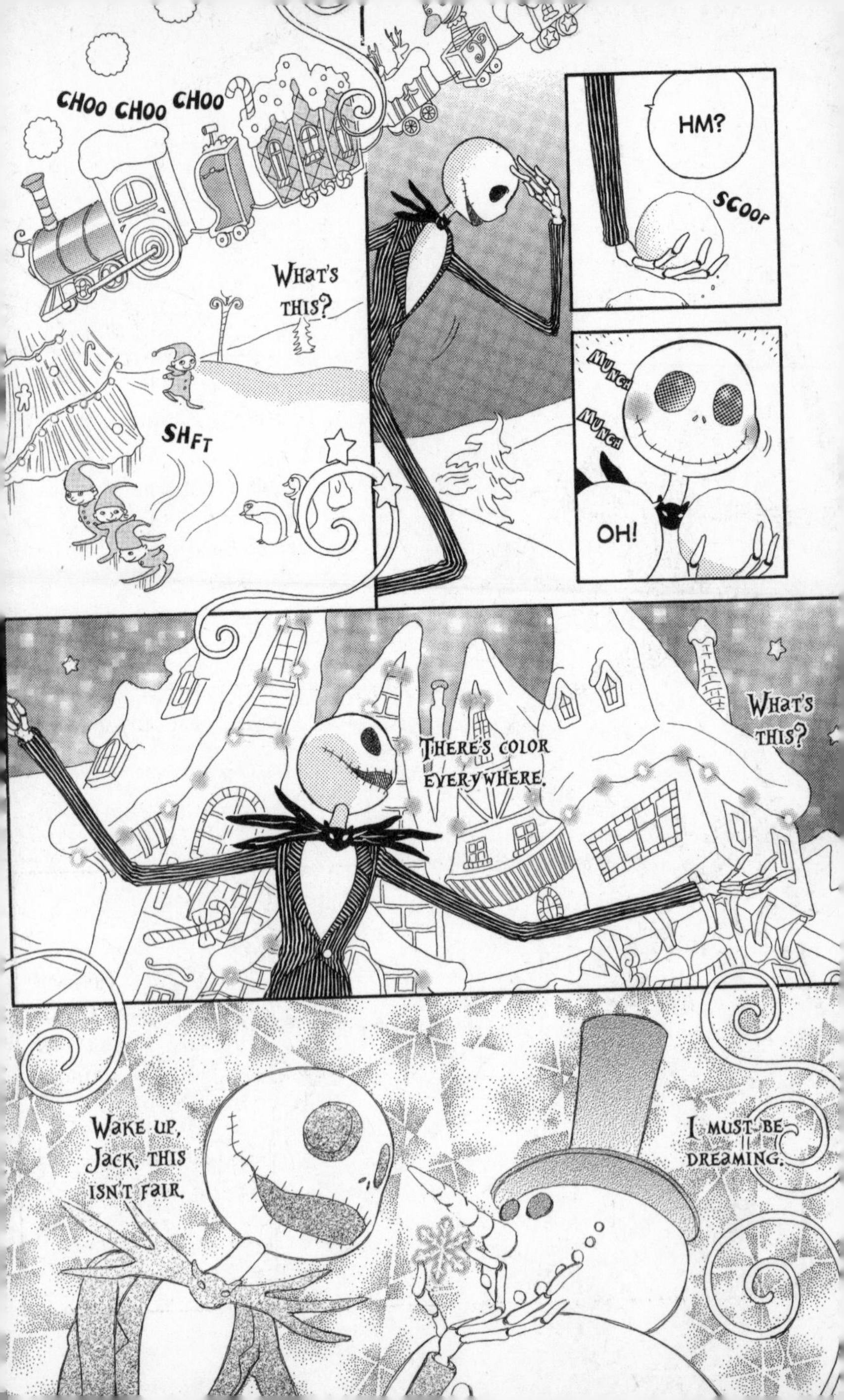
HM?
SCOOP
MUNCH
MUNCH
OH!
CHOO CHOO CHOO
WHAT'S THIS?
SHFT
WHAT'S THIS?
THERE'S COLOR EVERYWHERE.
I MUST BE DREAMING.
WAKE UP, JACK, THIS ISN'T FAIR.

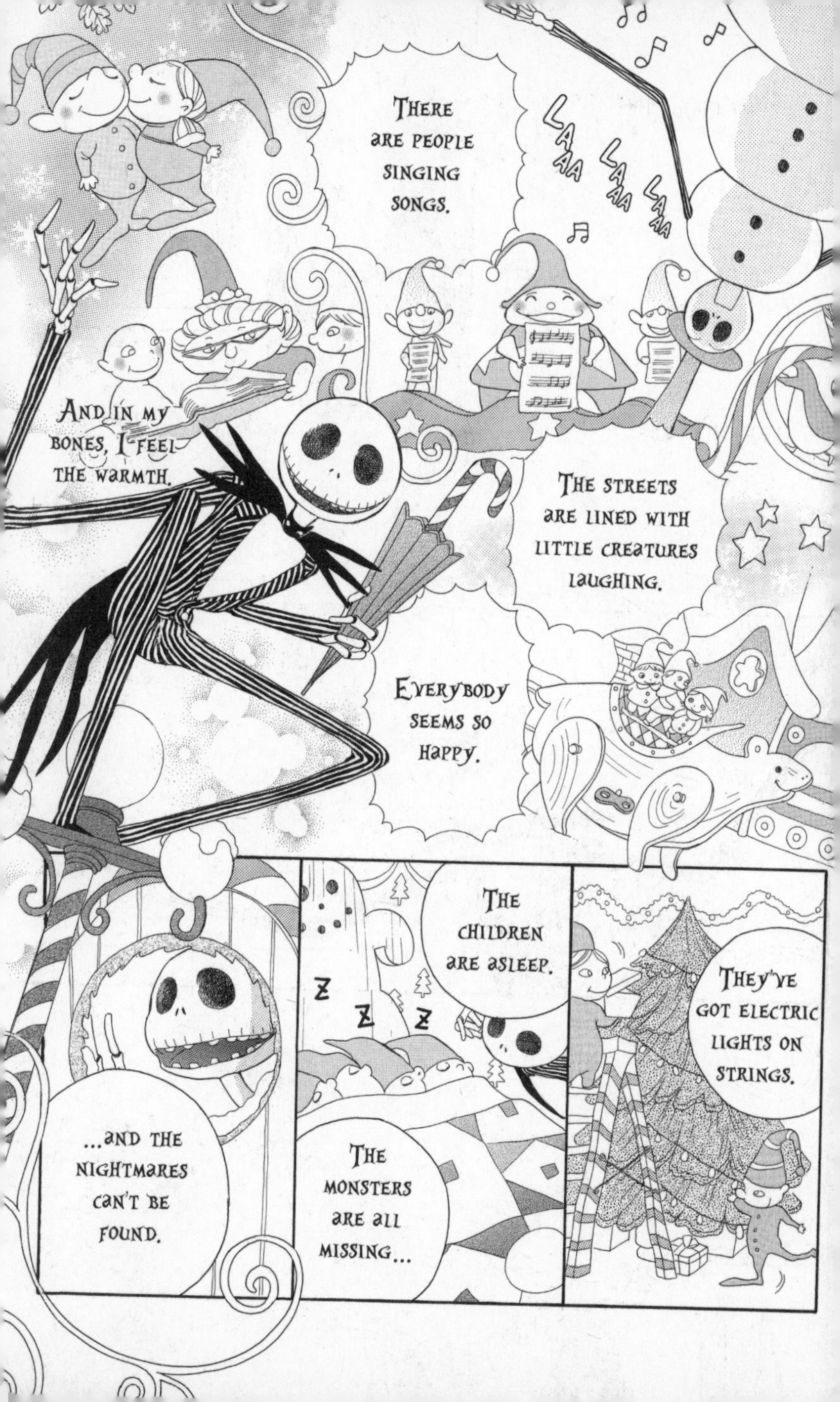
LAAA LAAA LAAA
There are people singing songs.
The streets are lined with little creatures laughing.
Everybody seems so happy.
And in my bones, I feel the warmth.
They've got electric lights on strings.
The children are asleep.
Z Z Z
The monsters are all missing...
...and the nightmares can't be found.

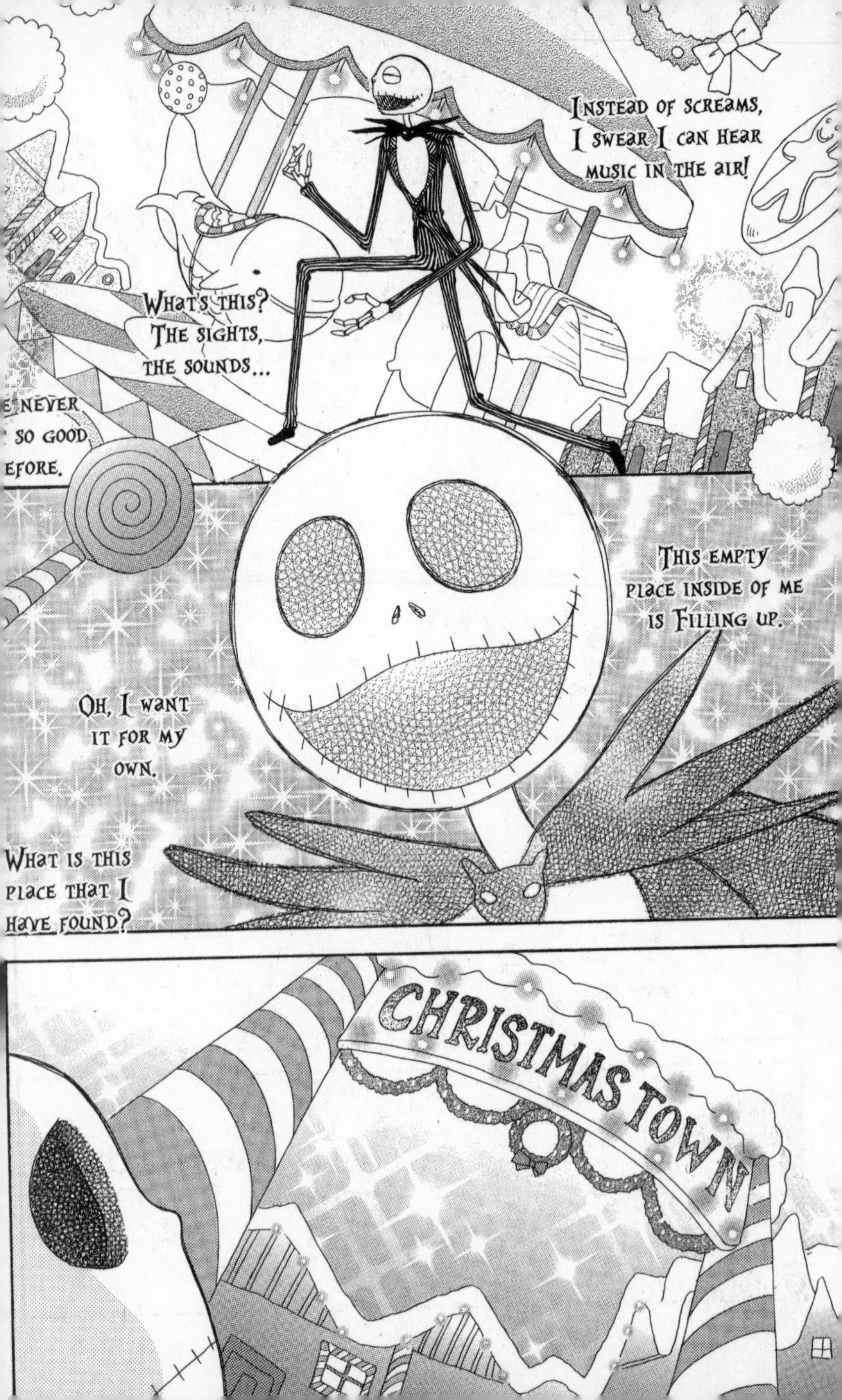
INSTEAD OF SCREAMS, I SWEAR I CAN HEAR MUSIC IN THE AIR!
WHAT'S THIS? THE SIGHTS, THE SOUNDS...
E NEVER SO GOOD EFORE.
THIS EMPTY PLACE INSIDE OF ME IS FILLING UP.
OH, I WANT IT FOR MY OWN.
WHAT IS THIS PLACE THAT I HAVE FOUND?
CHRISTMAS TOWN

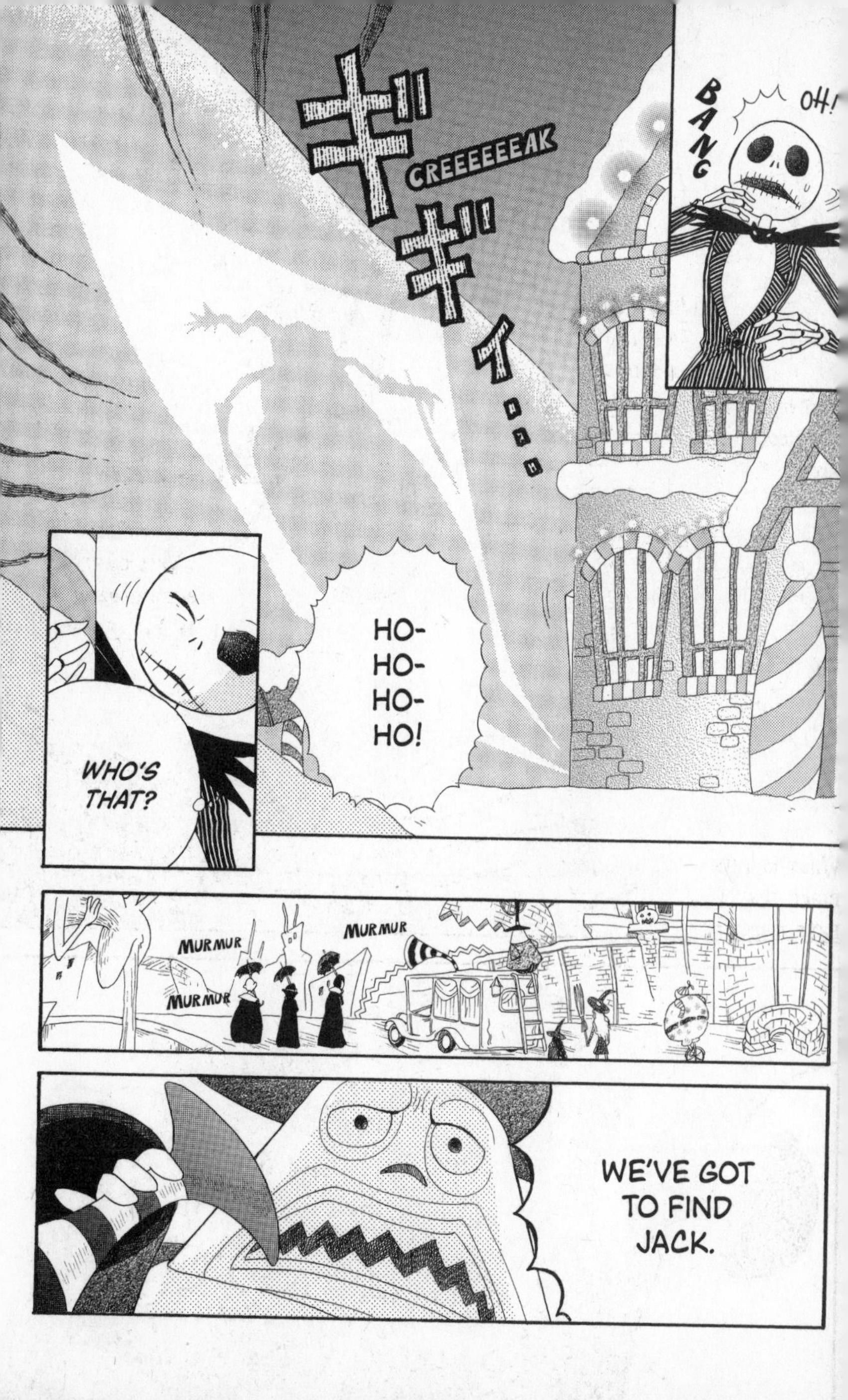

BANG
OH!
ギギイ
CREEEEEEAK
HO-HO-HO-HO!
WHO'S THAT?
MURMUR
MURMUR
MURMUR
WE'VE GOT TO FIND JACK.

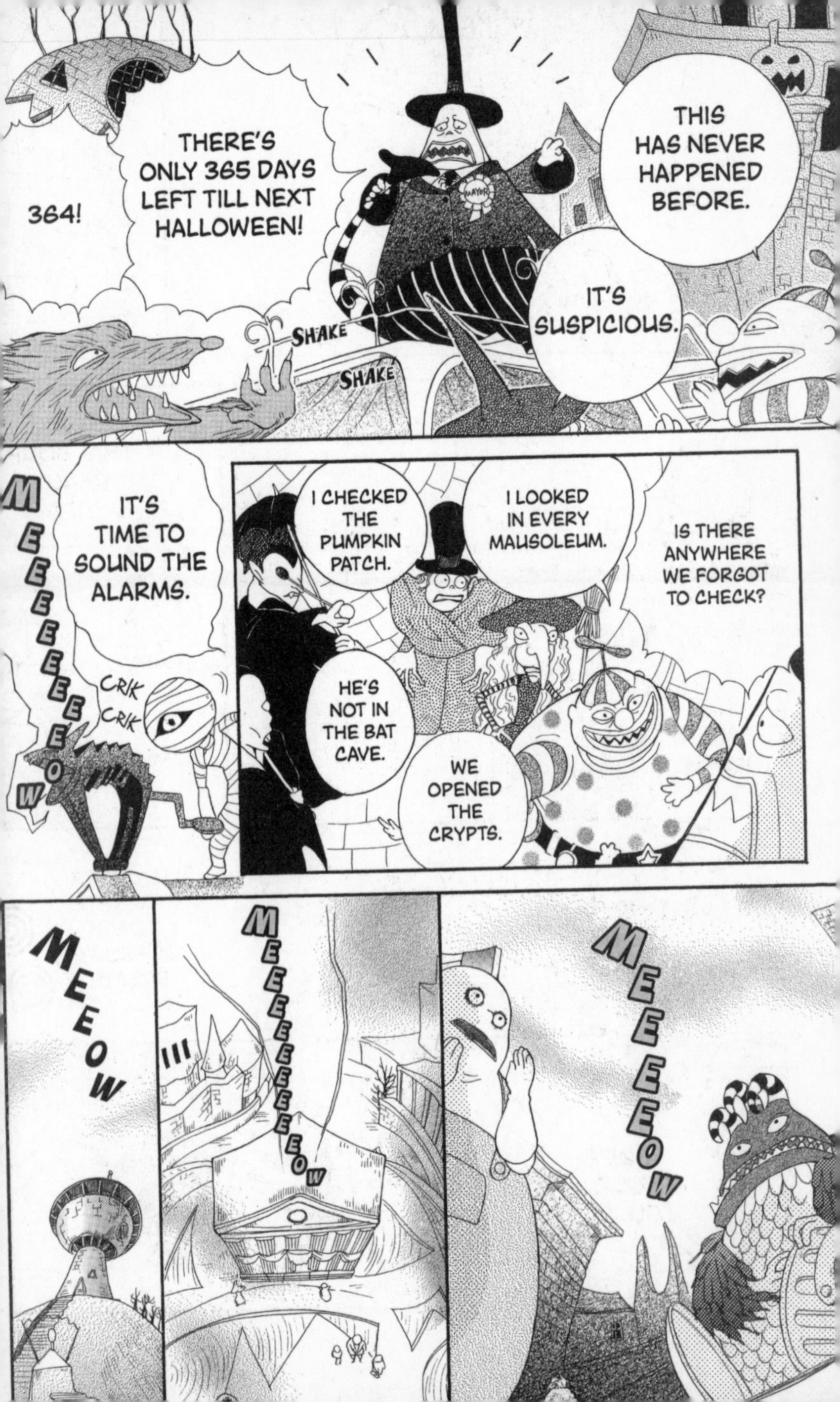
THIS HAS NEVER HAPPENED BEFORE.
IT'S SUSPICIOUS.
SHAKE
SHAKE
THERE'S ONLY 365 DAYS LEFT TILL NEXT HALLOWEEN!
364!
IS THERE ANYWHERE WE FORGOT TO CHECK?
I LOOKED IN EVERY MAUSOLEUM.
I CHECKED THE PUMPKIN PATCH.
HE'S NOT IN THE BAT CAVE.
WE OPENED THE CRYPTS.
IT'S TIME TO SOUND THE ALARMS.
CRIK
CRIK
MEEEEEEEEOW
MEEEEEOW
MEEEEEEEEEOW
MEEOW

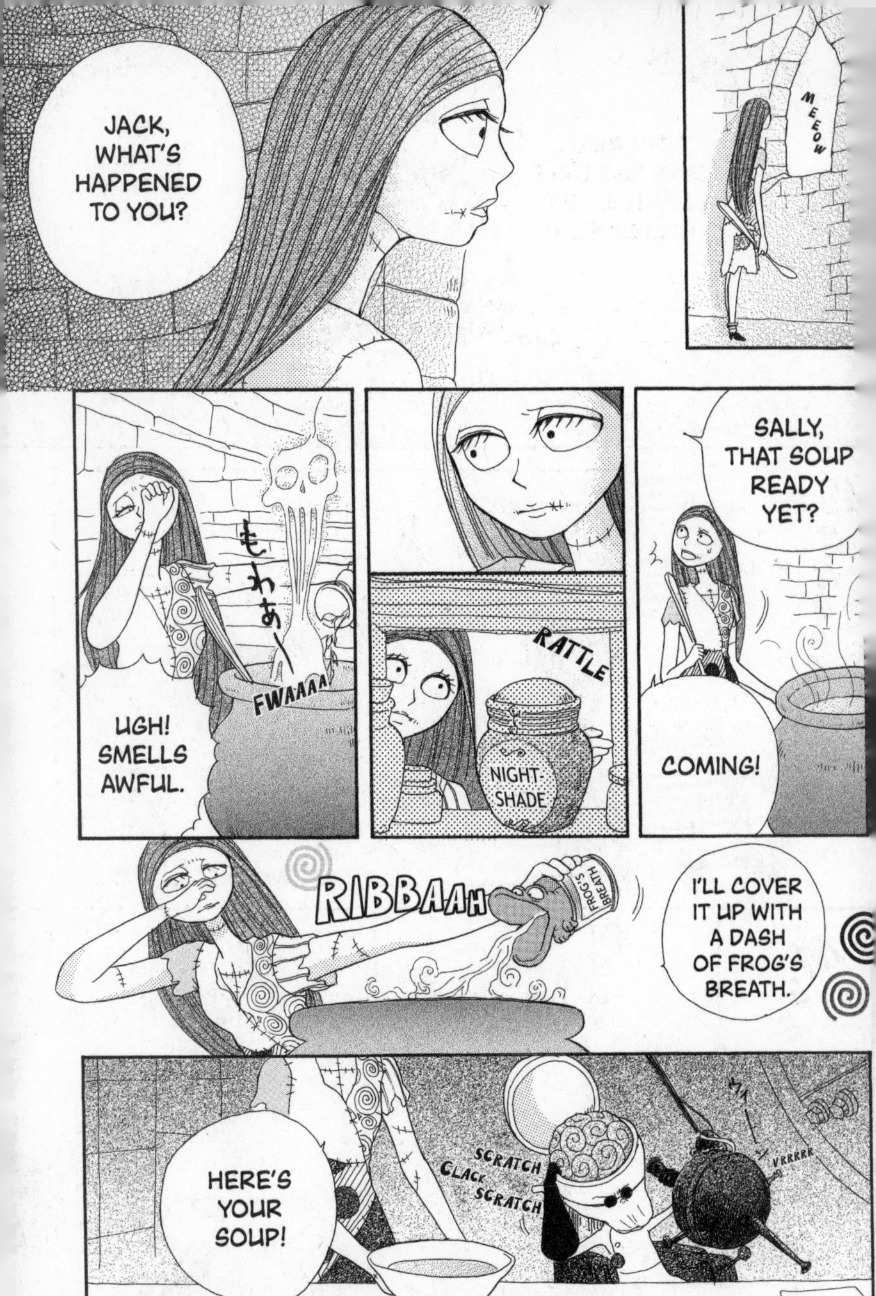
MEEOW
JACK, WHAT'S HAPPENED TO YOU?
SALLY, THAT SOUP READY YET?
COMING!
RATTLE
NIGHT-SHADE
もわあ〜
FWAAAA
UGH! SMELLS AWFUL.
I'LL COVER IT UP WITH A DASH OF FROG'S BREATH.
FROG'S BREATH
RIBBAAH
ウィーン
VRRRRR
SCRATCH
CLACK
SCRATCH
HERE'S YOUR SOUP!

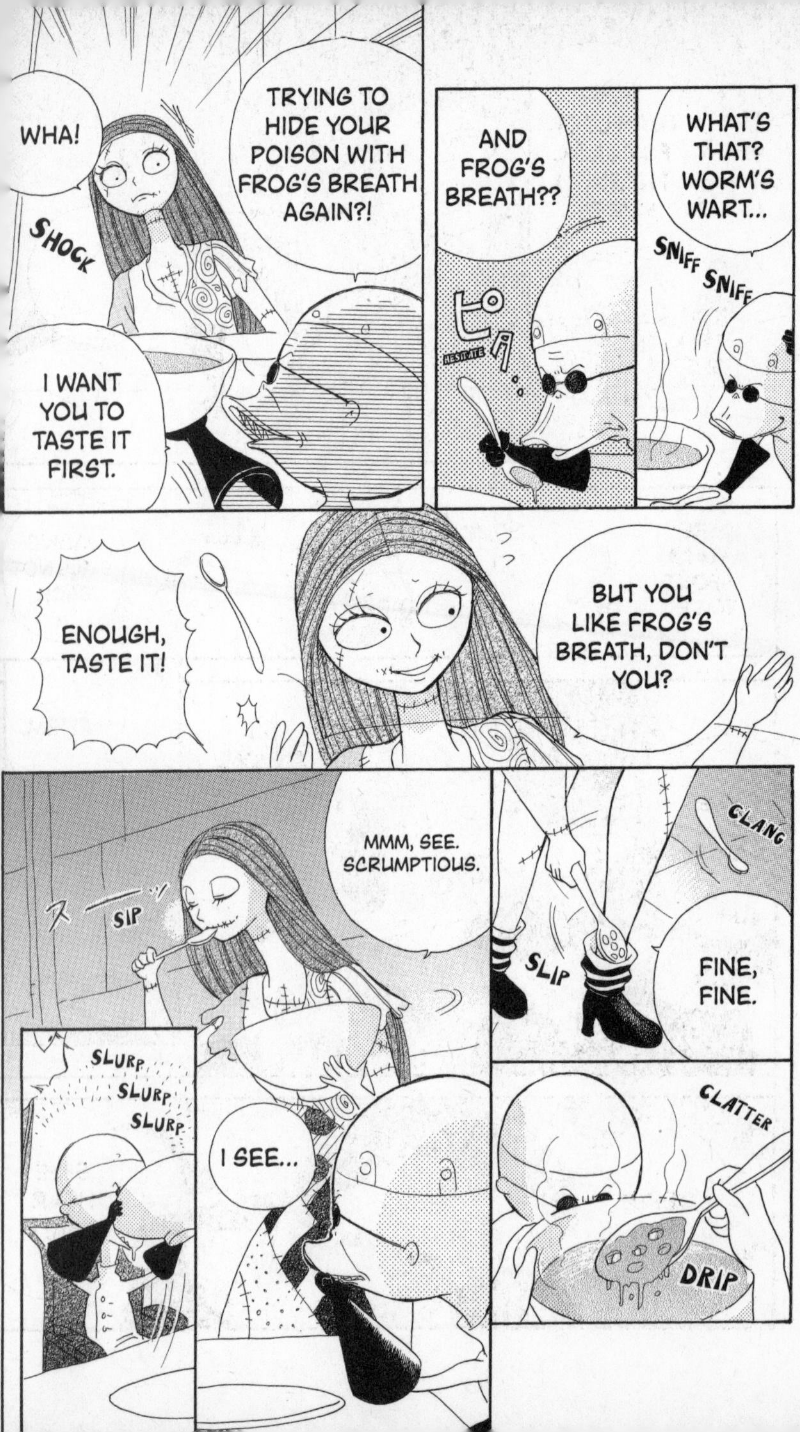
WHAT'S THAT? WORM'S WART...
SNIFF SNIFF
AND FROG'S BREATH??
ピク
HESITATE
TRYING TO HIDE YOUR POISON WITH FROG'S BREATH AGAIN?!
WHA!
SHOCK
I WANT YOU TO TASTE IT FIRST.
BUT YOU LIKE FROG'S BREATH, DON'T YOU?
ENOUGH, TASTE IT!
CLANG
FINE, FINE.
SLIP
CLATTER
DRIP
MMM, SEE. SCRUMPTIOUS.
ス
SIP
I SEE...
SLURP
SLURP
SLURP

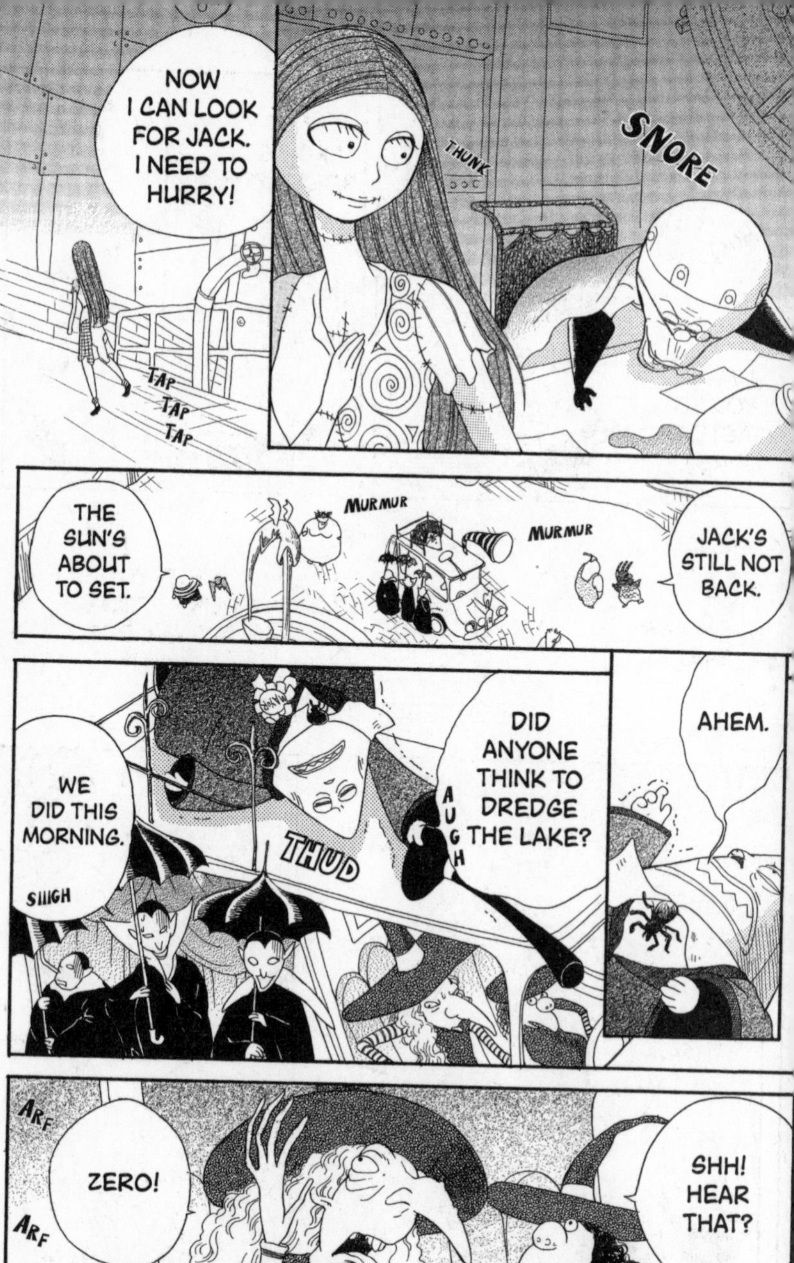
SNORE
THUNK
NOW I CAN LOOK FOR JACK. I NEED TO HURRY!
TAP
TAP
TAP
JACK'S STILL NOT BACK.
MURMUR
MURMUR
THE SUN'S ABOUT TO SET.
AHEM.
DID ANYONE THINK TO DREDGE THE LAKE?
AUGH
THUD
WE DID THIS MORNING.
SIIGH
SHH! HEAR THAT?
ZERO!
ARF
ARF

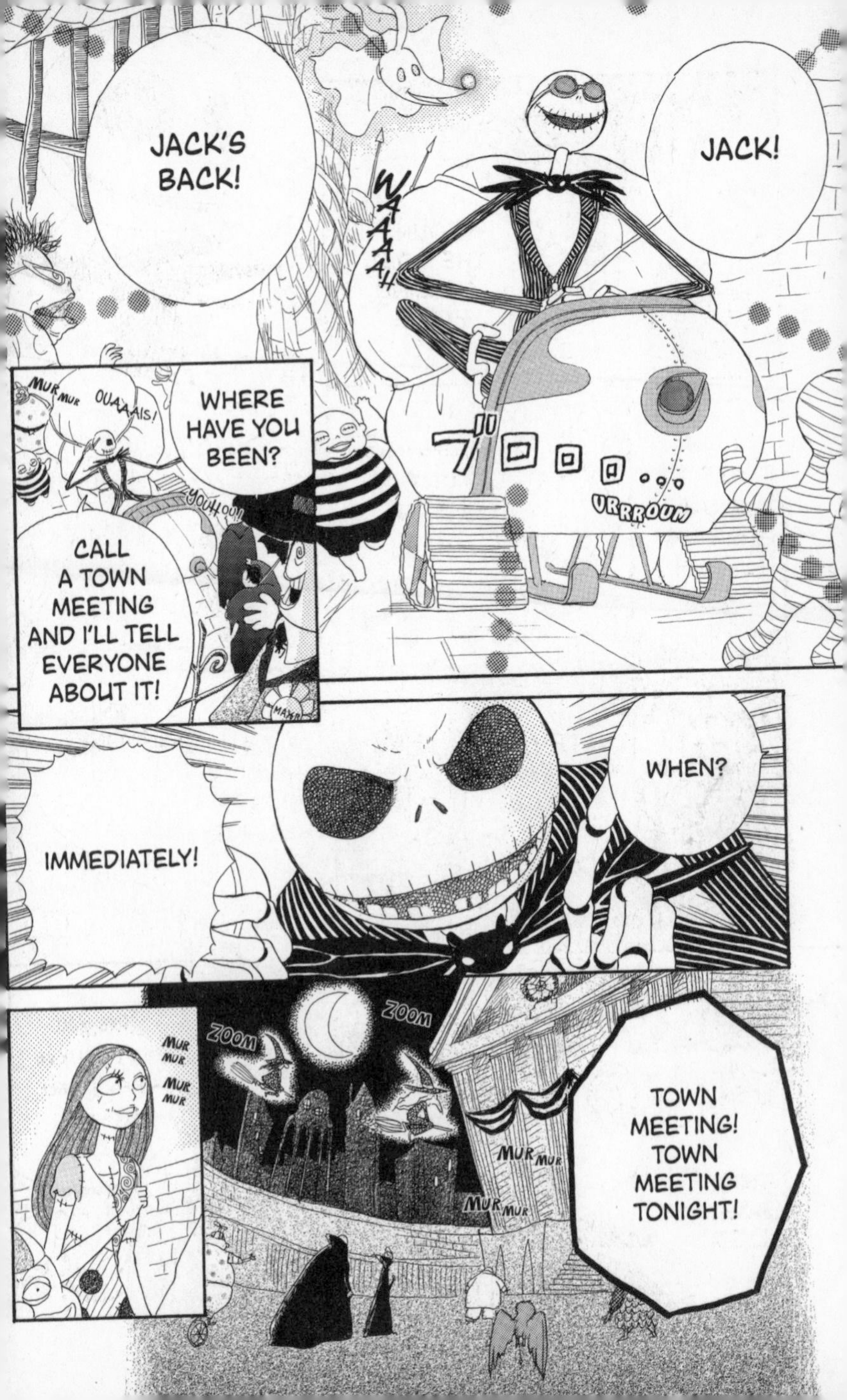
JACK!
WAAAAAH
JACK'S BACK!
ブロロロ...
VRRROUM
WHERE HAVE YOU BEEN?
MUR MUR
OUAAAAIS!
YOUHOU!
CALL A TOWN MEETING AND I'LL TELL EVERYONE ABOUT IT!
WHEN?
IMMEDIATELY!
TOWN MEETING! TOWN MEETING TONIGHT!
ZOOM
ZOOM
MUR MUR
MUR MUR
MUR MUR
MUR MUR

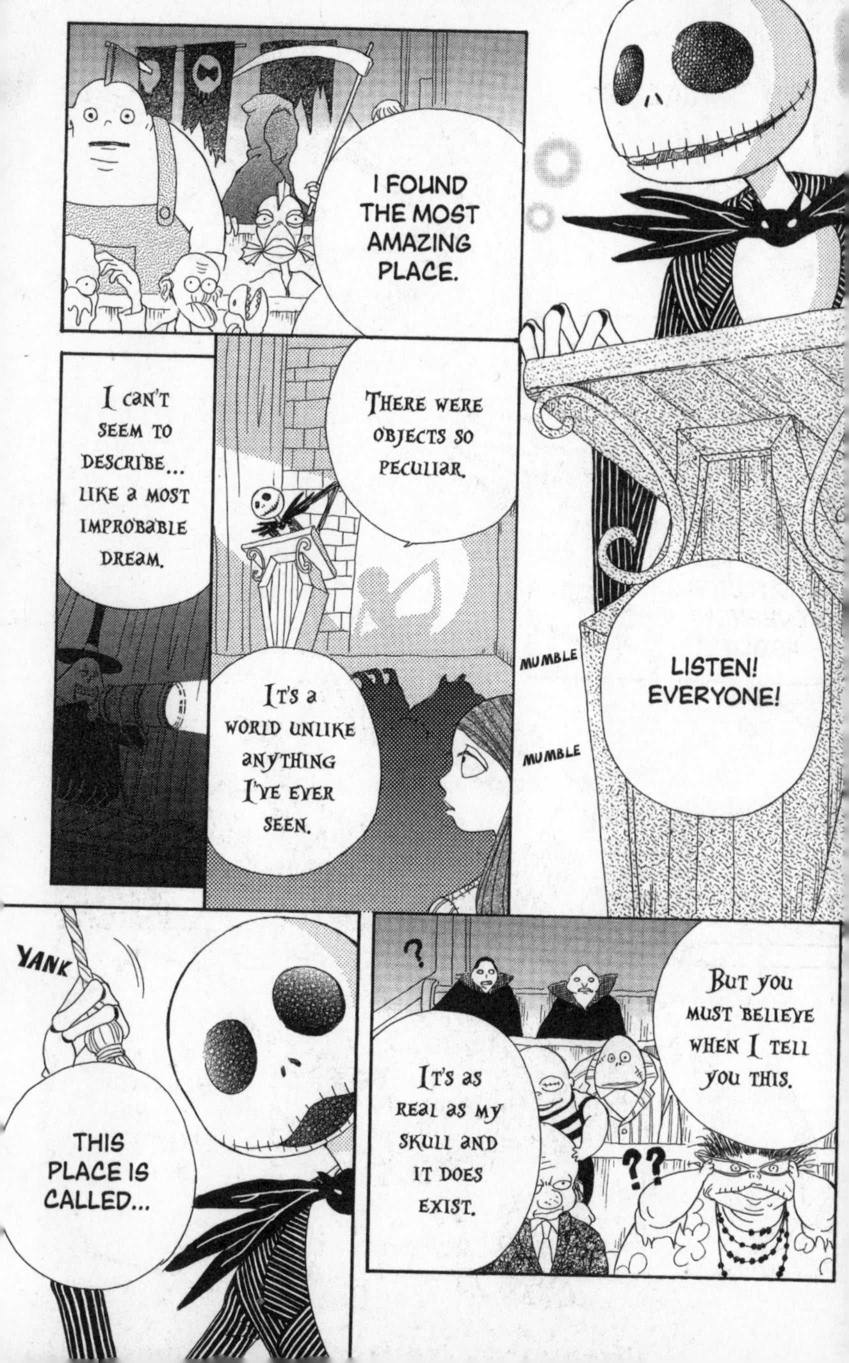
MUMBLE
MUMBLE
LISTEN! EVERYONE!
I FOUND THE MOST AMAZING PLACE.
THERE WERE OBJECTS SO PECULIAR.
IT'S A WORLD UNLIKE ANYTHING I'VE EVER SEEN.
I CAN'T SEEM TO DESCRIBE... LIKE A MOST IMPROBABLE DREAM.
?
BUT YOU MUST BELIEVE WHEN I TELL YOU THIS.
IT'S AS REAL AS MY SKULL AND IT DOES EXIST.
??
YANK
THIS PLACE IS CALLED...

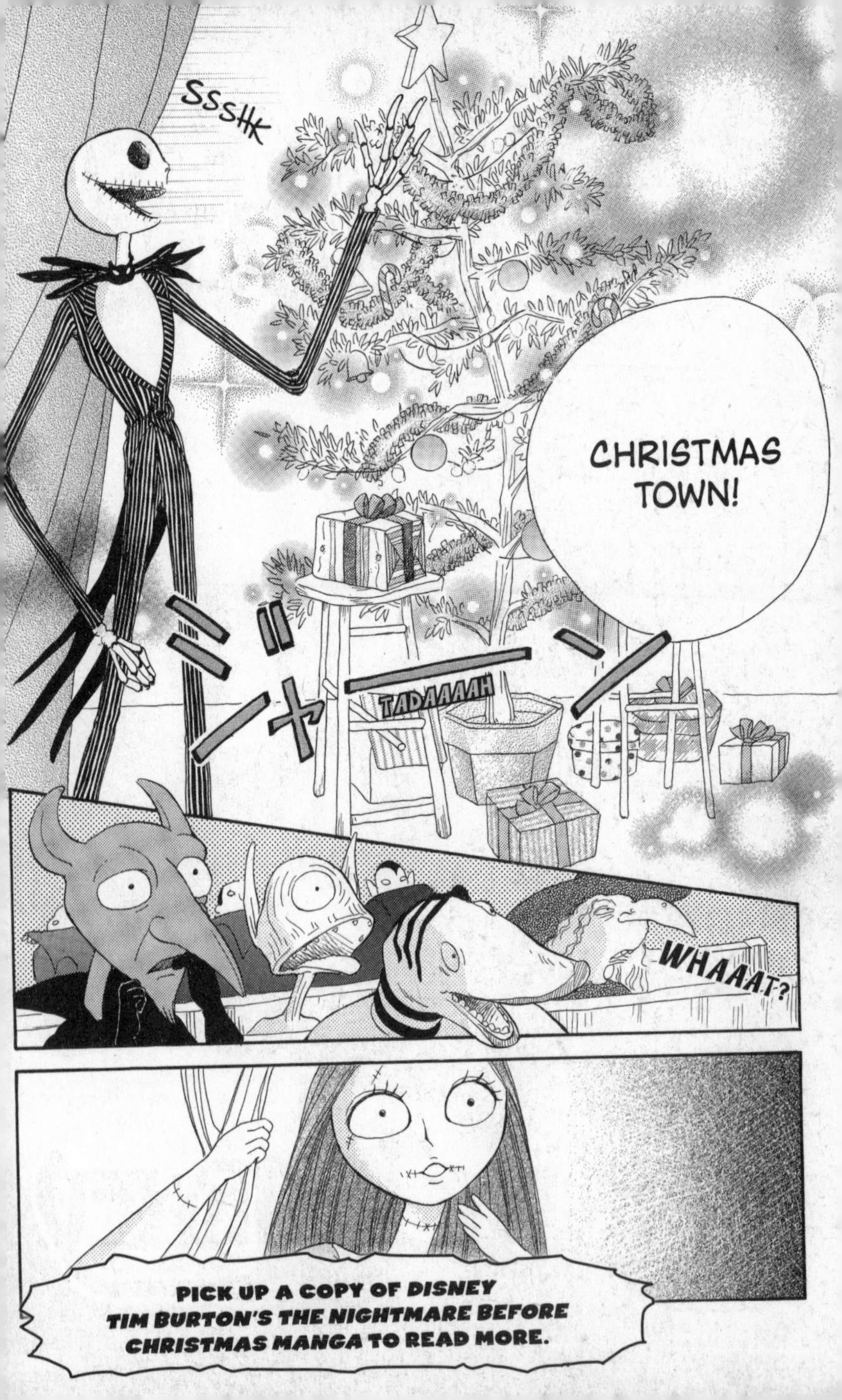
SSSHK
CHRISTMAS TOWN!
TADAAAAH
WHAAAT?
PICK UP A COPY OF DISNEY TIM BURTON'S THE NIGHTMARE BEFORE CHRISTMAS MANGA TO READ MORE.

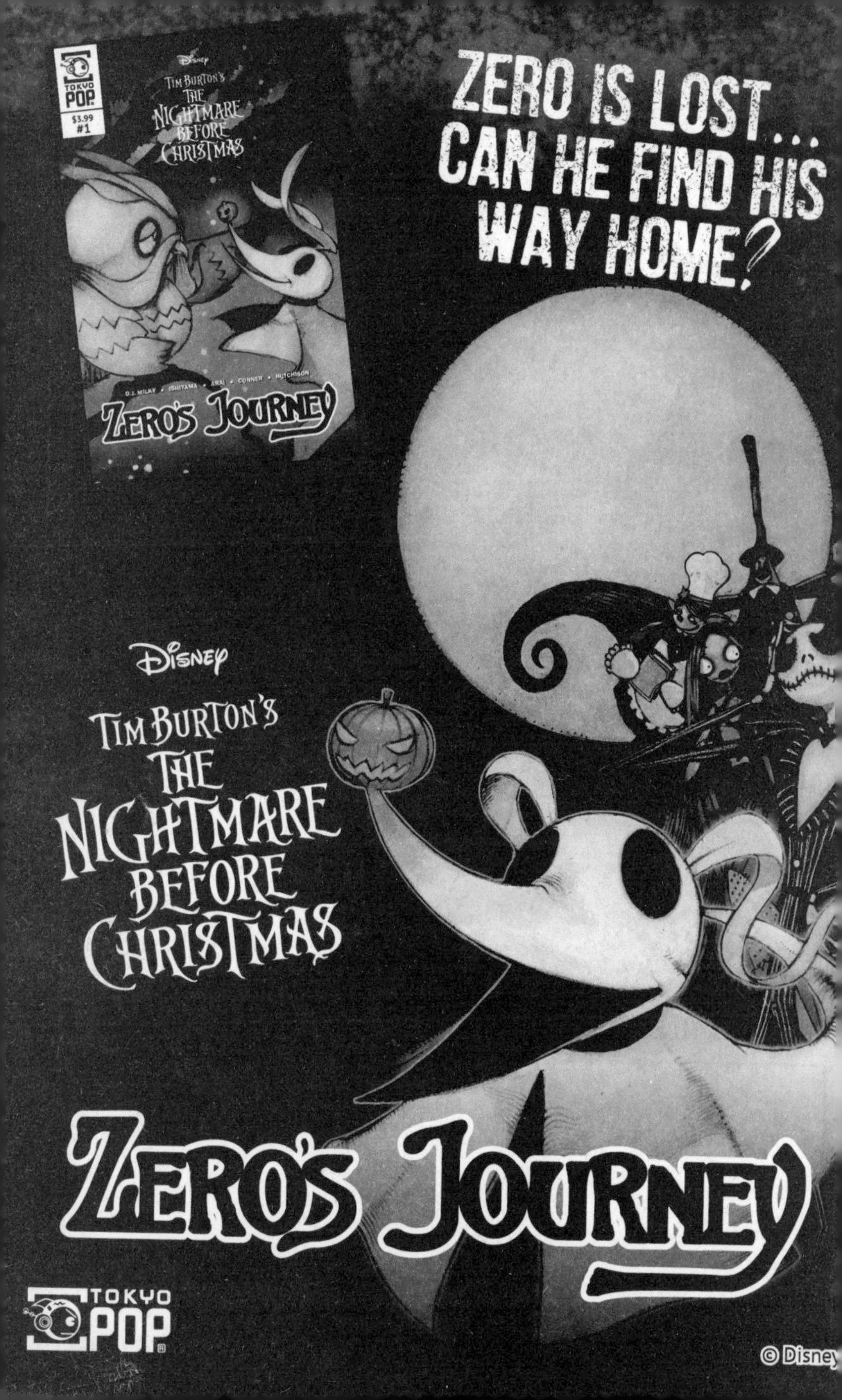

ZERO IS LOST... CAN HE FIND HIS WAY HOME?
TOKYO POP
$3.99 #1
Disney
TIM BURTON'S THE NIGHTMARE BEFORE CHRISTMAS
D.J. MILKY • ISHIYAMA • ARAI • CONNER • HUTCHISON
ZERO'S JOURNEY
Disney
TIM BURTON'S
THE NIGHTMARE BEFORE CHRISTMAS
ZERO'S JOURNEY
TOKYO POP
© Disney

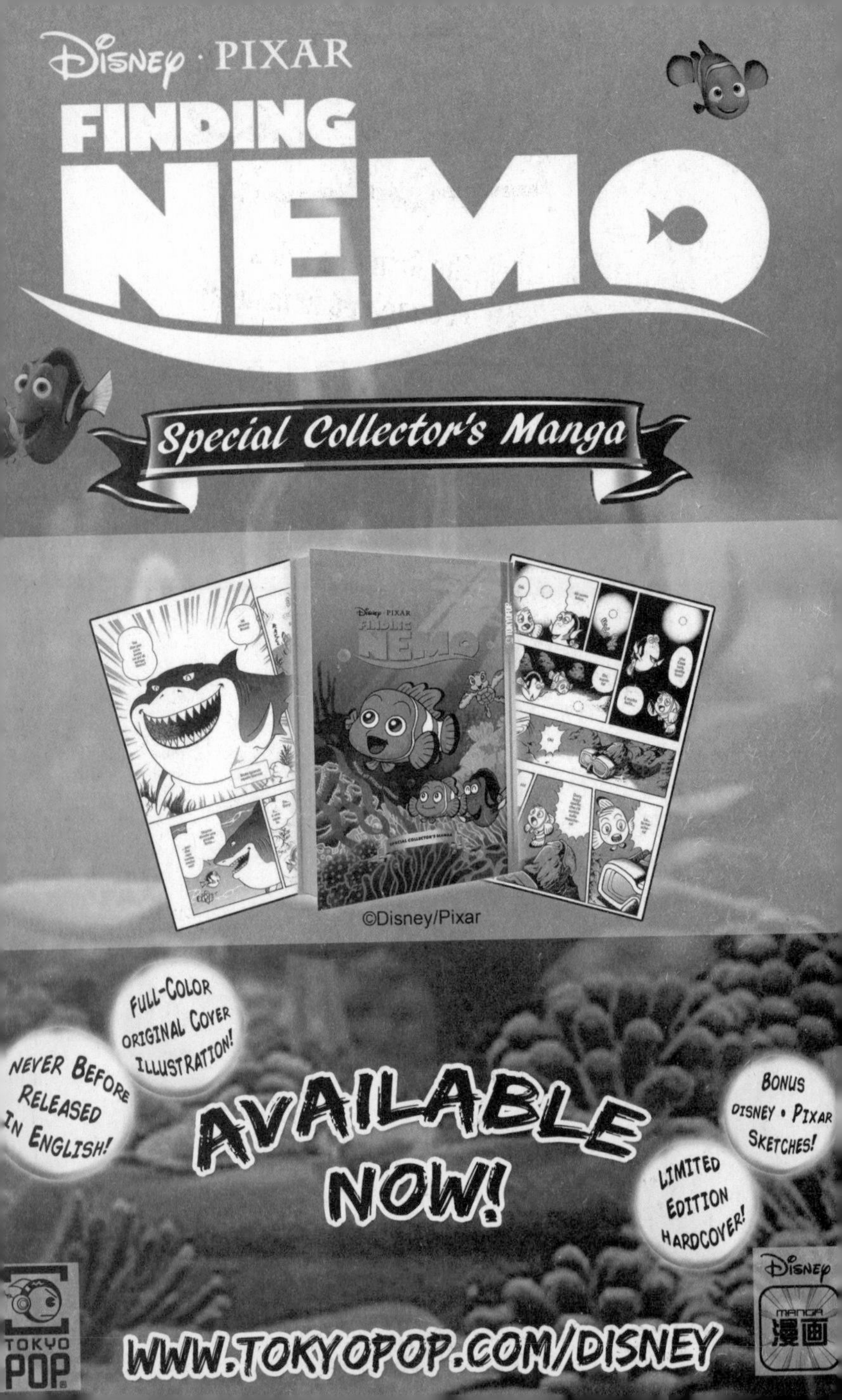
Disney · PIXAR
FINDING NEMO
Special Collector's Manga
©Disney/Pixar
FULL-COLOR ORIGINAL COVER ILLUSTRATION!
NEVER BEFORE RELEASED IN ENGLISH!
AVAILABLE NOW!
BONUS DISNEY • PIXAR SKETCHES!
LIMITED EDITION HARDCOVER!
WWW.TOKYOPOP.COM/DISNEY
TOKYO POP
Disney MANGA 漫画

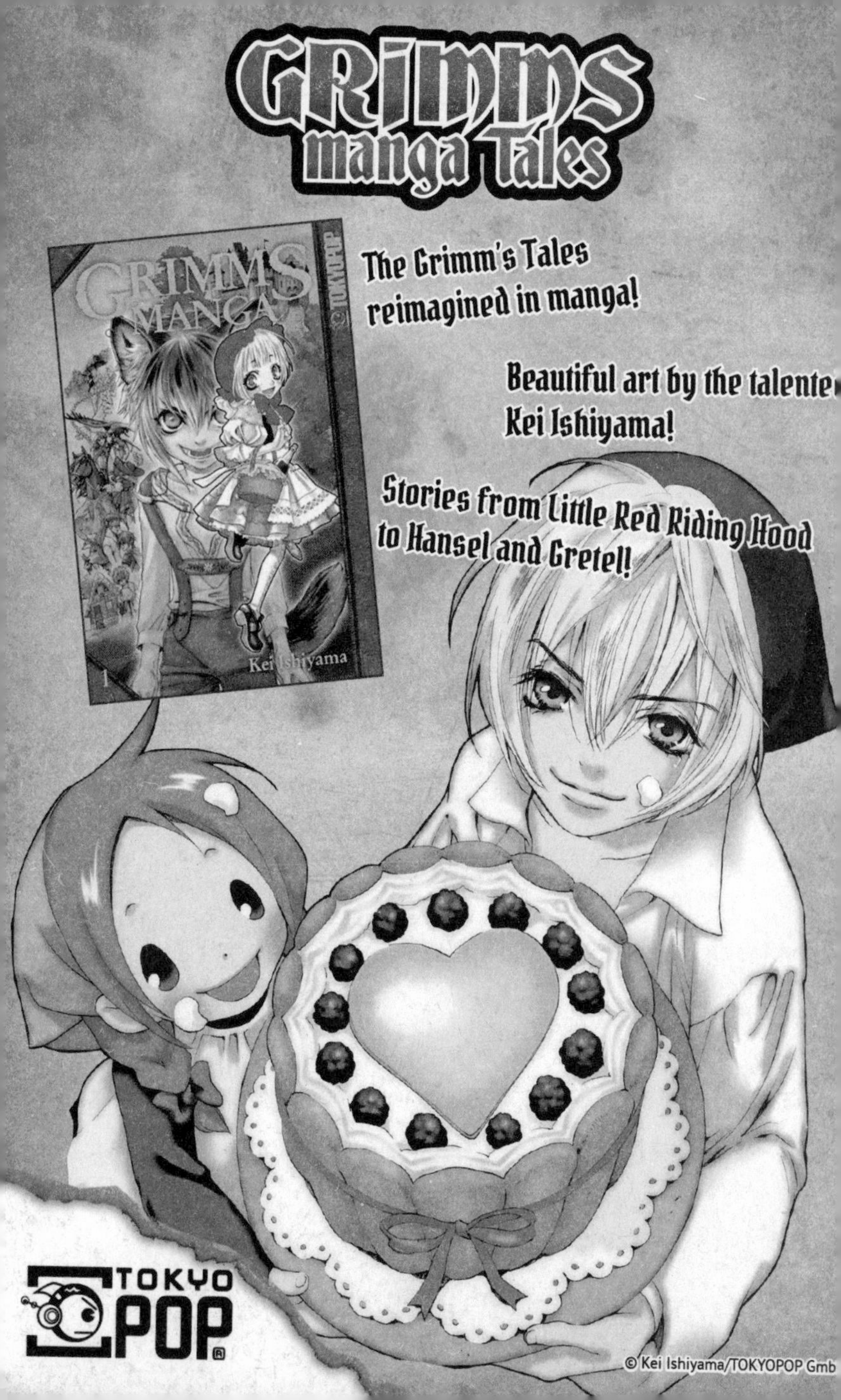
GRIMMS
manga Tales
GRIMMS MANGA
Kei Ishiyama
1
TOKYOPOP
The Grimm's Tales
reimagined in manga!
Beautiful art by the talente
Kei Ishiyama!
Stories from Little Red Riding Hood
to Hansel and Gretel!
TOKYO POP
© Kei Ishiyama/TOKYOPOP Gmb